Praise for
The Unseemly Education of Anne Merchant

"From the very first pages, I was spellbound by this deliciously dark tale of mysterious attraction, cutthroat ambition, and how far we will go to keep the ones we love."
—AMY PLUM, **international bestselling author**

"An original, breathtakingly written, and often chilling tale of what lengths people will go to for love. Joanna Wiebe has crafted a book that is unputdownable, so much so that I was forced to read part of it at work because I couldn't stop thinking about Anne and Cania Christy. (Shh, don't tell!) Joanna has officially made my instant-buy list."
—LINDSEY R. LOUCKS, **author of** *The Grave Winner*

"She had me at the introduction of the spooky setting—the kind of stuff readers can lose themselves in. Joanna Wiebe is a fun new author to be on the lookout for!"
—WENDY HIGGINS, **author of The Sweet Trilogy**

"School grounds shrouded in mystery, beautiful student body obsessed with the race to be valedictorian, and a gorgeous, infuriating, unobtainable guy. Welcome to Cania Christy."
—A.E. ROUGHT, **author of** *Broken*

THE UNSEEMLY EDUCATION OF ANNE MERCHANT

THE
UNSEEMLY
EDUCATION
OF ANNE
MERCHANT

By Joanna Wiebe

BenBella Books
Dallas, Texas

BenBella Books, Inc.
10300 N. Central Expressway, Suite #530 | Dallas, TX 75231
www.benbellabooks.com | Send feedback to feedback@benbellabooks.com

Printed in the United States of America
10 9 8 7 6 5 4 3 2 1

Library of Congress Cataloging-in-Publication Data
Wiebe, Joanna.
  The unseemly education of Anne Merchant / by Joanna Wiebe.
    p. cm.
  Summary: From the moment Anne Merchant arrives at Cania Christy, a boarding school for the wealthiest teens, she has questions that remain unanswered, including why everything is a competition to be valedictorian and what mysterious reward comes with that title.
    ISBN 978-1-939529-32-9 (hardback) — ISBN 978-1-939529-33-6 (electronic)
[1. Supernatural—Fiction. 2. Boarding schools—Fiction. 3. Schools—Fiction. 4. Wealth—Fiction. 5. Islands—Fiction.] I. Title.
  PZ7.W63513Uns 2014
  [Fic]—dc23

                    2013027277

Editing by Glenn Yeffeth
Copyediting by Debra Kirkby
Proofreading by Amy Zarkos and Michael Fedison
Cover design by Kit Sweeney Photography & Design
Text design and composition by Silver Feather Design
Printed by Bang Printing

Distributed by Perseus Distribution | www.perseusdistribution.com
To place orders through Perseus Distribution:
Tel: (800) 343-4499 | Fax: (800) 351-5073 | E-mail: orderentry@perseusbooks.com

Significant discounts for bulk sales are available. Please contact Glenn Yeffeth at glenn@benbellabooks.com or (214) 750-3628.

CONTENTS

one

WORMWOOD ISLAND

HERE'S SOMETHING NOBODY TELLS RICH PEOPLE: THEY die, too.

There's this sense, you know, this *misconception* that wealthy people are invincible. Like when Fortune 500 execs get cancer or something equally awful, they think they can coerce a massive, aggressive, bumpy tumor straight out of their body by throwing bundles of cash at it. As if you can swipe a black American Express card through your armpit, and—*ch-ching!*—you've just paid off the Grim Reaper, you've gloriously extended your life of leisure...and you've been given a bump in your Air Miles account to boot.

Idiotic.

But strangely common thinking among the wealthy.

In lovely, sunny Atherton, California—the most expensive neighborhood in America and my home up until, oh, yesterday—this notion that rich people are invincible is so prevalent, people go into a state of absolute shock when someone in our fancy 94027 zip code gets sick. Or crashes their Bentley. Or accidentally inhales Beluga caviar (which happens way more often than you'd think). I see it every day.

Scratch that. I *saw* it every day.

I saw it before my dad shipped me across the country to doom-and-gloom central, aka Wormwood Island, Maine, for what one might call a "fresh start."

I saw those delusional richies on a regular basis, back when I would sit quietly in the shadows at the top of the stairs and, with my sketchbook in hand, observe black-veiled parades marching somberly through the hallways of my house. See, our home is the second story of the Fair Oaks Funeral Home, where my dad's the lowly mortician and terribly paid funeral director and where we Merchants have the distinct pleasure of being the only broke-ass family for miles.

Yes, that means I'm *that* girl.

I'm the weird mortician's daughter. The creepy girl the kids at school call Death Chick or Wednesday Addams. The eerie girl they shy away from whenever I wear black or look unusually pale. The poor girl raised with dead bodies in the basement, zombies scratching at the cellar door, and ghosts around every corner. I'm that girl.

"No, you *were* that girl," I remind my reflection as I adjust a blue-and-gold tie over the crisp white shirt of my new school uniform. "Now you're just Anne Merchant, a junior at the Cania Christy Preparatory Academy. No one knows anything about you, which means—" I pause to tweak the tie so it draws a little less attention to my chest "—you can rewrite your history."

I am standing in front of a small mirror, which is on top of a small dresser in the small attic bedroom of the small cottage that's going to be my home for the next two years. I'll be here until I graduate from Cania Christy. Fingers crossed: I'll graduate as valedictorian. Becoming valedictorian is a critical part of my plan—my future hinges on it. If I don't graduate at the top of my class, I won't qualify for the scholarship money I'm going to need. But if—no, *when*—I graduate as the valedictorian, I'll be almost guaranteed a full scholarship to the school of my dreams, Brown. From there, my life is perfectly plotted: spend four years in undergrad, open a gallery in New York City, promote my own art while discovering new artists, and make enough money that my dad can leave behind his life of death to come out east for a fresh start of his own. Since I first put chalk to paper as a toddler, I've known my life's purpose: to create art. Art that presents a different version of the world to the world; art that looks closer. I lost sight of that vision over the course of the last two years, but it's back now. In full force. And to realize that vision, I'll need to be valedictorian. Which shouldn't be too hard. After all, I spent the first sixteen years of my life at the top of my class—the upside of being shunned as Death Chick is that you have plenty o' time to study.

Stepping back from the mirror, I assess myself. Turn left, turn right. And give up. I shake my head at my uniformed reflection.

"You look like some sort of *anime* floozy."

Everybody on earth has something they don't like about the way they look; for me, it's always been my one crooked tooth (which I've learned to mask with a closed-mouth smile) and my wildly curly blonde hair. That's *usually* what I'm up against. But today, I've discovered two new problems that had never seemed like problems before: my breasts. It's like they doubled in size overnight. This would not be a bad thing if I had a closet of clothes to choose from for my first day of school, but it is a significant issue given that I have only the uniforms that were waiting for me when I arrived here late last night. Uniforms that are decidedly form fitting. By which I mean they are decidedly three sizes too small.

Giving up, I button a cardigan over the shirt, trace my fingers along the golden Cania Christy emblem on it, mentally untie the knots in my stomach, and turn to fiddling with my wonky curls.

"Who would you like to be?" I ask myself lightly. "The daughter of a zillionaire turned yogi? The fabulously wealthy love child of a famous ballerina and a recluse artist?"

As if to drive home the point of who I really am and where I really come from—and the inescapability of both—a glint of sunlight shines through the attic window and reflects off my late mother's barrettes, which sit atop my dresser, sending a beam of light at my eyes. As if my mom's trying to get my attention from above. As if she refuses to be forgotten.

As if I could ever forget her.

It only takes the span of a breath, it only takes the lightest touch of my fingertips on those silvery barrettes, for visions of my beautiful mother's last moments to come rushing at me. The quiet desperation in her glassy stare when I found her on the kitchen floor. Her frail body hanging loosely in my arms as I rocked her and begged God for her life. The dampness of her lovely face as my tears rained down on her. I discovered her body when I was fourteen—well over two years ago—but the pain is so raw and the ache in my chest feels so *bright red*, it's as if she died yesterday.

My dad disapproves of my style of mourning. Particularly the length of time I've been in mourning and the life I've turned away from since she died. That's why I'm here. Because I can hardly breathe when I think of her. And because he is so used to death, he can't understand what's taking me so long to get back to my old overachieving self.

I pull my hand away from my mother's barrettes.

The sun disappears behind the clouds, leaving me to stare into the whiteness of the endless sea of fog separating me from the mysteries—the distant school, the sprawling campus, the teachers, the other students, the people on this island—that lie in wait.

Unlike rich people, poor folks know all about death. I know everything there is to know, from the temperature of the refrigerator they keep the bodies in to the weight of the thread they use to stitch eyelids tightly closed. I know that embalming fluid can be used for a cheap high. I know you instantly lose twenty-one grams of weight when you die. I even know the superstitions, like it's bad luck to have a mirror in a funeral hall because it traps the spirit of the dearly departed. If anyone should be comfortable with the idea of death, it's a mortician's daughter.

But nothing can prepare you for losing your mother.

Nothing can prepare you for the suddenness of a constant source of love and support vanishing so quickly. And so permanently.

"Annie!" my housemother, Gigi Malone—who, may I add, is certifiably crazy with a certifiably crazy dog—shouts at me from the bottom of two flights of rickety stairs. My door is closed, but this teetering cottage is so old and flimsy, it sounds like Gigi's standing right next to me and screaming into my ear. I can hear her little Pomeranian, Skippy, yelping wildly, just as he did the moment he met me last night. "You don't want to be late for your first day of school!"

I march on the spot for a moment, and the floorboards squeal. That's my way of telling Gigi I'm up without actually shouting back at her. You learn to communicate soundlessly under the constant weight of respectful silence in a funeral home. The year before my mom died, when she was in the hospital receiving treatment for what the docs called "rapid cycling bipolar disorder," my dad and I had the house to ourselves for nearly three months, and we might have spoken a half-dozen words to each other. Since her passing, things have become even quieter between us. But my dad was never one for words.

I hear Gigi walk away.

Then I slip on my knee-high boots, straighten my tights, smooth my skirt, and make a last-ditch effort to keep my shirt from busting open. I've got time for one more pep talk before I head downstairs and this new life of mine truly begins.

I start to tell myself, "You are a great artist," but my voice cracks.

So I take a deep breath. And I push out the loud voices that would hold me back. *They're all going to laugh at you. You're never going to fit in. You're still just Death Chick. Your dad can't afford to send you here, and you'll probably end up being shipped back to California when his check bounces.*

Squaring my shoulders, I stare harder into the tiny mirror on top of the dresser and, making every effort not to groan at my Einstein-inspired hair or to mask my crooked tooth with a slanted grin, say in my most confident tone, "Anne, you are a great artist. You are as gifted as any other student here. This is your chance to get your life back on track." Proving I'm not great at pep talks, I finish with, "So don't blow it."

As I open my bedroom door, leaving behind scents of shampoo and deodorant, and start down the creaky stairs, the smell of the sea—that slimy, green, salty smell—hits me with a wallop. *Welcome to Maine.* Small, square stained-glass windows line the narrow staircase that leads me down to the second floor, where Gigi's bedroom, the bathroom, and a tiny guest bedroom are; the windows extend down the next staircase, which is the main staircase, which will bring me to the living room and kitchen. When I pause to peer through the stained glass just steps above the main floor, I find the bluish-gray landscape of Wormwood Island distorted by red, orange, and green triangles. A permanent mist hovers two feet over the ground, running through a world of overgrown ferns, clouding moss-covered tree stumps, and wrapping like a thick cotton scarf around the beech trees that line the shores. There seems to be no beginning and no end to the island. It's as infinite as death itself.

"On the bright side," I say, gazing through the multicolored glass until my breath steams it, "you can hear the ocean here. *That's* like California." The glass squeaks as I rub the side of my fist through my breath-mist and see a break in the fog not fifty feet from Gigi's cottage. For the first time, I glimpse the outlines of a nearby row of houses and whisper, "Howdy, neighbors."

Out of the corner of my eye, I spy Gigi poking her head around the corner.

"You're talking to yourself, kid," she says.

Her voice sounds like a piano that's been played too long without tuning. Skippy races around his master's feet and barks at me with such force, his puffy orange body bounces a foot into the air; Gigi shoos him away.

Without looking at Gigi, I ask, "Who lives next door?"

"Don't you mind who lives next door. It's the Zins' place, but don't mind them."

"The Zins' place? It's one house?" The fog rolls along, and I can make out the connection between what appeared to be multiple small homes. I count six chimneys on the mansion's rooftop. "They must be rich."

"Everyone here's rich. Except you and me. But even I was rich once. Now I clean the Zin house and watch his kid when Dr. Zin's away on business, and they let me stay in this cottage."

"I wonder what sort of business he's in to afford a place like that."

"Not that you need to mind, but he's the head of admissions for Cania."

"Why's everyone rich here?" I don't know much about Cania or Wormwood Island—the decision for me to come here was made hastily—but I recall hearing something about the island once being a fishing village. Of all the wealthy people I've met, I can't recall any of them being fishermen.

Flitting her hands, Gigi mutters something and turns away.

Passing a growling Skippy, I follow Gigi through the front room and into the kitchen, which might have been nice twenty years ago, where I watch her shimmy onto a hard wooden bench behind the table before shoving half a piece of toast into her mouth. Glancing around, I notice a whitewashed curio cabinet, which holds what remains of an expensive-looking teapot collection. An open case on a shelf displays the last few pieces of silver flatware. The fingerprint-smudged glass of two cabinets reveals a wide selection of half-full liquor bottles.

Trying not to think much of the missing items and the booze—and trying even harder not to mentally weave a sad story of Gigi Malone, crazed woman in a stretched-out homemade sweater—I pour myself a cup of coffee as she leans over her crossword puzzle. I offer her a cup, too; she scowls and grumbles that I ought not to go around stunting my growth with caffeine.

I'm just over five-ten. Not exactly a hobbit.

"So my dad never explained why I'm living with you instead of in the school dorms," I begin, walking to the end of the kitchen and gazing out the garden window as I sip my coffee.

"Of course he didn't," she says under her breath.

Gigi's cottage may be old and small and the kitchen may be lined with plates commemorating the Reagan administration, but it has one redeeming quality: it's just feet from the edge of the east side of the island, giving a spectacular view of the endless Atlantic (when the fog breaks, at least). The lush land drops off sharply, suggesting a cliff. My gaze follows the island's dark green border as it runs mere steps from where I'm standing, behind the Zin mansion next door, and gets lost in the dense woods, only to appear again high in the distance, where the black slate rooftops of Cania Christy rise like the pointy teeth of a saw. There are no gentle slopes into the water, at least none that I can see from my vantage; there are just towering rocky cliffs, abused at their bases by hungry waves. It's rugged and harsh and absolutely perfect looking.

"You've only been here since last night," Gigi continues, "and already you don't like it."

"I like it. I'm just surprised. Does everyone live off-campus? I mean, there are dorms, aren't there?"

"You and the Zin boy are the only students living off-campus." Gigi shuffles her crossword around. "There are dorms, yes."

Her watery, drooping gaze rolls my way then trails out to the whitecaps of the ocean. A spot of toast with strawberry jam is stuck to her lip.

"But the dorms are full," she explains, chewing out each of her words in a slow, deliberate manner. "Headmaster Villicus approved your application a mere two days ago. You should be glad I opened my home to you."

"I *am*, Gigi."

"Because not many would do what I've done," she finishes sharply.

Our gazes meet and stick. To look in her eyes, you'd think she could be a hundred years old or five; she is at once a wise old woman and a lost child. The combination is, I have to admit, frustrating—the condescension of her wisdom fused with the weakness of her vulnerability. As if I should revere her and protect her at once. Either she's going to be a pain in the butt to live with, or I'm in a bad mood thanks to my intense jet lag. Or both.

She is the first to drop her gaze.

"Well, maybe something will open up at the dorm soon," I say. "In the meantime, Gigi, thank you for taking me in. It's—" I start looking around but stop quickly, which is the only way to keep a hint of believability in my tone "—nice here."

She doesn't look up. "You've got orientation today, right?" She scribbles over her crossword. I'm not even sure she's putting letters in the boxes. "Big day for you, between getting your Guardian and choosing your PT. Big day."

"Sorry?" This is the first I've heard of a *Guardian* or a *PT*. "What are those?"

Still staring down, her eyes dart left, right, up, and down. "Oh, pish posh," she sings, getting chirpy suddenly. "It's not my job to walk you through your whole orientation day in advance, is it? No. I've got strict orders from Headmaster Villicus. Let you bunk here. Stay out of it. And get paid."

"Is there something in particular you're staying out of?"

"Oh, what do I know? Your life! Your school! All of the above." Her expression can only be described as panicked when she looks up at me. "You're the first student I've had stay with me. Don't pay any attention to me."

With an odd smile, she shakes her stringy hair. Then she's on her feet, shoving me toward the front door, where Skippy has resumed bouncing and barking madly at me; this dog hates me. And I'm getting the sense that Gigi feels the same way, but she opts to growl and wave away topics rather than bark and bounce. After rummaging through the front closet, Gigi pivots on her heels and pushes a thick fisherman's coat at me. It smells like old fish carcasses. I take it and stop to look her in the eyes again, forcing her to look at me.

"Are we cool?" I ask.

"This is just a business arrangement," she says. Then her voice softens ever so slightly. "I can't say if it's a good thing you're here. But here you are. And I can't change that."

As I stumble out of Gigi's, a frigid breeze blows over my back, but I toss the fishy coat behind shrubs—I don't need to replace my *Death Chick* moniker with *Stinky Salmon* or something worse—and wrap a scarf around my neck. It's far too cold for September, but I have to remind myself I'm not in California anymore; beyond the fuzzy-looking trees and wide fern fronds is the cold Atlantic, not the warm Pacific. Breaking into a trot to keep from freezing, I dash up Gigi's gravelly walkway to the main road and tell myself not to run too hard or I'll show up at school sweating like the devil in a church.

The Zin mansion looms to my right. My hometown is filled with houses designed to make neighbors and tourists sick with envy, and it appears Dr. Zin's mansion was designed with the same thing in mind. But I'm not envious. Really, I'm not. After all, it looks like Dr. Zin's place, cloaked in fog, with sharply pitched roofs stabbing up through the mist, is about one lightning storm away from haunted house status. I turn onto the long, narrow, and empty road and start toward the school. In the distance, over the treetops and through the fog, I can just make out the peaks and steeples of the campus. Even from here, it looks nothing like the big-box school I used to go to.

"What did Dad get me into?" I ask myself and watch my breath freeze.

Until this morning, I'd heard nothing of getting a Guardian or choosing a PT, which, if I had my way, would be txt shorthand for getting Pretty Teeth or Perfect Tests. Having never been to a private school—never mind the most elite one on the planet—I guess it makes sense that I don't know. Maybe Guardians 'n' things are standard at these places.

"It'll be fine," I assure myself. "You'll figure it out."

That's when I notice it: a red line painted across the road right before the Zin property begins. The paint is bright. I near it. I spy layers of faded red below it, as if it's been painted and repainted weekly. For decades.

With a little hop, I cross it. I tell myself to disregard it.

As I start jogging, hoping not to be late, a loud Ducati whizzes by me, sending small rocks and twigs swirling into the air; I have to slow to pick a particularly wiry twig from the wilds of my hair. As I do, I hear the crackle of leaves underfoot and glance over my shoulder. A uniformed girl with a short brown bob and little bangs is walking far behind me. When I look again later, she's gone. I jog the rest of the way to school, alone on the road.

Cania Christy is one towering stone building backed by smaller converted houses and outbuildings, which I can barely distinguish beneath the slowly lifting perma-cloud that drapes campus. Just two things catch my immediate attention: the main building, over the front doors of which the name *Goethe Hall* is etched, and the silence. The campus is so noiseless that a part of me wonders if I'm a day early. I hear only the squealing protest of door hinges opening and closing and the caw of gulls muffled in the foggy seascape and absorbed by greenery that is so lush it's suffocating. In the rare moments a breeze blows a hole through the fog, I glimpse the odd student meandering silently into or out of Goethe Hall; I'm at once comforted to know I didn't arrive on the wrong day and curious to find that, without fail, every student is walking alone. It's a strange but welcome relief to think that this student body may be comprised of people similar to me, people who haven't always been in the in-crowd, people who are more focused on their goals and ambitions than on trying to be popular.

Perhaps there are no cliques here. Perhaps they're progressive enough at Cania Christy to ban bullying and the exclusionary cliques that help create it.

"Now what've we got here?" a girl with a drawl says.

I turn to find four girls in uniform watching me with their arms crossed. They're impossibly well groomed and flawless. Obviously besties. Proof that I was dead wrong about my anti-clique idea.

Their cool gazes roll up and down my body, assessing me in a way with which I've grown unfortunately familiar. Every girl knows this drill. These are the cool girls, ostensibly, and they have come to weigh and measure me. Their bodies, hair, makeup—even the way they rock their uniforms—are undeniable signs of their power on campus and their expectations of a perfectly charmed life, which their daddies will guarantee them. Like four slightly oversexed dolls, they stand at arm's length from me, thrusting out their cleavage, tossing their straightened silky hair over their shoulders, and pursing their pouty, glossy lips. Their skin is so unblemished it glows. Their eyes are so clear they might see right through me.

With my curls, crooked tooth, and stunningly empty bank account, I am their antithesis. Or, as I prefer to see it, they are mine.

I've never gotten along well with the popular girls. And something in their collective scowl tells me I'm not about to become the fifth member of this particular clique.

"You must be the new girl. The junior?" the ginger begins frostily, her tone warm like a Savannah summer but her eyes dead cold. Her followers—a Thai girl, an Indian girl, and a stark blonde—glare at me. "The California chick who thinks she's some sort of artist?"

"Unless there are two of us," I reply. My years of dealing with rich, bitchy, and beautiful girls have given me a bit of a bite. "Why? Are you the president of my fan club?"

"As if Harper would *ever* be your fan!" the Thai girl exclaims and looks at the ginger—evidently named Harper—for approval.

I narrow my eyes. "I just meant how do you know so much about me?"

With her friends mirroring her every move, Harper curls her lip and glares up at me. She's barely five-two but is filled head to toe with piss and vinegar. "Everyone knows about you."

"And *not* in a good way," the stark blonde adds, her words thick with a Russian accent.

"It's like when a circus freak walks into a room," Harper drawls. "It's hard for everyone else not to notice."

"Gee," I begin, "I'd love to hear more about how your parents met, but I've got to get to school."

I try to cut through the foursome, but Harper shoves her hand against my chest, stopping me. Not cool.

"Truth is, Merchant, we know who you are because it's not every day Headmaster Villicus lets in some poor chick with a crazy mom who killed herself." Harper smirks. "Word gets around."

"Well, you know nothing about my mother. But I'm sure you know *all about* getting around."

Removing her hand and pushing through their stunned crowd, I take the stairs into Goethe Hall two at a time and ignore the girls' voices as they tell each other that I'm not worth the hassle, that I'm ugly, that I totally need braces, and that I'm never going to get the "Big V," which sounds like something sexual but hell if I know. Inside the ornate Goethe Hall, I somehow find my way into the long queue where I try to shake off my encounter, try to stop seeing red, and wait impatiently to collect my orientation package from an old, wrinkled secretary who spits when she speaks.

"Did you say your name's Martha Cennen?" the secretary asks me as she shuffles through disorganized stacks of orientation packets. She smells like the bottom of an ashtray. She is wearing an enormous emerald brooch. Behind her, a dozen secretaries, also wearing massive pendants, type on typewriters, one finger at a time.

"No, it's Anne Merchant."

"Maybe you remind me of someone I used to know."

I sigh. "I'm a junior in the Fine Arts stream."

"A junior. Fine Arts. Tanner Chanem."

"*Anne Merchant,*" I correct.

"It's not Nate N. Nemrach?" Her gaze meets mine.

There's an odd, out-of-place playfulness in her expression. And then I realize where she's getting all those other names from.

"Are you just turning my name into anagrams?" I ask.

Like a caught child, she quickly shakes her head *no* and dives, with a giggle, back into searching the stacks. Or at least putting on a show of searching.

The ticking of single typewriter keys quickly becomes grating. Behind me, a Mandarin guy and an Italian girl—who are, like everyone else in the queue, coldly ignoring their peers—have started grumbling in their respective languages. I assume the wait and the maddeningly slow secretary are getting to them like they're getting to me. At last, the secretary pokes her head out of the pile of packets, lifts one victoriously, and yanks a sticky note off the front of it.

She reads the note, and a slow smile spreads across her face. "Message for you, Anne."

"From my dad?"

She shakes her head, but, before she can explain, a PA announcement interrupts her: *"All new students, meet at Valedictorian Hall by nine o'clock for your campus tours. All new students."* A glance at the clock shows it's nearly nine already, and I don't even know where Valedictorian Hall is. I look expectantly at her.

"You wanna go on the campus tour, don't you?" she asks me. I don't have much patience at the best of times, but she's *killing me.* She knows I have to go. It's like she's taking pleasure in dragging this out and watching everyone in line squirm as we wait helplessly for her.

"I'd like to go, yes."

She glances at the sticky note. "Is your dad named Mr. Merchant?"

"Yes."

She glances at it again. "Well then your dad didn't leave a message for you."

"Who did?"

Her grin spreads. It's yellow enough to be pure gold. "Headmaster Villicus. He'd like to see you. Which I guess means you won't be going on the campus tour."

Handing me my packet, she points me down a long, dark hall, which brings me to a set of empty wooden benches outside the headmaster's closed door. I take an uncomfortable seat, wait to be called in, and briefly admire a selection of Beksinski's beautiful nightmares condemning me from their frames on the walls. I start

absently reviewing my class schedule and syllabuses—all while
trying not to stew over my encounter with the girls outside and
failing miserably. It sucks to have *already* made enemies of what
are surely the most popular girls here, but it's not exactly new territory for me. I thought it'd be different at Cania—I thought I'd have
a clean slate and the protection of this school uniform—but tales
of my California life seem to have preceded me.

I can feel the slightly optimistic outlook I brought to the island receding like an ocean wave, exposing the oppressive heft of
my unshakable life story.

There are no rewrites in store for me here. No blank canvases.
What was will continue to be. That Harper and her pack of perfectly coifed skanks knew where I come from—that they knew
about my mother's sickness and subsequent suicide—reinforces
what a part of me already guessed: if I want a better life, I'm
going to have to fight for it. As Anne Merchant. Not as some
watered-down, poser, more acceptable version of myself.

A commotion at the end of the hall interrupts my thoughts,
and I glance up to see three silhouettes hurriedly heading my
way. Two are tall and lean, and the other is shorter and margin-
ally buff. It's clear that one of the tall guys is hauling the other
two toward Villicus's office, in spite of their reluctance. Their
bickering reaches me before they do.

"It's called the First Amendment," the shorter guy cries. His
voice seems to be holding back a laugh, and, as they come into
the light, I can see him grinning. "Freedom of speech. Freedom
to assemble."

"That's enough, Mr. Stone." One of the tall guys is, in fact,
a tall *man*, who is dressed impeccably in an expensive-looking
suit with a cashmere scarf and overcoat. His dark hair is brushed
elegantly away from his face, and his frosty blue glare glows against
his olive skin. Obviously, he's a member of the faculty. I hope he's
not my teacher, though, because it would be tragic for my GPA

if I spent my class time gawking at the teacher and stammering through my comments.

"I should be allowed to protest the Big V race," the Stone boy insists, "without your kid getting on my butt for it and without Villicus tearing me a new one!"

"Pilot, your picket sign read 'The Only V I Want Is Between Her Legs,'" the tall boy says and, frustrated, sits on the bench across from me. He drops his face into his hands and sighs. "That's not protesting. That's peacocking. Aggressively."

Pilot Stone smirks. His dark gaze dashes my way, and he smiles mischievously. I raise my papers in front of my face so it's not quite so obvious that I'm eavesdropping.

"Dr. Z, come on," Pilot says as he squeezes into the bench next to me, forcing me to shove down when there's hardly space to do so. He smells clean, and his leg and arm against mine are nice and warm. "I won't tell Villie about Ben here destroying my property—"

"Your property! It was offensive garbage on craft paper!" the tall boy cries out.

"—if you just let this whole thing go."

The negotiating stops quickly with a long, heavy pause. I wish now that I wasn't holding my syllabus up as high as I am so I could see their faces. Relying on my peripheral vision, I strain to make out Pilot's expression, but all I can see is that he is looking in the direction of Dr. Z, who is standing in front of Headmaster Villicus's office.

"Wait to be called in," Dr. Z orders before rapping on the door and abruptly disappearing inside.

I lower my syllabus to see Pilot mockingly salute the spot where Dr. Z was just standing and the tall guy with the swimmer's build—Ben, I believe his name is—run his hands through his thick sandy hair.

At once, both Pilot and Ben turn their gazes on me.

I have to tell myself not to blush. Because if these guys are even remotely representative of the male population in this student body, well, I can feel my optimism returning already.

two

THE BIG V

ADMITTEDLY, I'VE NEVER BEEN ASKED TO GO TO THE movies or for coffee. I've never held hands with a guy. And—unless you count a very strange moment when, at the age of eleven, after sketching a beautiful dead boy in his open casket, I kissed his cheek—I seem to have made it to and past my sweet sixteen without being properly kissed.

If *love and romance* were a credited course in school, I would flunk out.

If the tally of notches on your bedpost was any indication of your likelihood of finding love in the future, I'd be doomed to a life of collecting cats, culminating in death-by-suffocation-under-a-hoard-of-creepy-china-dolls.

But just because I haven't exactly allowed myself to become the human equivalent of a school bus—ridden regularly by everyone—doesn't mean a) that I'm dead inside or b) that guys feel dead inside when they look at me. I mean, I don't *know* what they feel. Probably nothing like what they feel when girls like Harper and her gang o' skanks walk by. But there have been times—memorable moments—when I've caught dudes looking at me in class. And, in grade eight, I heard a guy tell his friends he'd had a sex dream about me, which, I eventually admitted to myself, felt sort of cool. If it came down to it, I'd rather be smart than pretty, but a part of me would like to believe that, down the road, I might turn out to be both.

"First day?" Pilot asks me, breaking the silence.

Ben darts a glare at Pilot then averts his bright mint-green gaze in a way that makes me think he might never look at me again.

"I'm Pilot. You must be the new junior, Anne Merchant."

Great. Does everyone know my story? "Is it your first day, too?"

Pilot shakes his head and fixes his twinkling gaze on me. His irises are so black, they appear to merge with his pupils in an unsettling yet beguiling way. Everything about him is dark and masculine, from his ultra-short black hair to his rich skin tone to his wide, strong-looking shoulders.

"I came here last fall," he says. "From California. My dad knows your dad."

Before I can register my surprise at our connection, the door to Headmaster Villicus's office swings open, and Dr. Z looks out sternly. "Mr. Stone. He'll see you first."

"I'll catch up with you in class," Pilot says, smiling at me as he gets up. "I'm a junior, too—and a double major, so we'll have some classes together. I'll help you find your way around, cool? See you, Annie!"

The door has barely closed behind him when I breathe a sigh of relief. It was only moments ago that I was fretting over the extremely high likelihood that I would live a friendless existence here. I can't help but beam.

Which Ben catches me doing.

He scowls and looks away again. I close my lips to mask my crooked tooth, which my mom always said gave me character but which everyone else seems to be repulsed by, and refuse to let Ben get to me. I don't need everyone to be my friend. Just one person—just Pilot—will do, thank you.

I strain to eavesdrop on Pilot's conversation with the head-master, but I'm unable to make out more than the low rumble of mumbles. So I distract myself by rifling through my orientation packet. In catering to the greatest minds among the world's most privileged youth, Cania Christy holds itself to a standard of education that goes beyond the AP-level courses I had in public school. I used to take Bio; here, that's *The Ethical Dilemma of Euthanasia*. *Exploring the Science of Consciousness* is what regular schools would call Physics. And *A Critical Exploration of the Supernatural in Literature and Society* is Cania's version of English. Because I'm in the Fine Arts stream, I'll also take *Sculpting the Human Form* every Tuesday and Thursday afternoon and *Advanced Portfolio Development* first thing every day.

"Stomping the Devil's tattoo," Ben says out of nowhere. His voice is buttery—slippery and rich, like it's hard to hold onto, like it runs smoothly over everything it touches. Oh, God, I do not want him to have a sexy voice. In combination with his body, his eyes, and his sculpted face, it's completely unfair. "That's what it's called. What you're doing with your fingers."

There's no one else in the hall, so he's obviously talking to me. I realize then that I've been absentmindedly drumming my finger-tips on the arm of the bench. When I glance at Ben, I find that he's closed his eyes and tipped his head to the ceiling. Napping.

That's it? He just wanted me to stop drumming my fingers?

I tuck my hair behind my ears, take a deep breath, and very purposefully begin drumming again. Louder this time. And faster.

"I take it," he says, deigning to speak to me again, "you're not a music major."

I shake my head, drumming on blissfully. "Art."

And then I get his point: I can't carry a beat. My drumming slows to a stop.

"I'm an artist, too. A sculptor," he says. He must be a senior. There's a maturity about him that can only come with age. "Tell me, do you sign your work with your full name?"

Odd question. If I didn't know better, I'd think he was being friendly. But he's probably just talking to me because he's bored. Rich guys are always bored so quickly. That's what happens when you've had everything handed to you and have perfectly easy access to more of it at any time.

"I use my initials."

The corners of his lips turn up ever so slightly. "A.M."

"Yep. I guess you already know I'm a junior. Evidently, it's headline news, though I can't imagine why."

At the far end of the hall, a secretary appears in the darkness. For no apparent reason, she starts pacing, darting furtive glances our way every now and then like some strangely dressed, paranoid bird. Ben turns his gaze on her and waits until her back is to us to continue speaking, now in a hush I have to lean to make out.

"Because you're different from the rest of us," he says.

"Yeah, well, I was different from everyone back home, too, but."

"There are different ways to be different, Anne."

As the secretary darts another look our way, I internally smile at the sound of my name rolling off Ben's tongue. If I were to let myself entertain the idea of Ben being semi-decent, I would probably be lost in love with him in the time it takes to outline a pink heart on a canvas. There's an alluring formality about him, as if he's been raised to sit quietly at the dinner table while the chef serves him, as if he's been wearing a tie since he was a toddler. He sits extra-straight, he holds his jaw in a tight clench, his every move seems deliberate—not robotic. Deliberate. Elegant. At least, I'd think that if I let myself think that. Which I refuse to do. Because this guy showed me his true colors when he grimaced at my crooked tooth; if I am going to think of him at all, it will be casually and with indifference.

Yes, I command myself, *that's the way it will be.*

"I don't suppose you know all that much about being different, Ben," I say, careful to sound as indifferent as I wish to be. He arches an eyebrow, and I realize my tone may have been a little too cold.

"I'd say I know a lot about a lot, including being different," he replies. "Are you familiar with the Big V race?"

"Outside of the fact that it's being passionately protested?"

"It's only being protested by Pilot Stone." We sit in inhospitable silence for longer than I'd like—me trying not to feel consumed by the depth of his gaze, him quite likely wondering how he got saddled with my company—until Ben says, "I saw you running to school today. I passed you on my bike. You're fast. Long legs."

When my surprise shows on my face, he grins. His nose wrinkles charmingly. It's far cuter a smile than I'd have expected from someone like Ben, someone who's more of a starched-shirt guy than a funny T-shirt guy. Not that I care about his smile. Not that his extremely adorable crinkle-nosed grin really *affects* me, per se.

All at once, I realize who Ben is. The only way he could watch me run to school is if he was off-campus, too. Pilot had said something to Dr. Z about "his kid" shoving him.

"You're the Zin boy next door," I say in a breath. "And Dr. Z—that's Dr. Zin. Your dad."

"I assumed you'd pieced that together already."

I shake my head. He looks disappointed.

"I've been living in that monstrosity of a house for years," he explains. "No one's lived with Gigi in all that time. I would have thought she'd have mentioned me." Before I can continue with the small talk, Ben glances up the hall and lowers his voice.

"Look, A.M., I assume Villicus is going to assign your Guardian to you and get you to declare your PT."

Unsure why there's this sudden air of secrecy, I reply with a shrug, "Your guess is as good as mine."

"It's no guess. Most kids get assigned this stuff the second they arrive on the island—"

"The second?" I smirk at the exaggeration.

"—but yours is a special case."

"Special. *Right*." Of course, I know he's referring to my ghetto background.

"You're going to get assigned a Guardian right away. We all have one—well, everyone that's going for the Big V, at least."

"What's the Big V?"

"The valedictorian race. Listen," his mint gaze darts to the secretary again, and when she finally turns away, the pace of his speech quickens, "Villicus will explain all that stuff soon. Don't tell him I was talking to you."

"Um, are you okay?"

"Just do this one thing for me, will you, Anne?"

"I just—I don't even know you."

He flinches when I say that. The brass knob on Villicus's door squeals.

"Just make your Guardian happy," Ben whispers to me hurriedly through his teeth, like a ventriloquist, as the door starts to swing open, "and you'll be valedictorian next year. You *have* to."

Then, abruptly, he leans back against the bench and closes his eyes, as if he's been napping all this time. Pilot and Dr. Zin appear in the doorway. Pilot's eyes are wet and red, and he looks furious as he's ushered out. I'm hardly able to take in what's happening—with Ben's warning so fresh in my mind—as Pilot turns back and speaks boldly to our unseen headmaster. Ben slowly opens his eyes to join me in watching what follows.

"It's called free will," Pilot bellows, his voice deep but quaking. "I have every right to exercise it. And that means I get to make my own choices."

"Come along, Mr. Stone," Dr. Zin advises, taking Pilot by the arm.

Pilot shrugs his arm free and glowers at everyone but me.

"And I choose," Pilot continues boldly, "not to declare a PT, not to take a Guardian, and not to enter this BS race to become valedictorian. Let the rest of the students here try to impress their pathetic, uninvolved parents with some stupid title, but that's not how I'm going to live my life. And you can't force me. I will not declare a PT!"

In a flash, Pilot runs down the hall and, blankly, Dr. Zin turns his attention to Ben. He hands him a piece of paper.

"The headmaster was kind to you," Dr. Zin says stiffly to his son. I can easily see the resemblance now—it's not just their height, their hair, or their eyes but the formal way they speak. "He has not declined your application to assist Mr. Weinchler, in spite of your outburst. Take this form to the front desk for processing."

Then Dr. Zin turns to me and extends his arm toward the door, welcoming me to a room I'm pretty sure I don't want to go into. Not that I've ever had a reason to fear the principal. But because I just saw a rather tough-looking dude reduced to tears by the man on the other side of the door.

I expect Ben to half-smile or at least nod at me as I go in, but he's halfway down the hall even before I stand—confirming my worry that, in spite of what appeared to be a brief glimpse of the soft side of Ben Zin, he's as indifferent toward me as I need to be toward him.

Even before I spy Headmaster Villicus hobbling like the old man he is toward his desk, I am assaulted by the unbearable heat of his office. An enormous orange fire roars in the largest stone fireplace I've ever seen, belching smoke into the chimney but letting a small trickle escape from either side of the fire enclosure and rise to create a haze near the ceiling.

"Miss Merchant," Villicus greets. "Take a seat. Dr. Zin was just leaving."

My gaze follows Dr. Zin as, with a nod in Villicus's direction and none in mine, he retreats. The door closes with a faint click behind him.

"Sit," Villicus commands me.

He turns to me, crossing his arms over the back of his highback chair, and smiles. If you can call that a smile. His nearly brown teeth are crooked—much more crooked than mine—and his left eyebrow is permanently arched, with a large mole bursting out of it. It's taking everything in me *not* to stare at it as I approach. Not to stare at his bristly hair either or the hunch in his shoulders or the potbelly that he tries to hide under a brown suit that fits like a paper bag. It's as wrinkled as the cloak of a dead Franciscan friar, and I can smell the BO that clings to it. As the heat and odor make my head swoon, as I grip the wooden arm of my instantly uncomfortable chair, I flick my gaze toward the little window and inhale deeply through my mouth—like I'm breathing in the cool air.

He draws the shade.

In the dimness, he runs his stare over me again and again. Just as it seems he might be done looking me over, he drags his gaze up from my toes to my bare knees, all the way up, pausing where he likes and ultimately settling restlessly on the top of my head. Then his gaze drifts downward. For the first time, it occurs to me that these ultra-small uniforms are designed to give old men like Villicus something to feast their pervy eyes on.

I glance uneasily away, to an old framed map of Germany. Next to it, a cabinet holds what look like war medals, hundreds of them. Villicus's broad desk is bare except for a pen with a huge black plume, a jumbo hourglass that counts away the days, and a complex-looking case encrusted with flame-shaped sapphires.

"Thanks for inviting me to meet you," I begin, my voice cracking the excruciating quiet like a hammer on glass. "I have a few questions I'd love to get cleared up. For starters, I've been hearing a lot about Guardians and PTs, but I have no idea what those are."

My implied question hangs in the air.

"*Mizz Merchant*," he coos at last, "did you ask me to come to your office?"

He slinks around his desk and sits on it, just opposite me. Our knees are close enough to touch. I adjust my leg away.

"No."

"Then allow me to direct this conversation, dear."

I fold my hands on my lap.

"You do realize that, at Cania Christy, we accept only the best of the best."

"Okay," I say cautiously.

"*Okay*? Hmm."

Unsatisfied, he pushes off his desk and wanders behind my chair. There he stands, breathing heavily. With a short shudder, I stiffen as I feel his hands—his long, thick nails—brace my shoulders.

"Do you believe you are the best of the best?" he asks, still holding my shoulders.

I am frozen in his grip. "I've never really thought about it."

"Of course you have. Certainly your first art show must have given you a distinct amount of confidence in your abilities."

My pieces showed in an LA gallery when I was ten. "We didn't sell much."

"Not at that one, no," he whispers. His breath catches in my hair. "But at others."

I have no idea what he's referring to—I haven't had more than one art show. It occurs to me that my dad may have played up my successes to get me in here, so I say nothing and hope not to shatter Villicus's illusion. Besides, right now, I'm not thinking about art. All I'm thinking about is the unseemly presence of this man's hands on my shoulders. I try to slink out from under his hands, but his grip is unyielding. It's not that his touch is some creepy sex thing. It's worse. It's the energy he emits, something oppressive that's intensified the moment he nears me; it strikes something uncomfortable buried deep inside, an unplaceable but overpowering sensation, like a feverish nightmare exhumed.

At last, his hands slip from my shoulders, stripping away the sense of dread. He lurches toward his war medal case and stares through it while I try to shake off the memory of his touch.

"Let me be clear." He turns back to me. "Our admissions criteria are intentionally exclusionary, designed to keep out people like you. It is only by the kindness of those better than you that you are here today."

Don't react to his insult, I tell myself. After all, my housemother isn't exactly raving about me. And I'm sure my reaction to Harper this morning didn't put me in a great social position. Freaking out on the headmaster now could put a quick, ugly stop to this "fresh start."

"How do you feel when I say such things?" he asks, looking at me as if he knows me.

Sarcasm is my best defense. "What things?"

He smirks. "Very well. We might have had a rather enlightening conversation, but you insist on being a child. I am compelled to tell you that you are here today because you have a benefactor."

"A benefactor?"

"Senator Dave Stone—a friend of your father's—has made it possible for you to be here."

Villicus sits at his desk again and pensively temples his fingers under his chin while I put two and two together. Dave Stone is Pilot's dad. A cold wave of embarrassment rolls over me as I think of Pilot's dad telling him about the charity case he has to sponsor for this rich-bitch boarding school. To say nothing of how odd it is to learn that my dad, who spends all of his time in a dark funeral home, is connected to a senator. I know Atherton is filled with the country's wealthiest and most powerful people, but I didn't know my dad *knew* any of them.

"I'm sure you know that you ought to thank him." He waits for me to nod, and I comply. "He put himself out there for you. Cania Christy accepts only people of a certain net worth and only on invitation. You meet neither criterion."

Stiffly, I utter, "I'll be sure to thank him."

"And I'm sure I know *how* you'll thank him." Like perched black crows taking flight, Villicus's eyes narrow in the cloud-like gray of his face. "You'll thank him as all girls with your background thank men, especially men of affluence. And I do believe such appreciation will suit his tastes fine, nubile *fraulein* like you."

Tongue-tied at the shock of his comment, I can only blink. I've never even properly kissed a guy, and he thinks I'm going to sleep with some old friend of my dad's to thank him for sending me to this place? *In what world?!*

"Now, for the reason I actually called you here today."

"It wasn't just to insult me?"

Villicus snaps his fingers twice. His door flies open.

And in waltzes this skinny beanpole of a guy—this tall, lanky thing with pockmarks on his cheeks and probing, miniscule, steel eyes. His frenetic leer lunges toward me.

"Miss Merchant," Villicus says, "meet your Guardian."

three

MY GUARDIAN

SINCE FIRST HEARING ABOUT THIS WHOLE GUARDIAN idea, I've been naively filling in the blank after the word *Guardian* with the word *angel*. *Guardian Angel*. Part of me had expected that my Guardian would be ushering me through life here, helping me make decisions.

But this scrawny man-child is no guardian angel.

A mouth-breather no older than yours truly, he looks like someone you'd expect to crawl out from under the floorboards in a Wes Craven flick. Pale irises, greasy hair, and bumpy gray skin with little orange hairs poking out all over his jawline. I look from him to Villicus and back. A prerequisite to work at Cania must be that you be the ugliest son of a bitch alive.

"I'm Ted Rier," my Guardian says. He's got a German accent, just like Villicus. "You may call me Teddy."

"Ted is my newest assistant and the ideal Guardian for you," Villicus adds, just as my pathetic excuse for a Guardian shuts the door and scurries to take the seat next to me.

Trying to catch my gaze, Teddy lifts my hand and kisses it. It is impossible not to notice the white flecks in the corners of his mouth. It is nearly impossible not to cringe—yet I manage—

knowing my hand is so close to *that* or not to pull away too quickly when he smoothly says he's charmed to make my acquaintance.

"It would be great," I say as Villicus sits and Teddy opens his cheap-looking briefcase, "if someone could explain what exactly a Guardian is supposed to do. I assume there's a connection between a Guardian and a PT, but I'm fuzzy on both."

"If I may?" Teddy asks Villicus, who nods, allowing Teddy to field my questions. "Miss Merchant, first things first. I understand you attended a school prior to this one, and at that school you earned top grades."

"Top of my class and top of the Dean's List each year," I admit.

Teddy smirks. "I didn't know they had 'deans' at public schools."

"Which is supposed to mean what?"

Neither Teddy nor Villicus seems to appreciate my tone much. As if they're allowed to imply insults, but I'm not allowed a defense.

"You and I are on the same team," Teddy tells me. "If I have offended you, forgive me. But the fact is that you are familiar with and comfortable in an academic environment that breeds much lower expectations than Headmaster Villicus demands here at Cania Christy. You were a top performer in California. You excelled among the uninspired. But now you're among a new class of people. And you are competing for a title that, I give you my word, every student here wants more than you want to go to Brown on full scholarship."

I'm about to ask how on earth he could know that when I realize that my dad must have put that info on my application form. So I skip to my second question: "I'm competing to be valedictorian, you mean?"

Teddy drops a leaflet in the hand he kissed, which still feels icky. I read its headline.

"The Race to Be Valedictorian: Only the Supreme Survive."
Dropping the sheet momentarily, I look from Teddy to Villicus,

who is watching me with a small smile tipping the corners of his lips skyward. "Like 'only the strong survive'?"

Teddy glowers at me, and I immediately realize that this may be the one school on earth where "stupid questions" actually do exist.

"What I mean is," I backtrack, "if evolution—perhaps the most complex process in the universe, a process requiring unimaginable patience and rewarding natural talents—is all about the *strong* surviving, attaining the Big V must be an incredible challenge if only the *supreme* survive?"

Villicus stands and stoops behind his desk like a bird of prey, beady eyes glowing. He begins to speak—slowly, like one of those dictators you see in black-and-white films from the Second World War:

"I see that you have already adopted the vernacular of Cania students," he says. "The Big V, as the valedictorian title has become fondly known here, is the highest mark of academic honor one can receive in school if not in all of life's endeavors. Alas, who among this student body does not seek with full desperation the gift of the title valedictorian and all that it brings?"

I recall Pilot's teary declaration but dare not mention it now, not with Villicus knee-deep in a speech he has surely given a thousand or more times. Truly, my key consideration in coming here was that the prestige of being the valedictorian of a school of this caliber would seal my future. I am as desperate as any for the Big V. Maybe more.

"The stakes are high—higher than anywhere. Valedictorians at schools like Taft, Exeter, and Eton go on to Oxford, the Sorbonne, Columbia." Villicus's eyebrow arches up his long, turtle-like head. "But an Ivy acceptance is just the beginning for the Cania valedictorian. No student here has a parent who doesn't wholly wish him or her to graduate as the Big V. You recently saw Mr. Pilot Stone turn his back on the race, and I assure you: he is the only in the student body to do so. The Big V is, to be sure, a title that is *beyond* prestigious."

With the grandeur of an old actor, Villicus sweeps back his shapeless garment and takes his seat again. Teddy licks the tip of his pen, and I notice he's started filling in a form on a clipboard. My name is at the top of it.

"Miss Merchant," Teddy says, "do you wish to be considered for the title of valedictorian at the end of your senior year?"

He and Villicus wait for my answer.

This is a no-brainer. Memories of my father rush at me, images of him whispering to me that I need to try as hard as I can to become valedictorian. Even Ben, who had so little to say to me, had that to share.

"Of course," I say firmly.

Teddy ticks a box on the form. "Next," he says, "I will inform you of the three rules for becoming valedictorian."

"You would be wise to heed—verily, to *meditate on*—these rules," Villicus adds.

I listen closely. As uncomfortable as I feel with these two kooks, as frustrating as it is to feel controlled by them, and as much as I wish I could bolt from this insanely hot room, this actually is important. The Big V is becoming more important to me as each moment passes, especially as I realize that this is an intense competition—and what Type A doesn't perk up at the idea of competing?

The first rule is standard: I must have an outstanding GPA. *Obv.* Rule number two: I must follow Cania's communication guidelines to a tee. These are both table stakes; you cannot be considered for valedictorian if you fail to meet these two baseline expectations.

"What are the communication guidelines?" I ask.

"To begin, there is absolutely no fraternizing with the villagers," Teddy says. "No unsupervised phone calls. No Internet. No

personal computers, mobile phones, tablets, or other such techni-
cal nonsense."

"Sorry," I interrupt to their vexation, "but how am I supposed to research my papers without Internet access?"

"All papers are handwritten, and research is conducted in our
library."

"Where there are computers?"

"Where there are *books*. Now, the third and final rule,"
Teddy continues, bypassing my obvious concern, "is the critical
one. The deal breaker. The game changer. The one thing that will
set the superior apart. And it is this: you must sufficiently define
and excellently live by your *prosperitas thema*."

"What's a *prosperitas thema*?" I've only just said the words
when I realize I've heard of it already. "Oh, my PT."

Teddy points at the sheet dangling between my fingertips as
he explains, "Every student declares a PT, which is a statement
of the inherent quality each mortal possesses that will make one
a remarkable success in life."

Skimming the handout, I read that my PT is supposed to
complete the line:

> *When I grow up, I will be successful in life by using my*
> _____.

"So, it's essentially a statement of how we'll each be Most
Likely to Succeed," I summarize, and Teddy nods, though
Villicus sighs as if I've just summarized the *Mona Lisa* with a
single line about her smile.

"Once identified, your PT will be the ruler against which you
are measured," Teddy says.

Villicus piles on. "Candidates will be judged by their Guard-
ians at every turn on whether or not they are satisfying their PTs."
His eyes land on mine. "You must live and breathe your PT, Miss
Merchant, if you wish to become valedictorian."

"If you don't mind, what does that mean, practically speaking?" I ask. "How will I *live and breathe* it?"

"Suppose," Teddy offers, "your PT is to…be selfish to succeed in life."

"That sounds awful."

"I would grade your actions over the course of the next two years against that PT. I would expect you to skip to the front of every line, fail to share, sabotage the efforts of your peers, especially those who are most desperate, and—"

"Steal money from a beggar's bowl," I suggest.

"Precisely!" Villicus and Teddy exclaim.

"I was joking," I whisper. Neither hears me.

"Keep in mind," Teddy adds, "that everyone around you is making every effort to live and breathe their own PTs. You won't know it's happening. You won't know what they're playing at. But that is precisely what they're doing."

Evidently, our PTs are assigned to us by our Guardians. Guardians are selected from the faculty, the housemothers, even the secretaries. One Guardian for each junior and senior— freshmen and sophomores don't participate.

"I will be your shadow," Teddy says finally. "Naturally we'll be cohabitating at Miss Malone's—"

"Wait, what?" I interrupt. "You're living at Gigi's, too? With me?"

"Where did you expect me to live?"

"There's not even any room there!" I already know, though, that he must have claimed the guest bedroom, which is why I'm stuck in the attic.

"Miss Merchant," Villicus interjects, his tone flat, "you have put up more barriers in these past ten minutes than the average student does in their entire time on this campus."

"I'm just surprised—"

"*And* I've already considered," Villicus thrusts on, "the

possibility that you are not fit for this institution. Perhaps I ought to send you home. Do you realize that this morning alone I turned away a very wealthy man who implored me to let his daughter into the school? He's flying out here tonight by helicopter just to see if he can persuade me. And here you sit! Snarling. Making demands."

That shuts me up. Both Villicus and Teddy notice my reaction, and both smile; they share a joyless grimace. I'd love to be in a position to march out of here and stun them both, but with everything my dad gave up and all the strings he pulled to get me into Cania Christy, that would be a slap across his grizzled face. I wring my hands but know there's no use in fighting this.

"So we're living together, Teddy?" I choke out at last.

"The better to oversee your activities," Villicus says.

Teddy piles on. "You'll be graded at every turn. Morning, noon, night."

As a junior, I'm supposed to work with my Guardian to document the activities I've completed that prove I'm *living and breathing* my PT. Guardians track progress daily, weekly, monthly. And, on graduation day, if I've pleased Teddy, he will argue my case before the Valedictorian Committee, which, with just one member, is the smallest committee in the world: Headmaster Villicus. The student whose case is best argued will be named valedictorian. Along the way, we're supposed to keep our PTs private—no other students are allowed to know another's PT as that may give them an unfair advantage.

It's hitting me now, like lightning bolts shattering a gray sky, that Teddy is going to make or break me. He sneers at me like he knows I've just figured that out.

"Success does not happen by accident," Villicus says. "Success is borne of looking inside oneself, recognizing one's strengths, and making conscious decisions based on those strengths. That's what your PT is. Because mankind is rarely capable of seeing its own strengths or flaws, your Guardian will assess you and identify your PT for you."

I glance at Teddy. He just met me. How is he supposed to know my strengths and weaknesses?

Villicus goes on to explain that, although Cania has formalized and named the concept of the *prosperitas thema*, the greatest success stories of our time—even those who never set foot in this school—are each committed to a personal quality that has led to their success. Steve Jobs *was* innovation. Madonna *is* bold ambition. Warren Buffett *is* investment savvy. Oprah Winfrey *is* empowerment.

"Now, I see that you are already quite late for your scheduled meet-and-greet," Villicus finishes. "This evening, then, at your shared residence, Ted will determine your PT. And you, Miss Merchant, would be wise not to resist him."

By the time I race across campus through a rain shower that turns the quad into a slip-and-slide and, huffing, take a seat at the last open workstation in Room 1B of the stony Rex Paimonde building, I've already refused to let myself think that things can't get much worse. I'm learning that they sure as hell can, so I don't dare tempt fate. Instead, I rush to settle in, apologizing as I get my notepad out of my wet backpack, knowing I've interrupted their discussion. After all, I'm fifteen minutes late for a half-hour meet-and-greet.

But the teacher, Garnet Descarteres, this lovely blonde woman who's *maybe* twenty, smiles and tells me to relax, get settled, I haven't missed anything critical. She's so pretty, I have a hard time believing she works alongside fuglies like the secretaries, Teddy, and Villicus. She explains that it's her first year teaching here—

she's new, like *moi*—and that I should feel free to call her by her first name.

I'm about to smile when I glimpse someone I hadn't expected to see: Harper. And, just like that, things go from bad to worse.

In total, there are twelve of us in the Junior Arts Stream, and, although we'll have different classes, we'll all meet daily for a morning workshop with Garnet. I'm relieved to find Pilot here and all the more relieved that Ben isn't in this group—I've already guessed he's a senior, so I shouldn't have expected to see him. But a part of me, against my better judgment, did.

There's also a very smiley girl, who must have declared a PT to be as sweet as cherry pie because she couldn't appear more friendly and cherubic. The other nine students—including Harper and her Thai friend—engage actively with Garnet but practically snarl when someone else talks. Either everyone's taking the Big V competition ultra-seriously or they all declared PTs to be gigantic snobs in life.

"We were just introducing ourselves," Garnet tells me. "You'll have plenty of time to get to know each other at the dance this weekend, but why wait until the weekend to make friends when you can start now?"

At the mention of making friends, smirks and sneers appear one by one, like fireflies in the night, on the brooding yet beautiful faces of most of the students.

Harper whispers to her Thai friend, "Even if I were open to knowing this bunch of losers, ain't nothing gonna make me like Trailer Park Tramp." She gestures my way. I'm meant to see it; I'm meant to hear her. "We don't do charity in Texas."

Ignoring Harper, I organize myself and ask, "Are we saying anything in particular in our intros, Garnet?"

"The usual. Where you're from. What brought you here."

"We don't have to share our PTs, do we?" I ask, hoping to hear what the others will be "living and breathing" in the hopes of getting the Big V but knowing I'd have nothing to share yet.

No sooner have I uttered my question than everyone—even Pilot and the smiling girl—gapes at me like I just said Picasso is irrelevant.

"No, Anne," Garnet explains slowly, tucking a lock of her gorgeous blonde hair behind her ear. "Students are meant to keep their PTs private. Only you and the school's Guardians will know your PT."

"Unless you don't have one," Pilot tacks on. His eyes meet mine and he flashes me a bright smile. "Some of us choose not to. It's your right, you know."

"*Excuse moi*, Garnet," says a brown-haired boy with a tiny whiff of hair above his lip. He has a French accent so thick, it sounds like he's eating peanut butter while fighting a head cold: every sound he makes is stressed, dragged out endlessly, or shoved to the back of his throat. He glances from Garnet to me. "Do you think we should continue to tell all our specific details?"

"If you don't mind me adding, I was just thinking the same thing Augusto was," the smiling girl adds, tossing me an apologetic grin before looking again at Garnet. "I would appreciate some clear guidance, if you wouldn't mind, considering the, um, present company."

"Well, Augusto and Lotus," Garnet says, though she's clearly talking to all of us, "why don't you share as much with the group as you *think* you should, okay? Can we all self-edit? That's an important skill for an artist."

The introductions pick up where they left off before my interruption, with Augusto. He's from Quebec. His parents own luxury ski resorts in Montreal, Banff, and Colorado.

"Before I came here, I was very much in love with a boy," Augusto begins timidly, his cheeks flush. "The son of my own *au pair*. We could not share our love because my father is very traditional. So," he flicks his sad gaze at me and fidgets with his pen, "I was at one of our family ski resorts with my love. And, holding hands, he and I boarded off the most incredible cliff together, soaring into the crisp and cool air. It was, without question, the most profoundly amazing moment of my life." His eyes begin to water. "Unfortunately, my *mère* discovered us when we reached the bottom, and that was that. I was sent here after. I was a freshman at the time."

Pilot has an intriguing twinkle in his eye that makes me think he probably wasn't listening very intently to Augusto's tale of forbidden love. "Can I go next?"

"If you'd like, Pilot. Now, tell us, is your father the California senator Dave Stone?" Garnet asks.

"Until the DNA results come back," Pilot groans. "Yeah, he's my dad. Real shining star, that guy. Anyway, let's see, before I came here, I was at a prep school in sunny C-A, and I got caught up in some stuff my dad didn't want me doing. It wouldn't be good for his political career, see. So, long story short, I ended up here last November. Shipped away like so much riff-raff."

Next is Lotus Featherly, the smiling girl and the personification of the word *saccharine*. As she talks about her life before Cania, I begin to look around the table. To really look. And I notice this: all of the students are flawless. I'm not exaggerating. These kids are perfecto-mundo.

Not gorgeous, per se. Not models.

Just unblemished. And pristine.

Lotus is so free of acne, she'd put those ProActiv spokespeople to shame; her skin shines. Augusto's hair is almost too shiny. Pilot's teeth are *so* perfectly straight and white. Harper's figure is *so* Scarlett Johansson–voluptuous. They look like the untouched manifestation of perfect DNA. Flawless…and here I am. Swelling out of my little uniform. And with a crooked tooth and wild hair that's starting to frizz up thanks to the rain.

"What brought you to Cania Christy?" Garnet asks Lotus, snapping me back into reality.

Like a waterline has erupted, tears spring to the girl's eyes. Oh, no! There is no faster way to get on the Loser List than to cry publicly in school; that's what bathroom stalls are for. "There was a situation," Lotus whimpers, "and my dad was presented with an ultimatum concerning me. But he didn't take it seriously. And so my parents ended up sending me here." She drops her gaze and folds her hands. "It's for the best, but I desperately miss home sometimes."

Unspoken details hang in the air, details that would require a stealthy hand to grasp them without further upsetting poor Lotus. My hand has always been prone to shaking, so I don't press. Not with Lotus sobbing like she is. No one else seems to care much, anyway. Maybe Lotus is known for emotional overreactions or maybe they're as self-involved as all the richies I grew up with back in Atherton.

When it's my turn to talk, I keep the details to a minimum and close off every emotion I have about the death of my mother. My story may have arrived on this island long before I did, but that doesn't mean I have to confirm every suspicion these people have about me.

I begin, "I went to a regular school—"

"A *public* school," Harper clarifies under her breath.

"Yes, a public school in California. It was good." I pause as my brain skips past all the other stuff. "My dad thought it would be a good idea for me to come here because it's sure to look great on my transcripts."

Garnet half-smiles, but no one else reacts. The stories the rest of the kids tell are at least as vague as mine, but, unlike me, everyone seems to regard Cania as an undesirable last resort. Like Siberia for teens—somewhere they've been exiled to. Could it be that Cania isn't the ultimate prep school, isn't the sure way into the Ivy League? As if to solidify my suspicion, a guy with emo eyeliner tells his ill-fated story.

"My mom and the pool boy were vacationing in the French Riviera for the millionth time," Emo Boy says with a forced lisp. He strokes his long bangs away from his face. "So, I mean, what would you do if your parents were always leaving you with the maids?"

"Easy. Go clubbing," Pilot says.

"I know, right?" Emo Boy tugs his sweater cuffs over his thumbs and hunches into himself. "So I was at a rave, this mad-ass club, and, yeah, I'd taken some E—hello, it's a rave. And there was this bitchin' dancer in a cage, just slathered in glow paint, right?" His voice becomes muffled as, endlessly fidgeting, he shifts his fists over his mouth. "So I climbed up on some speakers. And I leapt out onto her cage. And it, like, dropped from the ceiling. And my mom had to come home early because I was in the hospital. And she was so pissed. So, yeah, here I am."

Harper's Thai chum, Plum, goes next. She was a child actor-turned-singer in Thailand before Cania.

"I was doing lines of coke with my dad's friend after some red carpet event," Plum says casually, pulling a compact out of her bag and swiping red lipstick on. "That man was more a dad to me than my real dad. Anyway, I passed out in the VIP lounge. The *effing* paparazzi took photos and plastered them everywhere. Bitches. So, yeah, now I'm here. No life. No shopping. Nothing but the Big V race and a dance every now and then."

Finally, it's Harper's turn. She openly shifts her bra to boost her cleavage and gazes at everyone but me, which is fine because it's taking every morsel of my brainpower to sort out what she's wearing. These uniforms are head-turning without modifications, yet she's replaced her white shirt with a superlow V-neck tank, "forgotten" her tights, and hiked her skirt up wicked high. (I should *not* know she wears a red thong, and yet I do.) Sure, she has sleek hair, a cool Balenciaga blazer, and accessories that would make Rachel Zoe look like a pauper, but nothing can mask the truth: she's over-the-top *sleazy*.

"This is my second year at Cania, y'all. My daddy said I should come here after last Christmas," Harper says. Stroking a thick lock of red hair with both hands, she stares into space. "We had what you might call a falling out. I wanted Santa to get me a pink Hummer, but my *stepmonster* said if I wanted to get around so bad I should try riding our expensive horses for a change. So I thought of this great plan, y'see, to get back at her for it. And, sure, I admit I overdid it and my plan sort of backfired. But I blame *her* for that. Whatevs. No one was really happy with what I done. I had to come here, and that's that."

As I'm imagining Harper's unspoken revenge attempt gone awry, her tone shifts. Her eyes narrow intentionally, like she saw someone do that on a bad TV drama once.

"But, well," she continues softly, "y'know how they say you can cut off a dog's tail, but you can't sew it back on?" Confused silence. "I think you *can*. And with my plans to get the Big V, I'm gonna fix my mistakes." She flicks a stern gaze at me. "Everybody best remember not to get in my way."

That single comment starts an uproar with everyone but me and Pilot. He catches my eye and, smiling, mouths, "Get used to this."

I stagger out of class and attend the rest of my orientation sessions, like *Using the Dewey Decimal System* (no Internet here) and *Living Your PT*. I survive lunch by avoiding the cafeteria; instead, I head down to the waterside, where I'm surprised to find dozens of kids sitting on logs and boulders up and down the water. Yet again, no one is talking to anyone else. No one.

The rest of the afternoon I notice that strangely cold behavior more. Everyone's totally separated by this insanely tense isolation. I'd been worried about cliques I'd have to wrestle my way into via demeaning rites of passage—sleeping in a frozen bra or making out with, like, a rock—but that couldn't be further from reality. Everyone here interacts formally. Coldly. Shaking hands when instructed but rarely meeting eyes. Twice, fights break out between kids who look so straight-laced and suburban—geeky, even—I have to hold my breath to keep from laughing. The only moments of relief come from Lotus, who happily pairs with me at one point, and Pilot, who seems to be smirking with me—like we're in on some private joke—every time I pass him on campus.

"What's so funny?" I finally ask him. It's the end of orientation day, and we're both leaving a workshop called *Help Your Guardian Help You*. Teddy was sitting next to me in the workshop; thankfully, Villicus called him to his office, and I haven't seen him since.

"Funny?" he asks, but he's smiling like even *that's* funny.

"Am I missing something?"

"Aren't you?"

"Do you only answer questions with questions?"

"Have you noticed that?"

Exchanging a smirk, we push through the doors. The air outside is like a wet slap.

"It's like living in a raincloud here," I say, buttoning my cardigan and longing for Gigi's fish-stank coat. "Is it always like this?"

"You'll get used to it." Pilot halts in his tracks, forcing me to stop, too. "Listen, I'm not weird, if that's what you think. I just wanted to talk to you more. Y'know, because it sort of feels like we know each other. Because of our dads and stuff."

"Totally," I say and watch my breath turn white before being absorbed into the misty air. "Your dad, like, got me in here."

"From what I understand, your dad did that all by himself."

"From what *I* understand, your dad is my *benefactor*."

"Ha!" he scoffs. Pilot and I start to stroll again. We meander across the quad, heading toward the dorms and passing grumpy kids accompanied, at times, by stone-faced Guardians. "That's the first and last time my dad will ever be called *bene* anything. I should've recorded it for posterity."

"Well, it was awesome of him. I can't say that I'd pay some random kid's tuition to a place like this, even if I had the money and thought her art was half-decent."

"Pay your tuition? Is that what you think my dad did for you?"

We stop again. Standing outside in this weather isn't doing my hair any favors; I can feel it growing like a Chia pet on my head.

"Isn't that what he did?" I ask.

"He supported your application, Annie. That's what makes him your benefactor. And, besides, people don't just pay tuition here."

"Well, Cania surely can't be the world's first *free* private school."

"That's not what I mean. Tuition here is beyond cold, hard cash." Nonchalantly, as if it'd be odd to be perplexed by such details, he lays it on me. "Your *dad* had to come up with your tuition. My dad wouldn't be allowed to pay your way if he wanted to."

But my dad doesn't have any money. Even a couple grand is a huge stretch for him. Of course, I don't tell Pilot that.

"Look, my dad told your dad about this place, which is a serious no-no. Secrecy is key—that's the only way to keep this place from turning into a slum." Grinning to take the edge off, Pilot explains that Villicus invites every student to Cania, which is why Villicus was stunned when my dad called him out of the blue and demanded he let me in. "When my dad told your dad about Cania, he broke the school's code of secrecy."

"There's a code of secrecy?"

"When you're dealing with rich screwballs, there are always codes for *everything*. You've gotta know the secret handshake, wear the club jacket, or flash the ring to get in anywhere worth getting into. Things have to be impossible to attain and insanely private for guys like my dad even to consider them. Even the people in that fishing village aren't allowed to cross the line to come on the school grounds. It's *that* exclusive here."

I recall the red line I hopped over this morning. "Yeah, my Guardian mentioned something about not 'fraternizing with the villagers.' That seems extreme and sort of mean."

"I think a marketer would call it *exclusive*."

"I think a villager would call it *mean*."

"You'll never know. Because you're not allowed to fraternize with them, remember?" His white teeth flash. "Anyway, there's only one person our age in that whole village, so it's not exactly like you're missing out on a bunch of hot dudes drinking the town dry every weekend."

Just ahead, some guy with his face painted white and his lips painted black—totally Goth—leans against the guys' dorm building and waves at us.

"Speaking of hot dudes, there's my roommate, Jack," Pilot says, taking my hand and yanking me toward him. "He's a senior, so don't worry, he'll be nice. You're not a Big V competitor for him."

Beaming through black lips, Jack turns to us as we approach. His dark gaze skips over my body and lands oh-so-obviously on my enormous 'fro. "Wow, either your PT is to raise rats in your hair or you lost a bet."

"Annie, meet Jack," Pilot says.

"It's just Anne, actually." I give Jack a slight wave. "Nice makeup. Does Halloween come early in Maine?"

Jack smirks and wraps an arm around my shoulder. "Okay, Afro Girl, you can stay."

"Lucky me," I mutter with a small smile as he releases me.

"I was trying to explain tuition to Annie."

"Ah, yes," Jack says, pulling out a cigarette and peering at me as he lights it. "Tuition. Not your usual twenty grand a semester."

I almost choke on my own saliva. The idea that my dad could pay anything close to that sort of fee is—it nauseates me.

"How much is it?" I ask, hiding a grimace.

A thin curl of smoke escapes Jack's lips as he chooses his next words with what seems to be great care. "Let's just say that if you want your kid to get in here, you pay. Big time."

Shooting a sharp look Jack's way, Pilot adds, "Traditional tuition wouldn't set Cania apart enough. Ivy League schools want the best, and Cania Christy does what it takes to prove it's producing the best—from the ridiculously motivated valedictorians it churns out to its code of secrecy to the *slightly inflated* tuition it charges."

"So how much is it?" I repeat. Just as I do, Harper and her posse stroll by, flicking their hair over their shoulders in perfectly timed unison. Is it wrong to want them to topple over in their six-inch Louboutins?

With equally tight grins, Pilot and Jack both shrug.

"If you have to ask, Annie, you can't afford it," Pilot says, chuckling.

By the time I head to Gigi's, crossing that red line again and trying hard not to look at the house the beautiful Ben Zin calls home, I'm exhausted. If the tiny, wobbly little cottage felt at all like home to me, I'd collapse on my bed and nap until dinner.

But it doesn't.

And the fact that Teddy's standing in the doorway, with his notepad in one hand and my abandoned coat in the other, watching my every move as I walk up the gravel path, doesn't help.

four

PROSPERITAS THEMA

EVEN AS NIGHT FALLS, THICK FOG STILL DRAPES THE island like the whole world's sadness has been sucked into this one spot and manifested as a permanent damp mist, which is turning light pink with the fading light of dusk.

I'm about to spend the school year in this dreary place, but it's not the weather I mind. I'm already getting used to it, almost as if I should have been born on the East Coast. I've always made my fun among the shadows, lived my life under a heavy cloud of mourning. This fog? This isolated island? This is nothing.

It's the people that'll take some getting used to.

Like Villicus, who, I can't help noticing, acts like he's running a reform school, not a prestigious prep school. And Teddy, who has spent the evening knocking on my bedroom door, sticking his pimply face in, assessing my activities, and reminding me that we'll determine my PT before bed. During the World's Most Uncomfortable Dinner—just Teddy, Gigi, me, and yippy Skippy—Teddy asks how my parents met, how we responded when my mom was first diagnosed bipolar, how much my dad knows about his clients at the funeral home. Pushing away his plate after just two bites, he schedules my first bi-weekly call with my dad for this

Friday. All the while, Gigi just looks on uncomfortably, as if she is reconsidering her decision to let me and my Guardian stay. (Can't say I blame her.) And Skippy—I thought that dog hated *me*! But Skippy barks at Teddy with such force and for so long, he actually loses his voice. It's only when Gigi turns in early, a shaking Skippy under her arm, that I feel calm for the first time in hours.

Until Teddy comes knocking on my bedroom door.

"We must get to the matter of your *prosperitas thema*," he says as he enters my room and looks slowly around. His voice squeaks often, like he's still going through puberty. "We shall declare and document it right now."

"Right now? Do you think you know me well enough to make a call like this already?"

"It specifically says in my Apprentice Guide that the subject's PT must be declared within twenty-four hours of arrival on the island."

"You're an apprentice?" My sucky, creepy Guardian doesn't even have any experience?

"Never mind that. Stand and face me."

I've barely risen from my chair when Teddy scoops my hands into his clammy mitts. "Close your eyes."

"Why?"

"So I may proceed with the reading."

"The reading?"

Teddy's reply is a cold glare. "Would you like to see these steps outlined in my guide?"

Reluctantly, I close my eyes. The problem with closing my eyes, though, is that it heightens my other senses—so, all at once, I can hear Teddy breathing loudly through his mouth, and I can feel the damp milkiness of his too-warm hands. He starts humming, and I open one eye a little to find him concentrating with his eyes closed. Like he's meditating.

"Close your eyes," he commands without opening his.

His fingers squeeze mine. I watch his thick, overgrown fingernails press deep into my palms, making me wince. As Teddy repeats his command, I glance at the Zin mansion lit by twilight beyond my window and allow myself to think not of Teddy but of Ben. Pretending Teddy is someone else—someone who I already recognize as the secret crush of my junior year—is the only way to get through this. I snap my eyelids shut and visualize Ben's thick hair, piercing eyes, and crinkle-nosed grin.

Moments pass like this. I've never had a reading done, but they're common enough where I come from that this isn't completely absurd. Just semi-absurd.

All at once, though, a shudder overtakes my body, and I'm caught off-guard by the strongest sensation of being *not entirely myself* any longer—of being invaded by some sour presence that lumbers its way around under my skin.

"Wait," I begin, but my voice catches in my throat.

I twitch involuntarily, as if my body is shaking out an intruder.

It's as though Teddy's reaching into my soul, and my soul is trying to shove him out. But that's impossible. Teddy is just a guy. The effect, the unnerving sense of having company under my own skin, can only be the result of some manipulated pressure point on my hands.

"Remain absolutely still, Miss Merchant," Teddy warns.

Keeping still is the last thing on my mind. A wave of nausea runs over me, and I suck my tongue to avoid getting sick right there on the creaking wooden floors, squeeze my eyes shut tighter, and tell myself to breathe. What's happening? Moments creep by. The sense that this might never end washes over me.

But still I stand, motionless, doing as I'm told, finally realizing that this—whatever this is—is the manner by which all students have their PTs selected. And I, like everyone else, am expected to stand quietly while I'm mysteriously, telepathically prodded.

Opening my eyes during a brief moment of calmness, I watch Teddy's long head rumble on his neck, teetering and bouncing like a bobble on the end of a radio antenna; his eyes are still closed. My stomach is once again on the brink. My skin feels tighter every second. And the idea, the absurd notion that Teddy could somehow be penetrating my soul, my aura, whatever you want to call it—that idea is flipping over and over in my mind. Without a resolution. My brain tells me it's impossible. My body makes a shockingly compelling argument against my brain.

"Yes." Teddy's tongue slithers. His tone is peril personified, but I'm glad for the noise, for the promise of this all being over soon. "I see it. It's you. I see your PT."

See my PT?

"Your soul is very old yet invigorated. It is…so seductive."

"*Gross.*"

"Hush now. A shadow hovers over you."

With a sharp, unexpected gasp, Teddy suddenly lifts my hands high in the air. My eyelids pop open. His eyes flash wide, glowing oddly, bloodshot beyond repair as his gaze fuses with mine. Briefly, in that moment, I feel, in spite of myself, as if our souls are real, as if our souls are touching each other, as if I can see his and—to my great surprise—it's not all dark. But then, without warning, he whips my arms down. *Hard.* So hard, I hear a *snap*, and my shoulders feel like they've popped right out of their sockets as he releases me.

With a howl of shock and pain, I hobble away. I balance myself after a spell of stumbling and lean against the foot of my bed, rubbing one shoulder, then the other. The only consolation, and it is a significant one, is that I feel like myself once again, even if I'm struggling to catch my breath, even if a dull creaminess coats my tongue.

"I have seen your PT. You have in your aura a tendency toward—" Teddy hesitates, standing in the midst of a great, long, *exaggerated* pause "—seduction."

I collapse against the bed and, baffled by the whole experience, start laughing. "Are you kidding me?"

"Miss Merchant," Teddy says, holding his hands up, "I assure you that your spirit does, in fact, lean toward a hypersexualized state."

"Or you wish it would," I counter, glaring up at him as the smile leaves my face. "If my PT were to sleep my way to the top, or whatever it is you have in mind, then tell me, dear Teddy, how would *you* grade me on that?"

He flinches. "You can't be suggesting…"

"Having your way with me here? Nightly stripteases in your bedroom, Teddy? Is that close to what you were thinking?"

"That would be an abuse of power! I would never!"

"I'll have you know that my uniform is as tight as it is because someone got my measurements wrong!" I get to my feet, wincing at the pain, and stride to the top of the stairs, gesturing for him to leave the attic. "I won't sign anything that says *that's* my PT. In fact, maybe I'm not interested in the Big V after all. Maybe I'll be just like Pilot and turn my back on this idiotic race."

"Wait!" Teddy cries, coming after me. "You need to do this, Anne." His expression is softer—almost kind—as he looks at me now. "There *was* something else in your aura."

"Surprise, surprise. What is it?"

"I would encourage you to choose the one I mentioned, though. It is your greatest strength. There are many ways to use your sexuality to your advantage. It doesn't have to be as obvious as you might think."

"That's BS. What was the other one? Tell me."

Reluctantly, Teddy nods. "It is because you are an artist that this is in you at all," he stammers, which, in combination with his thick accent, makes him that much harder to understand. "But I warn you that, although you are an artist in *this* life, you may not have been in other lives. Your soul has spent much longer in the role of the seductress than the artist."

"Teddy! Just tell me."

"Your alternative PT, Miss Merchant, is that you will succeed in life by looking closer. Beyond the surface. By asking questions and never accepting things at face value."

"Looking closer?"

I can't help but smile a little. It's *exactly* right. I feel it immediately, and knowing that Teddy was able to land on this assessment of my strength—a strength that one art curator once commented on—makes me wonder, for the briefest moment, if he was actually somehow in my soul, reading it.

"This might only cause you trouble, Miss Merchant," Teddy warns.

"It's perfect. Let's do it. What do I sign?"

"Very well." Teddy's voice shakes as he lifts the form to me. I scribble it down and turn to let him go.

"Not so fast," he says. Turning back, I find him lifting a long, silvery needle from his case and holding it out to me.

I stare at it. "What's that?"

"To seal the deal."

"To what?"

"We seal our official forms with blood at Cania Christy. It's in my guide."

"You're really funny tonight. But you should probably leave now."

Teddy just holds the needle out to me.

"So we're in the Middle Ages now?"

"Sarcasm is the lowest form of wit," Teddy says. "Signing in blood is a tradition of this school, a tradition that goes back generations." He thrusts the needle at me.

If I was alone, I might actually pinch myself to see if I'm dreaming because, so far, life at Cania Christy feels like life in a bad dream, like life on some planet filled with probing aliens.

"Everyone does it," Teddy states crossly. *Classic* that he would use the line teachers and parents have condemned for years.

"My signature isn't enough?"

"Thou must bequeath it solemnly!" he cries finally. With his hands trembling, with a hysteric gleam in his eye, he stomps on the spot.

"Teddy, come on! I mean, aren't I supposed to be questioning stuff? That's my PT, right? If I just gave in, wouldn't I be, like, in violation or something?"

Settling down, though his chest still heaves, he agrees. "I understand. Well done. But now that you've questioned it and learned that it is what you *must* do, you *must* do it."

Mental note: my Guardian will make up the rules as we go.

"What we have here is a learning opportunity," Teddy declares, taking my hand and pressing the soft pad of my fingertip. "Once you learn who's in control, I'll learn that you're worth fighting for on graduation day."

With the needle, he pricks my finger and squeezes a drop of my blood onto the lower corner of each form. I press my thumb into the crimson drop; as I pull away, I stare for a moment at the fingerprint I've left behind, at the lines that swirl around the center like the walls of some fiery tornado around its funnel, at the mark they use to identify criminals, not students. I look at the tiniest flecks that the lines of my fingerprint leave, and I think of how those ridges are designed to fire signals to the brain when a surface feels dangerously sharp, dangerously hot.

Not long after, Teddy heads to campus for an evening meeting of the Guardians, and, relieved to be alone, I bolt downstairs to the kitchen, where an old-school telephone—the rotary kind, black—clings to the wall. I need to talk to my dad. I need to know how much this place is costing him and if he has any idea he's sent me to a place where creepy Guardian-people crawl into your soul and suggest you get by in life on your back.

I pick up the receiver for the phone. But there's no dial tone. A quick glance shows me there's no cord connecting the two pieces.

"Ten bucks says Teddy took the damn thing with him."

Restless and still shaken by the PT exercise, I slide on my boots and Gigi's big, stinky jacket and head out the front door into the night air.

There are two ways I could go: up-island to campus or down-island to the *verboten* village. Creeping over the grass under the twilight sky and onto the road, I look north at the endless stretch and then south through the haze to where a distant village I'm not supposed to enter sits in wait. Behind me, I can feel the presence of the Zin mansion, where the golden glow of warmly lit rooms fills just enough ornate windows to make me long for a life as pleasant for myself.

I turn left. And, emboldened by my "look closer" PT, walk toward the village.

Taking their cue from the cool weather, the leaves have started changing color. Spots of orange and violet spread through the woods on both sides of the road, their colors diluted by the gray air, which is crisp enough to turn my nose and fingertips red. Outside the village, I spy a craggy wooden sign that shows the population: 212.

My PT may have given me the push I needed to head in this direction, but it hasn't empowered me to such an extent that I actually intend to go into the village. Given everything I've been told today, especially if I want to be valedictorian next year, that would be a career-limiting move worthy of detention, demerits, suspension, or whatever they do at Cania to punish disobedient students. Veering away from the village just as its old pale fishing shacks come into view, I head toward the flash of a lighthouse that passes through the woods on the west side of the island. On my way, I wander by a hillside spotted with enormous Cape Cod–style homes that are anything but what I expected the villagers to live in. These people are the inhabitants of an old whaling village, after all. They should live in shanties with dimly lit porches. They should have tattered clothes that reek of fish guts. And yet, judging by their homes, you'd think they were all millionaires.

"That's not fair!" a man hollers suddenly. I can't see him. He's somewhere far ahead, on the other side of the woods.

For a moment, I worry he's shouting at me, and I scramble away. But when it's obvious he doesn't know I'm here, I inch toward his voice, to the edge of the woods and to the top of a low cliff overlooking not only the vast, smooth ocean and the distant twinkling lights of the Kennebunkport coast but also the marina, which houses more mini-yachts than it seems to be built for. Standing on the dock below me, deep in a fiery conversation, are three men. Two I recognize instantly: Headmaster Villicus and the spectacularly handsome Dr. Zin. But I don't know who the third man is. He's Indian, and he looks truly angry—the kind of anger where you expect he might stomp on the spot while steam pours out of his ears.

Behind the trio, a sign warns visitors to report to Cania Christy or risk prosecution.

The men stand just a dozen yards away from me. At any moment, Villicus could look up and see me here, wandering the outskirts of the village like a prize moron, standing in the passing beam of the lighthouse. Sure, I live on the village side of the line, so I'd have an excuse if it came to that. But something tells me Villicus isn't one for excuses.

I duck behind a tree. Shielded by its thick, furry trunk, which gives softly under my fingertips, I peek down.

"But Lord Featherly promised!" the Indian man, who has a strong Scottish accent, shouts. Unmistakably new to the world of the wealthy, he wears dark-wash jeans, a Gucci-print shirt—collar flipped up—and an enormous pink-gold watch that flashes as he throws out his arms, exasperated. "He said you'd take care of me, Dr. Zin. Or are you just this old freak's lackey?"

"Lord Featherly has been loose with his information about this school," Dr. Zin retorts coolly, his voice low and smooth like a cocoa-dusted truffle, like a deeper version of Ben's. "And, allow me to remind you, he was in a different position than you are when he came to us, Manish."

"A different *position*? My company went public last year. Public! How rich do I need to be to send my daughter here?"

"We are not talking about *money*," Villicus interrupts. "You misunderstand the mandate of my institution."

"I just want what you're giving these kids," Manish says, lowering his voice. I inch closer to hear more. "My wife and I want it for our little girl. A future. As I said, I'll pay anything—"

"Our school starts in the ninth grade," Dr. Zin explains. "Even if you had been invited and were not acting with such impropriety, your daughter would not qualify on age alone."

"But her grades were exceptional. She could make a go of it as a freshman." He looks wildly between the two powerful men. "Lord Featherly said something about special tuition. I can give you anything you want. What will it take?"

"Frankly, there's nothing you could offer," Dr. Zin says.

"Please," Manish begs, dropping to his knees. He throws himself at Villicus's feet and wraps his arms around his old brown shoes. "*Please*. If you are the man I've been told you are, you *can* do this."

My eavesdropping is cut short when I hear leaves crunching behind me. My heart stops with a dull thump. My fingers claw into the tree bark. I close my eyes, and I freeze in place.

I'm sure I'll turn around and see Teddy. If not him, then some wild animal's about to maul me. I don't know which worries me more.

"Man," a girl says—and I promise, I nearly pee my pants. I suck my lips in to keep from screaming. "It's hard to hear them when they whisper, isn't it?"

Whipping around, I find a black-haired girl smiling at me as she lightly punts the kickstand on her bike. She tiptoes to my side, still grinning—she has braces—holds my arm, and peeks over my shoulder to spy on Villicus, Zin, and Manish.

"Oh, they look *mad*," she giggles. "Who's the rich idiot in the guido shirt? He looks almost as stupid as Villie."

I'm too stunned to move. Questions about who this girl is set in quickly. She's on this side of the line and she's friendly—so she's probably not from Cania. Not to mention that I'm sure I didn't see her at orientation today.

"Stop staring at *me*. You're missing the whole show," she whispers, her gaze fixed on the entertainment below. "That guy's laying it on thick. He's actually begging!"

"You're from the village."

Her black eyes flick in my direction. "Yep. I guess you'd better run away from me now. And I'll run away from you." She chuckles quietly. "Stupid rules."

Even still, I back away. My dad gave up way too much for me to compromise things now. As I back away, the girl turns to me. I'm taller than she is, but she's got a toughness about her that makes her seem larger.

"Come on. Be nice—*I'm* nice," she says. "Do you even know why the rules are what they are?"

I shake my head. Something about keeping things exclusive, but I don't say that.

"Exactly. You only know what Villie tells you. I've lived here my whole life. *I* know the rules. So trust me when I say that I know they're worth breaking. I know what I'm doing when I'm breaking them."

"Which you are," I say.

"Which you are, too. Or, what, did you miss that bright red line on the road back there? You had to cross it to get here, right?"

"I live on the village side of it."

Leaning against the spot I've given up on the tree, she fits her fingers into the same rivets I held in the bark and glances over her shoulder at me. Her eyes twinkle, and her skin is olive-toned, which makes her teeth, behind the metal, look very white. Unlike the kids at Cania, she's got a few blemishes, and her eyebrows are untamed.

"Oh," she says, "you're *you*. You're the new kid. The weird one."

"The weird one?"

"Aren't you?"

"Aren't *you*?" I fire back. "Only teen in a creepy village. Kinda weird."

Surprisingly, she beams. "I know, right? It's not just weird. It *blows*."

Manish's voice booms out suddenly, and I sidle next to the girl to watch the events unfolding below.

"You'll be hearing from my lawyer!" Manish hollers.

"It's imperative," Dr. Zin quickly cautions Manish, "that you keep this quiet."

"Impossible! Your policies are ageist and exclusionary. If my money can't get her in here, my money will shut this place down."

With that, Manish grabs his jacket and storms to a speedboat at the end of the dock. As he does, Villicus flicks his eyes up to exactly where the girl and I are standing—*Oh, crap!* Freaked, we both stumble backward, falling out of his sight to the mossy, crunchy earth. I hear her squeal, but I don't make a peep— because my heart's temporarily stopped.

Hushed, we wait motionlessly and soundlessly for the voices below to go away.

"He saw me," I finally whisper.

"He saw *me* for sure," she says, clutching her chest. "But I don't think he saw you. The tree shielded you. And I'm allowed to be here."

"Are you sure? If he saw us together, I think I could get in serious trouble."

"We both could," she adds, but it's obvious she's enjoying the excitement of the moment. She tears her hand away from her chest and sticks it out at me. Her white ceramic watch makes a clinking noise against her diamond tennis bracelet. "I'm Molly. Molly Watso."

"Anne Merchant." I take it and shake. A speedboat starts down at the dock. "So, what did you mean, I'm the weird one?"

"This is a small island, which is even worse than a small town." Rolling toward me, Molly chuckles. "I'd heard there was a new girl who was supposed to be different from the others. But don't worry. You're the *least* weird one up at that place, trust me."

"What makes them weird? That they're all flawless? Or that they're the evil offspring of, like, Rockefellers?"

"Both!" Molly laughs again. "So you go into the village when you're not supposed to. And you live with Gigi. What's your deal? Just a sucker for punishment?"

I get to my feet, dusting my hand-me-down jeans. Molly follows and hops on her bike.

"It gets worse," I confess easily. There's something calming and, well, normal about Molly Watso. "We've got these Guardians assigned to us. And mine—*Teddy*—is actually living with me at Gigi's. It's pretty close quarters. I had to get out for some air."

"Damn. I figured maybe Gigi would be your Guardian, but she's from the village, so that wouldn't work. Not really cut out for critiquing you twenty-four-seven." She arches her eyebrow. "But looks like your Teddy Bear isn't doing a very good job with that either."

We fall into a stroll through the woods. I'm heading back to the main road, and I imagine she's going to one of those enormous homes on the hillside.

"Hey, you know what the punishment is for us even talking, right?" she asks.

"Is it bad?"

"I'll take that as a *no*," she says, grinning. "You could be expelled."

"And what'd happen to you?"

"The worst."

"The worst?" I repeat. "The only thing worse than getting expelled from Cania might be having to go there in the first place." I expect her to laugh, but she doesn't.

"Exactly."

"I'm kidding," I say. "So, what would your punishment be?"

"Exactly what you said." She stops walking as we near the road. "I'd be forced to attend Cania."

"Attending Cania is a punishment? So, what? Is this place some sort of reform school?" I guess. Then another thought pops into my head. "Or, like, a mental institution for rich kids? Everyone there seems slightly off."

I don't add my concern: that my dad, after I fell into my depression over my mom's death, might have tricked me into coming here under the guise of starting fresh.

Suddenly, a gunshot—at least, I think that's what it is—tears through the air, bolting from the marina, ricocheting its echo, and sending me and Molly jumping out of our skin.

Molly nearly falls off her bike.

Another gunshot.

"Holy jeez," she stammers, balancing herself again. "This island is getting crazier every second." She skids away and calls back over her shoulder. "You okay getting home?"

Stunned, I think I mumble a *yes*. In a flash, Molly races to the hillside, shaking her head and shouting that she'll see me later. I can't believe she has the capacity to move. I'm frozen in place. By the time I'm able to move again, I stumble out of the woods and duck just as a Harley holding Dr. Zin and Villicus zooms by on the road below. It's not until they pass and I regain my composure that the sound Molly and I heard makes better sense.

"Not a gunshot," I assure myself. "It was the bike backfiring. Had to be."

That has to be it. Because the alternative is not something I can let enter my mind. Not if I'm going to keep my sanity here, in a place that, the more I think of it, could very well be a high-end asylum.

Back at Gigi's, under the dim glow of candles on my bedside table, my heart has stopped racing and I'm flipping through my student handbook, looking for clubs to join. It's occurred to me that the dreariness outside, the oddness of the day, my jet lag, and my strange encounter with Molly might have made me a little jumpier than usual. Those shots we heard? I've dreamt up a million more explanations. Could have been barking sea lions. Or wailing loons. Or someone scattering gulls. Or a starting gun.

"Yeah, a starting gun," I tell myself. "Starting gun for a running club."

Doesn't matter that, if the list of clubs in this handbook is exhaustive, there's no running club here. There is, however, every other club known to man. A Model UN. Something called the Pil-At-Ease Club. Economics Club. Glee Club. The Social Committee. Swimming. Tennis. Mathletes. *Everything*.

What will I sign up for?

"What would Mr. Ben Zin be likely to take?" I ask myself and just as quickly fling the handbook down. "Why am I even thinking about the snobby son of some gun-firing power tripper?"

Just before I blow out the candles, I hear a motorbike in the Zins' driveway, and I jump out of bed, flying to the window in time to see not a Harley but a yellow Ducati disappear under the Zins' porte cochere. For what feels like hours, I stand in the shadows, looking out my window, watching their house, watching lights fill and disappear from one window after the other.

In reality, I know guys like Ben don't associate with girls like me. He's a gorgeous senior; I'm a lowly junior. And I saw his reaction to my crooked smile. There's no denying that. If his grades were poor, at least I could console myself that he might one day deign to discuss persistence in stochastic environments with me—but he's set to get the Big V this year.

"Nothing could possibly interest Ben Zin in me."

I turn to the small mirror on my dresser. And I rub my eyes.

It must be the candlelight. Or maybe there's something in the water here that makes people look better than we otherwise would. Sure, I'm nowhere near as flawless as the other kids I encountered today, but I can't help but notice that I don't look quite as unfortunate as I normally do. Flattering light—that must be it.

Sweeping my hair away from my face and holding it high in a ponytail, I turn side to side to see my profile in the reflection. I look…hmm, not all that bad. It's sort of like being introduced to myself, like my brain is temporarily allowing me a second chance to make a first impression. I definitely look more like my mom than I used to (a good thing). I can see similarities with her bone structure, her eyes, and her lips. Sure, I've got a blemish near my jawline, but I'm sixteen! I'm supposed to.

Gradually, I let my eyes fall below my neck, but it's like this *chore* to get them there—to get them to my *actual* body, not just my face and hair, knowing that I'm about to check myself out. One part pathetic; one part intriguing.

Like a lot of girls, I guess, I've built an uncertain existence in the shadows of my most prominent flaws, which are the very qualities that make me *different*, which is only good on good days. But here I am now. Standing in my pajama shirt and undies. Tracing my fingertips over my collarbone in the dark. Dropping my arms to my side and letting my hand hover at the hem of my pajama shirt. Holding my breath, I lift it slowly. Take it off. And blush at my reflection. Because my body is so unrecognizable to me, it's almost pornographic.

"Not bad," I whisper, looking at myself as I never really have before. Something inside me stirs—not because I'm attracted to *myself*. It's something else. It's realizing, for the first time ever, that I may possess a teensy tiny bit of sexual power. It's realizing, in spite of my will to succeed based on intelligence alone, that Teddy might not have been entirely crazy to suggest my body could be a strong asset for me.

There's a knock at the door. I clasp my shirt to my chest and pray that Teddy doesn't come marching up the stairs to find me like this.

"Annie? You awake?" Gigi loud-whispers. "My feet are killing me. Would you massage them?"

I don't make a peep, and she finally pads back to her room. I slip my shirt back on and decide to force myself to sleep (because I'll be joining Ornithology Club, which starts at 7:00 A.M., which is 4:00 A.M. back home, which will feel *terrible* tomorrow). I reach to draw my shade. And at that exact moment, just as I let my eyes fall on the Zin mansion for what I thought would be a nanosecond, I glimpse someone standing at a window there.

No, not some*one*. Two people.

I can see only their silhouettes, but it's clear one is a man and the other a woman, and something tells me the man is *not* Dr. Zin. Too lean. Which means it's Ben. With a girl. A girl who is reaching for him … *not* in a motherly way.

The air empties out of my room. Everything deflates at the unmistakable sight of Ben with some girl.

"Of course he has a girlfriend," I sigh, drawing the shade. He was out with her tonight, and he brought her back to his place on that Ducati. "Of course."

And just like that, everything I thought I saw in the mirror disappears like the candlelight I extinguish between my fingertips. As I get into bed, my new confidence, like a stream of smoke, floats away, rising to twist around the beams of the attic ceiling and, in the darkness, disappear. Just in time for my door to squeak open. Just in time for Teddy to tiptoe up the stairs, stand over me, and scribble something on his notepad.

five

THE SCREAM

THE ART OF THE STRIPTEASE. REMOVING LAYER UPON layer of clothing to expose the flesh in small, seductive increments. Tantalizing. Like Salome's dance of the seven veils, Mata Hari's gradual shedding of nearly every garment save one, the burlesque dancer's beginning to end. Enticing…

…and clearly not something our nude model has even *considered*, given how rapidly he drops his robe. Blink and you'd have missed it.

Somehow I've made it through a night of tossing and turning, nightmares of finding my mom on the kitchen floor plaguing my mind. Somehow I've endured a broken coffee maker at Gigi's. And a cold sprint to school, during which Ben zipped by me on his Ducati—without even pausing. And an hour spent craning my neck as I watched the sky during Ornithology Club.

Somehow I've survived the night to make it to my morning art workshop led by Garnet. This week's lesson will be on the human form. Which is why a grown man now stands completely naked just beyond my reach—not that I'm about to *reach*.

Somehow I've made it here. To where a penis dangles in front of me.

As the swoosh of his robe leaving his body still reverberates, as we sit at our workstations with pencil in hand, twenty eyebrows go up and ten chins go down. Only yours truly and Garnet seem unfazed by this man's very exposed, very chiseled self. (And I'm sure Garnet's lack of surprise isn't due to the fact that she's helped her dad dress hundreds of naked cadavers.) To my surprise, even Harper is blushing. To no one's surprise, Lotus looks like she might cry.

"Feast your eyes," our model Trey exclaims, drawing his hand down his body. He's a member of the faculty, though you wouldn't know it to look at him. He's nowhere near as hard on the eyes as most of the teachers here. "I am man. Hear me roar."

Pilot, who sits across from me, snickers at the same time I do. But no one else makes a sound. Probably because they're all shocked, some with jealousy, some with fear—others, dare I read into Plum's pout, with lust.

Garnet simply sweeps the robe from the floor and tries to keep a straight face. "Thank you, Mr. Sedmoney," she says. "We appreciate you taking the time out of your teaching schedule to help us this week."

"I don't have any classes first period, so no worries." He swings his gaze around the room and settles on Harper, who is practically gyrating in her chair in an effort to get his attention.

"Well, then," Garnet says, "if you could sit still like a … like a *tableau vivant.*"

"Tableau vivant?" he repeats. "Mmm, French. Sexy." He rests his chin on his fist like *The Thinker* and gazes around the room from the corner of his eye.

Seeing Trey in his pose, Garnet seems at a loss for words, so she turns her attention on us, on the sea of crimson faces and wide eyes. "This is a refresher in gesture and proportion," she explains. "Learn to break the body into manageable pieces as opposed to … to … to trying to swallow the form whole." Immediately, she shakes her head; she seems relieved that none of us have the *co-jones* to laugh at what she just said.

We have a little under an hour to try *not* to stare at this man who seems intent on getting a reaction from us. He crosses his legs. Uncrosses them. Opens them wide. Stretches them long. Does everything but hold an arrow-shaped sign to his crotch and shout, "Look at this!" I painstakingly work to replicate his form on eleven-by-seventeen sheets of grid paper as Garnet strolls between our workstations, looking over our shoulders and offering advice before, returning to her desk, losing herself in her own sketches.

As the minutes tick by, Harper and Plum fall into one of those our-conversation-is-so-awesome-you-should-all-hear-it chats that I do my best not to listen to. It's about the dance this Saturday, which Harper's Social Committee is organizing and which I don't even want to think about. Unfortunately, those girls make it hard to ignore them—so hard that a few people, unable to endure another twang, squeal, or yip, demand they shut up.

"*Ferme la bouche!*" Augusto cries. "We do not care about your idiotic clothing for that idiotic dance."

"Idiotic *stripper* clothing!" Emo Boy tacks on.

Lotus frowns. "Please, everyone. Let's not argue."

"We didn't ask y'all to eavesdrop," Harper snorts. "Can't help if we're so interesting you've gotta pay attention to us."

Plum glares at Emo Boy, clutches her boobs, pushes them up, and adds, "Don't even play like you don't want this. You'd kill for this."

"If you mean kill myself to avoid going near it."

With a high-pitched huff, Plum leaps to her feet. She opens her mouth wide like she's about to shout something terrible, but she stops herself unexpectedly. And, to my surprise, sneers my way. "Oh, whatever!"

Shoving his hair out of his eyes, Emo Boy stands, marches up to Plum, and shoves her in the chest. Hard.

"No one wants *that*, you fugly has-been. And that's exactly why your PT's gonna totally *crash*."

"Crash?" She shoves him back with enough force that he loses his footing.

With that, Augusto's on his feet, too. I can't believe it. They're actually going to fight.

"Crash? Just like you did—" Plum lashes at him "—on that stupid dance floor—" another strike, but she just misses him "—with that *cage dancer*?"

Seriously. A fistfight.

It's insanely stupid to fight in the middle of class—especially with two teachers looking on, teachers who are grading us at every turn. But Augusto, Emo Boy, and Plum don't seem to care. They make one of those circles you see boxers make, side-stepping and holding each other's glowers as they lift their fists.

Finally, Lotus scurries to her feet and pulls Plum back. Reluctantly, Emo Boy and Augusto lower their fists. Garnet and Trey just watch—and I quickly realize that they're making notes. Are they grading the *quality* of the fight? Or could it be that at least one of those three has declared a PT to battle their way to success?

Stunned, I find myself locking eyes with Pilot. His expression is blank, as if he's given up on this school and the ubercompetitive people in it. Confused and wondering what's going on in his mind, I focus again on my sketch.

The room is tensely silent for the next twenty minutes. I run through sheet after sheet of paper, feeling like I'm getting closer to capturing something interesting beyond the lines of Trey's body, feeling myself fall into the groove. As I work up a frenzy, a cold sweat rushes over me.

"Five minutes, everyone," Garnet calls.

Shivers run through my arms. I glance up to see if someone opened a window, but as soon as I do, my head spins. Shaking it off, I see that, in fact, the windows are all closed—and almost everyone else has stripped off their cardigans and blazers. Perhaps I'm coming down with something because it feels like the cold is coming from my body itself, from my wrists; I pull my cardigan all the way up and over my fingertips, hoping to lock in some heat, but the shivering won't stop.

My breath is coming short and fast. Tiny, quick breaths that make my head woozy.

"You don't have time for the flu," I whisper to myself between chattering teeth and, trying to keep my pencil from shaking, look purposefully at Trey, demanding my body stop shivering.

But when I look Trey's way, there are three of him.

Squeezing my eyes shut, I look down at my paper. Bad idea. The lines are blurring together, duplicating themselves. Overlapping. Straight lines are wavy; everything is spinning. What I hear next, what I remember, is the thud of my body hitting the ground after some sort of freefall from my stool. I see a burst of light; I hear gasps all around. In the flashes behind my eyes, I see my dad leaning over me, petting my hair the way he used to when I would wake from feverish dreams. The cold sensation on my wrists, it's even stronger, like someone's rubbing ice cubes on my skin. My dad—he seems so real, almost touchable, and if he were to lean down and kiss my head now, I might even feel it. I wrestle to lift my three-hundred-ton head to his face.

"Anne?" A man's voice. A loud clap.

"I don't think that did it." A woman's voice.

Searing pain. Shooting in my skull. I try to lift my hand to my forehead and open my eyes, but I feel pinned down. Slowly, the ceiling of the classroom comes into view. And I find a naked man bending over me.

"Trey?"

He smiles and puts on the robe Garnet hands to him. "Dreaming of me, sweetheart?"

I just blink, trying to register where I am, who *he* is, what's going on. "What happened?"

"You fainted, Anne." Garnet's voice. I jerk my head toward her, but it hurts.

"We have you lying on the floor," Trey adds.

I wince as I realize all of my classmates' shadows are falling over me.

"Do you think you can stand?"

I nod.

"Lean on me," Trey says. As I lift my head, he wraps his arm around me. "One, two, three, up."

The room sways. I focus on a face in front of me: Pilot. Behind him, Augusto and his sad little moustache. Next to him, Lotus. I look slowly from person to person. The expressions on their faces are not what I'd expect.

"That's embarrassing," I say with a shy smile. But everyone just stares at me, wide-mouthed, as if I've turned my skin inside out. "It's fine. I'm okay." I pat my face, the back of my head, wondering if they're all staring at blood on me. I'm not bleeding. "Is there something wrong?"

"No, nothing, Anne," Pilot whispers, shaking his head like he's trying to shush me.

"What's everyone looking at?"

I turn to Harper, who drops her gaze. That's when I know something is up. I've only known Harper a day, but I'm positive she'd happily take any stab she could at me—so why's she holding back now? I glance at my hands, expecting to see something foreign, something alien, like scales or gigantic bruises. But they're just my normal hands.

"Let's get you seated," Garnet says, ushering me back to my workstation. Behind us, everyone shuffles away. "How's your head?"

"Why's everyone acting so weird?"

"You were muttering something when you passed out. It sounded like you said *Dad*."

The memory of my dad standing over me returns, but it's not nearly as strong or worrying as the sensation I have now— the sensation that something's up. "That's why everyone's acting weird?"

"No, it's—never mind. They're not."

"Yes, they are."

"They're *not*," Garnet states, her tone sharp before she turns to the class. "All right, let's start packing up, everyone. Trey will be here for the rest of the week, following which I will assess your work. Remember, based on these sketches, one of you will be selected to headline the Art Walk for Parents' Day this semester."

I leave class shaken. Pilot is just seconds behind me.

"Are you okay? I can't believe you passed out," he says as we step into the dark, syrupy fog. As if the fog isn't bad enough, a light rain has started to fall. Suffocating gray dreariness, when all I want is to *breathe*. "I've never seen that. Just *splat*. You fell right off."

"Yeah, I remember." A breeze blows under my skirt, soughing like whispered secrets through the fabric. "I've never done that before."

"You've never passed out?"

I shake my head and, through the rain, glance around the quad as we walk, trying to make sense of what just happened. I'm not a fainter. Even on the tea cups at Disneyland, while all the other kids were staggering off and dumping their guts into a garbage can, I walked off straight as an arrow and lined up for round two. But now this.

"I'm sorry, but I've gotta go," I say to him. It feels like the wet air is collapsing on me. Like Pilot, for all his welcome friendliness, is crushing me just by being near. I need space. "I have to go to the bathroom," I lie. "I'll see you later."

"Lunch," he calls as I race away. "Cafeteria. You and me."

Fine. Whatever. With nowhere to go, I head past Goethe Hall and to the nearly empty parking lot behind it, where I stop short, brace my knees, and thank God there's no one else here. The lot backs onto a steep hill that leads to the highest point on Wormwood Island, a flat clearing above a craggy, terrifyingly steep cliff. At the far end of the lot, I spy the Harley Dr. Zin was driving yesterday and the yellow Ducati I saw at Ben's house last night. I imagine Ben arriving at school today and confidently edging his powerful bike into that parking spot. The idea of him makes me feel better and worse at the same time, makes my stomach flutter and knot.

"Just breathe," I remind myself.

What started as a gentle shower has turned to rain, which is growing heavier as dark clouds roll in. This world, so shadowy, gray, and foreign to me, gradually stops spinning. The more I stand silently, the less freaked I am that I passed out. I have, after all, been uprooted and thrown into what feels like reform school. I had a terrible sleep. My internal clock is way off. A little fainting is called for.

With a long sigh, I trudge across the dim parking lot, pulling my blazer over my head to shield my hair from the rain. I amble to Ben's Ducati. Glance around. Make sure no one's watching as I trace my fingertips over the soft seat, covered in raindrops, and finally kneel to touch the steel muffler. I wonder what it's like to be Ben Zin. To be unapologetic and poised and perfect. I've never been any of those things.

While I'm lost in thought, a figure slides by the opposite end of the lot, right where I was standing only moments ago. I squint through the rain in time to see a man disappear into the bushes at the base of the cliff. The brush and trees shake as he ascends the hill; through a break in the trees, even with the rain coming down hard, I finally see who it is. I recognize his distinctive brown cloak.

"Villicus?"

He continues on, up. And I have a choice. I can escape what looks like the beginning of a thunderstorm, go to class, knowing the bell is going to ring in two minutes. Or I can follow him. Look closer at his activities. Begin acting on my PT, even if I'm not sure I'll convince Teddy this was all about my PT—not when my single purpose, at this moment, is to see what that strange old man is up to.

There's less underbrush on the hill than I'd expected. My boots and tights keep my legs from getting scraped as I make my way up, careful to keep my distance from Villicus, who walks superfast. He doesn't walk, actually; he slides and lurches and hobbles, moving with jerks and fits up the side of the hill that will take him—and me—to the flat clearing and the treacherous cliff there. Exposed to the rain.

My head is still spinning from passing out, and the exertion of climbing doesn't help. When I finally near the top, I quietly tuck myself behind a tree twenty feet behind him and hide myself in the tangled branches, which block most of the downpour.

Villicus looks out over the dark water, his back to me, his long coat flapping in the winds of the storm. He has a case—the jeweled case I saw on his desk yesterday—wide open at his feet; he reaches into it. If my ears aren't playing tricks on me, he's talking to himself in what sounds like a mix of Latin and German, his little mutterings intertwined with the whistle of the wind.

"*Sceptrum paremus. In cruor scribebat. Blut ist ein ganz besondrer Saft.*" A pause. "*Sie sagte unser Geheimnis.*"

I cower behind the tree, suddenly worried that he'll turn around at any second and spy me, suddenly regretting my decision to follow him instead of going to class, suddenly feeling like the world's biggest fool for eavesdropping on my headmaster when he has the power to expel me, to ruin my life. As a low rumble of thunder shakes the island, I hold my breath and freeze in place. Because it's too late to run now.

And then I hear a word I know, a name I recognize: *Featherly*. Lotus's last name. And the name mentioned repeatedly last night by that Manish fellow. Villicus says the name again and again; the soft, airy word is in stark contrast with the gruffness of the German. Villicus lifts the glassy object he's been holding into the air just as a bolt of lightning shatters the gray sky and reveals it to me: a tube with a pointy bottom, a pale label, and a silvery, heavy-looking top. It's filled with something dark, a viscous liquid that clings to its sides.

Finally, Villicus says in English, "For indiscretions, you pay your dues. Even God and Satan see eye to eye on this."

And, with that, he flings the tube out into the darkness, over the water. I watch it sail through sheets of rain until it disappears, swallowed by inky waves like a sacrifice to the gods of the ocean. Villicus snaps his case shut, lifts it, and, passing the shrubs and shadows that shield me, begins to hobble back down the hill.

Out of nowhere, someone screams on campus. That scream is followed by another. And then a shriek.

Villicus pauses to listen to the chorus of horror that sends chills through my bones. He's just steps from me; I hold my breath, grit my chattering teeth, and, drenched in rain, flatten against the shadowy side of the tree, praying harder that he won't notice me. Then, with a grin, he lumbers out of my sight. More screams—piercing, hair-raising, nightmarish cries—carry him onto campus. Then silence. Then the sound of me bolting down the hill and racing, heart beating furiously, to class.

six

THE MODEL UN
FROM HELL

TRUE TO HIS WORD, PILOT IS WAITING FOR ME WHEN I walk out of my morning lecture on the philosophy of consciousness, which followed *The Ethical Dilemma of Euthanasia*. Neither of which could hold my attention, not with the memory of those screams plaguing my mind all morning. Pilot is leaning against the lockers, which are plastered with Cupid and Death Dance posters. Whatever happened on campus to cause the screams, no one has spoken a word about it. If I didn't know better, if my brain wasn't seared with the fiery memory of those shrieks, I might think the whole thing was a fantasy, a hallucination borne of the eeriness of watching Villicus chant under a slate sky.

"You look like you've seen a ghost," Pilot says. "You still pale from passing out?"

"Something like that."

Together, we venture back out into the storm, which has slowed but not stopped, and walk to the cafeteria. Wondering if I should tell him about the screams and ask him if he knows what happened, I decide against it—for now. Not surprisingly, Pilot and

I are the only two on campus who are actually paired up; the rest of the students stay as separate from one another as possible, wandering around the quad like charged particles that can't touch.

And then we reach the cafeteria. Ah, the cafeteria. Let me pause for a moment to reflect on the beauty, the majesty of the Cania Christy cafeteria. First, its location is pristine, butted up against the shoreline. Second, its walls are comprised entirely of glass, which sets it apart from every other stone and brick building on campus and offers panoramic views. When you walk in, all you can see is the ocean and all you can smell is this insane aroma of whatever gourmet dish they're featuring—today, it's saffron seafood risotto. The lineups to get served are short. The plates are hot. The drinks are cold. The cafeteria ladies—well, okay, they look just like every other cafeteria lady, except they wear the same emerald brooches the secretaries wear. And the tables? They're next to an indoor stream that runs right through the room and cascades outside, where it careens down the shoal. Lovely.

If only I had an appetite.

"What'll you have, Annie?" Pilot picks up two trays.

"Not my name."

"Okay, what'll you have, *Anastasia*?"

Not even bothering to roll my eyes, I glance at the menu, looking for something simple. "What's in the club sandwich?"

"Basil-crusted shrimp. Kentucky hickory smoked bacon. Fresh avocado. And I think they serve it on toasted brioche."

I smother a laugh. So much for simple. I get the roasted beet salad instead and grab a table with Pilot, who's not hungry, either. Next to us—or, actually, four feet above us—sit the faculty; their table is an elevated platform. All the better to see the students from. I've never felt so watched over as I do at Cania. Back home, teachers trusted the smart kids, and I always just assumed that wealth bought you all sorts of privileges, like privacy, respect, and a willingness to look the other way. Here? I glance up at Villicus, who's peering at me—*oh, great*. Here, it's starting to feel like I can do no right. Like no one can.

"Like reform school," I mutter.

"What?" Pilot asks, spearing a ball of goat cheese from my plate. He shoves it in his mouth and chews. "Blech. Doesn't taste like anything."

"Never mind."

As if trained to ruin every moment I have at this place, Teddy walks in and takes a table near us. He pulls out his notepad and fixes his eye on me...because I guess there's a right way and a wrong way to *slice a beet*. Or maybe he's grading me on my ability to chew with my mouth closed. I can't be sure, but knowing I'm being observed from so many different angles doesn't give me warm fuzzies. Reform school. My dad definitely shipped me off to reform school—though the idea of Cania being a fancy mental institution hasn't entirely exited my mind.

Next to carefree Pilot, I must look like a paranoid schizophrenic. He yammers on endlessly, openly mocking the notion of being valedictorian. At one point, his voice gets so loud and Teddy's scribbling so furious that I wonder if we should leave.

"I'm not hungry anyway," I say. "Let's go."

"Oh, no, no, no," he chides, waving his finger. "We've barely even started to get you settled in here, Annie. Or, wait, what has Harper started calling you?"

"She's started calling me something?"

"Fainting Fanny."

"That doesn't even make sense," I groan, casting a sideways glare at Teddy as he notes my new nickname.

"No one said she's the cleverest girl around, but she's a shoe-in for valedictorian next year."

"She is?" I whisper, turning my shoulder to block Teddy from reading my lips. "Why?" I have a hard time masking my irritation.

"What? You don't like her already?" Pilot sighs. "God, why can't we all just get along? Look, Harper's all right. If you just let her have the Big V, everyone'll be fine."

"Well, that's convenient for you, but I actually want to be valedictorian."

"It's *not* convenient for me," he counters. His face pales, his voice falters, and his shoulders slump like a deflating balloon. "It's hard. My dad's not superenthused about my performance here, you know. He wants me to be valedictorian. He was supposed to be our next president, and here he's got this flunky kid who keeps screwing everything up."

"Wait, he was gonna be president?"

"It's more than a little screwy that you *don't* know that." Pilot frowns. "Anyway, that's not my point."

"Right. Sorry." I push a leaf around on my plate.

"It's like he wants me to fit into this little mold, but, I mean, I never asked to come here. *He* sent me here."

"So if no one wants to be here," I ask, "why is it so hard to get in?"

"Who said people don't want to be here?"

I stare at him. "You're kidding, right? Everything I heard yesterday about why people are here, it was all *brutal*. Vague, but brutal. Even *you* were vague."

"*Moi*? No way. I'm always straight up."

"Oh, really?" I say teasingly. "Because I seem to remember some crap about doing *something* your dad didn't like?" As I shake my head, he laughs. "So, spill it. Because, honestly, that could mean running with scissors or playing with matches."

"All right, if you must know, it did have something to do with fire." He drops his gaze. "There was a girl. In a house fire. I was driving by, and she was screaming so loudly, I could hear her over my engine—and we're talking a serious AMG engine. Loud."

"What happened?"

"I tried to save her, but I couldn't." He struggles to keep his emotions in check. "And the mental trauma that followed, knowing I could have helped her... it was too much to bear. I fell apart."

My jaw hits the table. "Pilot, that's incredible! You're, like, a hero. Why wouldn't your dad be extremely *proud* of you for that?"

"He thinks it was a stupid, reckless thing to do. And I guess he's right. I mean, I didn't save her. Anyway, that's not the point. The point is *I* don't want the Big V," Pilot continues. "*He* wants me to do it. Forget it," he grumbles. "When I fail, old pops'll finally get a taste of his own medicine. The hell he put our family through."

"Hell? What'd he do?"

As Pilot's mood shifts, in saunters Harper and her trio of perfect plastic friends. I glimpse them out of the corner of my eye; it's hard to look away. They're sparkly, shiny, sexy—like a roadside collision of money and physical perfection.

"I guess you wouldn't know," he says, and his voice chokes up. "The sex scandals."

My eyebrows hit the top of my head. "The what?"

"Don't make me repeat it."

I cringe but say nothing.

"*The Enquirer* called it 'The Sexcapade of the Century'."

"Your dad was involved in... a sexcapade?" I'm sorry, but it's hard to keep from laughing just a little. The word is ridiculous. The notion of such a thing is... come on.

"Behind the fall of every politician is the other woman. Or, in my dad's case, three other women. All caught on tape in the same bed." He fiddles with his napkin. "It was on Nancy Grace every night for a month. Made me sick. Anderson Cooper had him on the show twice. When the truth was exposed, my dad had to quit campaigning. So embarrassing."

As Pilot twists his napkin into a hundred knots, Harper and her gang claim a table close to the stream. I can't help but watch them, with their swaggers that belong in a red-light district. These girls. These devastatingly alluring girls. These inhumanly gorgeous girls.

Pilot catches me watching them. "Okay, so you're not interested in my dad's sex scandal, but you care about those sex-scandals-in-training?"

Underneath the table, he kicks my shin, but I barely react. I'm not superproud of my squirrel-like attraction to shiny things—their shiny hair, shiny lips, shiny eyelids, shiny cheekbones—but I can't stop staring.

"It's not that I *care*," I explain, though I'm still watching them, which isn't helping my argument. "They just look like walking magazine covers. Like *celebrities*."

"Like they have emaciated rat-dogs in their bags and tramp stamps on their butts?"

"Like they're made of glitter."

"I call them the Model UN from Hell." He kicks my shin again to get my attention and points to a silvery stand across the room. "Dessert table. I need a sugar rush. Come. Walk and talk."

As Pilot picks over the untouched dessert table—crème brulees, éclairs, chocolate mousse, raspberry torte—he names the members of the Model UN from Hell for me and details their backgrounds. Of course, I've already sat through classes with the coke-snorting vixen Plum and Little Miss Texas Harper. There's also a half-Indian, half-Croatian girl named Tallulah, who has bedroom eyes and puffy lips. And Agniezska, a hot little Russian ballerina who once dated the prince of Liechtenstein or something.

"Harper's their secretary general. The one making all the calls," he explains, sticking his finger into cupcake icing, tasting it, and putting the cupcake back. "Model UN. From Hell."

"Okay, I get the Model UN thing. But why are they from Hell? Because they're mean as snakes?"

Leaning against the wall, he boldly points around the room. "See this place? See how everyone's split up like they hate each other? One person per table?"

Yes, I've noticed. Everyone scowling. Everyone with their nose in a book or working on a paper.

"And see how you and me are the only pair here, and the Model UN from Hell, they're the only, what's the word...?"

"Quartet?"

"Foursome."

"Okay, *foursome*," I say and lift a crème brulee, cracking the top of it. "Do you have a point?"

"Everyone here hates each other for one reason only."

Casually, we begin strolling toward the Model UN from Hell and away, snacking absently and trying to hide that we're talking about them, watching them.

"Because their parents had to sign over their trust funds to get 'em in?" I laugh, but Pilot just grimaces. "I know, I know. Because they're competing for the Big V."

"Precisely. Because they've let themselves get sucked into this competition that makes each and every other kid here their enemy. That girl and those boys down there? They're going to go through high school never talking to each other, except to fight. Never making any friends. Hating everyone. You saw the fight in art class."

"So?" I ask as we pause near the stream. "A lot of kids hate everyone else."

"Because they're hormonal. Not because their parents pressure them to become valedictorian."

I shrug. "But it's a good pressure, right? Because being valedictorian here will get us into top colleges."

"Look who's been drinking the Kool-Aid!" He shakes his head.

"Fine," I concede. "Now back to the Model UN from Hell. Why from Hell?"

We both turn and watch them. Their matching red bras busting out of their cleavage. Their sex-kitten hair. Every day, they replace their standard-issue boots with whatever ultra-expensive, ultra-hooker shoes they have; today, it's Manolo Blahnik spiky boots.

"This, little orphan Annie, is *exactly* what makes them hellish, so listen up." He lowers his voice. I inch closer, so close his lips nearly touch my ear. "Their PT topics are all the same."

"Really?" We aren't supposed to know each others' topics, so this is juicy. Pilot's probably privy to a world of stuff I would never be just because he's *openly* not competing. Kids must tell him all sorts of stuff. "What's their topic?"

"Guess." If he didn't look serious, I wouldn't play along.

"To be … skanky cows?"

"Close," he says, half-smirking. "They will succeed in life by using their desirability."

"As in, 'they *are* desire'?" He nods. I scratch my head; it wasn't long ago that Teddy was suggesting I declare the very same PT. "Well, that's, like, not progressive. But I wouldn't call it hellish."

"No, their PT's not the point. That they have the same PT— that's the point."

I try to work through what he's telling me and wonder if I might not need an oversized magnifying glass like some cartoon sleuth. And then it hits me.

"So they're each other's biggest competition."

A slow smile creeps across his face. "Bingo."

"Which means they're competing with each other. But pretending to be friends. The only way Harper wins the Big V is if her friends go down."

"So-called friends," he clarifies. "Each one of those glittery chicks is just waiting for the other to fail. Watching her every move. Ready to tattle to Villicus if she screws up. Like mini-Guardians."

We collect our bags and coats from our table. Just then, Tallulah glances my way and smiles.

"Looks like someone's recruiting a new enemy. Or, sorry, a new BFF," Pilot whispers, chuckling. Then he dusts his hands together and sighs. "You *sure* you wanna be valedictorian, Annie? Or is it possible that, for the first time in my so-called 'disappointing' life, I'm taking the high road…and you should come along for the ride?"

As the bell rings, I race into sculpting class, my final class of the day. I'm the last to arrive except for the teacher. Only one desk is available. It's right next to Harper, who is smacking her gum; and it's right behind Tallulah, who, amazingly, is applying *another* heaping helping of lip gloss to her already glowing lips and nodding along with whatever Harper's rattling on about. Reluctantly, I slide into the seat next to Harper and start unpacking my bag. A two-way mirror along the far side of the room suggests that our Guardians are watching and grading us from the other side; this, I'm noticing, is a common feature in classrooms here.

"Good God, Tallie, I would give my fuchsia Halston peep-toes to see the sun again," Harper groans as she stares at the overcast afternoon sky. "I haven't had a tan in eight months."

"Maine isn't Dallas," Tallulah says.

"Gee-*ee*, thanks for that *excellent* observation. I hadn't noticed," Harper says. "You're starting to sound like my stepmonster. About as friendly as fire ants, she is. God, what does my dad see in her? Crunchy California type, y'know? Always yammering on about solar power this, sunscreen that. Hates tans. Hates me."

Her stepmonster sounds alright to me.

I scribble my name and the date on the top of my page as our instructor, Dr. Weinchler, and his assistant finally enter, wheeling a cart towering with something under a dust cloth. Harper goes on about a Tori Burch dress that her daddy's shipping out to her—a dress that, stop the world, may not even get here in time for the dance this Saturday.

"We're so gee-dee isolated here," Harper moans. "At least we have the dance to look forward to. Tragic how dull high school boys are, though. There's, like, maybe one guy on this whole island I'd even consider knocking boots with." She nods to the front of the room. Tallulah follows her gaze and, unable to help myself, I do, too. "But he's way too old for me. And, like, his name's actually *Ebenezer*. How lame is that?"

There he stands. Ben Zin. Ebenezer Zin.

He's our TA!

At exactly the moment I see Ben, before his gallingly flawless face even registers in my brain, before my stomach starts to turn at the idea that Harper might ever be with Ben, I recall the TA form his dad handed him yesterday outside Villicus's office. I watch him remove the dust cover from the cart, fold it, and, with Weinchler helping, lift a lengthy sculpture from the cart and place it on an oversized plinth near the chalkboard. It's his sculpture. His *art*.

OMG. He's an artist, too.

My heart sinks.

Thinking of the girlfriend I saw him with last night—she better not have been Harper!—I feel robbed. An artist. A sculptor. Good enough to TA. Why must Ben Effing Zin be so perfect, so totally out of my league? It makes my head swoon. Thank God I'm sitting, or I might pass out again.

"I could get Ben," Harper continues, convincing Tallulah. I glance at the Indian beauty to see her nodding passionately, but her eyes are empty. Does Harper know Tallulah's faking it? Does she know her little peons are desperate to get her kicked out of school, kicked out of the race for valedictorian? "But I'm too focused on the Big V to fiddle around with guys. At least, with guys who won't get me anywhere."

"You wouldn't make an exception for Ben?" Tallulah asks. "He's hot. His dad's ridunkulously powerful. And he's *really* rich. Like, Trump rich."

"So am I. So are you," Harper laughs. Then both girls look directly at me. "You, Fainting Fanny?" Harper strokes a lock of her perfectly annoying hair. I know what she's going to say before she even says it: "Not so much."

She was going for shock, trying to surprise me. But I'm not remotely surprised because this little hussy couldn't be more typical if she tried. I just roll my eyes at her uninspired jab and face forward; she and Tallulah exchange undeserved mini high fives.

"Eyes on me," Dr. Weinchler shouts, clapping his hands.

Weinchler is the antithesis of his TA. Old, gray, and stereotypically academic looking, with a soft face that resembles wax slowly melting. He looks like a caricature of a scientist. What little hair sits on top of his age-spotted head is wispy and even wilder than mine. His low voice cracks, but he doesn't seem to notice, so whenever he speaks, I strain to watch his wet, old lips move. It's like watching TV during a storm, when the volume keeps blinking out.

"This year," Weinchler begins shakily, the ruby pin on his lab coat sparkling, "your TA is one of America's brightest sculptors. Ebenezer Zin is a gifted representationalist. His collection of bronzes depicting the gruesome acts of plastic surgery, a searing tip of the hat to his father's former profession as an LA plastic surgeon—"

"San Mateo," Ben corrects. And I swoon a little more. After all, that's where I'm from.

"Does it matter?" Dr. Weinchler hacks into his sleeve. "Where was I?"

"My collection is touring…"

"Right! Mr. Zin's collection is currently touring major art galleries in Europe. As you see before you, he was kind enough to bring another work, entitled *Self Portrait with Company.*"

I. Am. *Stunned*. Ben is already touring the uber-exclusive galleries of Europe? He's barely eighteen. The idea of it makes me sick with envy.

"Thank you, Professor," Ben says. His voice—everything about him—is just as attractive as I remembered it, if not more. Which makes me feel worse.

As Ben steps forward, Weinchler claps his long, thin hands lightly, a pompous little clap, and encourages everyone to do the same. I clap, but I'm distracted with thoughts of Ben and his mystery girlfriend living some perfect life together in the future: him the artist, her the—*what*, nonprofit lawyer? He will be valedictorian for the senior class this year. And, after graduation, the two of them will move away to Yale or Harvard or whatever school for rich kids and celebrities they decide to attend *together*. Then? Off to some fabulous New York City brownstone. It's a no-brainer. I can picture it now.

And me—what is my fate? I can see it now. I will be a struggling artist, cast away from all "good" society after pissing off Villicus for God knows why or disappointing Teddy enough that I don't even qualify for the Big V race. I'll waste away at some community college, and there I'll have a sordid affair with a married prof who uses me to feel young again.

The only way to avoid such a fate is to become valedictorian. No matter what Pilot says. And no matter what hold Harper thinks she has on the title.

"Good afternoon and hello," Ben says, stepping forward.

His vibrant eyes scan the room, and sighs fan out among the girls. He paces in front of his small sculpture, which depicts five standing bodies intertwined—three humans dancing gaily, two skeletal figures engaging the dancers. One skeleton plays the flute.

I've seen this sort of sculpture before. Anyone with any interest in art history would recognize it instantly as derivative of a movement called the "dance of Death," which gained popularity in the fifteenth century. I'm relieved that Ben's sculpture doesn't floor me as I'd expected it to. It's been done, and done better. In this fact, I can take a little comfort. Ben may not be as amazing as I've started building him up to be.

"Let me explain to you," Ben begins, "what makes these good sculptures."

Definitely not as amazing! I had assumed that the boy was as arrogant as they come, but talk about pompous! To assume his work is "good"—to *call* it that. No need to compliment Ben Zin; he does that all on his own. As he launches into this endless harangue on the qualities of his art that match contemporary and traditional standards of what commercially successful art should be, blah, blah, blah, I can't help but think of how every single word he says conflicts 110 percent with what I believe art is meant to be, meant to do. Sure, he throws in fancy words to distract us— like *ontological perspective* and *Hegelian phenomenology*—but when you listen closely, you can almost hear his soul escaping through his mouth. He's completely passionless about his art.

"So, with that," Ben says, "tell me, who agrees that this is good art?"

Every hand in the room goes up—except mine. They've all been persuaded, and I wonder if maybe *Follow the Leader* isn't the PT for a few of them. But, well, that ain't my PT! Mine is to take nothing at face value, to get to the bottom of things. So I keep my hand down even as Harper scoffs at me like I must be the densest freak alive.

"Looks like all of you," Ben says without glancing my way and sighs.

"Wait," I call out as hands go down. Everybody grumbles like I'm holding them up. Gee, sorry, but if my dad mortgaged the family funeral home just to get me in here—which is all I can imagine he did—I'm going to milk every opportunity. He needs me to.

Ben looks at me. "Miss Merchant?"

"*I* disagree," I say. My voice doesn't even wobble, thank God. "Respectfully."

Indifferently, Ben plucks a fallen hair off his sleeve. "Go on."

"Because you referenced Hegel, you must know that Hegel said good art should express the essence of a culture. It's supposed to be the impetus for progress."

He raises an eyebrow. "Although you sound more like Danto than Hegel."

I argue that Danto might agree, though he's more of a pluralist—and we go back and forth on all this art history stuff, stuff I've read a million times. I know it inside out, know what he's going to say before he even says it. Who'd have thought those lonely Saturdays spent in the library rather than watching funeral processions would actually pay off?

"So," I conclude, "I'm at a loss as to how your sculpture is, as you said, good. It's derivative."

"By postmodern standards."

"By any standards. The dance of Death has been done."

At the front of the room, someone gasps. Harper scoffs. But I know I'm right, so screw 'em. And a quick glance at Weinchler shows me that he's nodding along with me, that he's agreeing. He's even taking notes! Finally, a positive note about me. I can only hope Teddy's on the other side of that mirror and that he caught this scene.

"Agree with me," I finish, "and we'll both be right."

And then it's Ben's turn to surprise me: he laughs.

"Well done," he says, running his hands through his fantastic hair. "I've actually hated this thing since the day Villicus commissioned it. Great argument, A.M."

So that does it. Not only am I validated by Weinchler, but *Ben* has agreed with me.

"I guess they taught y'all something in that public school," Harper hisses under her breath as Weinchler takes over the lecture. "Too bad it ain't near enough to get you the Big V."

"We'll see," I whisper back. And, for the first time, I actually believe it. I could be valedictorian next year. Brown, here I come!

seven

FIRE AND LIFE

I AWAKE WITH A JOLT FROM A VIVID, REPEATED NIGHT-mare. It's the middle of the night. My blankets are knotted, co-cooning me; I coiled them around my body like threads around a spool as I fought my way through long, tangled dreams that wouldn't let go. Even as the details of my nightmare fade rapidly, the basics of it and, even worse, the sadness it stirred within me won't let go, like claws digging into my breastplate.

I stare at the clock. Almost one in the morning.

I'd dreamt of walking up the back steps to our apartment above the funeral home. It was a warm morning—spring-like, with flowers in bloom and birds perched nearby. There was a siren, an earthquake warning in the distance; they'd sent us home early from school just in case. I turned the doorknob and stepped inside, but it was dark, the shades drawn. I glimpsed my reflection—pale, wide-eyed, hollow—in the hall mirror and called in a voice that echoed, "Mom?" On a small table, towering stacks of bills wobbled, bills from specialists and from that unimaginably expensive hospi-tal we'd been forced to pull Mom out of. I couldn't shake the sense that our house would explode if those bills fell, so I raised my hands to catch them—but at exactly that moment, the table transformed into an oven door, open wide. I stepped toward it. I tripped over somebody—my mom—lying at my feet, and I began to fall in.

I woke just before my head hit the oven door.

The dream has left me bruised inside, my head pounding. As if it repeated for days, not two hours, like round after round of a boxing match that the ref wouldn't call. Now, in a sweat, I stare into the black of my attic bedroom and sob quietly over the memory of my mother. Not just the mother who took her life that day. But the mother I used to have, the one who would repeat the stories she read during her breaks at the library, twirl my hair around her fingers, and teach me to dance in the kitchen when there were no funerals downstairs. The mother who grew up as I did; her father was a mortician—she and my dad met when he came to work for her dad. That's the mother I knew. The mother I had before that unidentifiable switch went off in her head and the psychiatrists stepped in.

I bury my face in my pillow, chasing away gloom. But the pounding in my head won't let up. I need an Advil, so I tiptoe down from the attic, slashing my hands through the dark corners where spirits could gather, just like I used to do back home to prove no ghosts stood there. Moving quietly to keep from waking my crackpot roomies, I rummage through the bathroom medicine cabinet until I realize that the pounding isn't coming from inside my head at all. I tilt my ear toward the sound.

Distant drumbeats.

I drift down the stairs. Standing at the front room picture window, with Skippy snoring behind me on the couch, I stare into the blackness of the night and see, beyond the forest separating all things school from all things village, bright orange sparks flying through the distant sky, over the village. Ashes. Low, vibrating drumbeats. I'm awake now, and I have no interest in returning to endless rounds of the same draining nightmare.

Slipping on a coat and a pair of boots, I grab a flashlight before I make the walk to the village, to the source of the fire. Around me, leaves rustle with the wind or with something more sinister. I can't be sure, don't want to find out, keep my flashlight shining forward, wonder if I'm out of my mind for walking in the dark like this, walking toward a mystifying fire in a village I'm sworn to steer clear of on a kook-run island I've barely settled into. But I can't help myself. I'm drawn onward.

Torches light the harbor, where villagers are sitting cross-legged in a circle near the water, a low stage set up in the middle of their ring. A dull hum. Bonfires on rafts float beyond the docks. Flames reflect off the water as if the ocean is on fire, as if Hell is rising up to consume Heaven. The crisp air reeks of smoke. The entire scene seems private, like some ancient tribal rite that will end in a human sacrifice—and who better to sacrifice than the disobedient girl from the prep-slash-reform school? I shake my head. Overactive imagination. But I keep to the shadows none-theless; tiptoe to a bench far enough away to watch without draw-ing attention; sit. The street lamps are out up and down the street. Relative to the vibrant gold of the fires, everything dark is nearly black, black enough to hide me.

Drums thump slowly. Heavily.

In the dim glow of scattered dying fires, vibrantly paint-ed men and women hold unlit torches; a tall man, illumi-nated and impossible to miss, inhales from a long pipe. Slowly, the drumbeat that pulled me here diminishes, and the pace of dozens of unseen rattles around the perim-eter of the stage picks up quickly, then slows. One by one, the villager torches are lit, and a fire spreads through their circle until it blazes like an enormous bullion ring. A leggy woman with white face paint and a cloth sling around her bare chest creeps through the ring, onto the stage; she is followed by two bare-chested men twirling large batons lit at both ends. Each time the fiery batons pass their faces, their eyes widen, their lips curl. I squirm.

A rattle shakes to a languid larghetto tempo. The painted woman is singing quietly, under her breath, so softly I can barely hear. Laying my jacket over my chest like a blanket, I listen as the woman's melancholy voice rises and falls, as the two men chant in a language I don't know. The crowd gradually begins to chant, too. The pipe is passed unhurriedly from person to person; only the drummers, who likely wish to avoid the slowing effect of whatever they're smoking, refuse it. The drumbeat intensifies, the sound of dozens of drums I can't see joining it.

The woman screams suddenly.

Startled, I recoil against the back of the bench; those who've smoked the pipe barely react. Swiftly, the woman pulls something from the sling around her chest, something small, like a baby. But the baby is motionless. (It can't be a baby. No way.) She lifts it over her head. The two men stop twirling their batons, and that tall man—gray-haired and huge, maybe six-five—enters the circle; he is carrying a large, flat rock. He places it at the woman's feet and backs away until he's absorbed by the blazing ring. Someone makes a crying sound, like a baby's, and then another and another, filling the air, filling my ears. The painted woman inches into a crouch—I can't tear my eyes away—in time with the drums, and the rattles quicken. She places the baby on the flat rock. Backs into the ring.

Only the shirtless men remain.

They circle the baby. I squint, praying that my eyes are tricking me, that what looks like a baby is actually just a dummy—because I will not be able to stop myself from charging through the fire and rescuing that child if it comes down to it.

The rattling accelerates. Becomes little more than quick sharp noises slapping one on top of the other—*chop shhick chop shhick*. A rising wall of sound.

"Free it!" someone roars.

Immediately, in unison, the men touch both ends of the baby with their flaming batons and set the thing on fire. It bursts into flames like it's made of gas-drenched straw.

I start to scream—it's just about howling from my lips—when someone clamps a hand over my mouth. That only makes me want to scream louder. I flail my arms, trying desperately to escape the hold of the stranger standing behind me. I finally free myself and fall off the bench, looking up with terror lighting my face to see *him* standing behind the bench, his mint-colored eyes glowing in the darkness.

"Ben?"

"You know, you actually seemed bright in class today. But I'm beginning to wonder if you aren't the dumbest person alive," he whispers, scowling. "What are you doing in the village?"

"You scared the hell out of me!" I say, panting, my heart beating an insane staccato. I throw my gaze at the men, who are tossing their batons at each other, back and forth over the burning body.

"You shouldn't be here," Ben says, his wide eyes reflecting the ring of fire. "Your Guardian will notice you're gone. He'll come looking."

"Did you follow me?"

"I saw you sneak out."

As I focus on Ben, I try not to pay attention to the fact that the rattling has stopped, the crying from the crowd has stopped. I try not to look at the stage again, but I can't help myself. The men grab the fiery body with their bare hands.

"Why did you follow me? To watch what I do and tell Teddy? I'm not even your competition. You're a senior."

"You think I'm telling you this because...I want to be vale-dictorian? Anne, you don't know what you're playing with here," Ben warns quietly. "If Villicus were to find you, he would punish you. And his punishments are...they're terrible." Then he glances at the stage and pales.

I follow his gaze to see Molly creeping toward us, her face painted bright pink with green stripes. She has her finger to her lips, shushing me, and is smiling her metallic smile. Turning back to Ben, I'm about to tell him to relax, but he's nowhere to be seen.

"Hey, you," Molly says to me.

On the stage behind her, the men leap in this strange, awkward way through the circle and race to the ocean. "A-ya!" they scream while the crowd looks on. They drop what's left of the baby on a floating bonfire, which finishes it off. As I sit on the bench again, she scoots up next to me.

"It's freezing out. Let's share some body heat."

I need a second. I need to wrap my brain around what's just happened. First, what I saw. Second, the arrival of Ben who was, to my surprise, following me.

At the center of the fiery ring, the huge man has returned, standing like an unshakable oak burst forth from the island. The harbor is silent save the crackling of fires.

"You have witnessed the cremation ceremony," the man says, his voice a deep baritone that carries so powerfully, I feel the earth rumble.

"You cremated it?" I whisper, turning to Molly, who's snuggling under my coat with me. "That baby?"

She furrows her brow. "What?"

"Please tell me it was already...passed on."

"What, you mean the dummy?"

"The what?"

"The bundle of straw. The one that represents a child." Molly shakes her head at me. "Did you think we burned real bodies in these ceremonies? Come on. We're not, like, barbarians. It's just a show."

A groan of relief escapes me. "Well, I didn't know. It's dark! It looked real. I thought maybe that was why Villicus keeps us away from you guys."

Molly chuckles, and we both shift to watch the man, who Molly explains is her grandpa and their shaman. With his arms extended, he fluidly pivots in the glow of the torches to address the whole circle. Now that my fears are allayed, I find myself torn between listening to Mr. Watso and wondering why Ben followed me.

"This is the final ceremony in the Festival of Fire and Life," Mr. Watso bellows, "a tradition unique to the Abenaki of this island they call Wormwood, this island that is *Ndakinna* to our great ancestors. It is a tradition that is just decades old but more meaningful than any ritual we have ever performed."

I feel Molly's eyes on me.

"You must be either crazy or stupid," she says when I finally look her way.

"So I've heard," I mutter. "Same with you. You know the rules."

"Let's blame my lapse in judgment on the Devil's Apple we were just passing around in the pipe," Molly chuckles.

"I thought it was, like, a peace pipe or something."

"Much better. Really takes the edge off. You've seen, like, salvia on those YouTube videos?" I say nothing, hoping not to reveal just how uncool I am. "Well, the Devil's Apple is like that, a natural hallucinogen that affects you for days."

"You smoke it together?"

"It's part of an Abenaki tradition. We're not just getting high." Bashing her argument to bits, she breaks into a fit of giggles.

"You blame talking to me on that?"

Snuggling against me, she sighs. "You and I both know it's not that. I just don't care anymore. There's practically no one left in our village. So I can't help but wonder why the hell I'm follow-ing rules that don't work for us."

"So, what's the point of the rules?" I ask, yawning. "Why keep us separated?"

"Oh man, Anne, I dunno. It's just been a rule for decades—it goes back to when Cania opened years ago," she sighs. "Initially, I think our village told the Cania people that they couldn't come onto our land. Then a line was drawn. And, since then, a rule we made has been turned against us. So now we don't question it. We're just supposed to follow it."

"Well, even if we get caught, so what?" I ask. "You'd be forced to come to Cania. That wouldn't be so bad, would it?"

"You'd be expelled, though. So I'd be stuck there alone with those snobs." We both chuckle at the idea.

Mr. Watso's voice lifts through the air again, interrupting us. "Cremation protects our souls and returns us to Tabaldak, our mighty creator." A single drumbeat begins.

"I wish it didn't have to be this way," Molly whispers, her voice filled with misery as she watches the ceremony. "We used to be this really proud island nation, you know? Even though we lost everything when we had to stop whaling, we still had pride."

"Well, I don't know about pride, but I've never seen such a cool ceremony before."

"Cool? It's garbage. There's nothing cool about it or this mental island. I wish we could just move away."

As much as I know we're not supposed to fraternize, I can't help but want Molly to stick around. "Your family must feel bad you don't have anyone your age here."

"You'd think, right? But look at him!" She flicks her glare at her grandpa. "He's our *shaman*. He can't leave. Refuses to. A captain goes down with his ship, y'know?" Then she turns to me, her eyes bright and slightly out of focus, the paint on her face glowing. "But what about me? I'm never supposed to have any friends? I'm just supposed to be this pathetic excuse for a teen-ager. In our stupid house. With our stupid fancy clothes."

"I love your clothes! You're lucky."

"Lucky?" She shakes her head. "Try bought and paid for."

"What's that supposed to mean?"

"You know, paid to lease the island to Villie and look the other way." She waves her hand in the direction of the magnificent homes on the hillside. "As if getting the finer things in life washes away the need for an *actual* life."

"What do you mean, look the other way?"

Pausing, Molly searches my face. Then she slides down, resting her head against me, fakes a yawn, and closes her eyes. "I'm just exaggerating. Blame the Devil's Apple again. Forget I said anything."

As if I could forget! I sit up straight, and her head bounces off my shoulder. She's frowning when she looks up at me.

"Look the other way? Look away from what exactly, Molly?"

But Mr. Watso's voice sails through the air before she can answer.

"My grandfather first welcomed the people of Cania to this island and signed the pact that would allow them access to this majestic land," he bellows. "Even as our village shrinks around us, as the young wisely abandon this place, we who remain must never forget the necessity of this pact that spared the lives of so many casualties of war and, when the whales were denied us, saved our people from starvation. That pact remains intact with our enduring silence."

Whoops and chants rise up around him, stretching across the ring of fire and through the smoke, into the murky darkness that hides me and Molly from sight.

"What's he talking about?" I ask, talking through my thoughts. Torches begin to sizzle in the water as the festival winds down. "Pilot said that the school's got a code of secrecy, but I assumed he was talking about something like the Illuminati or Freemasons have. Some secret society thing. Is there something bigger than that? Something Villicus would pay you to pretend not to see?"

"Anne—"

"Wait. And you guys needed to get paid because you used to whale but aren't allowed to anymore. Of course."

Molly glares at me. "Seriously, Anne, cool it."

"And the line, the red line that separates us." The pieces are coming together fast, though I wish they'd lock in place. I know there's more that I'm missing. "Are you guys keeping something secret...*from* us? From the kids up at the school?"

She clenches her jaw and glowers. "No. Not usually, at least," she finally says—reluctantly.

"Then you're keeping a secret *about* us? About the school? From other people?"

"God, who died and made you detective?"

A roar rings out through the air suddenly. My heart jumps, and Molly and I look up to see six feet, five inches of angry grandpa tearing through the throngs and charging at us.

"Molly Lynn Watso!" he roars.

Molly throws a quick apologetic glance at me as Mr. Watso storms our way. "Sorry," she mouths.

His face is red, his eyes bulging, his huge fists clenching. Startled, I get to my feet and back away. But Molly's already throwing her arms out in front of me; it's just a gesture, not enough to protect me from his ferocity.

"Gramps, don't! It's not her fault," Molly pleads.

"You will not do this! You will not bring on our demise!" he hollers. Then he yanks Molly's arm and tugs her away from me. He points at the men who've followed him and shouts, "Get that Cania girl *out of here*!"

But I don't need an escort! I spin on my heels and charge away, shaking, mortified. I race hard. Through shadows thick like cobwebs, my flashlight beam bounces frantically, barely cutting the darkness. I run for an eternity. When I finally slow to a pace my heaving lungs can bear, I wonder if my heart will ever calm down again. And I wonder if I'll ever see Molly again. Her grandpa's angry face is so clear in my mind. His bottomless bellow so deep in my ears. He shouted as if I were wielding a gun, not shaking in my boots. He glared like he *hated* me. But how could he? He doesn't even know me. I'm harmless! I'm just some artsy geek sitting alone on a bench in the dark. But it was like I was threatening his only grandchild's life.

Staring into the blackness beyond the beam of my flashlight, I know now there's something I'm meant to find out, some dark secret lurking, waiting to be discovered if I can just point my beam in the right direction and really, truly *see*. But at this exact moment, I don't see. I *hear*. I hear something in the woods, and I stop in my tracks as fear like cold, icy water cascades over my back and onto my legs.

I hear another noise.

And then I see them. In the shadows a few feet into the woods—feet from where I stand—two people. Two bodies. I silently beg for it not to be Ben and his girlfriend.

It's not Ben. It's a red-haired girl and a man; the soft moonlight glints off his bare chest, a chest I recognize because, just this morning, I drew it in class. My stomach drops to my feet as I gape at them.

"Trey Sedmoney," I utter. Nude model. Member of the Cania faculty.

No sooner have I said his name than he looks up from the redhead on her knees and locks his gaze on mine. A grin spreads across his face. And that's when I hear her voice.

"I deserve to win, don't I?" Harper asks him with her unmistakable Texan drawl. "Do you know anyone who's living and breathing their PT better than I am, Trey?"

eight

THE PRINCE

"COME ON. LIVE A LITTLE. YOU KNOW YOU WANNA SKIP study hall."

Pilot has correctly guessed that I'm in a bit of a funk today. He has no idea why, though. How could he? How could he know what I endured last night? That I was screamed at publicly by a huge man from the village just before I watched my fiercest competitor *engage* a member of the faculty, a man I had to sketch this morning, knowing what he used those parts for just last night? I can't exactly confess this crap to Pilot. So, after our morning workshop and after shaking off another bout of the chills, I tell him I'm homesick. And he says the best remedy for homesickness is skipping study hall.

"It's not like you can be graded for anything in study hall. I mean, you can, but who cares?" he insists as Harper glides by us and flips her hair, eyeing Pilot seductively.

Seeing her is all it takes to convince me to bail—to get as far away from this scene as I can when I'm surrounded on all sides by treacherous ocean. To say nothing of the fact that I'm hoping Pilot will open up to me about whatever it is the villagers are being paid to pretend not to notice. Perhaps it's just the student–faculty sex stuff—but something tells me it's more than that.

Five minutes later, Pilot and I are on the beach, sitting side by side on a huge fallen tree that's turned white and smooth with age and wind and countless waves crashing over it. Deadwood scraps litter the sand. The sun is out for the first time all week, and a family of sea lions takes in the rays on the rocks. Foamy water inches slowly up the shoreline, lapping at the shapeless feet of the lions. Amazing how mammoth they are, I think, and how little attention they pay to us. As if they haven't even noticed us, yammering as we are.

"Is it just me," I begin, "or are things weird around here?"

"Ha! Just follow my lead, and you'll be fine."

Pilot then proceeds to bring me up to speed on all things Cania Christy—from the teachers to avoid to the secretaries to kiss up to.

"Dr. Tina Naysi, the chem prof, looks senile but is actually, like, a genius. Trey Sedmoney—well, you already know him. He's caught groping at least one student every month, so watch your ass." He grins. It's the perfect invitation for me to tell him what I saw Harper doing last night, but I'd rather pretend it didn't happen. "There's no one in the front office worth trusting."

"The secretaries are insanely creepy. And immature."

"Yeah, just don't get in a fistfight with one of those fuglies." He cracks his knuckles and tugs a branch out from a tangle of mushy seaweed. "They've got nothing pretty to protect."

"Except their brooches. Those are stunning."

"Brooches?"

"Yeah. They all wear the same one. An emerald one. The cafeteria ladies wear it, too."

"Really?"

"And the teachers, but theirs have rubies. Except Garnet."

"They do?"

I stare at him. He's pulling bark off the branch. "You hadn't noticed?"

"Guess I'm not that perceptive." Then an idea hits him, brightening his face. "Hey! Maybe they all *have* to wear it. Like, their heads'll fall off if they take off the magical jeweled pin. Like that story about the woman with the yellow scarf or whatever, and her head fell off."

It's hard not to smile, watching Pilot pretend he's trying to keep his head on straight, watching him stagger off the tree to blindly chase an invisible head down the beach. When he finally collapses on the sand at my feet, he begins rehashing all these crazy stories from last year, chuckling as he impersonates teachers. I laugh along with him, but I'm surprised to find myself *watching* him more than listening. I notice the way his lips move softly as he speaks. His dark eyes glisten brightly, and his animated face is lovely and expressive. He's not as tall as Ben is, but that puts him right at my height, which could work—as long as I never wear heels, which I don't. Like everyone else at Cania, he's flawless, with skin that a magazine ad might call *radiant* or *glowing* but what I'd venture to call *candescent*, lit from within.

Hold on. I stop myself. What am I doing? Why am I pondering *Pilot?*

I guess I can't help it. He's nice, he's cute, and he's the only friend I've got now that Mr. Watso has made it abundantly clear I'm not allowed within a thousand-foot radius of Molly. But could Pilot Stone, son of a senator (albeit a sex addict), see beyond my crooked tooth and wild hair? Something in the way his eyes sparkle when he laughs with me makes me believe he could.

I feel a blush coming on—but it's quickly halted by an image my brain cooks up. Ben standing behind my bench last night. Warning me to get out of the village, which is considerate, I guess. But calling me dumb at the same time, which is anything but considerate. And he's got a girlfriend. And, who am I kidding, there's just no way Ben and I could ever happen.

"Unless you care about being graded," Pilot says.

I flinch. *What's he talking about?* I stopped paying any attention long ago.

"Do you?" he urges.

"Do I what?"

"Care about being graded."

"For what? Like, in general?"

"Did you just faint again?" he laughs.

I sigh. "I was thinking about—" I rack my brain for a lie. I can't very well tell him I've been mentally comparing him to Ben Zin. "I've been thinking about hearing things."

"Hearing things?" He looks intrigued. "Like, hearing voices in your head? Or are you tapped into *guicy jossip* already?"

I smile. "No. I've been literally hearing things. Like gunshots my first night here. And screams the other morning."

"Screams?"

"Yeah. On campus. You didn't hear them?"

He shrugs. "Maybe it was a bird. There's some crazy wildlife around here. Same for the gunshots."

"You think? Really?"

"Well, sure. I mean, the only other explanation is that you're on an island of screaming, gun-wielding murderers." Baring his teeth and making his eyes crazy-wide, he pretends to lunge for my neck. Shrieking, I push him back. "Anyway, I was talking about the dance this weekend, Miss Anne. The Cupid and Death Dance. Well, it's technically a masquerade, but whatevs."

"A masquerade?"

"It's not that serious. But, yeah, you get dressed up and wear a mask. And the theme is Cupid and Death, which is some sort of famous old masque from, like, Jane Austen times. That's all."

"Did you say we're being graded on it?"

"Yupper. Like everything here."

"Graded on a dance?"

"Everything that can be assessed is assessed," Pilot recites. "But if you, like *moi*, aren't hung up on the Big V, then, you know, it could be fun." Suddenly, he jumps down from the log. "Crap, I forgot I have to set up for my jazz class. I've gotta run. But, um." He shifts on his feet, fidgeting. "You didn't really say."

"Say what?"

"I mean, I guess I'm assuming you're not going with anyone else. When you could be. I dunno. Are you?"

I hold my breath. Is he asking what I think he's asking? If he is, that should be good, right? I mean, I've just been sitting here having this mini-fantasy about him. So I should want to say yes, shouldn't I?

"But," he sighs. "Well, I can't dance. Can you?"

If there's one thing I can do, it's dance. I have my mom to thank for that. But, recognizing Pilot's insecurity on the matter, I shrug. "I can't do the sort of dances they might have at an old-school masque, if that's what you mean."

"Cool. Well, if you're not worried about your grade or being embarrassed on the dance floor with me—because that's a given—then, will you go to the dance with me?"

A brisk walk away from the waterside is the impossibly ornate Valedictorian Hall. After some wandering, during which time I repeatedly try to remind myself that I'm *happy* to be going to the dance with Pilot, I find myself standing outside the front doors of that hall. Staring at it. I'd read about it in my student handbook and know already that it opens just once a year, just at the end of June, just for the graduation ceremony when the valedictorian is named. Yet I try the handle for the double doors anyway.

"Locked. Of course," I mutter, stuffing my hands in my blazer pockets.

I spy a bronze plaque behind thick vines of ivy traveling up the wall. Pushing aside the vines, I read the rhyme embossed on the plaque, which is a challenge because some of its letters are rubbed away:

-aled-ctori-n, you shine, you exce-,
Now to each of your peer-, bid a blessed f—well
From this isle of -ope to success, do proce-d,
Eve- active, ever after, with endl-ss Godspeed.

Honestly, the indoctrination machine here has been working overtime. For a moment, the geek in me thinks that perhaps the missing letters are part of some word game, and I start trying to piece them together—*VIA L SAR*—but give up when I glimpse someone I recognize walking by oh so silently. It's the girl with the bobbed hair; I saw her on the road on my first day. Our eyes meet briefly.

I watch her until she disappears around the corner of the building's stone walls and, not much later, come out on the other side, her gaze still fixed on me.

As she moves toward Goethe Hall, I look away from her, step back, and take in this underused, much revered building. Standing one extremely tall story high, Valedictorian Hall hints on its exterior of the magnificence of its interior. The surrounding gardens rise majestically and spread to the clean edges of beds with soil as dark as steeped tea; inside, I imagine a double aisle of darkly stained pews that gleam. A highly wrought chimney graces skyward; inside, I imagine an immaculate fifteen-foot marble fireplace. I stand on my tiptoes to peer through the stained-glass windows near the door, wondering why they keep such a building locked when it alone could attract tourists to the island, and hoping to catch a glimpse of something that might help me unravel the mysteries not only of this overelaborate building but also of the importance of the valedictorian race. A title so important they dedicate the most magnificent building on campus to it. A title so important they grade you at dances to see if you qualify for it.

The Cupid and Death Dance. This Saturday.

Admittedly, it felt somewhat cool when Pilot asked me to go with him. There was an embarrassing but flattering formality about it. But now the rush of that moment is wearing off, and my mind (my heart?) is starting to ask all these *questions*. As it asks, it drums up images of a certain green-eyed senior with whom I am *not* going. No, if Ben is going at all, he's going with his mysterious girlfriend.

"Anne Merchant, you are going with Pilot, plain and simple," I remind myself. "And that's good."

Pilot and I are going to have a nice, peaceful little night; he'll walk me home, ask to hold my hand, and we'll probably kiss on Gigi's doorstep. Nice. Peaceful. And as we have that sweet little kiss? In the mansion next door, Ben and his girlfriend will be in a sweaty, fiery tangle of passion.

I squeeze my eyes shut. "Don't torture yourself." I groan, reluctantly opening my eyes again and stepping around the side of the hall.

Where I find myself standing face-to-face with Ben.

We both jump at the sight of the other. But I'm not just startled; I'm *freaked out*. Did I say anything incriminating that he might've overheard? Did I accidentally mutter his name while I was thinking about him? Oh, damn, I hope not. I really must stop talking to myself.

"I thought you were someone else," he says, clutching his chest. I guess he's waiting for his girlfriend. "What are you doing, sneaking up like that?"

"I wasn't *sneaking* up. And you snuck up on me last night, so."

"That's different," he says. "That was to protect you."

"Protect me?"

"From yourself. You seem destined to self-destruct."

"Why? Because I questioned you in class?" Somehow, I've gone from pining over Ben to wanting to attack him, all in a matter of seconds. "Do you always lurk around like this?"

"I'm not lurking. I'm standing. Remembering something." For the first time, I notice that he looks disoriented. "The last time I was in this building."

"I thought they only let graduates in."

He brushes his hair back. "Someone I once admired graduated here. I was a guest."

Surprised by the intimacy of his revelation, I don't know what to say. "Well, sorry to interrupt."

And, with that, I walk by him, hoping I didn't come off as idiotic as I feel. But, out of nowhere, he grabs my shoulder, stopping me. In slow motion, I turn my head, lips parted, to glance down at the luckiest shoulder that ever existed, the one on which his hand now rests.

"I liked that you questioned me in class." He notices me watching his hand and quickly pulls it away. "Sorry. I didn't mean to—to touch you."

Soundlessly, I just shake my head.

"Your observations were good. For all the interest in the Big V here, there's much less emphasis on academics than on the PT. That you challenged me was … unexpected."

Stepping back, I look him in the eyes. "Because I'm *dumb*," I state coldly. "Is that what you mean? It was a good observation for a girl too stupid to stay out of the village."

"That's *not* what I mean. You should keep questioning things. It's a great survival strategy here."

"Thanks for the tip." It's my PT, after all.

"Just trust me. If you keep questioning things, you might find yourself walking out the doors of this very hall one smiling valedictorian," he adds, patting the exterior of Valedictorian Hall.

"Who said I wanted to be valedictorian?"

His eyes narrow. "You've been hanging out with Pilot Stone too much."

"Yeah, it's really terrible to hang out with nice people. I'm crazy that way."

"You don't think *I'm* a nice person?"

What does that mean? We don't hang out. Does he want to be friends?

"I *am* nice," he adds, part defensively, part in jest. "And full of great info about this place. For example, did you know that this is the only building on campus that isn't part of the original naval base?"

I glance at it. "It's a *hallenkirche*."

"Sixteenth century. Flown in brick by brick from Berlin and plated in copper." Looking intrigued, he takes a step closer to me. "So, when you're not reading Hegel you're studying German architecture?"

Cautiously, I shake my head. *He thinks you're a nerd. Quick, say something non-nerdy.* "Sometimes I read science fiction." *Dammit!* I've failed miserably, and now he thinks I'm a Trekkie.

A small grin plays on his lips. "Me, too."

"You do?"

"I'm in the library all the time. So, sci-fi. What else do you read?"

"Whatever there is," I say. "I was reading *Lord of the Flies* before I came here. It reminds me of Wormwood Island. You know, the way the kids are all stuck?" Not to mention that it wouldn't be all bad if a giant rock fell on Harper and crushed her like it did Piggy.

Something odd flickers in his eyes as he observes me. "Stuck? I hadn't realized you felt stuck."

"Don't *you*?"

"Ha! More than I can say." His eyes search mine, and I feel heat rising under my skin. "But, unlike those British school boys, we have strict supervision here and very strict rules to follow. So it's not quite the same. But close." After pausing like he's not sure if he should finish his thought, he finally says, "Try again."

Try again? "I read *1984* before that."

"And?"

"What do you mean, *and?*"

"Does it remind you of Wormwood Island, too?"

"Should it? You're the one who knows all about this school. You tell me."

"I'm not allowed to."

"You're not allowed to? Says who?"

"And something tells me I might not need to."

He pauses, glancing around as if someone might overhear. Or maybe he's just watching for his girlfriend. Then he takes another step toward me, closing the gap between us in one pace; I stop breathing. He's so close to me now, I can smell the sweetness of his breath and see tiny flecks of blue in his irises. The bell rings, but neither Ben nor I flinch. The subtext of this perplexing conversation has absorbed me completely, and I think it may even have drawn him in.

"*1984* was about Big Brother, mind control, relentless war. Is there any of that sort of thing going on here?" I ask.

After giving my assessment some consideration, he shakes his head. "Try again."

I wrack my brain. "*The Prince* by Machiavelli."

His smile falters; his bright eyes darken. "Rulers who create their own morals and sense of order? People who lie and cheat to get ahead? Yeah, you'll definitely want to study that one here."

"Why?" I ask.

"Any others?"

"*Why?*"

But just when things are getting interesting, Villicus steps out from behind the other side of Valedictorian Hall and stands directly behind Ben. Surely my expression tells Ben that we have unexpected company. He turns to face Villicus who, for such an old man, seems unusually large and powerful.

"Mr. Zin. Miss Merchant. Classes are about to begin."

Swallowing, I nod and glance at Ben. His face is blank.

"Mr. Zin," Villicus continues, "perhaps you might join me in my office to continue your literary discussion. Miss Merchant, off to class."

For the rest of the day, I replay my conversation with Ben—the good part, the pre-Villicus part—in my head. I replay it as I sit with Pilot at lunch. As I avoid Teddy's glare while walking through campus. As I run home after Meteorology Club, darting through the woods, over tree stumps, branches, ferns, to keep from being pelted by the rainstorm that's blown in with a muffled but ground-quaking growl. Darkness looms overhead as I run, and I welcome it, adoring each tiny black cloud (which I've just learned are called *cumulonimbus mammatus*) that stacks up next to its brother like coal briquettes, willing them to block out the sun for the rest of time, if they want to. I don't need the sunshine to feel good. I already feel good. No, I feel *great* out here, running at full tilt with the most unbelievable black sky dousing the earth. With a vast rainbow of crunching leaves in purple and orange hues under my boots. With the memory of Ben standing so close to me, smiling that charming smile, feeding me with tantalizing hints as if he knows how confused I feel right now.

Just as the rain begins to really pour down, I see the Zin mansion through a break in the trees ahead. My neighbor. My gorgeous neighbor who was actually nice to me today. I can almost hear the uncool, geeky girls around the world cheering. *Victory!* A small win, but a win!

I hurtle three felled trees in a row like a track superstar and say to myself, "He implied—he wanted—to be friends." There's no hiding my smile.

When I reach the impeccably manicured Zin lawn, I come to a short stop and, still shielded by the cover of trees, do a little dance. Then I glance at Ben's house, and my breath catches.

I duck immediately into the woods again, out of sight.

He's inside. Standing near a window in what looks like his kitchen. Thick raindrops cascade down the panes, exaggerating the warmth of his house, creating the coziest scene. He's facing me, but he can't see me. Because I'm hiding behind a tree, and because there's someone standing in front of him.

Some blonde girl with her back to me.

The girl I saw the other night. His girlfriend.

Through the driving rain, I see her lift his hands to her face, holding them near her mouth. I see him close his eyes. I can only imagine what she's doing, and it incenses me. Fills me with throat-tightening rage. Rage with myself for being so foolish. With Ben for being so taken. With that blonde girl for being so lucky. With Pilot for not being Ben. With Teddy for being everywhere at once. With Molly's grandpa for scaring her away from me. With my dad for sending me here. With my mom for dying and leaving me to deal with all of this on my own. All at once, it all rains down on me. This *rage*. This *pain*.

Closing my eyes, I lift my head to the black sky and let the cold showers hit me. My eyelids pop open. The sky looks like Hell and Heaven have switched places, like I am staring up into hot coals.

And, strangely, this view feels *right*. This anger feels *right*.

"Ben's not interested in you," I tell myself. I say it out loud. With the clearest voice. And I repeat it so it sinks in. Again and again, I speak the words that will tattoo this reality into the walls of my skull, where my brain can stare at that message all day until it finally starts to get it.

Ben's not interested in me. Ben's not interested in me.

Hunching to stay out of their view, I hold my breath, try not to look at them, and run through Ben's backyard, past his saltwater pool and lawn sculptures and outdoor kitchen, home to Gigi's, kicking myself for wasting the whole afternoon fawning over some random conversation with Ben. It's clear now that my obsession with Ben is entirely one-sided. But that doesn't have to ruin my life, nor does it have to make the dance with Pilot anything short of spectacular. It's better this way, anyway—one less distraction from my goals.

Now I *know*. Now I know, staring out the window at the Zins', that in spite of some fairy-tale–loving part of me that has clung to the hope that the prince might look my way—in spite of my Jane Austen–inspired faith that Ben might somehow be my Mr. Darcy—there is no denying it: he isn't. If Ben's a prince at all, well, the prince is taken. And I must get happy with the idea of being lucky to have, at best, the disappointing son of a would-be president as the man of my dreams.

nine

PORTRAIT OF
A BOY

IF IT WEREN'T FOR PILOT, I WOULD BE COMPLETELY LOST at Cania and burdened by the company of *only* Teddy (who isn't exactly the life of the party). But there Pilot is, day after day, all week long. Smiling at me in our art workshop, keeping me steady as, every morning around ten o'clock, I feel cold and dizzy at once. He's at Meteorology Club. At Ornithology Club. He's making me crack up—and Teddy frown—over lunch with impersonations and ridiculously exaggerated stories. Pointing out the heirs to billions who walk among us—the Hearsts, the Coppolas, the people who would be celebrities at any school but this one. Reminding me to take it easy, that the race for valedictorian, no matter how much I think it'll help me in life, isn't worth "wasting our fabulous young lives on." And, of course, distracting me from thinking about Ben. Not that he knows that.

Ben hasn't looked my way since our conversation outside Valedictorian Hall. Not once. Not in our sculpting class. Not in the halls when we pass each other. Not when he passes me on his Ducati each morning. Not even when he was in his backyard and I was in Gigi's. Not a word. The silence is excruciating. It's affecting my appetite. It's making me toss and turn at night. And the worst thing? Knowing that this silence means nothing to him. Knowing he doesn't even notice it, that he's too busy with his beautiful blonde girlfriend to see.

When I'm not thinking about him, I'm thinking about *her*.

Who *is* she, this mysterious girlfriend? The only blonde I know other than myself is Harper's Russian peon, Agniezska, but there's no way it could be her. She's so *vapid*. She chatters on about nothing as much as Harper does. What could he like in her? Sure, I don't really know Ben, but in our few interactions, he's seemed too intense, too smart for the likes of "Aggie." No, it's probably the worst case: Ben has a brilliant, sexy girlfriend with some kick-ass pedigree from Park Avenue—the long-lost sister of Tinsley Mortimer—and she's visiting him. That's why I never see him with her at school. She's staying in a beautiful suite in his house. Holding his hand in front of the fireplace at night. It's enough to make me want to die.

"So dish," Molly says. She's curled up next to me on Gigi's sofa. "What's the prob?"

It's Friday night, and I came home an hour ago to find Molly waiting at our back door. By some stroke of luck, Teddy isn't plastered to my side; he's at a teacher's event until seven. And Gigi, who I've discovered is a bit of a gambler, is at some makeshift casino night in the village. If either of them were here, Molly and I would be in so much trouble. It blows my mind that she had the *cojones* to come here. She doesn't seem to care, though. Says she can't be expected to "exist in a perpetual state of friendlessness," so screw them. That, and she promises to scoot out the back door the second Teddy or Gigi comes down the walk. With the cottage to ourselves, we set to searching Gigi's cupboards for a snack in place of dinner. Tonight's fare?

Microwave popcorn. Molly's eating most of it because I'm still not hungry.

"Dish?" I ask. "What do you mean?"

Molly tilts her head and scowls. "You think I can't tell you're all depressed? I can. Your expressions are, like, ridiculous."

"Gee, thanks."

"I'm just saying you should avoid playing poker. Seriously." Molly is tossing kernels in the air and catching them, one by one, in her mouth. Skippy is nestled at her feet; evidently, Molly's easy for the smelly little Pomeranian to warm to. "Are you still upset about what my gramps said to you?"

"It's not so much what he said as the fact that he wanted to kill me."

Molly smirks. "Can you blame him? Look at you. You're terrifying."

"Anyway, that's not it."

"Okay. So what, you haven't got a date for the dance?"

"The dance—ugh. You know about that?"

"Of course. It's, like, a huge deal at your school. And since I'm home-schooled, I sort of soak up every detail about *your* school. The first dance of the year. A welcome dance."

Ha! A welcome dance. I've never felt so unwelcome in my life as I do at Cania.

"Did you know they grade us on it?" I stare at Molly, who doesn't look surprised. "They grade us. On the *dance*—on how witty our banter is and, like, how sparkly our eye shadow is, I'm sure. All as part of this ridiculous valedictorian race, as if performing well at a dance could guarantee our success in life."

"What's ridiculous about becoming valedictorian?"

"It just feels so *controlled* here. And everyone's got these weird stories." She doesn't seem fazed, so I rattle on. "Everything we do is being watched and measured. I mean, isn't that what they do in serious lock-down reform schools?" It's *exactly* what they did when my mom was in the psych ward.

"You deserve a medal, Anne. It's only taken you a few days to feel imprisoned here. It took me, like, sixteen years."

"I'm not kidding, Mol."

"Okay, well, they don't normally have *dances* in reform school, do they?"

She watches my face, but I'm intentionally unresponsive—because I don't like any counterarguments to my theory. I *have* to believe I'm in reform school. Otherwise, what the hell is going on? I slowly chew a piece of popcorn. It needs salt, tastes like nothing.

"I don't think this is about the school, is it? I think," Molly pauses, "this is about the dance. Are you going alone?"

"No, I've got a date," I mutter, pulling a loose thread out of a throw pillow.

Molly's eyes almost burst out of her head. "Seriously?" She tosses the popcorn bowl on the coffee table—it nearly topples over—and scoots closer to me, gripping my calf and squeezing.

"Ouch!" I swat her hand away. "Is it that hard to believe I have a date?"

"You know I don't mean that! You're totally hot. It's just that you're all *enemies* at Cania." She waves her hand in the air, dismissing everything. "That doesn't matter, though. Tell me who it is *right this second*!"

I chew my lip. "His name's Pilot."

Molly's face pales. "Pilot Stone?"

"You know him?"

She has one of those what-should-I-say looks on her face, like her dear old nana's just given her a Barbie at her sweet sixteen party. "I know *of* him. He's got a good body, if you like that hulky sort of look. I know his dad's that politician."

"Right. The sex scandals."

"What if Pilot's a total sex freak? What if sex stuff, like, runs in his genes? What if Pilot spends all night groping you?"

"Excellent. That's very helpful. And he's too decent for that." As she's about to protest that groping isn't indecent between consenting warm bodies, I add, "We're just friends."

"Does he know that?" Molly leans against the sofa and strokes Skippy's fur. With a knowing smile, she follows up by asking, "Have you ever gone all the way, Anne?"

"Between studying and caring for my mom? Besides, I'm saving myself for Zac Efron." I pluck another thread from the pillow. "Why? Have you?"

She shakes her head like that would never happen, which is crazy because she's very pretty. "You've kissed, though, right?" she asks.

"Zac Efron?"

Throwing her head back, she laughs, "*Anyone.*"

"I have, yes, but it wasn't anything real," I recall, thinking about the gorgeous boy in the casket so long ago but not daring to confess his, um, *life status* to her. "At first, I was just sketching this guy. He was so striking, Mol, I just couldn't imagine a world without his face forever captured."

"He was sitting for you?"

I avoid directly answering her question. She doesn't need to know he was dead when I kissed him.

"And then, well, I couldn't help myself."

"*You* kissed *him*?" she asks with a big smile.

I nod. "He was so beautiful."

"Bold." Seemingly aware that I'm lost in a five-year-old memory, silly though it is, she lets her smile vanish. "I think you shouldn't kiss Pilot if he doesn't make you feel like that guy did." Our eyes meet. "Did you guys end up dating? Is he still in California?"

"No," I reply, absentmindedly stroking my lower lip as I remember his cool skin. "I never saw him again."

"You must be a terrible kisser," she says, trying to lighten the mood. I can't help but laugh. "Okay, so tell me what you're wearing to the dance. Tell me it's *gorgeous*."

If there's one thing I *don't* want to talk about, it's the sad state of my wardrobe, which has been, for the longest time, my mom's old clothes. I'm not ready to get dressed up tomorrow night. I don't recall seeing a glam gown tucked away among the well-worn jeans and old Disneyland tees in my tiny closet.

"Is it important, what I wear?"

"Is it *what*?" Molly looks like she's not sure if I'm kidding. "Anne, it's the Cupid and Death dance. It's, like, a huge tradition." She dips into the popcorn again.

"So I have to get dressed up?"

Molly swallows her popcorn slowly, like she can't believe she actually has to explain this. "Slightly." She stares at me, waiting for me to comprehend. "Here's the deal. 'Kay, it's this cool masquerade-type thing from way long ago. The girls all get dressed up, with like full-on gowns, big jewelry, big hair—that'll be easy for you. You've already got sexy hair."

I almost choke on my popcorn.

"The makeup. The shoes." Molly's getting lost in her fantasy, preening on the sofa like *she's* getting dressed for the dance. "The girls wear these sexy little masks—just to add to the mystique of it all. Isn't that deadly hot? The whole masque is based on this old story, this premise that Cupid and Death exchange arrows, or whatever. So people who hate each other fall in love, and vice versa. Every year. Every welcome dance. Same story."

"Do the guys wear tuxes?"

"Oh, the guys get devilish. See, the girls go as hot girls, right? But the guys go as either Cupid or Death. Most choose Death—sexier costume."

"It's a costume party?"

"No, it's a masquerade done by the wealthiest kids on the face of the earth." Molly sighs. "Which means it's all about looking celebrity-sexy. Don't you want to floor the room with how hot you can look?"

"I love you for saying that, Mol, but I've got nothing to wear. And, honestly, I'd prefer to just wear jeans and have a kick-ass time dancing."

Memories of summers with my mom flood my mind, and I find myself clenching my teeth to keep from turning into some sobbing friend Molly'll never wanna see again. But I can't help reliving those afternoons in the kitchen. After spending the morning with my mom at the library, where she worked and where I read, we'd get home and she'd turn on the radio. Sometimes she'd fall deep into thought, and I wouldn't hear from her for hours; other times—the best times—she'd challenge me to one-up her dance moves. Sounds lame, I know, to dance with your own mom, but she was a trained dancer who probably could have gone far had she not fallen for my dad and decided to stay in Atherton. Before she adopted the life of a librarian and mortician's wife, long before she and my dad welcomed me to their family, she was a beautiful, leggy ballerina.

Our kitchen's squeaking linoleum floor saw her take me through everything from tap and jazz to cool urban dancing. Sometimes my dad, who had no rhythm, would take a break from his work to judge us or watch the routines she'd choreographed. What wouldn't I give to get those days back? Just one of those days. Just for a minute.

Something out the front window catches my eye then, and my heart stops short before breaking into a sprint. Ben is on his Ducati, revving it as he waits for his front gates to open so he can leave his estate.

"What is it?" Molly asks, following my stare. When she sees him, she laughs out loud. "Oh, no, you don't. You like *him*! Ben freakin' Zin. No wonder you're depressed."

I exhale heavily, letting my cheeks puff up and empty. His bike takes off. Through the trees lining the road, I catch glimpses of him flying by, heading toward campus, and then he's gone. Cruising the island.

"It doesn't matter," I whisper, sagging into the sofa as Ben passes. "He's got some girlfriend from off the island visiting anyway."

Molly raises an eyebrow. "What are you talking about?"

"I saw him with a girl. In his house. *Twice.*" I frown and stare into space, mentally reliving those moments. "He used to live in Beverly Hills. He must have met her there. They're probably soul mates."

"A visiting girlfriend? From Beverly Hills? Here?"

I blink slowly, which is as close to confirmation as I can get. Every passing day, my imagination transforms Ben's girlfriend into better and better versions of the perfect girl. She's just one sleep away from being a Swedish princess turned eco-entrepreneur with a membership in Mensa.

"How do you know this girlfriend is not from Cania?"

"I can't place her," I sigh. "She doesn't look like any of the girls I've seen."

"In the whopping four days you've gone to school here."

"Five."

Molly rolls her eyes. "Whatever. So it sounds like you want to find out about your competition. Am I right?"

"She's hardly my competition. Or, I guess, I'm hardly hers," I groan. Molly just smiles at me. "Why? What are you thinking?"

That's how I find myself standing at the Zins' twelve-foot front door, holding my fist an inch from it, preparing to knock.

"Let's just see if she answers," Molly says for the third time.

"And if she does? We, what, head for the hills?"

"No—we interrogate her." Molly grins, but I can barely

breathe. "Don't worry. If she answers, we can say you're looking for Gigi."

So holding my breath, closing my eyes, and praying Ben doesn't come home to find me *interrogating* his girlfriend, I rap quickly. Twice. Then Molly and I wait. Try again. Wait. "Great, she's not here. That's that. Let's go."

"My thoughts exactly," Molly says. "Come on."

Ten seconds later, I'm pressed against the ivied trellis by the Zins' outdoor kitchen, right near the solarium that houses their pool, at the back of the house. Molly has somehow convinced me that we need to find hard evidence of Ben's girlfriend's existence. The only way to do that?

B&E.

"You are the worst influence," I loud-whisper.

I've never in my life considered breaking into a house, and yet it has taken little more than Molly's mention of it to get me here. If we get caught? I lie and say it's all for my PT. And pretend I've never met this crazy village girl.

Pressing her finger to her lips, Molly jerks her head at a window that's slightly ajar. "Do you want to find out about Miss California or don't you? No better way than to snoop through Ben's underwear drawer." She fakes a pensive look. "What do you think? Boxers or briefs?"

"What if he comes home while we're in there? Or what if she's in there, like, napping?" I chew on my lip nervously. "I'd die. Seriously. Keel over dead."

"Come on," Molly groans. "Don't play coy with me. You know you want to."

Pressing against the wall, Molly slinks like a cat burglar from a black-and-white movie until she reaches the window. I can only stare in amazement. Waving me over, she pokes her head in and glances around quickly, stirring up butterflies in my stomach.

"Forget it!" I whisper sharply. "Abort mission! We are *not* breaking into Ben's house."

But we break in anyway. Molly pulls the window open and pops the screen out. I can't very well leave her alone to wander in there all by herself.

"Nobody's home," Molly says as she hops in, dusts herself off, and stares around the room. "Ben will never know."

"How do you know his family's not here?"

Nervously, I prop myself on the ledge, swing my legs over, and, with a deep breath, jump into the room. We're in the library, the enormous curved walls of which are lined with mahogany bookshelves and filled with beautifully bound texts. A ladder travels up. A desk, presumably Dr. Zin's, is on the other side of the room.

"It's just Ben and his dad."

"Well, how do you know *his dad's* not here?" I ask.

"Dr. Zin's always away. Recruiting all over the world. So, what kind of evidence are we looking for? Long blonde hairs on his bed?" Molly asks. "Or short little pubes?"

"That is so not funny," I grumble, watching Molly disappear around the corner. "Don't go far."

"I won't," she whispers, peeking back in.

I have no idea where to begin. Here I am, nestled in the middle of a wealth of information, but none of it can help me—not the volumes by Goethe, Marlowe, Mann—because I haven't got the foggiest idea what I'm looking for. Evidence of the existence of a blonde girlfriend, whatever that might look like. Love letters? Erotic photos? I hope not.

There are two elegant-looking urns displayed on the marble mantelpiece of the fireplace. A large, old-looking book labeled *Ars Goetia* on a side table. An ornate bronze cross hangs over the doorway; next to it is a glazed Serenity Prayer stamped with the Alcoholics Anonymous logo. Framed photos are scattered across the walls, organized in that designerly eclectic way: sleek chrome frames blended with thickly molded antiques, all in different sizes. Almost every photo is of Dr. Zin with some celebrity or politician from the eighties and nineties. Cher. Michael Jackson. That Eurotrash singer, Pete Burns. In one, Zin's hovering over a smiling Geraldo Riviera, who's obviously recovering from a nose job. Three with Joan Rivers. One of him with Donatella Versace at Bill Clinton's second inauguration. Even one with Demi Moore.

As I wonder at the sort of life Ben and his dad have, a life of luxury so different from my own, I trail my fingers over the old book—*Ars Goetia*—that attracted me earlier. I lift its weighty, copper-flecked cover. The floor under me creeks, though the air is still and I haven't budged. A wisp of cool air glides by me, and the curtains of the window we crawled through billow in large shapes, as if an unseen child hides behind them. Steadily, I return my attention to the book, a grimoire, which is an ancient book on demonology, and open it. Its pages are thick with centuries of dust clinging to the oil deposited by the fingers of people long dead. Dog-eared pages lure me. The first is a listing of the ranks of demons, from mere devils to marquis to dukes to princes, each fitting somehow into the legions—or armies—of Hell. The photos show tattooed and bejeweled men, many nude, some seemingly in a state of decay, most baring their teeth, slick with blood, inexplicably vulgar.

"Creepy," I whisper, turning to another tagged page.

This one is an actual list of demons. One is named Paimonde— just like the name of the building where I have art class.

"That can't just be a coincidence."

A chime across the room startles me, shaking my bones in my skin. Panicked, I glance at the doorway but find it empty. I drop the cover of the disturbing grimoire, rubbing my hands as if that might wash away the eerie sensation flooding my body, and head to where the chime sounded from: the Mac on the desk. The chime was an email coming in. Dammit, why didn't I just go to the computer first? Surely Ben's got some photos of his girlfriend on here.

"Let's just pray she's not photogenic." I sit and shuffle the mouse to wake it up.

The screen fills with color, bright and vibrant in contrast to the darkness of this library and of the book I've just read; a row of icons lines the bottom. I hover over the iPhoto icon and click. Disappointingly, there are just four photos. I click the first one.

It's Ben and a dirty-blonde look-alike girl who can only be his little sister—thirteen, maybe fourteen. Ben looks exactly as he does now, except with a different hairstyle. The room they're in is decorated with a towering silver-and-gold Christmas tree, with Andy Warhol on the walls, with distinctive barrel chairs, probably the originals Frank Lloyd Wright designed, flanking the tree. Ben and his sister are smiling broadly, their arms around each other's shoulders; the formality that seems so characteristic of Ben now is nowhere to be seen.

"He looks happy."

Maybe the blonde was his sister visiting, I let myself hope. I glance at the doorway—still empty—and click the mouse.

The second photo is of Ben's sister by herself, smiling as she holds Taylor Swift's *Fearless* CD, a Christmas gift. The third is of her again, this time wrapping a string of lights around Ben, who has a bow on his head; Dr. Zin smiles just at the edge of the frame. And the final photo is of Ben's mom sitting between her kids in front of the tree. They all have bows on their heads. She looks so normal, so mom-like—not what I'd expected of the wife of a plastic surgeon—that it's almost like looking at my own family photos, the way we used to be. Playful, normal, a *family*. I can't help but wonder where Ben's mom and sister are now. Still in California? Did the Zins divorce?

"You alive in there?" Molly shouts, poking her head in and sending me through the roof.

"Molly! Are you trying to kill me?" I hiss. "Have you found anything?"

She wrinkles her nose. "Bedroom's clear."

Dammit. I'd wanted an excuse to check his bedroom.

"Checking the kitchen," Molly says.

"For what?"

She grins. "Snacks." And disappears again.

Turning back to the computer, I bring up a search window. As much as I want to know about Ben's love interest, I have more pressing questions to answer. I put my investigation into the details of Ben's girlfriend on hold while I start a new one: researching Cania Christy.

Now we'll see if this place really is a reform school. The school has no website, but someone must have written something about it at some point. Surely there's a tweet, a Facebook status update, Instagram photos. The thought of finding this critical answer makes me feel stronger. Go, PT, go! I enter my search and, glancing at the doorway, wait.

No results found for "Cania Christy."

I try again, this time without the quotes.

Did you mean Can I Christy?

Drum my fingers. On a whim, baffled that the school is so off the radar, I click on the Zins' bookmarks in the hopes that they've saved something meaningful there. A long stream of saved pages cascades down the screen.

Understanding the Power of Demonic Charms.

Using Dark Powers to Bring Down the Dark Ones.

A Complete List of the Princes of Hell.

Overcoming Demons: Why They Cannot Be Slain.

Inter-realm communication...

Ars Goetia for Dummies.

I click on the *overcoming demons* link and wait as the page loads *painfully* slowly.

Suddenly, something bangs in the kitchen, right next to the library, and a cold sweat rushes over my body as I imagine Ben walking in. My eyes sweep the room for a way out. *Quick Escape*

Route: door to the left leading into who knows what. Unless I can make it back out the window in time.

It bangs again. A cupboard door.

"That was me," Molly whispers loudly. "They don't have any good snacks, so I'm heading upstairs again."

I can't shake the feeling that we're seconds from being caught. But I can't leave yet. Because I would be crazy to go to the effort of breaking in only to walk away without *any* info—especially without some much-needed answers about Cania Christy, the villagers, and this island. There may not be anything online about this place, but surely the head of admissions has plenty of revealing documents on his laptop. Though why he left it at home when he went on his recruiting travels is beyond me.

As I'm about to close the browser to search their desktop for files, I see that the top half of the page I've been trying to load has come in. There's a curious illustration of a devil-like character flying over a city. In the bottom half of the page, a flash video is taking its sweet time loading.

Anxiously, I glance around the desktop while I wait and spy a notebook, which I reach for, brushing my thumb absently along the bottom of the pages. Flip it open. All of the pages are empty...except the back few, which are dark with pencil sketches. I know that trick: whenever I wanted to hide my drawings so my parents wouldn't see them and start raving about my talent—and embarrassing the hell out of me—I'd use the back pages of a book. Where no one would look.

Only Ben, with his artist's hand, could have drawn these images. A devilish man dragging another man by his ankle; something I can't decipher is written at the bottom. The next page shows a similar-looking man, but this time with a hoof for a foot; again, a scrawled phrase, but this time I can read it.

"Call me to do your bidding by name. And we shall craft a fitting exchange."

The next page is covered in tiny sketches that blend into one—
all featuring a demonic hoofed man. Ben had spent some time on
the words on this page, dressing each letter with Gothic flair. I
squint to make out the words. Something about writing in blood.
Something about craving security.

That's when I hear it.

The squeal of a door opening and the click of it closing down
the hall. It sends a fresh ripple of fear under my skin. I freeze. Goose
bumps spread over my body. My breath catches in my throat.

Someone is whistling. And it's not Molly.

There's no doubt about it: Ben is *back*. I thought I'd hear his
Ducati pull up but obviously not.

Gulping audibly and immediately cursing myself for it, I
inch away from the desk. But, at once, music sounds near me,
swelling through unseen speakers and overtaking Ben's whistling.
I don't know where it's coming from. In a panic, I look all over,
flustered. And then I pinpoint it.

"The computer," I whisper. The video on that page has *finally*
loaded and is now playing.

Ben's whistling stops abruptly. "Hello?" he calls.

I have one reaction and one reaction only. *Run!*

No time to consider how sick I feel! No time to think of how
scared, how stupid, or how my heart is racing at rocket speed. It's
the Quick Escape Route or bust.

Molly's upstairs, blissfully unaware that we're both about to
be caught, and I have to get her. I boot across the library. I can
hear Ben in the hall outside the library.

My escape route didn't seem quite so far away when I was
standing at the desk. But now it feels as distant as California.

I can't get caught here. No. I can't live with Ben knowing
what a stalker-freak I am.

I push myself harder and, sensing Ben nearing, bolt through
the far doorway, into total darkness.

There I pause for half a second—just to beat myself up. *You are never hanging out with Molly again!* Protected by the darkness, I lean toward the doorway to listen into the library. The music playing on the computer stops short: Ben's in there now, and he's paused the video. Any second, he'll see the room's open window and the absent screen, and he'll know someone's broken in.

"I'm so screwed," I mouth.

Hands shaking, I feel my way forward. I touch a banister and, trading mouse-like silence for speed, motor up the narrow staircase. I burst at last into a hallway on the second floor. My chest is heaving. Did Ben hear me? Is he behind me now?

"Molly!" I whisper as loudly and quietly as I can.

The door next to me creaks open. I have to bite my tongue to keep from screaming. But it's just Molly. Standing in the shadows of a linen closet. Her eyes as bulging as mine.

"Ben's back?" Molly mouths.

There's no time to talk. Grabbing her sleeve, I drag her to the nearest door and fling it open. We'll have to climb out a window and down the trellis.

But we don't even make it to the window. We stop short.

Dr. Zin smiles at us from a chair on which he is leisurely reading admissions documents. We've just barged into his master suite.

"Girls," he says coolly.

"Dr. Zin," Molly chokes out.

She thought he was gone; I had a strong gut feeling he wasn't. This is one time I'd *love* to have been wrong.

I don't even let the door bounce against the wall before I'm yanking Molly out and dragging her to the main staircase. Our feet can't fly down the stairs fast enough. Can't cross the marble foyer with anything close to the speed we need. Our hands can't grip the door handle to the huge front doors and throw them open without fumbling for what feels like half an hour before, at last, we tumble out into the foggy early evening.

And, just like that, we're racing full-force toward Gigi's. Heaving. Panting. Pushing as hard as we can. Molly pulls me past the house and into the woods that lead to the village. We keep running. We run until we both collapse breathlessly, panicked, kicking ourselves.

"Why did we run?" Molly says between gasps. "Why didn't we make up some story?"

"I'm sorry. It was instinct. I know there's no way Dr. Zin will just forget that a Cania girl and the village girl were snooping through his house."

"He won't tell Villicus," Molly assures us both. "He won't. He can't. He won't. Do you think he might?"

"I'm sorry. He's Villicus's right-hand man," I whisper to her, gasping for air. "Now you're going to have to go to school here."

"No, I won't. My gramps wouldn't ever let that happen," she says, struggling to breathe, choking up. "I guess this is what I wanted anyway. You don't break Villicus's rules without expecting punishment."

"All that hassle, and we didn't even find anything."

"I'm sorry. I knew we wouldn't," Molly says, her breath coming slower. "I guess I just wanted a little excitement. And escape. More than anything, escape."

"How'd you know we wouldn't find anything?"

"You guys aren't allowed visitors. Just your parents. And only on Parents' Day." Chest heaving, Molly cocks her head. "Wait, they didn't tell you that, either?"

ten

IN THE DARK

THAT NIGHT, I TAKE A MOMENT TO DO A QUICK TALLY OF the amount of sheer Crazy—with a capital *C*—I've already encountered at Cania Christy.

One, signing school forms with blood. Two, living on an island with a red line across the middle of it, an island where the villagers think *I'm* dangerous. Three, being graded constantly, even when I sleep and eat, by my uber-creepy Guardian, who *peered into my soul*. All in an effort to be valedictorian. As if that's some sort of brass ring. Four, crashing the villagers' top-secret cremation ceremony, where I learned that the villagers are being paid to look the other way. That, and getting bawled out by the village shaman just seconds later. Five, passing out in class and the recurring cold, woozy feeling I get at the same time every morning. Six, breaking into Ben's house. And getting caught. Seven, no visitors allowed except on Parents' Day.

That's more than enough Crazy for one lifetime, never mind one week. But something tells me it isn't half of it. How could it be that my former life spent worrying over my mom could seem like an extended vacation compared to this place? Even if Cania isn't reform school, it definitely isn't the school my dad was lead to believe it was. The only good news is that it's *finally* Friday night, time for Teddy to replace the cord on Gigi's ancient rotary phone so I can call my dad and ask him about this place. Of course, all good news comes with bad news in my world: Teddy will be standing over my shoulder throughout my call, listening to every word. So I'll have to be cryptic and hope my dad reads into the subtext.

"Fifteen minutes," he says as he dials the number.

"Generous." I take the receiver. I plan to bait my dad with questions like, "What did you think of the movie *Girl, Interrupted?*" Stuff like that. Things that will get him to confess that I'm in a nuthouse.

But, of course, things do not go as planned. There will be no such conversation tonight. Why not? Because my dad takes Crazy to a whole new level the moment he gets on the phone: he actually freaks out at the sound of my voice.

I can't believe it.

A man who works in isolation with dead or grieving people, my dad is normally the epitome of calm, collected, reserved. Right now, though, he sounds like a hyperactive child who's just dined on a dozen pixie sticks.

"Are you okay, Dad?" I ask for the thousandth time, watching the minutes tick by as he repeats how happy he is to hear from me. For a second, I worry he's confusing me with my mom. Maybe all that time spent alone in the funeral home has been screwing with his head. "Take an Ativan."

"I'm fine. I'm good. It's just so good to *hear you* say that, sweetheart." His exuberance doesn't even sound right on his voice. I can't imagine the expression on his bearded face because I'm sure I've never once seen him so delighted. "I hope you know how much I'm looking forward to Parents' Day next weekend. I've bought my tickets and booked my dorm room."

"Booked your what?"

"My dorm room."

"I thought the dorms were all taken. That's why I'm at Gigi's."

Immediately, Teddy grabs the phone from me and, pushing me away, whispers something to my dad as I protest. When he's done, he hands it back like it's normal behavior to shove me out of the way.

"Sorry about that, Dad," I say.

"Listen, honey, it's okay. It's my fault. But, sweetheart, it looks like I won't be able to stay overnight next weekend after all."

"Why not? What changed?" I shoot a glare at Teddy, hoping it stings him at least a little. I know what changed. I just can't believe Teddy has the authority to make it change.

"Don't worry about that. And, hey, about the dorm rooms. Forget what I said. If it's meant to be, you'll get a dorm room. It's in God's hands."

"In God's hands?"

"Sure, sweetie."

People talk about something being in God's hands when they're trying to get into med school or watching their beloved wife's mental soundness degrade before their eyes. Not when they're talking about dorm assignments. Doesn't God have bigger things to worry about than getting me into *student housing*?

"Whatever," I mutter. "That's not important. Just give me a sec. I have an, um, question about a movie."

"A movie?"

No, not a movie. I want to know why you shipped me out to some high-priced juvie. And what you gave up. What did I do wrong? Was it just because I was sad about Mom?

A timer goes off on my dad's end of the line.

"Sorry, hun. I'd love to talk about movies and everything—you can't even imagine—but it's been fifteen minutes."

"I think it's been fourteen."

"Sorry," he repeats, "but it'll have to wait until I see you next weekend, okay? Don't want to break the rules."

And, with that, Teddy pulls the receiver away from me and unplugs it. Pursing his skinny lips, he turns to me. "Your father is wise to obey the rules. You should follow his lead."

The last thing I want to do is listen to Teddy yammer on about what I *should* be doing, how I *should* be behaving. Taking the stairs three at a time, I bound up to my room and slam the door.

Desperate to distract myself, I root through my closet to plan my dance outfit, throwing clothes over my bed, wondering exactly how formal *formal* is. My pathetic wardrobe makes me want to jump off a cliff. Nothing; I have nothing. And the girls in the dorms? The Model UN from Hell? They probably have it *all*. Hervé Léger and Bottega Veneta party dresses. Emilio Pucci scarves. Marchesa clutches. Stella McCartney lingerie underneath it all. Swarovski crystal masks.

I'll be glad not to have loose threads hanging from my skirt hem.

Hours later, when I turn off the attic light and crawl into bed, I can't hide from my thoughts any longer. So I stare up at the beams, dreading the nightmares waiting on the other side and wincing to think of Dr. Zin's face when I flung open the door and saw him sitting there. *Ugh.* Squeezing my eyes shut doesn't drive the memory away. It's clear that I've compromised my future at Cania Christy just because I got jealous of some girl—some chick who is definitely not from off-island and who, for all I know, may be Ben's study partner. Restless, I get out of bed and pace my room. The floorboards creak, threatening to rouse the house, but Gigi hasn't come home yet, and I don't care if Teddy wakes up—it's not like his beauty sleep is helping him.

It's nearly midnight, but the sky is orange with light reflecting off the crescent of the coming harvest moon. As I draw the shade, I glance, as always, at the Zin mansion.

My breath catches.

Ben is standing directly across from me, a dark shadow in the same dimly lit window where he stood just days ago with

that girl. But he's alone. His luminescent eyes are the only hint
of color, the only indication that the silhouette is Ben, not some
wandering spirit and not Dr. Zin. A shiver runs down my spine
and up again, like hundreds of tiny angels are fluttering their
wings under my skin, under my hair.

Undeniably, Ben is watching me.

How long has he been looking? The whole time I was pacing?

Instead of backing away, I return his gaze. I lift my window,
letting in the chilly night air, hoping to apologize to him if he's
figured out that I broke into his house today. But he shakes his
head and points at the bottom of his window, telling me it won't
open. I nod and reluctantly shimmy the old window down again.

In this moment, the isolation of this island feels greater than
ever, and I imagine Wormwood Island lost in an ocean, invisible
from space, hidden below an omnipresent cloud. Perhaps Ben is
feeling something similar. But he turns away suddenly, and just
as I worry he won't return, he does; he raises a sketch so I can
see it—but, in the darkness and at this distance, I can *barely* see
it. Seems to be a face, but I can't tell. Did he draw me? Or is this
another one of Ben's valiant attempts to shed light on the murky
mysteries of a world he knows better than I? I shake my head at
him. I don't know what the image is, and I don't know what I'm
supposed to take away from it.

Saturday for me is spent worrying the phone will ring and Dr. Zin
or Villicus will be on the other end of the line, telling Gigi and
Teddy all about my B&E. When I'm not worrying, I'm studying, sketching, flipping through art books. Anything to take my
mind off the four-hours-away, three-hours-away, two-hours-away
dance. By the time the sun sets, I've sketched so much my hand

hurts; when I look down at what I've produced, I know none of it can be used to help me at school. Because I've created a stack of sketches that are, without a doubt, Ben look-alikes.

Ben standing at the window.

Ben on his Ducati.

Ben leaning against an oak in the quad as I saw him do once.

"Obsess much?" I ask myself.

When I hear a rapping on my door, I flip the sketches upside down, looking for any trace of my fascination with Ben, anything to give me away.

"Come in," I call.

But Teddy is already halfway up the stairs, as if knocking is a formality and privacy an illusion. He pauses, peering around; I can see only his skinny head poking up like a groundhog. His rat eyes look at me, leer around my room, and return to me. Bracing the desk, I wait for the bad news: I'm out. And Molly's in.

"It's almost dinner time, Anne."

I sigh, relieved. "I'll be right down."

Rather than leaving, he comes to the top of the stairs and invites himself in. I suck on the inside of my cheek to keep from growling, amazed at how imperceptive he is. Is he lost? Does he actually believe his role as my Guardian entitles him to walk around my room as he pleases?

"So," he drones. "I've been noting your behavior all week."

I put my pencil down. He wants to have a conversation. And I suppose I should give him what he wants, considering the power he wields.

"And have you been satisfied?" I ask. "You've been watching from behind the two-way mirrors, I believe."

He drags his hand along the footboard of my bed, wanders to a far wall, returns to my bed and rubs a bed knob between his palms. *Mental note: Bleach bed knobs.* Wanders more. Stops just feet away from me.

"Your academic performance means very little to me. We need to talk about your PT," he says coldly. "I'd like to propose to Villicus that we change it. Several of the other Guardians agree. Trey Sedmoney in particular has encouraged me to have this discussion with you."

"Change my PT now? I've spent the whole week trying to live by it."

"As I suspected, it is not coming easily. But it ought to. It should be built into your nature."

I lean back in my chair and glare at him, surely failing to mask my intense irritation. "If you're suggesting I go with the one you first proposed…"

"Let me tell you," he prattles on, waving his finger, "there are girls in your class who have exceedingly better PTs than you."

"The Model UN from Hell?" He's been hanging around me enough, he knows I'm referring to Harper's crowd.

"I could rate you very favorably," he says, his soft voice sending shivers up my spine, "if you could be so obliging." Then he lowers his hands to his pants and undoes the top button.

My mouth drops open, but not in the way he wants it to. "You're disgusting."

"I'm your meal ticket."

"There is no way on God's green earth that I would ever do that. Get out."

A simper morphs his mouth as he zips his pants again. A part of me thinks I see relief wash his face, as if he was just playing the part of a revolting pervert. Which can't be true.

"If only we were on God's green earth, Miss Merchant." And he leaves.

eleven

CUPID AND DEATH

JUST A MINUTE AGO, IT WAS 7:15, AND I WAS EATING oregano-heavy spaghetti while avoiding Gigi's curious gaze—the tension between Teddy and me thicker than the gray haze beyond the kitchen windows.

"How is it possible that it's eight already?" I ask my reflection now, sweeping pieces of my hair up loosely in my mom's barrettes, trying not to let myself fall into a depression as I silently beg for her to be here. Just for a moment. Just for my first dance. The list of challenges I'd kill for her guidance on is growing longer by the second. The memories of our afternoon dance-offs, of the tap and hip-hop sessions she adored guiding me through each summer, are a numbing sort of torture. "Don't do that, Anne. Don't ruin your mascara."

Rubbing a spot of cream blush into my cheeks, I try to feel as joyful as I'm starting to look. Smudge eye shadow on. Darken my lashes. Tend to all the odds and ends of being a girl as expertly as possible given my untrained hand and poorly stocked makeup case. All in an attempt to camouflage a flaw more noticeable than my crooked tooth.

My outfit.

Resigned to never being the pretty one in the room, I clasp a long strand of costume jewelry around my neck, remind myself that I'll need to be witty to keep attention on my face tonight, and step back to see my reflection. But this mirror's too small, so I head to the bathroom downstairs. As I enter—and shudder to hear Teddy whistling while he dresses, because *of course* my Guardian has to attend tonight, too—the doorbell rings. For a brief, heart-stopping moment, I think it might be Ben. Well, I don't really think it will be; I just *hope*, based on a small bit of residual happiness I have about that moment at the window last night. I lean toward the staircase to listen.

"Delivery," the woman at the door says.

Sighing, I step back into the bathroom and almost drown in a wave of depression when I look in the mirror. *Ugh. Forget it!* I'm not going. I slump onto the side of the bathtub and rest my head in my hands. There's no point going to a formal dance in this excuse for a skirt, which is almost as old as I am. And my blouse? I've seen the Model UN from Hell wear nicer shirts for Pil-At-Ease Club.

"Annie! Come down here," Gigi shouts.

What now? I drag myself past the mirror again, refusing to look in it. *Just stand Pilot up*, I think as I stomp down the stairs. *It'll be better that way. Less embarrassing.*

"I had no idea you were running deliveries," Gigi says to the delivery lady. "Here Anne is now."

I glance at Gigi and then over to the delivery lady, who's standing behind her. But it isn't a delivery lady. It's *Molly*. Smiling Molly. Shaking-her-head Molly. Desperately-*shhing*-me Molly. Trying-to-hide-our-secret-friendship Molly.

"Can I help you?" I ask her. I'm wearing my best poker face, but Molly's exaggerated frown says it all over again: I have no future in poker.

Gigi mumbles as she passes me up the stairs, "I'll tell Teddy the delivery's from your dad. But after tonight, you don't speak to Molly again."

At the top of the stairs, she turns, shakes her head, and closes her bedroom door behind her. When I look at Molly, who's holding a big white box, I nearly burst out laughing. Molly just grins and holds the box out. Far behind her, I think I spy that quiet girl with the short bangs standing on the road, but the shadows engulf that spot before I can be sure. So I turn quickly to Molly.

"Sounds like Gigi knows we've been hanging out," I say with a grimace and glance over my shoulder to ensure Teddy's not watching. "Did you hear anything from Dr. Zin? Did he rat us out?"

Molly simply says, "Delivery, Miss Merchant."

"What? Whatever. I'm totally glad to see you. I am in serious need of girl help." As demonstration, I curtsy in my old skirt.

"Package for Miss Annabelle Merchant."

I frown. "What's going on? Who's Annabelle? I'm *Anne.* Molly, what's up?"

"Sorry, do I have the wrong person?" Molly widens her eyes and runs them over the address on the box. "Maybe it's Cinderella I'm looking for?"

"You wouldn't be far off."

"I'm serious, Anne," she says, lowering her voice and nudging the box toward me.

"What do you mean? You don't know my name?"

"Geez. I thought you Cania kids were supposed to be smart."

"I'm confused."

"Can you just play along with this whole delivery charade before Teddy comes out? Now you say 'why, that's me' and I say, 'please sign here.' Look! I even have a clipboard." Molly frowns. "Please sign my clipboard. And then march upstairs, get that hot body dressed, and have an amazing time."

"I am dressed," I groan.

"No. You're not."

"Yes, I am. This is it. I'm not kidding." Still holding the box, I sign the clipboard to play along. "My wardrobe is really this pathetic, and, yes, if you're wondering, I do want to die."

Molly looks me up and down. "This was such a good idea," she breathes, smiling. "I'm going straight to Heaven for this one." And then she turns, jumps off the steps, and hops on her bicycle.

I holler after her, "You forgot your box!"

Smiling over her shoulder, Molly shushes me and calls out in her best loud-whisper, "Go steal Ben away from that chicky, you gorgeous thing. Then meet me tomorrow morning at ten, in the woods by the marina, and tell me everything. And don't say I never did anything for you! I should be sainted for what I'm doing."

The problem with sainting is that they don't hand those titles out to people until years after they've died, until well after someone's lived a totally virtuous life. So you don't get to become a living saint for performing one-off miracles.

But if there was a way to canonize a living, breathing teen girl or a competition for whom in the whole wide world should be sainted, I would stand on the tallest of mountains, the highest of hills, and proclaim that Miss Molly Watso of Wormwood Island *must* be a strong contender.

But, I have to admit, it'd be hard to climb a mountain in the heels I'm wearing right now.

"Come on!" Teddy bellows as he marches over the red line to campus, annoyed that I can't keep up.

I have questions—lots of them. I've had them since the moment I placed the long white box on my bed and opened the lid to reveal the most welcome gift I've ever received. Questions like how on earth Molly got her hands on strappy, gold-studded Jimmy Choo stilettos. Or how she had in her possession a Prussian blue Carolina Herrera trumpet-style gown that clings to every curve I'm still getting used to on my body. Or where on earth she found a thin golden mask with a dramatic plume of three feathers in three shades of blue. Or how she knew that I'd need all these things from her and delivered them just in the nick of time.

But I don't want answers to those questions. No, I don't want to spoil the closest thing to a magical encounter with a fairy godmother—a sixteen-year-old, non fairy, non godmother—I've ever had. I'm going to take this blessing without question, make it up to Molly however I can, and, best of all, hold my head high at the dance.

Even if I am walking into that dance with Teddy.

"I'm not going to keep stopping to wait for you," Teddy shouts at me as he marches along the road to campus.

"Don't let me keep you," I call back, wobbling as I get used to these heels.

"It is my job to stay by your side." He stops, hands on his scrawny hips. "*Des Chaos wunderlicher tochter!*"

When I look at him, boney in his tuxedo, I realize there's a reason they call them penguin suits. He looks like a malnourished, angry penguin.

"Why do you have to stay by my side?" I reply, stomping by him. "No other Guardians do that."

"They ought to!"

His lips form an invisible, crooked line as his eyes slide over my body like black eels navigating seaweed. I try not to gag at the memory of this afternoon, of him in my room. Trust Teddy to ruin tonight for me. My first dance, and, thanks to Molly, I finally look like I'm supposed to be here. I've got a legit date and a mask and everything. But I'll feel gross all night knowing Teddy's watching me. Knowing what he's thinking.

"I should have been by your side when you received your delivery," he spits.

"Why? What does it matter?" I stare ahead, begging for my

legs to move faster so I can escape what could easily turn into an inquisition. Molly and I are getting too casual with our inter-actions; we'd be smart to take Gigi's advice or we'll both be in trouble soon.

"You know damn well why," he says. I refuse to respond.

The hypnotic beat of a drum machine set behind brittle, rau-cous tones and an echoing voice guides me and Teddy, marching in silence, through the campus gates. The music is coming from the other side of Goethe Hall where the dance is set up in the middle of campus, on the grassy quad. Over the course of the week, I've overheard Harper telling everyone within earshot all about the massive castle-like structure she was going to have her lackeys on the Social Committee build from scratch in the quad; the dance is inside the castle, and I'm certain Harper will find a way to have herself crowned queen before the end of the night. But I don't care. Let her be queen. I'm here to enjoy myself—no matter what Teddy or Harper or anyone does.

As we walk around the side of Goethe Hall, I spy the castle, and my irritation with everything immediately washes away.

I've found myself in a pop-up book, in a fantasy world where the overwhelmingly massive ginger-and-rose moon watches from just steps off the inky shoreline, wisps of charcoal clouds drift-ing over it, their edges blood red in the moonlight. In front of the moon, the school buildings are jagged black cutouts, like the devil's claws clutching at a fiery light. And here, just feet away, is the entrance to a perfectly imperfect castle—or the remains of one: tens of thousands of gray papier mâché blocks in various sizes, made to look like the stone of an old castle, encase a vast dance floor. Blocks are missing, ostensibly knocked down over the ages, leaving craggy gaps of all sizes through which crimson moonlight flows. Candlelight glows within. A colossal chandelier is suspended from the ceiling, which is itself comprised of white-washed beams wrapped in silvery lights. I hate to admit it, but

Harper's outdone herself.

As if to lighten the darkly romantic ambiance, a trio of fresh-men boys, obviously putting aside the Big V competition for the night, walk by, dressed in enormous white diapers and holding arrows; one of them whistles at me, making Teddy scowl and giv-ing me a nice boost of confidence. Those boys seem to be the only Cupids here. All the other guys, I notice as I stop to take ev-erything in, are dressed as various interpretations of Death. The usual black cloak and scythe—*dozens* of those guys. Some interest-ing Deaths, like an empty pill bottle and a puffy tornado with little trailers in it. One guy is dressed as an old-school cartoon bomb with *Acme* stamped on it, while, standing next to him, another is costumed as a glowing ball with spikes coming out of it.

"A virus," I say with a laugh and point him out to Teddy.

"Childish," he replies as a George W. Bush walks by and beams at me.

"*He* can't be sitting well with Little Miss Texas."

"Annie!" Pilot screams across the dance floor. His voice car-ries over the band. Heads turn.

"Remember, you're with me tonight," Teddy sneers, putting his arm around me.

Balking, I shove him off. "I'm not here with *you*, Teddy."

"It's my role as your Guardian! Your second shadow. Grad-ing you all night long."

"Don't ever touch me again," I snap, biting hard on the end of each word as it leaves my lips.

Teddy's eyes narrow, his sneer stays put, but he storms off. Just as Pilot arrives, panting. Golden candlelight glimmers in his eyes as he takes my hands. Shaking off the memory of Teddy's vile touch, I do my best not to turn five shades of red while Pilot looks me up and down.

"Wow, nice mask. You look effing fierce," he says with a broad smile.

"Thanks," I breathe. In my heels, I'm much taller than he is. "You look decent yourself."

"Decent?" His eyebrows hit his hairline, but I just smile and shrug. He wears a suit—the conservative suit of a politician's son—and carries a bright red scythe. "Okay, I'll take it. Come sit? I'm sorry I couldn't come pick you up, but Teddy was adamant that he had to walk you here."

"Just count yourself lucky that you don't have a Guardian."

Around the perimeter of the room, the faculty watches us. Between them, those freaky secretaries, the lunch ladies, and a sprinkling of women I've never seen—presumably housemothers from the dorms—all stand, staring at everyone with what I'm starting to recognize as the mask of the Guardian: a deadpan gawp. There must be a hundred adults here, one for every junior and senior, plus a few extras to monitor the sophies and freshmen who aren't yet being graded for the Big V. They're all a reminder, a walking, talking, pen-scratching, clipboard-reading reminder, that this is no ordinary dance. Clipped to their boards are charts for grading our clothing, composure, conversation. They know our PTs by heart, which will factor into our grading. To drive home the point that tonight is still very much part of the Big V competition, at the back of the castle, standing in a small, dim balcony a dozen feet above us, is Villicus; the silvery lights on the beams near his narrow skull reflect off his pupils, transforming him into a golden-eyed shadow, a leering rat atop a pillar of black onyx. It's hard to tell, but it looks like he's watching me with Pilot.

Shuddering, I turn toward the band, which is comprised of five kids from a music club, with surprisingly cool lead vocals by Plum. Those are the only people I recognize, though. The girls on the dance floor are all masked. And most of the guys wear makeup.

"Getting dressed up makes the night easier," Pilot explains, walking me to a table. "The costumes. The anonymity."

"But they're grading us, so nothing's different," I say, glancing again at Teddy, who's prowling the room with his eyes on me. Feels like I'm being stalked by a skinny, horny cougar. "Competition as usual."

"We can pretend, though." Pilot grips my hand. "I mean, we're still teenagers in high school. We still wanna…"

"Knock boots?" I laugh, doing my best Harper impersonation. "You know what I've wondered? I get the whole junior–senior competition, but why don't the younger kids hang out? They don't have Guardians yet. They're not being graded."

"Well, they have parents," Pilot says, walking me to a table in the corner where a few others are seated. "Their parents are already pressuring them. So, yeah, they're as deep in this competition as any of us, even if no Guardian is keeping score."

As if to help Pilot make his point, a sophomore boy in a black cloak rips the mask off a freshman girl and throws it down. As he stomps on it, the girl shrieks and, tearing his scythe from his hand, jabs him in the gut.

Ben is nowhere to be seen. In a way, I'm relieved. But that relief switches to irritation when, arriving at the table, I see that Harper, Tallulah, and Agniezska are here, watching me from behind their flashy masks. Harper's in an orange mask meant to look like the Texas Longhorns emblem. Tallulah's mask must have cost serious money if the jewels on it are real. Taking home the skanky award is Agniezska, whose mask is transparent with tiny white diamonds on it—just like her skintight dress, under which she does not wear pasties or anything to cover the darker areas of her naked body. If I were Teddy, I'd ask to swap with whoever her Guardian is. No challenge there. All three girls smile at Pilot, as do the guys sitting around the table. In fact, everyone in the room is totally accepting of Pilot because he's the only one they're never in competition with.

"Anne, long time no see," shouts Jack, who's exchanged his usual Goth kid gear for a pimp-style red suit with white, feathery angel wings. A blend of Cupid and Death.

"I think you mean *Fainting Fanny*," Harper snickers.

"Right. Because I fainted once," I deadpan. "Clever."

"Yeah, that's so obvious, Harper," Jack adds. "Your insecurities are really showing."

"God, can we please get along tonight?" Pilot begs.

"What're you talking about?" Jack asks. "That's impossible. It's obvious these girls are in full competition mode. I just can't believe all four of you have the same PT."

Four of them? Plum's onstage, so Harper, Tallulah, and Agniezska make three. Whirling in her chair, Harper glares at Pilot. And then at me. And then at Pilot again.

"What is Jack talking about?" she demands. "I thought you said her PT was to act like Inspector Gadget or some bullshit?"

When did Pilot talk to Harper about my PT? That's private. I told him that in confidence.

"Sorry, Jack," I say, "but I don't think we do."

"So, wait," Jack says with a confused look on his face. Then he leans back and claps his hands together, grinning broadly. "Wait, wait, wait. Anne, are you saying you're not even trying to be sexy tonight? That's not even your PT?" He guffaws. "And you're kicking their asses!"

I turn red. Bright red. Tomato red.

Cheers on the dance floor distract us all, and everyone around the table leaps to their feet. The song has changed to an even louder, faster one, a twist on a Beyoncé song I half-recognize, sending the crowd into an absolute frenzy of joy, a craze I hadn't even *considered* these normally uptight, bitter kids could produce. Flailing arms. Shaking, jumping bodies. Hoots, hollers, bellows. Laughter and screaming—good screaming—like I haven't heard in ages. It's my first dance. And, Harper and Guardians aside, it's already *so much better* than the ones I've seen in eighties movies, which just so happen to be the ones I've based my expectations on: boys leaning against one wall, girls against the other. This dance is night-club fabulous. Way too fabulous for me to even consider sitting down. As much as Pilot obviously wants to avoid the dance floor, I can't. Not when I want to do much more than *observe*, not when dancing is the one thing that makes me feel normal…cool, even.

"What do you think?" I ask him. He just shakes his head. The longer I stand, my shoulders bouncing, my toes tapping, gazing out over the rapidly filling floor, over the manic crowd, the paler his complexion grows.

"Annie, please," he begs, frozen, as others pair off to dance and groups form on the floor. A smile creeps across my face. "No, really. I'm the worst." Still, I say nothing but dance up to him. He cringes. "I love the music. Hate the dancing."

When he sees I'm not about to give in, he reluctantly pushes my still-empty chair back in. I grin and tug at his hand, hauling him smack into the middle of the dance floor.

Brilliant that everyone's masked! Anyone with reservations about dancing publicly *must* go to a masque. Overcome by a sense of liberation like nothing I've felt in years, I let loose. Fully. And completely.

"I love this song!" I shout over the music to him.

He laughs nervously, but, the more I move, the more he opens up to the idea of dancing. Soon, his side-to-side step gets a bit freer, looser—cooler. Laughing, I pull out my California street-dancing swagger, which is insanely tough in this dress and heels, but I can't help myself. This song is begging for some *boom-pop*, and I am *all over* that.

"Man, you've got soul! You're awesome!" Pilot shouts. "You even make me look good." Then, with a laugh, he throws down some Running Man, and I try to follow, but my dress is so tight around my thighs that I just end up laughing and falling into a side swipe—which, shockingly, Pilot mirrors.

"I thought you hated dancing!" I holler at him.

He shrugs. "I used to have a massive crush on Julia Stiles! Watched *Save the Last Dance*, like, ninety times." Then he throws his head back and hoots. "Did I just admit that?"

As I pull out some pretty simple b-boy breaking, I can't help but notice that the floor is clearing out around us—but the others aren't leaving; they're backing into a circle. To watch us and cheer us on. Kudos to Pilot for not freaking out, for working out a valiant attempt at popping and locking that inspires me to do the same. A few kids clap, and Pilot and I exchange wide grins.

Until.

Until I see that Harper, Tallulah, and Agniezska are watching from the sidelines, staring from behind their flashy masks. Inch by inch, Harper pulls her longhorns down from her eyes, revealing a glare that is like no other I've *ever* received. Enough to stop me in my tracks—if I wasn't having such an awesome time.

Unfortunately, the song finally comes to an end and switches to something slow. Jack strides our way, clapping along with a few other people; at the same time, Harper, fuming, storms right at us.

"Nice moves, Merchant!" Jack laughs as Pilot and I grin and pretend not to notice a seething Harper. "Bod. Brains. Bustin' it. Thank God they're grading you, but too bad for your competition."

"Pilot," Harper interrupts angrily, "dance with me. Now."

She whirls in a huff—a gorgeous, shimmery, irritated huff that gets more frantic the more Jack laughs at her. Pilot has been holding my hand, but, to my surprise, he drops it and follows Harper.

"You're going?" I mouth after him. But he just looks sorry. I guess I can't blame him. Harper's crazy-looking enough right now that if she told *anyone* to dance with her, they would—anything to wash that freaky look off her face. She probably bullied Pilot into telling her my PT, too.

"Classic! Well, then," Jack says, smirking as he saunters to my side, "if your date's dumb enough to leave you all by yourself, dance with me?"

Hearing that, Harper stops in her tracks. She and Pilot turn back.

"No way," she says. "That's not how it works, Jack."

But I'm already taking Jack's hand. "You don't make the rules," I remind her. "It's a *dance*."

"It's a dance at Cania Christy, Fat Fanny," Harper hisses. "I'm sure back in public school, you'd dance with anyone, spike your punch, and have threesomes in the bathroom." Says the girl who screws teachers in the woods! "But this is the Cupid and Death Dance."

"So what?"

"You shouldn't even have danced with Pilot! You can only dance with people who can't stand you—like the story for the old masque goes."

I remember Molly's comment about Cupid and Death exchanging arrows, but nothing about this.

"That leaves you free to dance with pretty much anyone. Except Pilot. And, I guess, Jack, since he seems to have a thing for you."

"Hold up. If those are the rules, and if you two hate each other," Jack begins, looking slyly from me to Harper, "can we watch you dance together? Maybe with a little less clothing."

Harper snorts at him. "Why don't you find a corner and dance with your right hand, Jack?"

"Happily. Just know I won't be thinking of *you* when I do it," he replies. Then he turns his grin on me, bounces his eyebrows, and strolls away.

"And me?" I ask. "I should just stand here?"

"Why do you even care about dancing? You suck."

"You're wasting the whole song!" I cry, rolling my eyes. "Assign me my detestable partner already, Harper."

"You are so useless!" She grabs Augusto by the arm as he wanders by. "Dance with Augusto. Go clump around those Amazon feet over there with him."

With a small smile, Augusto drags me into that *boring* high-school box step: forward-side-together, backward-side-together. What a joy. Minutes pass in silence. From time to time, I think I spy Ben—but it's never him. I won't see him tonight. Here I'm all dressed up, and there's no one to impress. And now that Jack's gone and taken his compliments with him, a part of me just wants to go home. Quit while I'm ahead.

"You enjoyed sketching the naked teacher in our workshop?" Augusto finally asks, breaking the silence. I nod. "You fainted, though. I cannot blame you. There is much pressure in this place, but I did not think you were feeling it yet."

"I didn't faint because of any pressure. I was just feeling…off."

Truth is, I don't know why I fainted or why, every morning, I have to fight to keep from passing out.

He nods. "Then it's because of what happened to Lotus. I felt off about that, too."

"Lotus?" I repeat. "What are you talking about?"

"But, no, I'm wrong. She was not yet expelled that morning. So that could not be it."

"Lotus was expelled?" I lean away from Augusto and look into his eyes. "You mean Lotus, that nice girl?"

"Yes, Lotus Featherly. She was expelled Tuesday after our workshop." Augusto shrugs as the song finally ends. I realize I haven't seen Lotus in class since Tuesday morning. "You are not paying much attention, are you?"

With that odd insult, Augusto bows and leaves me standing in the middle of the dance floor as *Touch Myself* begins. Confused, I'm about to return to the table to ask Pilot about Lotus—what such an angelic girl could possibly have done to be expelled— when Harper marches up to me and tries to stare me down. But she's about three inches shorter than I am, even in heels, so it doesn't quite work.

"You ready to take this on?" she asks. Not asks. *Demands.*

"Take what on?"

"This!" She runs her hands up and down her body. "Right here. Right now."

"Wait. Are you saying what I think you're saying?"

She wants to battle. She wants a dance-off. For a moment, I'm stunned. But as everyone begins to take notice, as I spy Teddy scribbling frantically on his board and Villicus watching from above, as I feel a new wave of frustration with this place where even dances are graded and nice people like Lotus get expelled, my shock disappears. It's replaced by something I much prefer: the will to win.

"If your PT really is to use your bod to get ahead," she says, "dance like you mean it."

With a short slide, I close the distance between us and peer down into the little slots in her crystal mask. Ever so coolly, channeling an inner seductress Teddy and Jack have convinced me I possess, I whisper to her, "That's not my PT. But I'll do it anyway. Just to destroy you."

That's how I find myself in the first real dance-off of my life. I start it off, beginning by sliding into and out of an exaggerated S-shape formed by sitting deep in my right hip, rolling up to my left, arching my back, and smoothly busting out my chest. To warm things up. I pause for good measure, making deep eye contact with guys in the crowd, who clap when I do. I'm not sure where this is coming from—these are not moves my mom ever taught me. It just feels natural.

When it's Harper's turn, she breaks quickly into bumping and grinding an unseen pole. Although she's got almost no butt, she bounces it like she does. She dances like a cheerleader. Which is good. If you like cheerleaders. Her walk is perfectly timed—1,2,3,4—and her hip rolls are orchestrated. I respond with a smooth belly dancing–inspired gyration. She comes back with a drop to the floor and some strange chest-bouncing move that hurts my eyes.

I'm unimpressed, and it shows. Both she and the crowd notice my attitude—but while it gets under Harper's skin, the crowd laps it up, begging me for more.

Growing irritated, Harper tries to get in my face, but she's got no game. Finally, I wave my hand like *you stink*—steeped in swagger—and, as I step it up with a final sequence that my mom actually did choreograph way back when, the crowd erupts.

Tearing off her mask, Harper casts a fiery glare in my direction and storms off, followed closely behind by her gang.

I'm surrounded immediately by people patting my back. Teachers are nodding and scribbling on their clipboards. And, as I'm floating on euphoria, as everyone clears away, I see, across the room, just beyond the crowd, Ben. My heart stops the moment our eyes meet. Neither one of us moves; this moment is an almost identical replica of our brief encounter last night. But, unlike when we were separated by physical walls, there's no reason now to keep our distance. There's no reason for Ben not to approach me or, for that matter, me him. Still on a high, feeling as though I might be invincible, I decide to go for it. Smiling broadly, I take the first step toward him—but Pilot is suddenly at my side again. I glance away from Ben just long enough to know that, when I turn back, he'll be gone. And, sure enough, he is. Sighing, I close my eyes and reluctantly open them to look at Pilot. My heart is pounding like mad.

"That was insane, Annie," Pilot shouts into my ear, wrapping his arm around my shoulders. "You can bet Teddy will use that display in his argument for the Big V for you."

"I don't think it'll help much. If I had the PT Teddy wanted me to have, it would."

Pilot escorts me back to the table, which is, thankfully, empty.

My head swoons as, taking a chair, I relive not only the image of Ben turning away from me—perhaps he thought my sexy dancing was cheap—but also Augusto's comment about Lotus. Pilot's beaming as I pull my mask down, let it hang around my neck, and get straight to the point.

"Lotus was expelled," I state.

"Lotus, yeah." He blinks. His smile awkwardly shrinks. "So? Let's talk about those moves. You had me working up a sweat just watching you."

"What do you mean, so?"

"So, one less junior to compete with," he says dismissively. "I think half the guys in here were pitching tents watching you."

"I'm serious. Why was she expelled? She was a *doll*."

"You want a drink? I can go get us something."

"Do you know what she did, Pilot? Why she was kicked out?"

"Anne!" he exclaims, erupting suddenly, standing, and shoving his chair. "I'm not going to explain this place to you. You act like you're in some regular old high school. But you're not. Are you that dense?"

"I knew it. I'm in a reform school." That's the only kind of school Lotus could possibly be dismissed from.

"No, you're *not*," he sneers. "You're in an intense competition with kids who'll do anything to get you expelled. That's what you're in. Got it? Now I'm getting a drink, and then you and me are gonna dance, even if Harper doesn't like it." He throws a glare over his shoulder, where Harper's standing, watching us. "Then, we're not going to talk about this crap anymore."

"Pi—"

"No, you listen to me. If you're going for the Big V, you don't get to complain when it hurts people. Got it?"

With that, he disappears, leaving me dumbfounded. And leaving an empty seat next to me that Harper, watching me with the strangest doe-eyed gaze, takes.

"That didn't look like fun," she drawls, scooting the chair closer while I stare after Pilot. It's hard to hear her over the music. "Nice work on the dance floor. I guess I'm having an off night."

As if attached to Harper by invisible rope, Tallulah and Agniezska arrive at the table, flanking her and turning their sharp smiles on me.

"So, we're dying to know," Tallulah says. "Do you like him?"

"Pilot?" I ask. What a ridiculous thing to talk about when my mind is somewhere completely different. Sighing, I try to clear my thoughts and play along with them. "Sure. He's nice. Whatever."

"Well, let me give you a tip," Harper adds, "because I'm sure you're new at this." She lowers her voice and checks that Pilot is out of earshot. "First, since he hates the Big V, you should think twice about it."

Could she be more transparent?

"Two, let your hair down. Guys love when girls have their hair down."

The thought of taking my hair out of my mom's barrettes is laughable. My hair will fly in a billion directions. But Harper has already lifted her hands to my ears, holding them below my barrettes. She's reaching out to me; that's a good thing, right? Even though I slaughtered her on the dance floor, she's trying to be friendly. Her little friends are genuinely smiling. Maybe they could be nice. It would be rude to deny her attempt to befriend me, wouldn't it? I'm not exactly Little Miss Popular. Who am I to turn away an ally? Even if that ally is part of the vulture-esque Model UN from Hell.

"May I?" Harper asks.

It's like being locked in the headlight of an oncoming train, looking into Harper's eyes. Frozen, with all three beautiful girls, girls who would never consider befriending me in the past, smiling at me, I surrender and nod. Harper unclips the four silvery barrettes and sends my thick, curly hair tumbling over my shoulders.

"There." She places the barrettes on the table and smoothes

my hair. "Doesn't she look hotter'n hell's door hinges now, ladies?"

Feeling my neck and shoulders relax, I sigh. "Thanks."

As the next song starts, Tallulah and Agniezska pair off, leaving me alone with Harper. Maybe this is a turning point in our relationship. I know I don't want to be her friend; I don't want to be a member of the Model UN from Hell. But tonight. Tonight, I want to have a good time. Without conflict. Is that too much to hope for?

Harper shoos away two nervous-looking sophomore boys before they even have a chance to ask us to dance. "We need some girl time," she tells them, absentmindedly rolling one of my barrettes in her hands. "Y'know, some people are saying you're gonna headline Art Walk and even be a contender for the Big V. Can you believe that?"

I swallow.

"You really think you can make it to the Big V?" She looks perplexed. "When you're up against me? And even with Pilot not wantin' you to get caught up in it all?"

I glance at the beloved barrette she holds so casually and remind myself to play nice. Who knows what this hotheaded Texan could do if worked up enough? A change of topic is in order.

"So, will your parents be coming to Parents' Day next weekend?" I ask.

"My daddy wouldn't miss a chance to see me for the world." She clenches her jaw. "He wants me to get the Big V more than anything."

"That's nice." *Put my mom's barrette down. Right now.*

"I would never even have come to Cania if it wasn't for my stepmonster," Harper continues. "My daddy needs me back home."

"Is your stepmom coming, too?"

"Unfortunately." Harper's face goes blank. Gone is her wide-eyed and obviously feigned innocence. "Guess some people don't get it."

"Don't get what?" My voice breaks.

"That they don't belong on this island. And that they should leave." With that, Harper snaps one barrette in half. My mouth drops open. She snaps another.

"What are you doing?" I cry, my voice barely audible with the drums beating madly. I grasp for my remaining barrettes. Just miss them. She snaps them both.

"Wake up, you reject," she hisses. "You don't belong here. And you're ruining everything." She brushes the pieces of my broken heirloom onto the floor. "*Wake up!*" And storms off.

twelve

CONSEQUENCES

I WAS WRONG. I *CAN* MARCH UP A MOUNTAIN—OR AT least a steep hillside—in these heels, if I'm angry enough.

Fuming, I head to the cliff where I watched Villicus the other day. My motivation for climbing up here is simple: I want to get as far away from that dance as possible, and I don't want to go home. I just want to escape. To a place where it's dark and calm. My first thought was the parking lot, but a bunch of kids were making out there. So I marched on and up. To the one place where I can stare out at the enormous sky and hope to feel my mom looking down. Where the echo of my voice might reach her, and she can call on some angels to help me out here—maybe even send a lightning bolt to zap Harper like a Kentucky-fried bitch. But, no matter how I beg, there is no lightning. Only a chilly breeze that grows fiercer the higher I get.

The air is filled with competing sounds. A cover of a My Chemical Romance song pours from the castle; loons and sea lions, which ought to be asleep, sing their lonesome odes below; my breath heaves as I storm up the hill, giving myself hell for wimping out with Harper. At the summit, I unstrap my borrowed shoes—the words *Property of Molly Watso* written inside them—

and look out over the endless black waters. My toes curl into the cool, damp grass. My bare heels rest on a flat patch of icy cold rock. Shoes in hand, I creep to the edge, where Villicus stood, where the pulsating moon beckons me as though it has a secret to share. I peer over the cliff, listening; my head swoons with the waves crashing below. Here I stand, staring down a 100-foot drop, inches away from a fall that will mean death, the ultimate escape from the bitches and freaks at Cania.

"It's not worth it."

I recognize his voice without even looking back at him. What's *he* doing here?

"What do you know?" I ask. But, heading his words, I stumble away from the cliff, leaving the waves to clobber the black granite, to wear away at it chip by chip. The wind thrusts wide wisps of hair across my face when I turn to see Ben, who is just feet away, cloaked in the dark shadows of darker trees. I'm not in the mood for him. I don't need to feel like an idiot any more tonight, thanks.

"What are you doing up here?" he asks. He looks gorgeous in his suit, and that only makes things worse.

"I didn't realize this was private property."

"I didn't say it was."

"What are *you* doing up here?"

He shrugs. "You left the dance?"

Pressing my tongue against the back of my teeth to keep from saying more, I nod. I need to forget about Harper, not rehash it all.

"You weren't having a good time?"

I shrug.

"You've lost the ability to speak?"

I huff. "No. I'm just—it doesn't matter."

Sighing, Ben passes me, a current of air carrying his aroma as he glides by and walks to the very spot I was just standing, inches from the edge. There, he gazes at the water below.

"I used to love dances," he says. "I used to go to my sister's recitals all the time." He faces me again. His eyes are fluorescent green against the gray sky; his expression tortured. "Jeannie took ballet. Jeannie. That's my sister."

He's obviously struggling with some old memory, some homesickness I could relate to, if I wanted to. But I don't. I don't want anything more than to be left alone. Especially by Mr. Hot and Cold himself.

"You remind me of Jeannie sometimes," he says out of nowhere. "And not just because you won that dance-off back there."

The revelation nearly knocks the wind out of me. I stare at him, wondering why he's so damn hard to pin down. His emotions must run on a dial, and he's just turned it from Complete Asshole Mode to Charming Mode.

"Because I'm blonde?"

"How do you know Jeannie's blonde?" Then he smiles. "Oh, yeah. The break-in yesterday. You saw her photos on my computer."

It's bad enough that he knows I broke in, but that's he's calling me on it? Now, when I already feel like jumping off a cliff?

"What else did you see?" he asks. The moonlight on his face reveals his mystified expression.

"Nothing," I lie.

"Nothing?"

"What does it matter?" The wind whips my hair across my face and into my mouth, making me cough. Damn Harper for breaking my barrettes! "I saw a web page," I growl, shoving my hair away. "Some photos of your family."

"That's it?"

"Your sketchbook. And a freaky old book about demons."

"Did you read it?"

"Read it? Why would I?"

"Because your PT is to look closer," he says, gliding toward me. I stumble backward with surprise, but that only brings him forward even more. "Tell me you read it."

"How do you know what my PT is?"

"Everyone's PTs are saved in a spreadsheet on my dad's Mac, which you'd know if you were any good at looking closer."

"My PT is private!"

"My whole *house* is private."

He rushes toward me now, and before my heart can skip a beat, before my brain can process the fact that he's near, his incredible face is little more than an inch away from mine. I gasp, trying to step back further, to stay at a distance where he won't see my crooked tooth and judge me again like he did before. But he catches me by the waist and pulls me against his chest.

"But that didn't stop you from breaking in," he finishes, gazing into my eyes disarmingly.

"You're wrong, you know," I stammer, trying to find my voice and winded by the surprise of feeling his body against mine, his hands on my back, tortured by the presence of his beautiful lips so near mine but so out of reach. "I looked for answers on your computer."

"Then what did you find?"

I shake my head. "I don't know."

Am I *supposed* to be looking for something? This isn't the first time Ben's implied so. He tilts his head and inches his face close enough that our lips nearly brush.

"You *should* have read the whole book," he says. "Every book on our shelves. I can't—" he sighs, his eyes flooding my face "—I can't *give* you the answers."

"What answers?" I gasp. This closeness to Ben, when he is always so unimaginably distant, is clouding my mind and compromising my focus.

"I can't risk everything. You have to try. I thought you were smarter than this."

"...smarter?"

Exactly the word to wake me from his trance.

Worst of all? He's right. I'm an *idiot* for falling for his charms time after time. And the moment I let that fact hit me, the moment I remind myself that I am hopelessly brainless around him, I shove at his chest, trying to free myself.

But he refuses to release me. "That's not what I meant," he says, his low voice rumbling over my face as he grips my wrists behind my back. "You always misunderstand me. Just hold on a second."

Even as I wriggle, I notice that his breath is sweet like cotton candy. His eyes unimaginably clear. His skin glowing. When he turns his head a fraction and the moonlight slips over the side of his face, he radiates a soft white light. I stop wrestling.

"Oh, my gosh," I whisper, locked on him.

"What is it?"

Our eyes meet. And slowly, before I can stop myself, I say, "You're *perfect*."

He thrusts me away. I stumble, barely keeping myself from falling, as he retreats.

"No," he says. It sounds like a warning. "I'm not."

Again, I'm an *idiot*! I've lived my life with a perfect GPA and was once called an art prodigy. Yet, somehow, I'm totally mental when it comes to Ben Zin.

"You of all people," he sighs, running his hands through his hair wildly. "You're an artist! You should want to look beyond the surface. Find the greater truth. Look at all the layers and reject them, one by one. Don't you get that? You must *try* to see beyond the illusion of normalcy they create."

"Normalcy?"

"I've hinted at so much already, Anne."

"Hinted? You call those hints? A few book titles outside some hall? You're so unbelievably cryptic, it's like talking to Gollum!"

That comment obviously throws him off but only for a moment.

"Look, I've been doing my best to help you. I got in trouble for it, too." He fidgets with his suit sleeve. "Why did you bother breaking in? Weren't you looking for exactly what's inside *Ars Goetia*?"

"It wasn't my idea. It was Molly's," I blurt. And, with that, my confession is just *spilling* out of me. "She said we should find out about your girlfriend. We saw you leave. And we just thought…" I search the moonlit horizon for a way out of this. "It was stupid."

"My girlfriend?" His smile makes a surprise reappearance. "And who exactly is my *girlfriend*?"

"You tell me!" I holler, exasperated as I throw my hands in the air. The shimmery Jimmy Choos in my hand reflect the moonlight. "That blonde girl. The one in your house the other day."

He says nothing for an eternity. So I don't, either. Instead, I stand silently in the wind, waiting for who knows what. Beating myself up for abandoning Pilot at the dance. Silly me. A perfectly nice guy with a good head on his shoulders likes me, and I'm in a shouting match with an unattainable snob who takes every opportunity to trash my intelligence.

"It doesn't matter," I stammer, ending the silence, ending it all. "I'm going to be smarter going forward."

"You saw me with her?"

"I don't want to hear a word about it." It's bad enough that I've spent the last few days stressing over it. It's bad enough that I've told myself Ben couldn't have a blonde girlfriend, that I've convinced myself it was his study partner. If Ben actually has a girlfriend, he can keep it to himself. I've suffered enough tonight. "I'm over it."

"Over it? Why? Because you've found *true love* with your reckless boyfriend, Pilot?"

"My what?"

"Be careful with him."

"He's neither reckless nor my boyfriend. He's *good*. He never makes me feel like you do, and he doesn't judge me for my flaws. *That*, and he's above this whole valedictorian race."

"Wait a second," Ben says, shaking his head. "What makes you think *I'm* not above the race, but he is?"

"Because you're so hateful! You keep to yourself. You never say hello. You're just like everyone else. Except Pilot."

For a second, Ben looks like he's had the wind knocked out of him. For a second, I wish I could take it back.

"That's what you think? I'm hateful? You don't... you don't feel any sort of connection to me whatsoever?" he asks, his eyes narrowing as he moves closer to me, sending me staggering backward again.

My heel hits a rock, and I lose my balance, regaining it just in time to keep from falling but not before my shoes fly from my hand and down the dark hill. *Great.* Now I'll never find them.

"Well, tell me," he continues, "how would you feel if you lived day after day on this island? With the bullshit rules, signing forms in blood, a fucking mausoleum for a graduation hall, expulsions around the corner for everyone—just as you start to care about them."

"Care! You?"

"Yes, care! I'm capable of it, you know. Let me prove it."

That gets my attention. That's interesting.

"How will you prove it?" I ask tentatively, hoping against hope that he'll pull me close to him again.

"With advice, which is all I can give you," he storms, stuffing his hands in his pockets like he's trying to control himself. "Do what your Guardian says. Work for the Big V. And, for God's sake, stay the hell away from Molly. You *will* get caught."

I. Am. A. Fool.

"Thanks, Ben," I begin soberly. "But I already have a Guardian giving me all the advice I can take. Keep yours. I don't need it."

Clenching my teeth, I whirl and race down the hill, refusing to yell at Ben or let him yell at me for another second. I hear him call my name, but I ignore it. In the shadows, I trip on one of my abandoned heels, which scrapes the bottom of my foot. Wincing with pain, I stumble, grab the shoe, and glance back at the mountaintop. But I can't see him.

"Of course he's gone," I sniffle.

Of course he doesn't care to follow me or make sure I'm alright. Patting around in the darkness for Molly's other shoe, I feel tears heat my face; they blur my vision, and I lose patience looking for the shoe. It's gone. So I hike up my dress and race down the remainder of the hill. The bottom of my foot is bleeding as I stumble onto campus, begrudging the music that I'd danced to an hour ago, begrudging everything that has been taken from me tonight.

Sunday morning. There's a sparkly Jimmy Choo on the landing outside my bedroom door when I head downstairs. I've got to meet Molly in half an hour down at the marina, and I need to get a coffee. Last night kicked the crap out of me.

I pick up the shoe. Read Molly's name inside.

Freeze in place.

As it occurs to me that someone has found the missing shoe and returned it to *me* when *Molly's* name is written inside, as the implications of this returned shoe dawn on me, I hear a noise downstairs.

Someone is weeping.

I creep down the stairs, avoiding the step that creaks, and

pass Teddy, who's glowering at me in the living room.

Gigi is sobbing at the kitchen table. Her crying stops short, and she shifts in her chair to face me as I enter the room. Mascara streaks her face. In her hand, she swirls a glass of whiskey around some ice cubes.

"It's done," she says. "The last child in the village is dead."

Her words rush at me with so much force, it feels like they're pulling the walls in around us. Stunned, I wait for my brain to make sense of what she's saying. I wait to be crushed.

"Villicus left her no choice," she continues. "It was Cania or ... death."

My throat doesn't work. My brain can't catch up. It's too much. I must be sleeping. Except I'm not. This is happening.

Molly.

"What do you ...?" My voice falters. Cania or *death*?

All at once, in an alarming montage, I see Molly standing outside last night, with that white box in her hands. Poking her head in the door at the Zins' on Friday, smiling her metallic smile. Waving to me as she biked away.

Gigi sputters, "Molly's dead now. What are we supposed to do? What have we become?"

I see idiot me, carelessly leaving Molly's shoe on the hillside. I see Teddy, standing at his bedroom window last night, watching Molly say we should meet for a gossip session this morning. Turning, I walk into the living room, walk up to Teddy, and deliberately bring my hand across his face with all my might—or at least I try to. He catches my wrist midair and stares me down.

"*You* did this to Molly," he states bitterly. "You both knew the rules. But you decided to break them."

Yes, I'm to blame for breaking a rule. But it was a ridiculous rule. And it was Teddy who told Villicus what he saw; I wouldn't be surprised if Dr. Zin was behind this, too. Behind the death of an innocent kid who broke a rule no one can even explain. The punishment is so preposterous, so out of whack with the crime that I *know* now that there's more to this island and the people on it than I've been told. I know, glaring into Teddy's hate-filled sallow face, that I'm in a high-priced insane asylum. And if I believed in it, I might even be convinced I'm in Hell itself.

thirteen

LOOKING CLOSER

THERE'S NO ANSWER AT THE ZINS', NO MATTER HOW many times I ring the bell, pound on the door, or shout over the driving rain for them to let me in. It's hailing now as I run from their house toward the marina, knowing already Molly won't be there. I run at breakneck speed up to campus, to the middle of the quad, where I slump against a tree and try to catch my breath, to arrange my thoughts. But I can't. My heart's beating so fast, it's impossible to do anything but run even more.

The hail won't let me stay outside, though, so I'm forced to look for refuge.

Every door is locked on campus except the dorms, the cafeteria, and the library. Swinging the door open, I burst into the bottomless quiet of the library, wheezing, and hear a resounding *shhh* that sends me looking for a stairwell to escape into. What am I doing here? I need to know if Ben's dad was involved, if he told Villicus that Molly and I were in his house. As much as I wish I could forget, I haven't forgotten the gunshots I heard last week. I can't forget Dr. Zin was there.

But I need more answers than just that. I yank open the heavy door to the stairwell and, rushing in, stop to process a thought. If

Ben knows everything he says he knows about Wormwood Island and Cania, then he needs to tell me what exactly is so horrendous about this place—aside from the obvious—that Molly would rather she be dead than attend this school. "Molly's dead," I finally let myself say, even if only in a whisper. I must be in shock. Because I don't cry. I owe it to Molly to keep it together until I get some answers. If at some point I feel like crying, then I'll have to shove it down deep and let it out later. I collapse against the cold concrete-block wall and stare across the landing. The hood of my yellow rain slicker cushions the blow as my head bobs against the wall.

Molly's dead. And I'm expelled.

The expulsion is nothing. I don't care—I couldn't possibly care about that right now. It's all about Molly. A girl I knew for less than a week but who, in that time, was more a friend to me than anyone I've known in years. And how did I repay her friendship? Shuddering, I close my eyes and relive that moment in the darkness last night, as I halfheartedly patted around for her shoe and then ran away empty-handed. Knowing her name was inside it. It's enough to send me flying up the stairs, as if I could run away from what I've done, from my responsibility in Molly's death. Up, up, I run, until I'm on the fourth floor, the top floor, where the staircase ends at a single steel door. I throw it open and burst into the room.

The first thing I notice is the cold.

The second is that I'm not alone.

"Anne? Is that you?"

The only person on the entire floor, Ben is sitting on a hard wooden chair with his head in his hands. Over his head is a sign shaped like an arrow that reads "Religion" and points west. A stack of books sits on the study carousel beside him, a reading lamp shining down over him, glowing yellow, bringing out the shadows that ring his eyes. He looks as exhausted as I feel.

"Have you heard what happened to Molly?" My voice is surprisingly clear and strong. He nods. "I need to know if your dad was involved."

"Shh," he says, pressing his finger to his lips. "Inside voices in the library."

"Was he? I need a straight answer."

"My dad?" He shakes his head, but he doesn't look surprised. "Not this time."

"But he's done crap like that before?"

Reluctantly, he nods. "He's been involved in expulsions and similarly ugly situations. It's his job. There are rules he has to play by."

"Did he tell Villicus that Molly and I broke into your house? That we're friends?" *Were* friends.

Again, he shakes his head. "My dad's had a change of heart recently. He doesn't tell Villicus anything he doesn't have to."

So it was that bastard Teddy. If it wasn't for me and my stupid Guardian, none of this would have happened to Molly.

"Why don't you sit?" Ben offers. "You can't stay long because I'm expecting Lizzy, but—"

"I'm fine standing," I huff angrily. But a moment passes, and I make my way over to him, taking the chair on the opposite side of the small table. "Who's Lizzy?"

"An old friend. That's just her nickname."

The books on the tabletop are old and picked over. Some have tattered corners and age spots, faded spines, and tea-spattered edges. Titles like *Bedeviled Constructs of the Reformation* and *Diabology: Better the Devil You Know.*

"Why are you reading these?" I ask.

"Is that what you really want to ask me?"

"I want to know why Molly died."

"Because she was killed."

"That's not an answer."

"It's my only answer. I don't *know*, Anne." His eyes meet mine. "What's this change in you? You're finally ready to start asking questions? And you start with the hardest one."

"Why weren't there any other kids in the village but Molly?"

"There used to be," he says. "But the villagers slowly started moving away, back in the fifties, I guess. The ones who've stayed rarely have children. The elderly have stayed, too, for Mr. Watso. I guess they'll go now."

"That doesn't answer my question."

"Is this an interrogation?" he asks, but I respond with a blank glare. "They want off this island. Villicus needs them, though, and he pays them so well, his generosity would be a hard habit for them to break."

"Why does he need them?"

"Why not?"

"Is it because this is an asylum?"

He frowns at me. A chill courses through the room though no windows are open.

"I know you want some answers, but I really don't think you could handle them." Sighing, he adds, "And I wouldn't risk it."

"You have no idea what I can handle!"

"I know what *I* can handle. The repercussions would be… unbearable. I'm sorry, it's out of my hands."

"Fantastic, Ben. Thanks for the help."

"Hey, you had a chance to find the truth. You were in my library on my dad's computer."

"I saw photos of your family! That's nothing."

Flinching, he looks away. "Maybe not to you, but it's something to me. Photos of my last Christmas with my mom and sister. That's everything to me."

I finally nod. "Okay." I fidget. "I'm sorry. You're right."

"You don't have to say that."

"I *am* sorry, though," I say, and my voice cracks to prove it. With everything that's just happened, I'm starting to feel seriously emotional. And the mere mention of Christmas with family only reminds me of how much I miss my mom. Why does everybody have to die? My throat tightens. "I'm so lost."

"You're just not in the know right now," he says gently. "The only consolation is, I think, that you're a fighter." His hand on his knee is close to me, and I watch it shift as if he's about to reach for me but won't let himself. "Jeannie was a fighter, too."

"Why doesn't she go to Cania?"

Shifting away from me, he says, "She passed away. She and my mom did. In a car accident."

"Oh, my gosh. They died?"

"We were in California at a black-tie event for some celebrity client of my dad's. He had a few too many, and then he drove us back to the hotel. Or tried to." He rubs his hands over his face. "You know what that's like, of course, to lose part of your family." I'd almost forgotten that he read my file. "I once thought that that was what drew me to you, that you'd lost your mom, too. But I know now that it's more than that."

"I'm not sure what you mean."

"I have to be cryptic, A.M." Smiling softly, he adds, "Do you really think I come off like Gollum?"

Footsteps pound out in the stairwell, and the door flies open, hitting us with a sudden gust of warm air. There stands Garnet, her face flushed like she's been running and crying at the same time. I suppose she's heard the news about Molly and is trying to round up kids for a grief counseling session.

"Well, hello, you two," she says coolly. "I didn't expect to find *you* in here, Miss Merchant."

Hold that thought. She *didn't* expect to find me? She's not rounding up kids.

"Garnet," Ben breathes. Their eyes meet. "I was just telling Anne where to find a book she was looking for." His suddenly blank stare darts at me. "Second floor. Check the stacks."

"Oh. Thanks," I say, confused, and get to my feet. I adjust my rain slicker as Garnet and Ben stare my way. Are they waiting for me to leave? I shuffle my feet a bit. "Um, okay. See you guys later."

"See you tomorrow morning, Anne," Garnet says. "I'm announcing the Art Walk winner first thing in class. We'll see how you fare."

Nodding like a robot, I glance from her to Ben once more before exiting into the stairwell, leaving them behind in the frigid darkness. The concrete steps blend into one gray blob as I race down as quickly as possible, recalling the strange expression on Garnet's face and the shift in Ben's mood when she arrived. As if *I* was the intruder. As if I was an annoying little girl the big kids had to shoo away. Bracing the cool handrail, I stop short near the doorway to the first floor and look up to the fourth again, my head dizzy and my chest heaving.

This is the moment when I realize who Ben's blonde girlfriend is, who the person nicknamed *Lizzy* is.

"No way," I whisper, covering my mouth. "But she's a *teacher*."

Following Gigi's lead, I retire to bed early that night. It's been a long day, and I'm ready to cry into my pillow for Molly, but not before Teddy stops me on my way up to the attic.

"The master has demanded to see you in his office first thing in the morning," he says. His tongue slithers in his puny black mouth.

"The *master*?"

"The headmaster," he corrects. "I have strict instructions to walk by your side from Gigi's front door to his office door. So don't try any funny business."

"What does he want with me? Is he going to off me, too?"

"You'd better watch yourself," he warns, his beady eyes bright. "He wants your confession."

"My what?"

"Your confession about your relationship with Molly Watso."

Fine!, I think, slamming my door. I'll be expelled tomorrow morning, shipped back to California, and there I'll force my dad to come clean about sending me to a rich-kid asylum. *Fine by me!* I'll tell him and anyone who'll listen every little detail about this nuthouse, from signing forms in blood to pitting students against each other. I'll tell him how Harper performs sexual favors for teachers to win the Big V. How Garnet is having an affair with a minor. How I may be the only student at this school who isn't *screwing* some teacher to get a grade—and how, if Teddy had had his way yesterday, that wouldn't even be true. How they're so evil here, good people like Lotus get expelled and Molly would rather die than join the student body.

Exhausted by it all, I turn out the lights. It's time for a cry. It's time to let out everything I feel about what's happened to Molly. As I pull back my covers, though, I stop short. There is a hard-cover book half-tucked under my pillow: Machiavelli's *The Prince*. Its jacket gleams.

I squint in the darkness of the attic. "Hello?" I whisper. "Who's there?"

Flicking on my bedside lamp, I pick up the book and a note falls out, flitting down to my duvet.

Here's the book you were looking for.
~Ben

Wondering if Ben's watching me right now, I head to my window, fully expecting to see him at his. But I don't see him at all. What I see makes my voice catch in my throat.

There she is. There's Molly. Waving up at me before darting into the shadows.

My voice finally escapes, and I scream once, short and tight, then leap into bed and throw the covers over my head, breaking immediately into the prayer my mom used to say with me when I was certain I'd seen a ghost in my bedroom doorway. I chant it until I fall into darkness: *Now I lay me down to sleep.*

fourteen

MY SOUL TO KEEP

IN AN EERILY SILENT ROOM, I WAKE UP WITH A START AND sense that I am not alone. Ben's book is under the covers with me, where I still hide, where the air is stuffy, humid with my tears. Outside the covers? I have no idea. And that is the worst part of falling asleep with your face covered—waking up to darkness, waking up to the awareness that someone could be standing right over your body, waiting for you to slowly inch the covers back, waiting to ambush you. I hear the floor groan near the staircase. I *know* I am not alone.

There is someone in my room.

But at least they're near the stairs, not hovering over me. And perhaps they don't realize that they're dealing with a girl from a funeral home, a girl who learned to shine a flashlight on the monsters under the bed, to swipe her hand through the shadows just to prove there's nothing to fear when it comes to things that go bump in the night. A girl who, in one quick motion, is whipping the covers off and thrashing her head in the direction of the intruder. Which I expect to be Teddy. But which is categorically *not*.

"Molly." I say it in a whisper. For a reason I'll never understand, I don't scream when I see her leaning against the newel post at the top of the stairs, smiling a lovely straight, white smile at me.

"*Shh*," she whispers. Her voice sounds completely normal. She looks…completely normal—except her braces are gone. She's not ghostly in any way. The opposite, in fact. Even from feet away, she appears filled with life, vibrant. I rub my eyes and gape at her again. "They said you were dead." I shove my covers off the rest of the way.

She shrugs. That response stops me in my tracks. It's a surprisingly nonchalant thing to do when someone suggests you're dead.

"Molly?" My chest is abruptly heavy with dread. "What are you doing here? Are you…a ghost?"

"I don't want you to blame yourself," she says, sidestepping my questions. "And I don't want you to be sad. I know I'm going to be okay, but I need you to look out for yourself now."

"What—?" I stammer, struggling to form a coherent thought.

She smiles softly. Without a sound, she begins backing down the stairs, keeping her pretty brown eyes on me the whole time, that small grin playing across her lips but, otherwise, such a mystifying expression. Clearly, she wants me to follow her. And I do. Like little mice escaping the attic, we quietly creep down the stairs, Molly staying five or so steps ahead of me and watching me, watching me. The stairs that bring us to the main floor of the cottage practically disappear under my feet, I am so fixated on her, on assessing everything about her and comparing it to what I know of ghosts and of humans, wondering which side she's on. And then she's leaving through the front door, and the moment I turn my eyes away to slip on my boots, she's taking off at full speed, running with all her might, wailing into the wind, "Follow me, Anne!"

Stumbling, fumbling to get my boots on, I hobble as I race after her. The fog is hanging low, and it clings to my bare arms, neck, and face as I follow Molly toward the village, where the dim glow of a hundred torches turns the sky orange and where smoke mixes with fog. Drumbeats again, just like before. Molly runs faster than I knew she could, never even pausing for a breath, only glancing over her shoulder every other minute to make sure I'm still with her. And I am. I'm chasing an apparition into a village I'm sworn to steer clear of. Yet I can't turn away, can't stop. Even though I know I should. In the village are people who hate me, who likely blame me for what's happened to Molly, but I'm running toward them all.

I come to a short stop near the bench where Molly and I watched the fire festival. Ahead, Molly runs up to a woman sitting in the ring of torches, a woman who must be her mother. Just as I wonder if anyone else can see the ghost of Molly, her mother puts her arm around her, pulling her close and kissing the top of her head fiercely.

"What took you so long?" I hear her mother say. "Every second with you is so precious, sweetheart."

Like last week, Mr. Watso is in the middle of the circle of torches. But unlike last week, the dancing woman and the two shirtless men are nowhere to be seen. And unlike last week, the ring of people is small. A moment later, I see where the rest of the villagers have gone: in the darkness beyond, out at the docks, nearly fifty people are loading up a dozen mini-yachts. Two boats have already set sail, and I can just make out their floodlights glowing as they head west, toward the mainland. Am I wrong, or am I witnessing a mass exodus of the villagers?

"Our dear Molly has arrived, at last," says Mr. Watso.

His tone couldn't be any gentler, couldn't be any different from the rough roaring of last week's encounter. It's a tone I recognize because it's exactly the tone that everybody who's ever given a eulogy at the Fair Oaks Funeral Home has had. He's lost someone; he's in mourning. But how could he have lost Molly if we can all see her?

Then he glances my way, spying me shivering in the fog. "It looks like Molly wanted her friend here, too."

She nods. "I did," she says, smiling at me. "My only friend."

I return her smile and taste a tear that rolls down my cheek and between my parted lips.

"Without further ado, let us begin the cremation."

It's hard to say what happens next because it's almost too much for my brain to process. A great fire is lit in the center of the ring. Mr. Watso says beautiful words about his granddaughter. Molly's mother weeps; Molly whispers in her ear. Others in the circle cling to each other. Another boat shoves off, the passengers on it waving solemn good-byes. Mr. Watso lifts a long body wrapped in cloth over his head, managing the weight effortlessly, just like I've seen so many pallbearers do with caskets. A foghorn sounds in the distance. The wrapped body is gently placed in the fire, and Mr. Watso, overcome with sorrow, chokes out a *good-bye*. Everyone is sobbing now. Including me.

I tear my eyes away from the cremation in time to see Molly begin to flicker just like the flames, in time to see her glance my way with that small grin that comes and goes. And then her mother is clinging to no one at all, her lonesome wail rising into the air. Molly is gone.

"The cremation is complete," chokes Mr. Watso. "Let us pause to remember Molly Lynn Watso. Let us pray that the spirit of my grandchild finds rest in the eternal beyond."

Villicus taps the hourglass on his desk, and a burst of sand flows down. His perma-arched eyebrow is high on his head this morning as he looks at me and waits for Teddy to fold his long body into a tiny chair placed off to the side. The jeweled case I saw

Villicus carrying the other day is on his desk again, looking pol-
ished and new.

I am waiting patiently to be expelled. I am numb.

In any court, this case would be thrown out and the detectives
and lawyers humiliated. Because I haven't confessed to a thing. And
the only evidence Villicus has to any wrongdoing on my part is either circumstantial—that shoe they found on the hill could have
been worn by Molly herself—or provided by a witness I'd rejected
just hours before the shoe was discovered (that is, Teddy).

But there's no court here. And I'm the only one doing any
sort of investigating, which says a lot. Villicus is free to make
whatever judgments he'd like. Just as I'm free to make whatever
judgments I'd like about him—the most important right now being that he played a role in the death of Molly Watso. No one has
said who did it—hell, she might have killed herself—but Villicus
is at least indirectly culpable. It was his institution that was so terrible that Molly chose death over it.

Crossing my legs and folding my hands over my knees, I await
expulsion. I should be overjoyed to be leaving. But I feel nothing.
I'm sure I went into shock last night, and I have yet to snap out of
it. If this isn't a nuthouse, as I strongly suspect it is, this expulsion
will show on my transcripts when I apply to Brown—but that
doesn't matter now, not like it used to.

"Miss Merchant," Villicus says finally. Pressing his fingertips
together, he rests his chin on the steeple they form. From the corner
of my eye, I see Teddy mimic him; he looks exactly like a praying
mantis. "You have been made privy to the punishment Miss Molly
Watso received for breaking our rules."

I nod, biting my lip hard enough to draw blood. The image
of Molly flickering last night at her cremation ceremony is all I've
been able to think about in the few hours since then. The only good
thing that came from witnessing that ceremony is that I've now
got a couple of theories as to why there's a rule to keep villagers

and Cania kids separated. My first theory is that it's got something to do with living and dying, though I'm not sure *exactly* what. The clues I have are unbelievable at best. Molly was alive in my room last night. She was flesh and bone, same old Molly, with the only difference being that her braces were gone. I have no idea how she was alive like that, but she was. And then, as Mr. Watso said, she needed to be cremated so her body and spirit could be released. As if the village itself holds some sort of reincarnation power. I get it now. The villagers have creepy powers. Creepy enough to make it necessary that they're separated from us. Why Molly would be killed, though, makes little sense to me.

My second theory is that, in fact, this is some high-end, hugely experimental psychiatric facility for kids. All the students at Cania are mental patients. Villicus is the head administrator, Teddy my very own Nurse Ratched. That even explains what Dr. Zin, a legit doctor, albeit a plastic surgeon, is doing here. We patients need to keep out of the village because villagers smoke that Devil's Apple stuff, which aggravates our fragile minds and causes hallucinations, like what I saw last night. The hard part is getting my head around the idea that *I'd* be locked up. I'm not crazy. Now that I'm out of here, I guess I'll never know which theory's at least close if not spot-on…but, wait, do you get *expelled* from mental hospitals?

"Let us proceed to your punishment," Villicus says.

"My expulsion."

Villicus and Teddy exchange a look.

"Your father worked very hard to get you into this school," Villicus says. "It has been a long time since any parent showed such tenacity and persistence. I do not recall when I last heard someone threaten my life as he did."

"I do," I say. "The man on the dock. Manish."

Villicus's eyes narrow. "Good. Confess your sins now, while you can. I assume you were with Miss Watso that night, eavesdropping."

"What does it matter? Just expel me and get it over with."

"*I* dole out the punishments, miss. Not you," Villicus says. "And your punishment is not what you expect. You are not expelled." Something in his tone makes me think I'm going to wish I were. "However, you *will* be punished. Ted?"

Standing and clearing his throat, Teddy flips open a manila envelope and reads. "In light of the school's interest in retaining the contributions of both Anne and Stanley Merchant, I do hereby recommend that the punishment for Miss Merchant, in the matter of The Molly Watso Offense, be the refusal of admission to Parents' Day for Stanley Merchant. And, for Miss Merchant, the completion of ten additional hours of club time, to be served this week."

Club time?

No Parents' Day for my dad?

"That's it?" I ask, astonished. Mental institution. Definitely. "Molly is dead, and I'm pulling extra club duties?"

"You understand," Villicus says as Teddy closes his folder, "that Miss Watso's punishment, although seemingly disproportionate to her crime, was given to protect my students. The villagers have had a long-standing pact with this school. The punishment fits the crime."

The secrecy pact. Between the villagers and, evidently, Villicus. Is he going to tell me what it's all about, why Cania would pay seemingly exorbitant amounts to keep the villagers quiet? Exhaling slowly, I try to keep my face from revealing my thoughts. Glancing at Villicus, I peer into his eyes, but it's like touching hot coals.

"The club on which you are to serve as penance for your sins is the Parents' Day committee, led by Harper Otto."

Under Harper's supervision, I spend my after-school hours on Monday making flowers out of tissue paper and my lunch hour on Tuesday creating gift bags with the other poor saps on this committee: the Model UN from Hell, Pilot, and two sopho-more girls, both of whom look exceptionally pissed off. I wonder if any of these people know what's happened to Molly or if they'd care if they did. They're all so indoctrinated by Villicus to hate the villagers, they'd probably spit on Molly's grave, if she had one.

Harper has already proven a total tyrant to work under. "Fainting Fanny, I thought you were supposed to have an artistic eye," she hisses as she tests the springiness of a ribbon I've just curled. She sweeps the whole pile of ribbon into a garbage can. "Start again. God, is it any wonder Garnet made me the lead for Art Walk?"

Oh, right, that. So it turns out that while Villicus was giv-ing me my "punishment" Monday morning, Garnet was award-ing Little Miss Texas for her attempts to draw the human form. (To look at Harper's stick-figure sketches, though, I can't help but think Garnet was awarding for Best Effort.) Harper has taken *every opportunity possible* to remind me that Garnet chose her. Un-fortunately for her, I don't care. My dad's not allowed to come to Parents' Day anymore—a fact that they wouldn't even let me tell him—so who do I have to impress? Nobody.

"Don't be mad, Merchant. With talent like mine, things like this just drop right into my lap."

"And here I thought *you* were the only thing dropping into laps."

I can almost hear her growl as her face reddens. "Everything I do, I do to win," she proclaims. "I can only hope for your sake that you're better at your PT than you are at art." With the huff of a spoiled princess, she spins on her heels, pauses to collect herself, and saunters back to her gang.

"Don't worry about Harper," Pilot whispers. "She's not all bad. She can be cool."

I glare at him.

"In that complex, hard-to-understand way," he adds.

"Sure." I eye Harper up as she swaps a tube of lip gloss with Plum. "Every time I see her twirling her hair around her finger, I think, gee, that girl sure is *complex*."

"Wow, you doing okay? You've seemed kinda pissed the last few days."

"My dad can't come to Parents' Day," I confess. I haven't wanted to talk about it. Pilot wouldn't understand if I told him about Molly, either, so what's the point in saying anything? I don't need anyone else to know I broke that rule. "It sucks. He was really looking forward to it."

"Oh," Pilot says. "I thought maybe you were still feeling bad about ditching me at the dance on Saturday."

I look up to find him smiling. "I said I was sorry. Hold a grudge much?"

"I'm kidding!" he laughs. "Anyway, it's too bad about your dad, though I admit I'm jealous. I *wish* my dad wasn't coming this weekend. The pressure he puts on me. I'm relieved when he leaves."

I pull the blade of scissors along a ribbon and produce a too-tight curl.

"That's no good!" Harper shouts at me from across the room. "This ain't rocket surgery, Merchant." Then she reaches into her pocket, pulls out a key, and marches up to me. "There's a box of pre-curled ribbons in the storage shed between the dorm buildings. Maybe you're the kind of artist who needs to copy examples. A paint-by-number type."

I take the key and leave. Retrieving the ribbons is easy enough, but I'm in no rush to get back to taking orders from the Secretary General from Hell. And standing right near the dorms with a perfectly good excuse for being there, I decide to find out what exactly I'm missing. There must be a reason I've been kept at Gigi's.

It's as silent as a tomb in the girls' dorm when I inch the oak door open and step inside. It's dark. Frosted sconces glow up and down the hall on the first floor, up the stairwell, casting more shadows than they uncover. Cautiously, I step into the foyer.

"Hello?"

No answer. I put the box of ribbons down.

The thickly glazed floor creaks underfoot, and I find myself falling into old funeral-home habits, holding my breath to counteract the creaking while I move down the hall as quietly as possible. Lined on both sides with tall fir doors on which dried flower wreaths hang, the hall leads to a luxurious common area, the only bright space in the building. Checking over my shoulder and peeking into the cracks of each open door to be sure I'm alone, I tiptoe in and let my feet sink into the dense cream rug. Three pink-crystal chandeliers are suspended from the ceiling, reflecting light off silver-framed mirrors and scattering diamonds over the plush purple lounges, over the cozy corners lush with pillows. Tall windows line the far wall, which looks out over the ocean. This common area is, by far, the prettiest room I've seen at the school—austere but girly, conservative but lush. Thrilled, I'm about to step further in when the floor above creaks. I pause, hold my breath, waiting for voices. But there's nothing.

With the heaviest sigh, I sink into a posh highback armchair that's more comfortable than it looks. On the table next to me is a stack of books. I absentmindedly grab the top one and flip through it without even glancing at its images or words, absorbed by the serenity of the room, which, the more I sit in it, feels a tad like the reception area at our funeral home, just with pillows and a heavy rug added.

As I'm about to return the book to the pile, I glimpse its title: *The Many Lives of the Girls of Cania Christy.*

Intrigued, I open the book again. It's filled with thick pages slathered in photos, stickers, poems, clippings, and small captions. Like a yearbook, but more detailed. Like a nondigital Facebook. As I flip through, I realize each page is dedicated to a girl. Plum is smiling in a school photo; little magazine photos of her on the red carpet, standing next to other Thai celebrities; magazine clippings and a newspaper article written in Thai. The next page is a senior I recognize. The next, a freshman. The next, Harper.

"Blech." I quickly flip the page.

The next is Lotus. I smile to see her; I barely knew her, but I miss her anyway. Since the moment I heard about her expulsion, I've had a sick feeling. That feeling's only grown worse.

Suddenly, there are voices down the hall. Thinking fast, I close the book and stuff it up my shirt, determined to read it in detail later if only to better know my enemies. I tuck my shirt into my skirt, button my blazer, and creep to the doorway to listen. As the girls walk up the stairs together, I skulk down the hall, grab the box of ribbons, and head across campus. One step closer to living a new twist on my PT: uncovering the secrets of the students of Cania Christy.

fifteen

THE SCULPTOR

"TODAY, YOU BECOME SCULPTORS," WEINCHLER AN-
nounces.

On cue, Ben pulls the dust cloth off a cart filled with oyster-
colored blocks of clay. I haven't seen him since he and Garnet
basically shoved me out of the library on Sunday—even if he did
later sneak into my room to leave that Machiavelli book there—
and I'm feeling strange about him. I'm feeling strange about everyone. But it's different with Ben, knowing what I know about
his relationship with a teacher.

"I will put you in pairs—don't complain—and you will take
turns experiencing the faces of each other," Weinchler explains.
"Next class, you'll start sculpting busts. I am certain you will disap-
point me, but, nonetheless, we must put ourselves through the exercise." He pulls a list out of a binder and peers at it from the bottom
of his eyes. "I've divided you into pairs alphabetically."

As long as I don't get stuck with Harper, I can survive this
assignment. All afternoon, I've been walking around with the
scrapbook I stole from the girls' dorm in my backpack, and I
have a feeling she's going to suspect something's up. I mentally work through the students with last names close to mine:

Tallulah Josey, me, Mark Norbussman, Harper Otto. So either
Tallulah (ugh) or Mark (cool) will be my partner.

Weinchler reaches my part of the list. "Angela, you're with
Tallulah. Anne, you're with Mark."

Yes!

Ben leans into Weinchler and whispers in his ear.

"Yes, good, excellent," Weinchler replies to Ben before turning to me. "Anne, Mr. Zin has just pointed out that Mark is at a
meeting with his Guardian."

I feel the blood drain from my face. The next on the list is
Harper.

"But Mr. Zin is willing to stand in as your partner."

Surprised at the turn of events, I nod, but a wave of dread
comes over me so powerfully I think I might be sick. Paired with
Ben? *Seriously?* Sure, there are good parts to this. Now I can ask
Ben why he stole into my room. That, and I can, like, touch his
face for half of the class. But let's not forget the bad stuff! One, his
sordid affair. Two, my crooked tooth. The exposure! The vulnerability! I have to put myself in his hands, literally, knowing every
one of my flaws will come shining through. *Ev-er-y one of them.*
And I've seen his work, so I know how eidetic he can be.

I swallow down my anxiety.

The chair next to Ben squeals like a cat with its tail caught as
I pull it in. Around us, the rest of the students shuffle noisily as
Weinchler tells us to sit down, stop talking.

Ben doesn't seem to know that I know what's up with him
and Garnet. He's as casual as I've seen him, as casual as a decidedly formal guy like Ben can get.

"I figured I'd go first," he says. "Sound okay?"

I nod, but I feel awkward. I crane my neck to move my face
closer to his hands. I'm reminded, looking at him this close, of
my comment the other night on the mountain, when I told him
he was perfect. And his response—his cold response. It helps me

build a virtual wall now, a wall that will keep him out and keep me safely in. I tell myself Ben has an amazing capacity to be a complete jerk when I'm at my most vulnerable. Forget him.

With a sigh, he braces my face—his hands are warm—and looks into my eyes. "Will you relax? I've done this before. Let *me* lead."

"We'll see how comfortable you are when I'm squishing my hands against your face."

He grins. That grin threatens the structural integrity of the wall I'm trying to build. "Your skin feels very malleable, if it's any consolation."

"Thanks. I think."

I close my eyes and breathe in the scent of his hands— *Wonderful!* No, wait. I'm not allowed to think that way. I need to take a chill pill and convince myself Ben is…I dunno, some sort of gremlin or serial killer or something else I should run far, far away from. But it's like my skin is one of those blue plasma balls you see in science shops: the moment his fingers touch me, cell-sized explosions go off under my flesh and sensations like tiny, bright electric currents race all over me. His fingertips trace my face—the cheekbones I'm finally growing into, the lips I hope steal attention from my crooked tooth—before running under my hair, where his touch becomes firmer, like a massage. He's done this before. And I'm eating it up. Which I must put an immediate stop to. Build that wall.

"So I have a question for you," I say, my eyes still closed. I feel his fingertips hesitate on my skin before proceeding.

"Are you sure you want to ask here? If I recall correctly, you tend to jump right to the hardest questions."

"Why would Molly choose death over attending Cania?"

"Like I was saying."

My eyes flit open. He's staring at me, unimpressed, with an eyebrow arched. For a moment, we just eye each other. And then he deliberately slides his thumbs over my eyelids, and I'm in darkness once again.

"Nothing relaxes me like sculpting," he says, keeping his voice low so no one can hear. "From exploring my muse just like this to shaping the clay. It's the only way to forget everything."

"What's to forget?"

"Exactly what I just said. *Everything.*"

Weinchler shouts something at a pair of students who are arguing loudly.

"So," Ben continues, "did you get the book?"

"You mean the one you left on my bed? After breaking in?" I roll my eyes, but they're closed, so the effect is lost.

"You broke into my place first." His fingers rest on my lips now. "Did you read it?"

He pulls his hands back. I open my eyes.

"Not yet. I've been slightly preoccupied by the recent death of my friend."

"And yet you're still here."

"What do you mean by that?"

"Surely you've wondered why Villicus let you stay, Anne," he says.

"Do you wish he'd expelled me?"

His palms are pressed against my cheeks. "I think you know I'd like to be your friend."

I scoff. I certainly did not know that.

"I've tried not to be, of course," he concedes. "I've been *warned* not to be. But you are surprisingly hard to stay away from."

"Because I'm your neighbor?"

"Sure. That's why."

I press my lips firmly together to keep from smiling. After all, moments of happiness with Ben inevitably lead to a typhoon-speed downward spiral of uncertainty and self-loathing. No use getting my hopes up, even if he's suggesting what he seems to be.

"Because I remind you of your sister," I offer as an alternative to the more exciting reason. "I'm sorry she passed away. And your mom, too. They looked like really nice people in the photos I saw. You guys looked happy."

I can't help but wonder—pulling on my Psych 101 hat—if our mutual losses aren't part of what draws us together. Certainly I'm drawn to Ben because he's gorgeous, untouchable, and artistic, but there's more connecting us, something deeper. Something I felt from the moment I saw him outside Villicus's office. Something I may have felt long before I ever met him—as if we knew each other in another life. For God knows why, Ben just *makes sense* when he rides his Ducati around the island by himself or stands forlorn in a window. Even his relationship with a teacher, something doomed from day one, makes a small bit of sense. The same thing that separates me from everyone else here—a life lived in the shadows, darkened by an unhealthy familiarity with death—separates him, too.

"If you don't mind, how long ago did they pass on?"

It couldn't have been more than a year ago, given how old he and his sister looked in their Christmas photos. Though why she was smiling over a Taylor Swift CD from years ago, I can't figure out. His hands move to my neck, his fingers tracing my jawline and sending shivers over my body.

"A little over five years ago," he answers.

Bit by bit, ever so gradually, as if any movement might disturb us, I open my eyes only to find Ben's closed. As he looks now—peaceful, with his distractingly gorgeous eyes closed—he reminds me of someone I can't quite place.

"But, Ben," I say, "she looked nearly fifteen in the photo. And you looked like you do now. How could she have passed away five years ago? She would have been ten."

Ben opens his eyes. He says nothing but pulls his hands from my face and looks at them as if they're different now. Running them through his precisely tousled hair, he breathes deeply.

"She was actually thirteen in that photo. And thirteen when she died."

"Five years ago? But weren't you older than she was?"

"Yes. I was sixteen in that photo."

A clap at the back of the room startles us both.

"You are all terrible, horrible sculptors!" Weinchler shouts, storming to the front of the room. His outburst is made uglier by the fact that no one has even started sculpting yet, so how could he know? Ornery old bat. "You need additional reading assignments, so everybody back to your desks and open your text to chapter four."

I pull away from Ben—but, in a flash, he reaches for my hands. I don't know why. To try to explain?

"I don't understand, Ben," I say. "It doesn't add up. How old are you?"

He hushes me by fixing his intense gaze on me. As I think he's about to share something, he slides his hands over my wrists, stopping just under my cardigan sleeve. His eyes, pained, hold mine as he gently strokes the tender undersides of my wrists, where my pulse races, giving me away to him but to no one else—no one in the room could even see him holding me from this angle. His fingertips stay just at the edges of my cuff, just far enough under my sweater to be…more than familiar.

My smile vanishes. I scan his face as he lifts my hand to caress his cheek.

"Is it coming back to you?" he asks.

"I'm not sure what you mean," I stammer.

"*Me*," he says. "I thought you might have recognized the drawing I showed you the other night, when we were standing at the window. But you still don't know, do you?"

And then he pulls away, looking bashful, and Weinchler shoos me back to my desk, where I try to catch my breath.

Wintery winds blast my face, still tingling from Ben's touch, when I shove open the building door after class to head to yet *another* Social Committee meeting. My heart is racing so fast that my head can't keep up. Class today was the first time I've talked with Ben without the whole thing ending in intense frustration for me. If I didn't already know about Garnet, I might even believe that Ben was starting to feel something for me. But he's not. So I'll settle for friendship, which doesn't really feel like settling.

As I hurriedly button my coat as high as it will go and bury my smile in my collar, I zero in on Pilot crossing the field with the girl with the bobbed hair. Noticing me, he waves her good-bye and heads straight for me, his grin brightening his face. I watch him jog my way. He's all boy, through and through. Not complicated whatsoever.

"It's cold." The white of my breath puffs in front of me until the fog consumes it.

"Not a fan of winter?"

"It's barely fall. Who's that girl you were talking to? I've seen her around."

"Who, Hiltop?"

"Hill-top? That's her name?"

He chuckles. "She's Austrian. She can't help what her parents named her."

As we walk to our meeting, I find myself lost in thought—Ben thoughts—while Pilot chatters idly. I laugh with him every so often, nod, say "Uh-huh" and "Oh, really?" and other meaningless phrases that are enough to feign engagement—to cover the obsession my brain and body have with Ben—until finally we're at Goethe Hall and Pilot's opening the door.

"Another thrilling Social Committee meeting, m'lady." He adds a flourish of his hand.

Curtsying, I smile up at him. "Why, thank you," I offer in my best Southern accent.

"Wait—wow." He suddenly pushes his hand against my chest so he can look at me better. But he's keeping me in the blustery winds.

"Pilot, what the hell? It's freezing out." I swat him and walk into the foyer, watching his face, expecting a joke. "What?"

"*You.*"

I flinch. "Me? Nice. Thanks."

"No, really." He's pointing at my mouth.

Backing away on instinct, I raise my hands in defense. "What are you doing? You're freaking me out."

"*You're* freaking *me* out." He really looks freaked out, too. His fingers stretch toward my face.

"What's wrong? Stop it," I demand.

"It looks fantastic. You look really great," he breathes, peering closer. "I knew there was something different about you."

"What are you talking about?" I smack at his hand as his fingers brush my lips. "Stop touching my mouth."

"Smile for me."

"What? No."

"Smile, Annie. You'll like it."

"Are you crazy?" Now I'm starting to get freaked. "Is there something wrong?"

Panicked, I run my tongue along my teeth, fearing I've lost one. That would be even worse than having a crooked tooth—having a big gaping hole in my smile like some sort of backwoods yokel.

Then I run my tongue over my teeth again.

"What on earth?" I breathe.

For as long as I can remember, I've felt one bump when my tongue moves over my teeth. One bump that represents my jagged tooth, my most nagging imperfection.

That bump is gone. My teeth are smoothly, perfectly aligned.
A smile lights Pilot's face. "Do you feel different?"

With my mind racing, I just shake my head.

"Well, something's changed. What happened to you?"

That's a great question: What did happen? How did it happen?

"What classes did you have today?" he asks.

"Why? What does that matter?"

"Did you touch anybody? Did you pass out again?"

I frown. "And, what, smash my tooth on the floor? Knock it
straight?"

"I just—"

"Stop talking!" I exclaim and press my hands to my ears,
squeezing my eyes shut. "I need to think." I hear my voice inside
my head. I hear a million things inside my head. Then, opening
my eyes, I lower my hands from my ears. Pilot is still smiling. "I
had sculpting class," I whisper. "I was paired with Ben."

"Well, Ben *is* a remarkable sculptor."

Could that be it? Pilot's joking, but could there be some truth
to it? Could Ben have resculpted my teeth? *Impossible.*

"I'm serious," I say.

Panic sets in. Is Ben some sort of witch dentist? No, it can't
be. This must just be another hallucination—but then why is Pilot
seeing it, too? It's *real*. This actually happened. Does that mean
what happened with Molly the other night is real, too? I stumble
back against the wall; the foyer is spinning. To keep from passing
out in front of Pilot, in front of the few others now walking by, I
shove through the doors and break into a sprint.

"Wait!" he calls after me.

"I'm not going to that stupid club today," I shout back. The
idea of taking orders from Harper for the rest of the afternoon is
unbearable.

He quickly catches up. "That's cool. I won't go either."

"You'll get in trouble."

"Hello? I don't care about that, Anne," he says. "I'm going wherever you're going."

The problem is that I don't know where I'm going. My mind is in tatters. My tongue has been stroking my tooth repeatedly, and I'm finding myself torn between loving the idea of having a flawless new smile and hating the idea that Ben simply took the liberty of *fixing* me. How he managed to do it is another question entirely. That he did it at all, that's what's plaguing me as I race Pilot away from campus.

"I need a doctor or a dentist," I say, panting. "Do you know any?"

"Dr. Zin," he says. I glower at him. "Anne, the village is empty. No one here ever seems to get sick." He shakes his head and throws his hands in the air. "There's no one that can help you. I'm sorry."

The skies open above us as we stand on the road to the village. I'd be a fool to go back there anyway, considering what happened to Molly when we broke the rule.

"I just want answers," I say, a sob escaping my lips.

Softly, Pilot nods and pulls me to him. I'm surprised at how quickly I cling to his warm, muscular body and how tightly I hold him. I can't help but wonder why—*why!*—just when things were going well with Ben did he have to prove, once and for all, that I'm not good enough for him, that I'll never be good enough for him? Pilot would *never* do that to me.

"Sometimes there are no answers," Pilot offers as a consolation. "What if you stopped torturing yourself with so much looking? What if you just accepted that, although things don't make sense in a traditional way, everything's fine and your life here can be wonderful?"

Nodding, I back away and take Pilot's hands in mine, smiling at him through the rain. "It could be wonderful," I agree, sniffling. "You're right."

If I'd accept Pilot's affections instead of resisting and seeking something that truly moves me, I'm sure life here would be a breeze.

As I work to convince myself of this, I glance down at our hands in the rain and notice they seem melded somehow. Meshed. But not in that romantic way you read about in romances. The edges of his hands are plainly blurred around mine, like the lightness surrounding blotches of paint in a watercolor. I squint and he notices.

Grimacing, he pulls his hands away and stuffs them into his pockets.

sixteen

THE MANY LIVES OF
THE GIRLS OF CANIA CHRISTY

WITH THE NUMBER OF CANDLES BURNING IN MY ROOM, you'd think I was holding a séance or re-creating the Festival of Fire and Life. But I am doing neither. It's been a long, hard day—wait, who am I kidding? It's been an endless, *anguish*-filled couple of weeks, with new homes, new schools, friends made and lost, more punishments than I've ever received in my life, and the cruelest sort of kindness from a boy I should never have looked at twice. It'd be traumatic for anyone.

So I've done what any warm-blooded American girl would do. I've gathered every candle I could find, put a depressing CD on a stereo I've hauled up from the living room, replaced my school uniform with comfy sweats, and curled up in bed with a book. Not just any book. The scrapbook I swiped from the dorms earlier.

I trace my fingertips over its title: *The Many Lives of the Girls of Cania Christy.*

The cottage is quiet. The lights are out. Gigi already shouted her goodnight to me, and Teddy left my room after his final assessment of the night ten minutes ago. Even Skippy has stopped

198

yipping and settled on Gigi's big brass bed. It's so quiet, you can almost hear the cover of the scrapbook creak when I open it.

Inside, I see the same photos, scraps, and stickers I saw at lunchtime. Plum singing. Lotus smiling; I pause again on her page, taking time to read a newspaper clipping pasted under her freshman-year school photo:

Kidnapping Turns Tragic

The body of Lotus Jane Featherly, daughter of Lord Marshall Featherly, was recovered early this morning from the Thames, just six days after Miss Featherly was abducted from her London mansion.

Confused, I turn the page and see Tallulah Josey smiling at me. A note card that looks like a party invitation is placed to the right of her photo; I open it to discover that it's no party invitation. I should have recognized it instantly. I've helped my dad fold thousands of these.

"A funeral program."

Hiltop P. Shemese is next, but her page is empty. There's just a photo of her in uniform, smiling softly. No stories, no clippings, no photos of a past life.

Agniezska is a few pages down. Bright, colorful photos of her in *The Nutcracker* and *Swan Lake*. She's breathtaking—a little too thin, but stunning onstage. I'd feel a twinge of jealousy if I didn't quickly spy a magazine clipping with the headline, "Anorexia Claims Prima Ballerina Agniezska Kytian, Dead at 70 Pounds." In the story, Agniezska's mother-slash-manager is referenced as pushing her daughter to the brink, forcing her to be thin at all costs.

I flip back to Plum's page. There, I see newspaper clippings in Thai layered over photos of her rushing through throngs of fans, bodyguards all around. Everything is in Thai, so I can't read the details. One of the photos speaks plainly to me, though: Plum and a much older man, sprawled across a velvety chaise longue, champagne bottles and glasses smashed around them, a powder-covered mirror on the table. It's her and her dad's friend. It's the scene she described taking place before she came to Cania.

A candle flickers next to my bed. My breathing halts.

I flip to Harper's page. In her largest photo, she looks depressed. She has acne. She weighs at least twice as much as she currently does. Her hair is stringier, not at all the silky red hair I envy today. I can't breathe as my eyes dart over the many clippings on her page and land on the label of a pill bottle—a prescription for Vicodin. And then on a note card with a speech on it, the number 4, presumably the fourth card of the speech, at the top:

> *What can we make of my baby girl's last moments? We might look at the lasso she'd tied around the neck of Misty, my wife's prize stallion, and we might assume she had ill intent. Did she think she could strangle Misty? Did she feel so voiceless in her own home or so desperate for the thing she wanted most—not the pink Hummer, but my attention—that she was brought to such a lowly state? I'll never know. All her stepmother and I will have is the vision of finding her the next morning, on our return from the city, with that unfathomable gash on her head where Misty kicked her.*

The card ends there.

The hairs on my arms and the back of my neck are standing at attention. A shudder has been running up and down my spine repeatedly since I read Lotus's clipping, running like a car on a never-ending roller coaster. I don't know how many more death announcements, eulogies, and funeral programs I read. I don't know if I close the book or not. I don't know anything. The one thought I have hasn't quite reached me yet. It moves through the darkness of my room slowly, deliberately, like the Grim Reaper wading through a sludgy pond to reach me, like he's been wading toward me for days, has jerked his way up the stairs, and is finally here, his slender, long arms extending toward me. I want to back away from him, from my one unavoidable thought, but he keeps approaching, nearer and nearer until I'm in his cold, wet grasp.

It can't be.

Breaking the silence is a knock at my door; startled, I scream *loud*. I hear my door swing open, and I know Teddy's rushing up the stairs, so I stuff the book under my duvet and do my best not to look as *fucking crazy* as I suddenly feel. I can't handle him being here. I need to be alone. To think.

Because it can't be. What the scrapbook was telling me can't be true.

"What?" I shout at him. "Teddy, get out of my room!"

"Don't talk to me that way."

"Get out!"

"Why did you scream?"

"Get *out*!"

"Have these candles been burning all night?" he demands. I glance at the clock. I've been sitting in stunned silence for hours. "You're going to start a fire."

Fine by me. I'll start a fire. I'll burn this whole place to the ground and it won't matter. *Because.* I can't finish the thought. Teddy goes from candle to candle, puffing each one out and taking his time as he does it.

"Please leave," I beg.

"With your attitude," he says as he walks back to the stairwell in the darkness, "you're never going to be valedictorian."

Valedictorian? As if that matters!

"Can you *please* leave now?" I implore through gritted teeth.

"Not until you lie down."

I throw myself down on the bed. "Now?"

There's a creak on the stairs. The door clicks closed. I'm alone again, in the dark, with this book of death in my quivering grip.

In the time it took for Teddy to blow out all the candles in my room, the thought—that one thought—has made its way into my mind. That doesn't mean it's *sunk* in yet, but I've realized it.

The perfect-looking students at Cania. So angelically untouched by acne, fat, and everything else normal teenagers endure.

The tuition. Only for an *extraordinary* purpose would people like Manish beg and offer anything to get their children into this place.

The isolation from the rest of the world. We are all alone here. No visitors allowed. Only the villagers are here with us, and they've made a pact with Villicus, they've been bribed into secrecy. Secrecy about something hugely valuable. Something that's so clear to me now, so horrifyingly clear.

Molly died. But she was in my room, in the flesh, that night; and she was in her mother's arms that night. It wasn't until a body—her body—wrapped in cloth, was cremated and, as her grandpa said, her spirit was freed that she disappeared.

She was dead. And yet she lived again. On this island.

Lotus died, too. So did Harper, Plum, Agniezska, Tallulah—everybody at Cania Christy. Augusto went off a cliff before he came here; was it a skiing accident? Emo Boy leapt onto that dancer's cage and ended up at the hospital; could he have gone to the morgue? Pilot tried unsuccessfully to rescue a girl from a house fire; could he have died in that very fire? Could it be?

It must be. Every other half-ass theory I've had fails to piece together like this one does. It must be.

Every single student at Cania Christy is dead.

"But…But wai…" I don't want to think about what comes next. But it's too late. My brain rushes there instantly. And what I realize next hits me with a powerful *whoosh* that plasters me against my bed.

Every single student at Cania Christy is dead. And so am I.

seventeen

DEATH AND THE MAIDEN

"ANNIE, YOU LOOK REALLY TERRIBLE," PILOT SAYS FOR the eight-hundredth time today.

He has no idea what I know or why I look at him so strangely, like I'm seeing him for the first time every time.

"I can't believe you're still pissed at Ben. Your smile looks awesome. I'm no big fan of the Zinanator, but you should thank him."

You're dead, I think, staring at him, knowing I have enormous rings around my eyes from the most sleepless, unimaginable night ever, a night spent fixating on my new reality. *I'm at a school for dead kids.*

But I can't say that. Not to Pilot. Not to anyone.

All day, my mind has turned over so many possibilities, I've barely noticed a thing going on around me—and yet, at the same time, I've noticed everything. Their translucent skin. Their flawlessness. I spent ten minutes in the cafeteria today just staring unabashedly at a skinny freshman with bright blue eyes and long blonde hair, a perfect angel without the wings. I watched her move. Wondered how she got here, how she died. The scrapbook she's probably in is under my pillow at home, but I didn't pay any attention to her last night. I was too caught up in the death stories of the people I know here.

I've spent the day wondering if this is purgatory. Or Hell. Or Heaven.

I've wondered how exactly I died. Because I can't remember. Is that normal, to be unable to remember how you die? Is that why they made that scrapbook, why they clipped those stories and pasted in pieces of their eulogies?

I've wondered if my dad's dead, too. How else did I talk with him on the phone? And am I still on earth? I must be. The parents are all coming this weekend. Surely they're not dead, too. Surely that's not how Heaven works: kids die, parents die, and only on select weekends are they allowed to see one another.

I've wondered if the other kids know they're dead, hence the need to keep villager kids separate from Cania kids. But if they don't, how could one explain the scrapbook? I can't. They all know they're dead—199 students are allowed to know they're dead…and I'm the only exception.

Correction: I was the only exception.

Why me? Why shouldn't I know?

Most of all, I've wondered if I'm crazy. I'm *alive*. I feel it. Pilot's alive. I feel it when I smack at him as he makes some idiotic face that's supposed to be an imitation of me pissed off. He's flesh and bone and blood and brains, just like me. He's heart and soul and *life*. Just like me.

And I have a new zit today! *Ha!* Take that, Death.

I'm torn between believing my hunch and believing my eyes. If I believe my hunch, this must be Heaven, in spite of Harper's presence. If I believe my eyes…

"Have you even seen Ben today?" Pilot asks me. He's stuffing gift bags with tissue flowers as we sit on a tabletop at the Parents' Day meeting after school. "You could always ask him if he's, like, a magician or something."

I'm trying to refocus on the conversation. I've been observing Pilot more than I've been listening. It's like déjà vu. I remember watching him, not listening to him, last week on the beach, when he asked me to the dance, back when I was still blissfully ignorant. That morning, we sat near a family of sea lions; they didn't notice us because animals don't notice spirits. Except for dogs, which yelp at them—like Skippy does every time I come around. He also yelps at Teddy. But he doesn't yelp at Gigi. So does that mean Teddy's dead, too? And Gigi's alive?

When did all the others find out they were dead? A week after their arrival? Two weeks? Is there some test going on here that I'm not passing, something I should be doing to prove I'm *allowed* to know that I'm *dead?* Does everyone know that I don't know? That must be why I'm at Gigi's. Because if I lived at the dorms, I surely would've found out last week. It took me about two minutes in the dorms to find the scrapbook. And one minute of reading it to *get* it.

"Earth to Annie?" Pilot sings. "*Ben*. You know, Ben Zin? The guy who changed your teeth? Your neighbor."

"What about him?"

"Have you asked him what happened?"

I haven't wanted to think about Ben. When I caught him looking at me in the hallway this morning, I immediately headed for the girls' bathroom. For some reason, the idea of Ben not being *real* makes my brain want to shut down, to block it out, even more than I want to hide from the fact that Pilot, Harper—everybody else—are deceased, are physical manifestations nothing like you'd expect of spirits, but spirits nonetheless. Fleshy spirits. Of all the questions that have entered my mind, Ben's life status is the one I promptly shut out.

Naturally, I have millions of questions about my own death. Why don't I remember dying? The best explanation—the sane explanation—is that I'm making all of this up. That I'm not dead. Nobody is. That book I found was just a morbid joke a bunch of rich bitches put together; Hiltop's page was empty, probably because she knows such a joke would be in very poor taste. Molly's cremation was just the hallucination of a girl with a family history of mental illness and the recent secondhand-smoking of some Devil's Apple.

"No," I finally say to Pilot, glancing at Harper and her gang, who are obviously whispering about the two of us while they frame Parents' Day signs in glitter. "I haven't talked to him."

I've spent all day biting my tongue and hiding my expressions during moments of intense realization, moments when I wanted to scream loud and hard and tear out of whatever room I'm in. Walking through the hallways and bumping into kids, knowing they're all dead. This, what I'm about to ask Pilot, is the closest I've come to speaking of what I suspect—what I'm not certain of, but what I suspect.

"Annie." He holds two tissue flowers to his chest and smiles. "Look. I'm a late bloomer."

That act alone stops the wheels in my mind from turning. Why did this perfectly nice, fun guy have to die? He said he got here last year, so he died when he was just fifteen? Feeling my lip start to quiver, I bite down and taste blood. We have blood. Why the need for blood? Why the need for sleep? Maybe we're not dead at all. Maybe I really am just going crazy.

Mental diseases are genetic, after all.

What's more likely? That I'm at a school for dead kids...or that I'm afflicted with a disease I'm in denial about, a disease similar to the one my mother coped with?

That's it. That's got to be it. I'm losing my mind.

"Never mind," I say, swatting the flowers from his hands with a smile.

"Hey, you lovebirds," Harper calls to us. "More work. Less flirting."

Pilot and I both blush.

It's devastating to know that my mind is already slipping away from me, but at least that means everyone here is still alive. The idea sends a wave of relief over me, a wave that carries me toward Parents' Day that very Saturday.

No, we're not dead.

Dead kids can't stand in uniform out in the quad, shivering with the cool breeze whipping off the Atlantic, waiting for their parents to arrive on a yacht we can see making its way up the island. And dead kids can't slouch on the stools next to their sketches and watch as Dr. Zin and Ben stroll side by side, taking in the various displays.

"Why are you even here, Fainting Fanny?" Harper scowls as she takes her place at the entrance to the Art Walk. "Your dad's not coming. And your sketches suck."

Garnet approaches us, and Harper's attitude abruptly changes.

"Harper," Garnet says, "good work on organizing Parents' Day."

For a split second, Garnet darts a glance in my direction, and I wonder for the hundredth time if she made Harper the Art Walk lead as a warning to me, now that I know about her relationship with Ben. She's telling me to keep quiet or she could easily destroy my life here. I get it—message received, loud and clear. I'm not saying a word. And with the scare I gave myself this week, I almost don't care about Garnet and Ben; my mind obviously needs to focus on fewer things—to stay healthy—which means there's no room for boys, especially confusing boys tied up in affairs with teachers.

"I'm sorry to hear your father won't be joining us, Anne," Garnet says. Her expression is sincerely sorrowful. "I can only imagine how heartbreaking that must be for him."

As Dr. Zin and Ben near, I watch Garnet's gaze chase after Ben, who's pretending to admire the sketches but whose gaze returns to her again and again. They're obviously in love. And I don't care. Nope, just a healthy, clean frame of mind for me— no Bens allowed. Even when he ignores my sketches and stands alongside Garnet, who whispers in his ear, I refuse to care. That said, I still want some answers about what he did to my teeth. He's not getting off that easily. If he can answer that question, then I'll ask him about the troubling math problem that is how he could have been sixteen when his sister passed away five years ago.

"Ben!" I call.

Both Ben and Garnet turn coolly in my direction.

"What is it?" he asks. His tone is unmistakably icy.

"I have something I need to ask you."

Flicking a glance at Garnet, he sighs and walks over. But before I can get a word out, he's leaning in and doing one of those loud-whisper things Harper does, where everyone in a ten-foot vicinity can hear.

"Sorry if you're confused, Anne," he says, "but I am *not* your friend. Got it?"

Then he sweeps away. Garnet follows him.

Humiliated, I tell myself no one can see my chest heaving. Surely no one's looking. But, no, they're *all* looking, from Harper to Dr. Zin to Augusto, who's sitting next to me on the other side. Harper smirks. Augusto drops his eyes.

"Miss Merchant," Dr. Zin says, taking this awkward moment to view my work. "Perhaps you would be heading this art show if you spent more time on your craft and less breaking into people's homes." And then he walks away.

Great.

Keep it together. Everyone's a jerk because of the Big V competition. Chill. Don't start crying—if you cry, so help me, Anne...

A foghorn blows out on the water. Within minutes, the yacht has docked and parents are rushing off, bounding up the white staircase from the campus dock to the quad. The Glee Club, led by Pilot and Plum, begins singing the school anthem, backed by the Horn Club and Handbell Club. As the parents reach the quad, they glimpse their children at this display or that and rush to their sides, throwing their arms around them and weeping madly. I can't help but notice that they're all overreacting almost as much as my dad did on the phone with me. Both Harper and Augusto, who are on either side of me, jump to their feet and let themselves fall into the embraces of their adoring parents.

"Heading up the Art Walk!" Harper's dad exclaims. "You're a shoe in for valedictorian if you keep this up." Even her step-monster gushes over how lovely she looks, how beautiful her sketches are, how desperately they miss her back in Texas. Harper eats it up.

Augusto's parents are worse. In spite of myself, I stare at them as they sob, sniffle, and drool over each other. There's something familiar about all the parents. Something in their expression I recognize but can't place.

"Next fall, *mon vieux*, you will be leading Art Walk," his mother, a squat Quebecker, says as his father blows his nose with a silky handkerchief. "It will be a splendid senior year."

"I tried." Augusto's face crumples. With another meaningful sigh, they all embrace again.

And here I stand. Alone. Shivering in the wind, rubbing my arms, trying to look unfazed, and suddenly missing my dad as if I haven't seen him in years instead of just two weeks.

"Little orphan Annie?"

Glancing over, I see Pilot and his dad, Dave Stone, looking every bit the politician, walking my way. Blinking away tears and hoping my eyes aren't red, I muster a warm smile.

"Dad, this is her," Pilot beams.

"Miss Merchant," Dave says, extending his hand to me. "I see Stanley's little girl isn't so little anymore."

"Nice to meet you." I shake his hand quickly.

The way Dave's gaze washes over me in my uniform, I can't help but feel exposed, dressed up like a common fetish in front of a sleazy politician. The tip of his tongue rolls over his bottom lip, his eyes linger on my low vest and then slide up my neck, over my lips, to my eyes. I dart a glance at Pilot, wondering if he's picking up on his father's wandering eyes, but he seems happily unaware. Given what he's confessed about Dave being disappointed in him, I wouldn't be surprised if Pilot felt honored to know the girl he took to the dance was being ogled by his dad. Anything to impress the old man.

"It looks like your time here so far has helped," Dave says. "The exercise alone is putting a lovely color in your cheeks."

"Oh," I mumble, confused by his comment.

"Will we see you later? Perhaps after the symposium in Valedictorian Hall?"

The symposium is only open to parents. After it, there's a whole day of activities planned, activities I'm supposed to participate in even though my dad's not here. But suddenly, I don't want to participate. Suddenly, I want to run home, dig the scrapbook out from under my mattress, and pore over it again. I've refused to look at it since convincing myself that nobody is dead, after all—that my mind is to blame for everything that's so bonkers around here. But what Dave said, that the exercise has put color in my cheeks, struck me as more than odd. As if he saw me without color in my cheeks.

What kind of people have colorless faces?

The kind of people who sit on my dad's cold steel table with embalming fluid running through their veins.

I need to read *The Many Lives of the Girls of Cania Christy* again.

Senator Stone takes one last look at my legs before heading off to the symposium in Valedictorian Hall. Without a moment to lose, I'm gone, racing back to Gigi's.

eighteen

THE QUICK AND THE DEAD

THERE ARE FIVE STAGES OF GRIEF THAT MY DAD EX-plains to every mourner who enters our home. I've heard them a million times. The first stage is denial. I'm pretty sure that's what I've been in all week: denial. Because the moment my fingers brush the cover of *The Many Lives of the Girls of Cania Christy*, I know for a fact that I am dead and so are they. There are hundreds of things I don't understand about this new reality of mine, this state of existence no doctor can diagnose and no words can describe, but I know for a fact that it is very, very real.

What drives it home? The expression I recognized on all the parents' faces. I *knew* I'd seen it before. And I had. On the faces of all the mourners I've painted through the years. That grief-stricken gaze was just mixed with something today. With shock, disbelief, fear, and desperation.

Next, I can expect anger. And then bargaining. Depression. Acceptance. Not sure when those kick in. Maybe they won't happen at all. Maybe grieving is different for dead people. Surely the rules of grief don't apply here. No rules apply here but gravity and whatever Villicus makes up. Tucking the scrapbook into my bag, I race down the attic stairs and almost make it through the kitchen, on my way out the back door, when I see Gigi slouched at the table, weeping into a glass of water. Scratch that—the slouch of her eyelids means it's vodka, not water. I stop short and stare at her, instantly infuriated.

"Are you alive?" I demand. My voice is sterner than I'd expected it to be, which must mean anger is setting in. I'm ready for answers now. I know what's going on, and it's time everyone fessed up.

She sobs. "I miss Molly."

"You didn't even know her. Are you alive, Gigi? Answer me."

"Everyone's leaving, but someone has to stay. Watso has to stay. I have to stay. We made a pact. Villicus will take back everything if we flee." Staring up at me, mascara running down her face, Gigi blinks, sniffles, looks like a sleepy barn owl. "Every day, we invite him back to the island, calling him here by name. Every day, we keep his secrets for him."

"You're not making sense."

"But it was our island before he came here. The perfect location. A forgotten island in the wealthiest country in the world. My grandfather wrote the treaty with Villicus when he got here just after the war ended. Did you know that? He showed up when Germany surrendered," she slurs. "There was a battle on our shores, where the navy was stationed. The soldiers died. And my own mother was killed—she was just a child. Then Villicus helped her. It was his foot in the door, you see. Her death was the beginning of his reign here. No one's supposed to know that, but now you do."

"That's impossible. That would make Villicus, like, a million years old."

"No, not a million. But older than he looks." She finishes her vodka with a loud gulp.

"You're drunk."

"I should never have taken you in," she whimpers. And then another round of sobs bursts out of her in short gasps. "But I was so desperate for the money, to save enough to help others off this island and out of his grip. I had to take you. Villicus needed a place to put you. He wanted you so badly."

Up until this moment, I've been gritting my teeth, frustrated with this drunken old woman I've never liked, frustrated that she's keeping me from returning to campus for answers.

But now. Now I'm interested. Let the interrogation begin.

"What do you mean, Villicus *wanted* me, Gigi?"

"I can't tell you."

"You can do anything you want to."

"I can't. Villicus owns my tongue, just like he owns everyone and everything else here."

"No man can own another."

"Keep telling yourself that, kid."

"So you're just going to keep his secrets? Look around you," I hiss. "Whatever reason you had for keeping anything secret, it's gone. Dead. What do you have to lose? You said it yourself. It's over."

"You don't have any idea. He's beyond powerful."

"Why did he want me, Gigi?"

"I can't—"

"Why did Villicus want *me*?"

Her mouth opens like she's about to confess everything. But her eyes zoom in on Teddy racing by the kitchen windows to the back door, which he throws wide open.

"What's going on in here?" he exclaims. His appearance at exactly the most inconvenient moments is starting to alarm me. Who the hell is Teddy? "Gigi, what are you saying to this girl?"

The ice in her glass clinks as she trembles. Her watery, terrified eyes roll over my face.

"Nothing," I say dismissively. "Just the idiotic blathering of a pathetic old drunk."

Villicus has a purpose for me here, and I need to know what it is. But first, I have to get this damn book back into the dorm common area before someone notices it's missing. Breaking in is easy—the door's open—but breaking out is more challenging. Because a Texan who looks angry enough to breathe fire out her nose is glaring in the dorm foyer as I try to leave.

"What are you doing?" Harper demands. "Plowing up snakes?"

The good news is she has no idea what I'm doing. I've already returned the book, so, unless she finds it and dusts it for fingerprints—unlikely—I'm in the clear.

"What do you care?" I ask, stalking out the door. She races after me and pulls at my arm.

"What are you trying to do?"

"I'm not trying to *do* anything," I say coolly, glaring. "What are *you* trying to do? Tell me!"

"Lordy, you don't know anything!"

"I. Know. *Everything.*"

"You know nothing." Her expression shifts from suspicion to amusement. "Whatever you think you know, even if you're right, is just a tenth of what you need to know to survive here." She flips her once-stringy hair over her shoulder. "Now help me set up the gift bags for the parents before I tell Villicus on you."

We're both fuming as she marches stiffly ahead of me to Valedictorian Hall, where Agniezska and Plum are sitting, hands folded, at the little table set outside the hall's front doors. The gift bags Pilot and I stuffed with tissue flowers line the tabletop. Tallulah is walking around the bags and dropping something in each one.

"What's *she* doing here?" Plum sneers.

I find myself looking closely at Plum, this former child star who overdosed on coke at some nightclub. Until the gift Tallulah is adding to the bags catches my eye.

"What's that?" I ask, but I don't wait for an answer. Everything everyone says here is ambiguous crap. If I want the truth, I have to find it myself. So I grab a bag, dig under the tissue, and yank out the gift: an engraved pewter apple with a bite out of it.

"Anne!" Tallulah shrieks. "You're not allowed!"

"*The world was founded on an exchange*," I read before staring at the girls. "What the hell does that mean? Like, Eve and the apple?"

Swiping the apple out of my hands, Harper snarls. "Apples go on teachers' desks. You're at a school. Hello? It's so obvious."

"That's not what that means."

"Enough!" she fires at me before jabbing her finger in the direction of a storage room I've been in and out of all day, at the rear of Valedictorian Hall. "Go to that closet and get the box of school pins. We need them for these gift bags."

"Give me the key."

"You are such a bee in my bonnet," Harper grumbles. "I left it on the door jamb of the closet. Put it back when you're done!"

I march to the closet. Mumbling to myself, I pluck the key from over the door, push the door in, and pocket the key, striding expertly through the long, dark closet I navigated all morning, even with mops, brooms, and buckets scattered everywhere. Near the shelves, I pull a dangling cord, and a bare bulb floods the room with yellow light. Lining the walls in teetering towers are crates and bins labeled with peeling masking tape. At the end of the closet, Villicus's booming voice in Valedictorian Hall shakes the wall, and I can't help but roll my eyes. Villicus. The idea of him sends a surge of hot blood rushing through my veins.

Hang on.

"What's the matter with me?" I whisper to myself.

In my fury, I nearly overlooked the fact that Villicus is giving a secret speech *on the other side of the wall* right now. Unfortunately, there's no easy way into Valedictorian Hall from this closet. Fortunately, I've got experience with B&Es. And, overhead, an air duct leads into Valedictorian Hall.

It is extremely *Law & Order* of me to go to these lengths. To stack six crates soundlessly like stairs that I climb until I can reach the ceiling of the closet, if I stretch. To use the flat part of a key to unscrew the vent cover. To wiggle the cover free gently and, taking care, pull it down almost silently, setting it softly on a shelf next to the box of school pins I *should* be retrieving. I grip the inside of the vent, sticky with decades of dust, and, with a thin gasp, hoist myself up, feeling the crates rattle under me but remain, thankfully, vertical. My height makes it possible to fit in, but a part of me wishes I was still the scrawny girl I once was; my hips barely squeeze into the narrow duct. For a half-second, I experience a mild bout of claustrophobia, but I shake it off because time's a-wastin' and because, hell, since I'm already dead, I don't really have to fear dying in here, do I? As noiselessly as possible, I shimmy through the dark, groaning air duct, heading toward Valedictorian Hall and expecting, with every inch I move, to see a light shining through the vent at the end, telling me I'm almost there. The best I see is a dim glow, which barely creeps between the vent cover's slats.

When I make it to the cover and peek out into Valedictorian Hall, I realize why it's so dim.

I'd expected the room to be lit like any other room. But, instead, candles burn in little groups up and down the long hall, where hundreds of parents and teachers sit on folding chairs, staring at Villicus, who struts in front of a tall wall of some two hundred tiny drawers.

The vent I'm looking through must be fifteen feet up the wall. Anxiously, I crane my neck to better see Villicus. But he keeps hobbling out of my limited view. The few words of his speech

I catch reveal no well-guarded secrets, no insights into why he wants me here. He's just talking random Cania crap, adding his somber voice-over to an otherwise eerie scene in which shadows flicker across the faces of parents who can't tear their eyes away. They watch Villicus like they're in a trance, like someone's captured them in a spell that keeps them from blinking. Around the perimeter of the room, portraits of valedictorians are suspended midair, hung on invisible line attached to the vaulted ceiling. On the side opposite me, secretaries swarm, giggling with each other; as much as I wouldn't wish death on anybody, I can't help but think it wouldn't be so bad to learn those secretaries are dead, too.

I want to see more, but it's so dark, and when I shift, the ducting squeals. The majority of the room, straight from the pages of *Beowulf,* is in shadows. I can just glimpse a handful of parents, their expressions indistinguishable under the candlelight. But I manage to make out some faces. Directly below me, a Japanese woman dressed in black stifles endless sobs as she keeps one hand on the empty seat next to her; the other hand clutches a circle of beads from which tassels dangle. Next to her empty seat is a manly-looking woman. Cancel that! It's a man dressed as a woman. I'm about to write him off as one of those eccentric billionaires you hear about, until I see, in the row behind, a couple who look equally out of place. They appear homeless, with tattered clothing, wasted expressions, gaunt cheeks. Beside them sit the very definition of the odd couple: a devastatingly debonair man holding the hand of a woman so enormous, she is almost suffocating inside her chins.

Where are the fabulously rich parents I'd expected? The CEOs and oil magnates, Botoxed women and too-tanned men? Now I wish I'd paid better attention to these parents earlier, back on the quad. A man glances up at the ceiling, exposing his face to me. "I Love Porno" is tattooed to his forehead.

What on earth?

Before I can peer any further into the darkness, before I can even start to make sense of this abnormal group, a long, lumbering *creak* interrupts my thoughts. The sound is coming from inside the air shaft, right under my arm. It's followed by a shake—and the duct dropping almost an inch.

"Oh, shit," I whisper, gently shifting against the opposite wall of the duct just as the shaft groans again. This thing is going to fall any second, and everyone in Valedictorian Hall, including Villicus, will know I was eavesdropping. Even if I can't be killed, I'm pretty sure I'll be both humiliated and in serious physical pain.

As cautiously but quickly as I can move, I hold my breath and inch backward. Leaving the air duct is slightly more complicated than entering it. Because it's so narrow, I can't turn my head enough to see where I'm going; I can only go straight and depend on the glow of the light from the closet and my feet scraping along the duct to keep me from tumbling out in a pain-packed heap. Just as my toes come upon emptiness—the opening in the closet ceiling—the whole shaft moans so loudly, I worry the parents in Valedictorian Hall heard it. Exactly the impetus I need to shimmy out the rest of the way *pronto*!

Lowering my body out of the shaft in the darkness, I dangle my legs and point my toes, lowering myself as far as I can go and realizing, as I do, that I should've added another row of crates. I'll have to let myself drop at least two feet, and that could send the whole makeshift staircase tumbling down.

Okay. You can do this. Just try to control yourself as you freefall.

With another groan of the duct, I release my grip and fall. And keep falling well beyond the two feet I'd expected. I land in a slump on the floor.

My staircase of crates is gone.

The room is dark. But I left the light on before I went into the airshaft.

This can only mean one thing—one thing that makes the pain of my fall disappear.

Someone's been in here since I went up.

I scan the darkness for company. "I'm just getting some pins for Harper," I say. As I straighten up, my hip groans from my landing and gravel crunches under my shoes. I wince, step forward, and nearly leap out of my skin when something brushes my face. Reaching for it blindly, I feel a crunchy mop-head and sigh. But at that moment, I hear deep breathing.

"You thought no one would see you," Teddy says. *Teddy!* Where the hell did he come from?

As I take another step, I can just discern the outline of a metal shelving unit. And then, all of a sudden, Teddy's bumpy face. He stands a foot from me, leering, his beady eyes lit bizarrely behind the shadows. Gasping, I stumble backward and topple over a bin, breaking my fall on its lid.

"Teddy!" I blast, keeping my voice as low as I can while shouting. "You scared the living daylights out of me."

"What are you doing in here?" he hisses. "You're *not* just doing Harper's bidding."

"Who are you? Harriet the Spy?"

"I am your Guardian," he snaps, glaring down at me. "Are you trying to get expelled? You are seconds away from losing all hope of even being *considered* for valedictorian, Missy!"

"You have no proof," I say, getting to my feet again, "that I am not in here getting something for Harper. Just ask her."

He leans back for a moment, considering my excuse. But, in a flash, he lurches at me and pins me to the metal shelves. His sticky hands wrap around my wrists; he's stronger than he looks, I realize, as the sharp corner of a box digs into my spine.

"I saw you," he scowls. "I saw you with my own two eyes from inside the hall. And I heard you fall out of that shaft."

"Get away from me." I wince. "I was looking beyond the surface you all expect me to accept. It's my PT! There's nothing wrong with it."

"You were breaking the rules. Again."

Bits of Teddy's saliva fly over my face. He smells like doused campfire. His wet lips brush against my nose when he leans closer to me, but I dodge him, trying not to gag.

"Don't force me to scream. I will."

"And who would believe you? Nobody. You barely even exist here."

"Then you should barely feel this," I fire, thrusting my knee up and hitting him exactly where I know it will drop him. I bolt for the far door and, tripping over a garden house, burst into the dreary afternoon air, panicked but relieved to be free.

"Annie?"

Huffing, I glance quickly to the right. As my eyes adjust to the daylight, I see Pilot standing wide-eyed, smiling at me until he sees the state I'm in.

"What happened? You're covered in dust."

"Come on." I grab his hand and begin limping away. I can't be here when Teddy comes out.

"Harper's looking for you," he says. "And I wanted to ask you something."

"Walk and talk, Pi."

"We're planning a get-together up at the beach tonight. North shore. An exercise in decompression, if you will. Post-Parent Pressure Day. You in?"

Tugging his arm, I nod vehemently, willing to agree to anything just to get away from this building.

nineteen

THE TUITION BATTLE

THE FORECAST CALLS FOR SLEET. I'LL HAPPILY SIT IN a hailstorm, if I have to, just to get away from spending the night under the same roof as Teddy.

So, after dinner, when all the parents—from crazy-looking *I Love Porno* dad to Harper's surprisingly nice-looking parents—retire to the dorms, I meet Pilot at the school gates to head up-island.

"You came," he breathes. "I wasn't sure you would."

"Why not?" I ask as we start walking north of the school, passing the hill where I watched Villicus dispose of who knows what that day; where I stood screaming at Ben, back when I still had anything resembling hope about him; where someone—probably Teddy—found Molly's shoe and used it to trigger her death.

"Honestly? I was worried my dad creeped you out today," he confesses.

Even though I'm not feeling particularly cheery, I laugh. "I wondered if you noticed."

As we walk, clouds roll in overhead, replacing what little was left of the golden twilight with a dark gray smear. A yellow Ducati—*his*—zooms by.

"So tell me," I say to keep from thinking of the fact that Ben, who evidently detests me now, didn't even pause, "is there an unspoken truce going on tonight?"

"More like a temporary cease-fire." Pilot's idly dragging a branch. "No Guardians. No grading. No competition. Just us. It's exactly what I need after the stress Lieutenant General Stone put on me today."

"Was it that bad?"

"It was terrible. Every second word out of my dad's mouth was *valedictorian*." He rolls his eyes. "Good ol' *vale dicere*. The idea of wasting my life on that single achievement. Seriously."

"He knows you don't want to be valedictorian, doesn't he?"

"It's not that simple."

Pilot's voice is drowned out as, just ahead of us, Ben's Ducati rounds a curve in the road, appearing again from behind a stand of bushy pine trees and racing our way. It roars as he revs the engine, lifting the front wheel inches off the road, slamming it back down and, seconds later, whizzing by us. Leaves scatter. I step on one, and it crunches under my shoe.

"Show off," Pilot mutters. Then he looks at me. "Listen, tonight's about getting away from all that valedictorian stuff. Starting now." With that, he pulls two mini bottles of vodka, the small bottles you get on airplanes, from his coat pocket. Holding them between his fingers, he tips one toward me. "Can we do that?"

"Sure," I say, smiling.

Truth is, I think I've finally figured out why it's important to become valedictorian: it's the ultimate act of *normalcy*. How better to pretend your child hasn't died than to not only see them go to school but to set the same goal for them that every other overachieving high-schooler on earth has? To be valedictorian. It's such a common aspiration, such a simple way to pretend life is as it was. The thought of it makes my eyes water, knowing how far we'll go to hold onto any sense of normalcy—however tenuous—just to lessen the pain of losing someone we love. I know that's all my dad wants for me. I know he'd do anything to sustain the illusion that I'm alive and well.

Of course, there must also be parents who care only about status, about knocking out the competition so they can prove what skyrocketing investment portfolios and custom homes in the Hamptons can't: that their offspring, the fruit of their loins, even postmortem, is the best. What floors me is the willingness of the kids to play along. It's taken me a while to figure that out, but that's because there are so many impossible curiosities to sort through. I have to attack them one at a time. My hope is that, tonight, Pilot will help with a few straggling questions. Surely he knows more than he's let on.

Nodding, I tug one cool bottle from his grip. "Straight vodka?"

"You don't think you've earned it?"

I've earned it and then some. Twisting the lid off, I think, *Here's to our pathetically short lives*, and, nodding at Pilot as he rests his bottle on his lips, tip it back. I shudder. It's like drinking window cleaner. Or diesel.

"It'll hit you hard. But it doesn't last long," Pilot wheezes, wiping his mouth on the back of his hand. "Nope. Never lasts long enough." As he chuckles, I finish my bottle off—fast, before I can taste it, before my tongue can react to it. He does the same and, wiping his lips, softens his expression. "You holdin' up okay, Annie? You seem like you're doing an awful lot of *looking closer* lately."

"It's hard not to."

"So," he tilts his head, looking curious, "you found anything interesting?"

"Depends what you mean by interesting." I'd call what I've discovered shocking, stomach-churning, even horrifying. But not *interesting*.

"So you've found something, and now you need to find everything?"

"Does everyone talk in code around here?"

"Not always. Just with you. Just since you arrived." Tossing his empty bottle into the woods, he rubs his hands over his ultra-short hair. "Have you cracked the code yet?"

I'm closer than ever to getting the answers I thought I wanted. But, suddenly, I don't want them—not yet. Because my head is exhausted with the revelations of the day. Because I don't feel like being serious right now, like interrogating or investigating or using my brain in any way. I just want to unwind like a normal sixteen-year-old would. In the absence of knowing what such unwinding might look like—lack of experience—I say nothing.

I simply take off running.

What am I running from? From Pilot confirming everything and, in one short breath, eliminating any hope that I might be wrong? What am I running toward? A beach filled with dead kids.

Tossing the branch he's been dragging, Pilot chases me. Suddenly we're racing, laughing as we push ourselves. Minutes later, we arrive at the sandy beach at the northernmost tip of Wormwood Island, where dozens of kids mosey around in the sand, their shoes off as if it's ninety degrees, not thirty, their arms slung over each other's shoulders. I can't help but compare tonight to the dance last weekend, where we danced under the pressure of Guardians grading us, where we scrapped and jabbed because we were so caught up in the race for the Big V. A vanity race. Here, tonight, on this beach, there's none of that. Just giggling. Someone strumming a guitar. Y'know, *unwinding*.

"Looks like these bitches are already *crunk*," Pilot laughs.

"We're late for the party." I grin. "Better catch up."

Tugging his sleeve, I pull him toward the crowd that's formed around Jack. It's something I never would've done before—not here, and not in my previous life. But, like Pilot said, we need to decompress. And I'm too aware now, too frustrated by the fuzzy areas around my suspicions, too bewildered by the forces focused on oppressing me to care. I'm too far gone to play by the rules I've played by before. Excuse my French, but fuck the rules. Fuck competing with everyone just to make our parents proud or to make them feel better about *our* deaths. Fuck Teddy, Villicus, Dr. Zin—hell, even Ben. And if Harper doesn't like me, fuck her, too. And Plum. And the whole Model UN from Hell with their big, nasty boobs and obvious desperation.

Jack's holding a bottle of something. To his right, a few guys try to build a bonfire out of driftwood. Down by the water, Tallulah and Mark Norbussman are soaking wet after tumbling into the water while wrestling. Everyone roams in every direction, crossing to the dark woods that flank either side of the beach, meandering to the waterside, where the last streaks of daylight on the horizon make the shallowest waters glow with a pale golden hue.

"Jack!" I shout into the wind as we near his crowd. He waves us over. "What've you got there?"

"Hey, you sex bomb! You, too, Anne," he shouts with a loud laugh. "It's tequila. Tequila!" Hoots and bellows of joy fill the air.

Reeking of booze, Harper runs up out of nowhere, guffaws, and pulls Plum, who's near me, to her chest. "Y'all ready to get hog wild?"

"Let's do it!" Pilot shouts.

"Tequila!" Jack bellows again. He rifles under a stack of blankets and finds a basket, opening it to reveal a dozen more bottles. "And lots of it."

"Pilot!" Harper hollers, even though she's standing directly in front of us. Leaning on Plum, who's laughing for no reason, she grabs Pilot's collar and stares him down. "Pi, I have to say, you've been doing *such* an amazing job."

Blushing, Pilot glances from her to me and mutters in my ear, "Social Committee stuff."

"Really," Harper continues, her drawl blending into one hiccupy stream of soft sounds, "you're going above and beyond. I'll square up with you later."

"Anyway," Pilot interrupts, gently pushing her away. "You've never had tequila, have you, Annie?"

"No." I glance back at Harper, who's whispering in Plum's ear. They break into a fit of giggles. "What was Harper talking about?"

"Don't worry about her," Jack slurs. "She's drunk."

"So are you."

"And you should be, too," he laughs. "Come on. Take off some of those layers, Anne, or I'll make you play strip poker with me. Christ, who wears a winter jacket to one of these things?"

I *should* loosen up tonight. Why not? I'm dead now. I don't have to be the artsy geek anymore. I can be anything. Do anything. Reading my mind, Jack fills a shot glass with golden tequila that sloshes over the sides and hands it to me.

"The best way to relax, gorgeous."

With a blush, I take it. Jack's quickly filling another shot glass and then more until everyone in our huddle is listening to Harper count down *three, two, one*. And we drink, polishing off our glasses, gasping; I hold my stomach to keep it down.

"Another!" Plum hollers. Everyone cheers and the rest of the crowd hustles over to join us. Shot glasses appear from nowhere.

"Aren't we supposed to have salt and lime with tequila?" I ask.

"Not with this stuff, Fainting Fanny," Pilot teases, wrapping his arm around my shoulder, warming me as the wind rolls in off the ocean. "This is the best. Straight from Jack's dad's last distillery, which just so happens to be the *best* distillery in all of *Meh-hee-ko*."

"Wait," Jack cries out, his warm breath freezing in white puffs as the sun, at last, completely disappears below the horizon. He waves his hands to stop the conversations up and down the beach. "Wait, wait, wait! Everyone, this next bottle of *extra añejo* requires a toast. My dad wouldn't have it any other way."

"May your life be long and useful like a roll of toilet paper," Tallulah shouts, holding up her glass. "And if not, may you end up on Wormwood Island. Let's drink!"

"*That's* not a toast," Jack says. Then his gaze falls on Pilot, and his tone turns theatrical. "Mr. Pilot Stone. The one person on this whole island who doesn't give a crap about the Big V. My hero. Will you do the honors?"

Pilot grimaces, rolling his eyes, but a bunch of people clap, and everyone turns to him. I find myself leaning away as if trying to stay out of a photo, but his hand around my shoulder keeps me from breaking free.

"Thank you, my good man," Pilot says, mimicking Jack's affected speech. Jack bows dramatically, and Pilot faces everyone, steering me along with him as he moves. Seemingly on cue, a sophomore finally ignites the pile of driftwood nearby, and a fire sparks in the center of it, traveling out and up until it roars, crackles, and spits.

"Welcome, everyone," Pilot says, "to the Festival of Fire and Life."

I know Pilot's kidding, but the mention of the villagers' festival, which I didn't even realize any of these Cania kids *knew* of, instantly reminds me of Molly. Conjures an image of her. Unearths one of the big things I've been hiding from. The memory of following her that night from my bedroom down to her cremation ceremony, where her grandfather lowered her former body onto the fire, where her new body flickered in her mother's arms before disappearing. They said the fire released the spirit of the child from the power of the island. If the only way to release a child from the island—to keep that child from staying alive in the form Molly was in that night, in the form we're all in right now—is to burn their former body, that must mean that all of our bodies are stored on the island somewhere; only when those bodies are destroyed can we permanently *die*.

My dead body is somewhere here.

It could be right under my feet.

I slowly lower my gaze to the sand, a wave of dizziness—thanks to the drinks—making my head swoon. In the flicker of the fire, I'm half expecting to see a long, boney hand reach up from beneath the sand, to feel its deathly grip around my ankle, to be pulled under the earth where hundreds of decomposing bodies will writhe and claw at me. But no hand reaches up. It's just sand. Even still, the thought of it rattles me. It's made the fact that I'm dead—*dead*—much more real. Without thinking, forgetting that Pilot's midway through a speech, I knock back my shot.

Everyone stares at me.

Pilot laughs. "Easy, Annie! I'm still giving the toast."

If the blood hadn't completely drained from my face to my toes already, I might blush. But instead, I just gawk at him, shockingly aware that I'm dead, wondering if we have to stay on this island in order to live or if we'll ever be free again, amazed at how eerie he looks in the firelight.

He laughs nervously. "Where was I? Oh, yeah. This crazy-ass fire festival and this fine tequila are brought to you by the lovely folks at Jack's dad's Agave Shack, the only business Villicus allowed him to keep."

Wait . . . *what?*

"To Jack's dad!"

"And his tequila!"

"All our parents gave up much more than money to get us in here," Pilot adds slyly, glancing at me from the corner of his eye. "Businesses. Homes. Rumor has it that, not too many years ago, a mother even gave up her own thumbs. Which brings us to my favorite Cania Christy tradition."

"Tuition Battle!" Harper shouts. A few others copy her, and a chant begins: *Tuition Battle. Tuition Battle.*

"Yes, it's time for the much-honored Tuition Battle. Time to compare notes." Pilot concludes, "Let's see whose parents gave up the most, proving that they love them most."

A half-minute later, the chants have died down, I've had two more shots, and I'm sitting on a blanket with Pilot, others settling around us. I'm stunned by what's about to happen. These students who have been a complete mystery to me are now going to swap stories about what their parents gave up to get them in here.

The Tuition Battle. That's what they're calling this.

On my first day here, Pilot and Jack told me tuition was about more than money. But I'd thought they just meant an obscene amount of money. Now this atomic bomb's been dropped on me: my dad—everyone's parents—actually gave up *colossal* possessions. Businesses. Power. Limbs! And who knows what else?

What did my dad give up to have access to his dead daughter, if only briefly?

Did he ship my body here? Do I need to be on this island to live here? Do I need to be burned to leave this place? Can I live elsewhere? Was Lotus's body burned when she was expelled? At once, the reality of Lotus's expulsion hits me. Her last day was the day I heard the scream on campus, the day I watched Villicus chant, say her father's name, and throw a tube into the ocean. A vial. A vial of blood.

"That's all this island needs," I whisper. "Our blood. Our DNA. To re-create us."

I marvel that an island could be so enchanted. But my wonder turns to worry quickly as I consider the possibility that the island doesn't have the power to breathe new life into kids. Perhaps someone here can perform such magic. As unbelievable as that sounds.

Imagine having that power, I think. Imagine being able to approach a father who's just lost his little girl and offer him the chance to see her live again, walk again, talk again. Everything you never got the chance to say, you can say now. Every kiss you withheld, you can give. Every angry word you said, you can undo. Most people would give anything for one more day with someone they love. What might an *entire* second chance at life be worth to a grieving parent?

"Before we play this, Anne," Pilot says, nestling on the blanket next to me, "we need to get something out on the table. I mean, you know, right? I saw you watching me the other day, and I figured you'd figured it out."

"I *know*?"

"Do you?"

I haven't actually admitted what I know to anyone. Haven't said the words out loud yet.

"You mean... you mean..." But I can't finish my thought.

"Uh-huh," he says, his tone meaning-laden. "*That's* what I mean."

"*Dead*," I whisper, finally meeting his black eyes. "Everyone here died."

He sighs, but then he turns to the settling crowd and shouts, "Hey, guys, she knows! Annie knows. We're all clear."

My mouth drops open. All at once, two dozen heads turn my way. Under their amused stares, I slowly exhale and nod. With that minor confirmation of such a major fact, they shrug and turn away. Being dead and then alive again is old news to them.

"Pi," I whisper, shocked, "why did you tell them that?"

"Because it would've been a seriously dull night if we had to keep talking in code, don't you think? It's *good* that you figured it out."

"It doesn't feel good."

"I can imagine. Ignorance is bliss, right? Hey, maybe you can move into the dorms now. Be my neighbor. We've still got two years together... *until*."

Jokingly, though I can't see the humor, he closes his eyes and crosses his arms over his chest, like he's in a coffin.

"Are you saying we don't get to live beyond graduation?"

"I thought you said you'd figured all this out, Anne-Ban."

I'm amazed at how quickly the veils have dropped. All this secrecy. Gone, just like that. There was a moment earlier tonight when I thought I'd have to weasel the answers out of Pilot, get him good and drunk so he could fess up the way my dad used to talk about drunken mourners spilling their guts about everything—the mother they secretly hated, the lover they furtively kept. I thought I'd have to torture Pilot for info. Quite suddenly, he's giving it up so easily.

Too easily.

Speaking of easy, Harper jumps up, bounces to the front of the fire, and shouts out, "Well, someone get Merchant a medal!" She breaks into an undeserved fit of laughter. "All right, all right, it's good that she knows now. 'Course we can't go telling Villicus she knows, or the poor dear might get in trouble. And no one wants that."

"No one wants that more than you!" Jack shouts.

Harper grins and shrugs.

"Villicus will talk to her about it later, I'm sure," Pilot adds, pulling me closer. "So let's just go on with Tuition Battle, all right?"

I quietly ask him, "Why shouldn't Villicus know I know?"

"It's just... it's complicated."

"Try me."

"This is a pretty big secret to keep, Anne. It's the reason no one's allowed to know about the school, the reason my dad got in trouble for telling your dad."

"But why would he think I can't keep it quiet?"

"Villicus just needed to know he could trust you before telling you."

"Why would he think he can't trust me?"

"*Shh*, the battle's gonna start."

"Okay, okay," Harper says as I contain a growl over the ongoing, relentless secrecy, "so, y'all will get a chance to come up to the fire and explain your tuition, then we vote on whose parents gave up the most to get them in here. So, okay."

She takes a moment to pull her hair back so the rising winds don't whip it over her face.

"As you know, my family's got more money than God. Oil money. The *best* kind of money."

Letting his hand rest for a noticeably long time on my knee, Pilot whispers in my ear, "Did you know Harper got kicked in the head by a prize-winning horse?"

"Why can't he trust me?" I press.

"Pilot, you and your girlfriend need to *hush!*" Harper shouts, her drawl extra-thick thanks to the tequila. "So, here's my tuition. My daddy, because he loves me so damn much, more than he loves my stupid stepmonster, agreed to do *this!* He told Villicus he'd cause at least ten oil spills every year. And!" Swiping her hands through the air, she cuts everyone off as the whoops begin and as my jaw drops for the second time in as many minutes. "*And* he agreed to make it seem impossible to clean them up. A-a-and, when he finally did get around to cleaning them up, he'd only use chemicals that are as bad as the oil." Gleefully, she claps. "That's what my pa agreed to do in exchange for a second chance to love me. Top that!"

The roar of a dozen kids shouting erupts; others clap, less impressed. With a fake curtsy, Harper returns to her spot, but not before shooting a glare my way.

I'm stunned silent.

Next, Jack describes how his dad signed over twelve distilleries and breweries, retaining just the tequila factory in Mexico. Twelve of them. Handed to Villicus on a silver platter. All in exchange for giving Jack a second chance at life.

"So tuition isn't just about money," I ask Pilot, with my throat tightening around every word, "and it isn't just about signing over businesses, either. It's about…?"

"It's about testing the lengths parents will go to for their children," Pilot says as if I'm boring him. "How 'bout Jack? Know how he died? He was poisoned by his personal chef."

The Tuition Battle rages on. Tallulah's father, a famous movie director, was forced to get a sex change. Mark's former supermodel of a mother had to gain and keep on *exactly* four hundred extra pounds; every hour—night and day—she weighs herself to ensure she's on track. The billionaire parents of a senior named Tom agreed to become homeless so he could attend Cania.

Why would Villicus want that?

Why would parents be so willing to do that? Especially if graduation will end our lives?

This must be the hundredth time I've asked myself that very question. But it is the first time I've actually come up with an answer. And the answer changes everything.

twenty

THE ICE STORM

I KNOW NOW. I KNOW WHY PARENTS GIVE UP EVERYTHING—
and then some—to see their children come to Cania. It's not just
for the chance to extend one's life a little on the island.

I know why the valedictorian race means so much.

I know why they call it the Big V. Because its rewards are as
big as they come.

I know now. *Only the valedictorian gets to live again.*

It's a lottery like no other. With a highly priced ticket to
match. Little wonder the Big V race consumes our every action
and thought.

"You okay, Annie?" Pilot tries to concentrate his unfocused
gaze on me, leaning in.

I am anything but okay, I think, as Pilot watches me. His face
is almost above mine, closer than it's ever been, and oddly intimi-
dating. Like Ben's breath, his is candy-scented. Like Ben's skin,
like everyone else's, his is luminescent, translucent. The acne, the
scars, the extra weight, the broken bones of our previous lives,
they're all gone. One glance around the beach reminds me that
everyone is flawless, above mere humanity, above mortality. The
bonfire sends flecks of ash soaring through the sky.

If those flecks landed on us, would they burn us, I wonder? Can we be hurt?

But my tooth. My tooth was still crooked before Ben sculpted it. And I've had a few zits already here. I briefly entertain the idea that I'm still alive when the memory of my dad's overly happy voice hits me like cold water. He'd only be that happy if he thought he was never going to hear my voice again.

"Annie?" Pilot asks, his voice low. "What about you? Will you go next?"

Should I tell him I don't know, that I'm terrified of what my tuition might be? If I play along, if I act like I'm knee-deep in knowledge rather than just starting to get my toes wet, Pilot might reveal more, which is exactly what I need him to do.

"Why don't you go next?"

"Why don't *you*?" he presses.

"Hey!" Jack shouts. "Alistair Bloomberg didn't show? His tuition is the best."

"Maybe he got expelled," a sophomore adds.

"I wish," a senior tacks on. Even though he knows, as I know, that expulsion is death.

"Who's Alistair Bloomberg?" I ask.

"His dad's the one with the *I Love Porno* tattoo," Pilot explains. "Did you see that guy? Seriously, Villicus outdid himself on that one."

"Why would Villicus want that?" I ask cautiously, half afraid of the answer, half afraid of what my reaction will be to it. "He doesn't get anything out of a tattooed head. Or oil spills. Or sex changes. Or—"

"Get anything? Are you talking about money again?" Pilot chuckles. "Anyone with money knows nothing's actually about money. It's about power."

"But money is power."

"Power is *everything*. When you have power, money follows.

That said, when money comes easily, like it does here, it gets boring." After running his finger along the inside of the glass, he licks it and scans the blanket for more. "Say you could ask a bunch of billionaire parents for anything, Annie, wouldn't you get creative? I mean, if you'd had people sign over businesses, jets, private islands, anything you can imagine for decades, if you were running the highest-grossing private corporation in the world—which is exactly what Cania is—wouldn't you want more than money?"

"I wouldn't want someone to tattoo their forehead."

He chuckles like I'm *so* simple-minded. "Villicus has the luxury of asking for whatever he wants. Sometimes, he ups the ante. Keep things interesting, y'know?"

Knowing my dad has no money to give, I instantly picture him with a tattoo on his forehead, and I want to cry. The worst part is that I know he'd do it, too. I know that, if Dr. Zin sat down across the kitchen table from him and said he had to carve the outline of a swastika into his face, he'd do it. For me.

"Hey," Pilot smirks, "you're not drinking your tequila."

We both glance down at my glass. Without hesitating, I knock it back. But it's not strong enough. Once you know you're dead and battling for a new life, nothing's strong enough to wash the stunning awareness away. Laughing, Pilot leaps to his feet and tugs me up with him.

"Come on!" he says. "This battle sucks; I've heard all these stories. Let's go spook some deer in the woods." And he breaks into a run.

Just inside a dense wooded stretch off the beach, I reluctantly catch up with Pilot. Standing together in the midst of trees turned black now that the sun's disappeared, we're breathing heavily, listening to waves crash down by the shore. In the distance, Coast Guard boats are whizzing around. Pilot explains that they're looking for the body of a missing billionaire; I correctly guess the billionaire is Manish, the flashy man I saw yelling at Villicus and

Zin weeks ago. Before gunshots tore through the air. I'm getting tired of being right. And I'm getting tired of the callous manner in which everyone seems to think about life, death, and murder around here. Even Pilot.

"Doesn't this feel good? There's so much to feel still, don't you think?" Pilot tilts his head to the sky, hidden somewhere above these countless tree branches, and inhales deeply. "You'd never guess we were anything but alive."

"How did you know I knew?" I ask.

"I figured it was only a matter of time."

"Why didn't you talk to me about it? Before tonight, I mean?"

"We're not supposed to. Villicus's orders. And I wasn't sure you knew until tonight."

Taking me by surprise, he turns to me suddenly, grabs my hands, and pulls them to his mouth, kissing my palms. My jaw drops, and I almost rip my hands away—until I notice the tears in his eyes.

"Oh, Annie." He kisses both my palms again, his lips trailing lightly over my skin, his dark eyes closing. "I died before I ever had the chance to." He pauses, sighs. "I'll never know what it's like to be close with a girl."

I stiffen.

"Look at you," he breathes, opening his eyes again, releasing my hands, and tenderly unknotting my scarf. "You're all bundled up like it's the middle of winter."

"Pi, what are you doing?" I ask.

His gaze meets mine, and there's no missing the redness, the emotion rising to the surface.

Standing here, letting him remove my scarf, I wonder if I could fall for him, if I could love him. God, that would make things easy. He's my closest friend, the one person with whom I've spent every spare hour at school, the only person who would open up to me about the secrets of Cania. Sure, he thinks of himself as the disappointing son of a narcissistic, power-hungry politician, but that doesn't mean he actually *is* disappointing. And he likes me, that much is clear. Judging by the glimmer in his eyes, he likes me a lot. So why shouldn't I be with Pilot?

Ben.

The moment I think his name, I shake my head.

"What's wrong?" Pilot asks, taking my scarf in his hands.

"Um, nothing." I notice my breath is coming faster, and so does he. But he's misreading it.

He smiles sheepishly. "You're unbelievably sexy." Placing my scarf on the boulder behind us, he reaches for the top button of my coat, holding my gaze as he does. "There's something about you. You don't even know the effect you have on men."

I just want him to stop. All I can think is *Ben.*

Shut up, I tell my stubborn brain. Ben is with Garnet—he's seeing a teacher. He explicitly told me today, in front of everyone, that there's nothing between us. He lives right next door to me, and yet he never walks with me to or from school or offers me a ride on his precious bike. And every time I see him on campus, he's cold. Let's not forget that he took the liberty of reshaping my entire smile to better suit his need for perfection. So what if he left a book in my room? Ben's father is in cahoots with Villicus. Sure, sure, Pilot's father is no stellar example of what a man should be, but—okay, fine, scrap the dad comparison.

Ben is dangerous. Pilot is safe. There's nothing wrong with safe. Safe's good. If you want your boyfriend to be there for you, you choose a safe guy to be your boyfriend. Or am I going to be one of those dimwit girls who falls for the risky, elusive, unattainable guy in the hopes that she'll be able to change him? No. Not me. Pilot has only ever been friendly with me, and he obviously likes me; as he presses himself closer to me, I can feel how much he likes me. Even wants me. Nice, safe, loving Pilot is the only way for a smart girl to go.

I glance down to see that Pilot has unbuttoned my coat and pushed it aside. He's positioned himself between my legs and is gazing at the curves under my shirt. Back at the beach, Jack is calling for us, heading our way.

"We should go," I stutter.

"I haven't told you about *my* tuition," Pilot says, not meeting my eyes. "I win the battle every time because what my dad exchanged for my life here is so major."

"Oh?" My voice chokes. I can't help but notice that his hands are on my waist and that his fingers are sliding beyond friendship territory.

"Villicus forced him to confess his sexual affairs publicly." His stare rolls over my collarbone, up my neck and down again. "He had to hold a major press conference. It ended any chance he had of becoming president—the most important thing in the world to him. But he did that for me, Anne." His gaze, at last, meets mine. "I guess he must believe in me a little."

With Jack's voice nearing us, I can't think of much other than how badly I want Pilot to remove himself from between my thighs—before the whole school gets the wrong idea about us. He's just drunk; I can forgive him for acting like we're together. But everyone else, including Ben, will hear, and then my fate with Pilot will be sealed.

"Pi, we should get back to the beach."

"He may still be president one day," Pilot says, as if he's trying to convince me to want to stay here with him. His palms roll over my hips. "God, you feel so good."

"It's gonna rain. And we've been telling these sad tuition stories and drinking. I just…"

His dark eyes burn. "If I could just be close to you, my dad might respect me."

I catch his hands just as they're moving up my back, and I pull them away from my body. "I can't fix your relationship with your dad." With an awkward half-smile, with my heart thumping in my chest and with all the sensitivity I can muster, I bring my legs together, pushing him back. Rejecting him. "I'm sorry. This is not about your dad. This is about me."

No, turning Pilot down has got nothing to do with Dave Stone. It has everything to do with my heart. My brainless, wasted heart. But I can't deny it and I won't hurt Pilot by leading him on now that I can feel how badly he wants to move from friendship status to something else.

"But there were all those signs," he says, looking both puzzled and drunk. "You laughed at my jokes. You held my hand."

Just then, Jack jogs in and stops short as he looks at us in our very unfortunate position. "Hope I'm not interrupting anything." Neither Pilot nor I say a word. "Come on, Pi. Plum wants to sing, and we all wanna dance. We're waiting on your musical talents."

"I'm coming," he says, backing away from me and looking in every direction but mine. He stumbles as he walks and clutches Jack's arm for support.

Suddenly nauseated—I've never had to turn anyone down and sure as hell didn't want my first to be Pilot—I follow behind. At a distance. But just within earshot of the guys.

"Not a bad gig you've got, buddy," Jack mumbles to Pilot, his voice low. "Get some ass from the blonde in the woods. And get blown by the redhead for your troubles."

The two take off in a run. I don't even want to know what Jack was talking about.

I stagger back to the beach, but I don't join the others. Instead, when I reach the bonfire, I stop and stare into it, numb, as the singing and dancing commence far ahead.

The fire. It's the only thing that released Molly from this island.

Robotically, I stick my hand smack in the middle of it—testing my theory about the impossibility of injuring these new, perfect bodies of ours—and watch the vibrant flames rise up to lick it. I feel the pain. I soak up the pain, wondering how long my hand would need to stay in for my skin to char. And then I pull it out, inspecting my flesh immediately. Sure enough, my skin is bright red and tight, even close to blistering near my pinky finger. But, within moments, the redness disappears, the pain disappears, every indication that I've just burned myself severely enough that I should be on the way to the hospital right now disappears. I turn my hand over, amazed to know that I was right, that this body, though *real*, is different from a human body. And then, from out of nowhere, Ben places his hand on mine.

"Didn't your parents ever tell you not to play with fire?"

Fifty feet away from where I stand, staring in *shock* at Ben Zin, looking from him to his hand, which is still on mine, an impromptu concert has broken out, stealing everyone's attention and leaving me to feel, for perhaps the first time ever, that I can actually talk to Ben without being intruded on. Plum is standing on a huge fallen tree, belting out some song, with Pilot as her backup. The rest of the crowd is dancing, cheering, singing along; I can barely see them, tucked away on the other side of the bonfire—which means they probably can't see me.

Where the road meets the beach, a yellow Ducati is parked. If that bike wasn't sitting right there, providing solid evidence that its rider is in the vicinity, I wouldn't believe my eyes or the sensation running under my skin at Ben's touch.

All night, I've watched for him furtively, hoping against reason that he'd show up here, mentally replaying the cold way he addressed me in the quad today and balancing that with the hint of interest he showed in speeding by me and Pilot twice on our way here. And now, here he is. No Garnet in sight. Just Ben. Taking my hand in his.

"Because it doesn't appear you have a partner," he begins, grinning in his gorgeous way, "any chance I can have this dance?" Placing his hand on my lower back, he pulls me to him. His cool breath moves my hair, sending shivers over me. He smells ethereal. His sea-colored gaze is ethereal. The airy way he floats in and out of my life is ethereal—like he might drift away the moment I get close to him—and that is the problem. "If you'll have me as a partner."

But I can take no more.

Freeing myself from his embrace, I back away from Ben's impossibly alluring expression. I don't give a damn if he's beautiful or if I'm hopelessly crushing on him. I'm not going to let him keep throwing my heart around.

"Why did you come here?" I demand. "Why, when you made it so clear today that you loathe me?"

"Is it bad that I came?"

"You *told* me we're not friends. You embarrassed me in front of everyone, including your dad. It was mortifying, Ben. And, icing on the cake, you're dating *Garnet*. A teacher."

"No, I'm not. Let me explain."

"I saw you two. Don't lie to me."

"We *were* dating. We dated for two years. But we're not now."

"I don't want to hear it. I can handle you being in love with someone else. I can handle you being caught up in some sordid teacher–student affair. Because at least I can still be friends with you that way." I begin backing away, which I realize I should have done from the start. "But you took even the hope of friendship away today."

"Surely you noticed that it's only when Garnet's around that I'm cold to you. Unfortunately, you misread that. It's not because I care for Garnet. It's because I care for *you* that I've acted as I have," he says, following me until the heat of the bonfire warms my back. "It's the only way to protect you."

"I don't need your protection!"

"Oh?" He thrusts his hand into and out of the flames. "A girl who can take care of herself doesn't play with fire."

"Don't talk to me like I'm an idiot."

"For the last time, I don't think you're an idiot," he says, softening his tone though his eyes still flare. "I think you're brilliant. I think, in fact, that you've figured it out."

"I have."

"You have?"

"You just said you thought I did!" I fire. "Why do you look so surprised?"

"I'm not surprised," he says, lowering his voice and pulling me away from the bonfire. "I'm scared. For you. What exactly do you think you've figured out?"

Dropping my voice to mock his, I whisper, "That we're all dead and brought to life again."

His face blanches. A drop of rain hits his nose. "Vivified."

"Sure. *Vivified.* What's the difference?" I glare at him.

"*Brought to life again* sounds like we're in our old bodies. But we're not. We're spirits in new versions of our old bodies."

"I know that, too. The point is that I'm not dumb after all, am I?"

"I never said you were," he says. "But, tell me, do *they* know you know?" He stabs in the direction of the dancing mob.

"What does it matter?"

"Do they?"

"Yes!" I cry as two freezing raindrops hit me hard.

What little color Ben had in his face drains away. "Okay, okay, we've gotta get you out of here. I'll get my dad to call your dad."

"Wait, why?"

"Look, Teddy's already pissed that you left the house without checking in with him," Ben says hurriedly. "He came to my house and demanded I lend him my bike so he could look for you. If he knows you know about vivification, Anne—"

"Shouldn't I be allowed to know I'm dead?"

"It's not that simple."

"Why not? Stop talking in puzzles and just tell me!"

"I want to. That's all I've wanted to do. And I might. Tonight. But not here."

I grab his arm and hold him in place. "What don't I know, Ben?"

His silence is an answer of its own. There's so much I don't know. The truth about our vivified selves is just the beginning. Perhaps even the reward of the Big V is just the beginning.

"Let's get out of here." He starts tugging me up the beach, toward his Ducati.

We make it about ten steps from the bonfire before the sound of singing halts and the cheering stops. Shaking my arm free, I turn to see what's happened—only to find everyone glaring at me. Worst of all? Pilot's staring at me with this *expression* that crushes my heart. He dashes off the boulder and, like a wounded deer, bolts into the woods.

"Way to go, Anne," Harper shouts, racing after Pilot. "You ruin everything."

Another drop of rain hits me. Another, and another. I glance from the sour faces of the group to Ben, who's waiting for me to follow him, to the sky—just as the clouds that have been looming, the clouds that have threatened to bring the promised sleet, burst open.

Within the span of a few breaths, it's raining full force. Icy, sharp rain that tears at my skin.

"Party's over!" Jack shouts.

The sleet douses the enormous fire while Ben lifts his jacket over my head, while the beach clears of people, while everyone rushing off shoots angry glares at me, glares that feel worse than the icy rain. Soon, they're all gone. And Ben and I stand silently—tensely—in the storm, facing the ocean and watching hundreds of millions of ice pellets hit the water's uneven surface by the second. The raindrops thicken into frosty sheets. I don't want to move. I don't want to take a step in any direction. Every time I move, it seems, some horrific realization rushes at me. Maybe if I just stand here. Maybe if I just close my eyes.

"We have to go," Ben says. "This is supposed to be a serious ice storm. It's not safe to be out here. And we need to take care of your situation."

A rumble of thunder. A clap of lightning tears through the clouds, and something else tears at my chest.

"Get away from me," I whisper when he reaches for me.

"Anne, I can tell you're upset, but we've got to get you home." I shake my head. He attempts to negotiate. "Can we at least get on my bike and go somewhere dry? You're shivering."

"No."

"Then can we walk? We can't stay here."

Reluctantly, I nod. "I don't need you to hold your jacket over me."

Leaving the beach and his bike behind, we walk back down the island, paralyzed by the tension, wondering, I think, if the other will break the silence. Up and down the narrow, winding road, icy rain collects on tree branches and leaves, building on itself, rapidly crafting dagger-like icicles that drip downward like the stalactites of a long dark cave lit by bolts of lightning. A motorbike roars down the island, making its way over the ice-slicked roads, its sound nearing.

I feel Ben's gaze on me. I feel his hand approach mine and pull away, sensing I'm not ready to be touched. At least he's perceptive.

"You have to tell me why you did it," I say finally, stopping and forcing him to do the same. We peer at each other through sheets of frosty rain that collect on our hair, freeze on our eyelashes, and coat our clothes. "What made you think you needed to fix my tooth, Ben?"

"Is that what you wanted to talk to me about today?"

I don't reply, which he accurately takes as a *yes*.

"I'm so sorry, Anne. I'm sorry because I couldn't risk Garnet finding out that I care for you. And I'm sorry because, well, if I changed anything about you by touching you, it wasn't intentional. I've just never touched anyone like you, not since I came to Cania."

"What does that mean, *like me*? Is this about my *situation*?"

"Look," he begins, catching my gaze and holding it even as cold rain streams down his face, making my heart drum loudly enough that I can hardly hear my own thoughts. At the same time a clap of lightning splits the sky above us, he takes my hands in his. "Look at us." Then he glances down tellingly at our entwined wet hands. "Look at this."

With my teeth chattering now, I follow his gaze. Just as when Pilot held my hand and I could barely tell where our flesh met, Ben's hand against mine looks strangely blurred. As if our skin is melting together, the edges smudged.

"Vivified, we're more spirit than we are flesh, you see, so the lines blur," Ben shouts over the rain. "He takes vials of our blood—he gets the morticians to do that. Blood from our remains. And he uses our DNA to re-create us here because he can't create us from thin air. He doesn't have that power."

"Who's *he*? Villicus?"

Ben nods, but I can't help but shake my head.

"Impossible!" I cry.

"Just listen, will you?" Ben fires back. "It's all true. All of it. Including the fact that I shouldn't have touched your face in our sculpting class that day, Anne. But, God help me, I wanted to be close to you. I feel as if I've been dreaming of you all my life. I can't help the way you make me feel, and I gave in to my desire to touch you. But I didn't mean to change you! I'm sure it was just part of your transformation, Anne, into the perfect manifestation of your DNA."

I tear my hands away. "You think I'm *so* imperfect."

"Don't take that the wrong way!" he exclaims. "I wasn't trying to *fix* you. I am fascinated by everything about you." He pulls me fiercely into his embrace, catching me softly before I slam against him. Giving into him, I find my body fitting perfectly into the crook of his arm, my face nestling easily into the warmth below his strong, beautiful jaw. "I suppose I inadvertently sculpted you into exactly what I see when I look at you," he says softly, his voice hoarse. "Pure perfection."

But before he can say another amazing word, a Harley rounds the curve ahead of us and screeches to a halt, nearly skidding out on the icy pavement. I turn to peer through the rain.

"She came after me," Ben mutters as the biker dismounts.

The biker pulls off her helmet, and I groan the moment I see her. "Garnet."

"Just let me take care of this," he says to me as I draw away, "and then I'll explain everything. Okay?"

"Ben!" Garnet calls from the opposite side of the road. "I have to talk to you."

"We've talked about this enough," he calls back.

As beautiful as ever—maybe even prettier lit by lightning—Garnet flicks her gaze at me. I realize how crazy I must look in this ice storm, like a drowned rat compared to Garnet, with her soft golden hair and creamy complexion. The rain is only starting to touch her.

"It's not going to be that easy," she says, more meaning behind her words than I can possibly fathom. "I've given up too much for you. I won't leave now."

Another rumble of thunder moves through the air, so close the ground shakes. Clenching his jaw, Ben steadily nods at her before turning to me.

"This'll just take a sec. I'm really sorry," he explains, his eyes pleading with me as he hands his jacket to me. "Cover your head with this. You're, um, soaked."

A flicker of the grin I love passes over his face, and I take his jacket, knowing for certain now that I look like death warmed over. Who cares? I *am* death warmed over.

The road is slick when Ben starts across it. As he strides across the ice with a confidence only the unbreakable have, a flash of lightning tears through the sky and hits a power line nearby. Sparks fly through the air. The power line snaps free.

"Ben!" I shout to warn him.

He and Garnet glance up. We all watch as the liberated black rope, filled with a violent electrical current, twists in the freezing midnight air, sparks exploding as it touches down on the road once, and again on a tree, bouncing wildly from object to object, threatening to take out everything in its path. Just as it flips again in the air, surges wildly, soars in hundreds of directions at once, and then careens *toward me*, Ben's eyes lock on mine.

I'm helpless to it.

With my next breath, it will hit me.

I squeeze my eyes shut and brace myself, preparing to be electrocuted right here on this road, right in front of Ben and Garnet.

But it doesn't hit me. I hear a violent zap. Then nothing at all. I throw my eyelids open to see a spray of golden orange light all around Ben, who crossed back to protect me. It hit *him*.

As bulbs in the street lamps burst—one, two, three, four—all the way down the island, as zaps and sizzles echo against the trees, as I stare and stare at what the electricity is doing to his body, it comes to an end. At last. Leaving no trace of the damage it's done. Because it leaves no trace of Ben.

He is simply gone. Vanished.

"More spirit than flesh," I utter, staring at the blank spot where he just stood.

He's disappeared. Into thin air. Where his feet were, just a blink earlier, now lays the spent wire, sleeping quietly in an unmoving curl. Unable to comprehend enough to even scream, I squeeze my eyes closed again and try to talk myself into opening them, but I can't. It's all madness on *that* side of reality. It's safer in my mind, where it's dark and cool and quiet.

"But nothing can kill him, right?" I call to Garnet, expecting my teacher to teach me. "He's vivified. He gets more than one body, doesn't he? More than one chance?"

"He's *mine*," she sneers. "I came back for him, and I'm not leaving without him. Don't fool yourself." Then she straps on her helmet, mounts her bike, and speeds back down the island, leaving every question unanswered.

In the blackout, with the sky stone gray, with the rain coming down in torrents, I run back down the island, avoiding the ice on the roads, uncertain where I'm going but certain I'm looking for one person: Ben Zin. He's somewhere out here. He must be. Just as Pilot and Harper are out here commiserating, swapping stories about how terrible I am.

"You don't just *disappear*," I convince myself through gasps for air. "There must be rules to vivification. Constants. If–then laws. *If your blood is on the island, then you are vivified*. Like Ben said."

I focus on finding Ben. The ice in my hair is heavy as I run. It separates my curls into thick dreadlocks that splay at the bottom, the wet ends slapping my chin and shoulders, spraying droplets of water into the air as I pass the gates of the dark campus and charge on. The Zin mansion soon becomes a barely discernible outline behind the black rain, with just a small glow in one of the windows to give away that someone is there, burning a candle. Is it Ben? Is that remotely possible?

Veering from my course, I steal up to the window, peeking in to see Dr. Zin, Gigi, and Teddy sitting together, with Skippy curled on Gigi's lap and snarling at Teddy.

But it's just those three. No Ben in sight.

Stopping for that one second, I let myself listen briefly to the thoughts flitting like colonies of rabid bats through my head. Garnet said she came back for Ben. From where? And what if the electricity actually killed Ben for good? What if he's really *gone*? A whimper escapes my lips. I clutch my hands over my mouth—but not before something scrapes at my arm. No, doesn't scrape at it. *Clutches* it. And yanks me from the window.

If my hand weren't on my mouth, the entire island would hear me scream.

Desperately, I claw at my unseen attacker.

I slip on the grass as rain pelts me from every direction. Finally freeing myself, I scramble away from the person, who is cloaked in darkness, and glare in its direction. At first, I see only a shadow, a glowing outline of a tall man. And then Ben's eyes. Bright green. Illuminated. He steps out of the shadows, his finger pressed to his lips.

"*Shh*," he whispers. "They'll hear you."

I gasp to see him. Never has his skin appeared so translucent. Never have his eyes been so brilliant, so glassy, so bewildering. Pulsating behind him, the vast darkness of the cloaked moon and the endless tempests cling to his every limb like long, thick fingers seducing him back into another world. The world of the dead.

I rise slowly, inch by inch, feeling a hot wave rush from my face to my toes and back up before he grins a grin that says *yes-I'm-alive-and-as-deathly-gorgeous-as-ever*.

"Don't be mad. Or scared," he says slowly, extending his pale, long fingers before me like a Good Samaritan approaching a street dog.

"I'm not." But I am. My whole body quakes.

"I need you to come with me. Come away from the house. Before Teddy senses you're home."

"Senses?"

"He's connected with you. Happens with every Guardian. They latch onto part of your soul when they first read you, and they never let go."

Terrified, the best I can do is move from a slumped crouch to my feet. Still, I back away from him, watching him closely, not sure what I'm feeling, why I'm so frightened suddenly, but recognizing the sensations scurrying under my cold, wet flesh. The same sensations I felt back home when I would get up in the middle of the night for a glass of water, knowing ghosts lurked around every corner, watching me with their glassy stares, darting out of sight the instant I glimpsed their trailing white hems.

"Anne…"

Then he lunges at me. He tugs me out of view, away from his front-room window. Because I don't want to be found out, I don't scream. But my eyes are feral, my expression wild as he hauls me violently behind his house, behind Gigi's, down to the water's edge, down where rough waves crash fiercely and mix with pools of water running to the shore. The slick rocks under our feet cause us both to stumble, but he continues on until we arrive alongside the ocean. Surrounded on three sides by dense, tangled woods. Our shivering bodies protected from view. Our riotous voices muffled by the storm. Streams of icy water run down both our faces, soaking our clothes, making our teeth chatter, as he turns and faces me at last.

"Let me get a few things out there now," he says, standing no more than two inches from me, so close the toes of his shoe fit between the toes of mine. His warm hands brace my shoulders. He waits for me to agree, but I don't have the capacity. "First thing, it's over between me and Garnet. Over. Don't look at me that way. It's *over*."

"She doesn't think it's over."

"She came back from her new life for me."

"Her new life? We're all dead!"

"Don't you know yet what the reward of the Big V is?"

"It's a second chance at life, I think."

He nods and waits for me to draw lines between the dots.

"Are you trying to tell me Garnet was a student here, and she graduated as valedictorian?" As I shout over the rain, he confirms everything—even the guesses that I dream up on the fly as, one by one, murky clues turn into solid puzzle pieces that snap together. "She had a second chance to live a real life. Off this island. And she gave that up to come back here. For you."

"We dated when she was a Cania student, back when her name was Lizzy. The valedictorian changes their name when they start their new life. She graduated last June. She wasn't gone longer than a few weeks before she asked Villicus if she could come back to Cania."

"As a teacher."

"Which requires that a person be in a certain state."

I'm not sure what he means, and it shows. "You're not saying she's not alive, are you? She *died* to be with you?"

"It's worse than that." His face blanches. "Much worse."

twenty-one

BEN ZIN

THUNDERCLAPS STRIKE LIKE APPLAUSE ABOVE US.

"Ben, what could Garnet have had to do to join the Cania faculty?"

I think of Trey Sedmoney and old Weinchler. Putting Trey's indiscretions aside, I can't help but think that they seem like rather normal teachers. There's nothing unusual about the faculty. The secretaries, on the other hand—they're another breed of human entirely.

"Let's just say she gave up more than her life."

"Her family's fortune? A private island?"

"*More.*"

Suddenly, two people walk through the trees behind us. Ben drags me to the wet forest floor as we wait for them to pass.

Through the falling ice, loose branches, and moss, I can just make out Pilot and Harper. He's still seeking comfort, and she's still giving it to him, probably filling his head with all sorts of lies about me, turning my one friend even more against me.

They recede into the darkness, leaving Ben and me alone, side by side, on the damp earth.

"Anne, please know that Garnet isn't the one for me, in spite of what she thinks and what she's done. The only reason I ever entertained a relationship with her was because she reminded me of a blonde girl who once kissed my cheek. Which brings me to the second thing I wanted to tell you. I'm sorry I was so rude to you today. And I'm sorry my dad was, too."

"It sucked," I confess under my breath.

"The reason we were rude to you today was to protect you. The only reason I've ever been anything but… cordial, I guess, is because I wanted to protect you."

Freezing water runs over my lips as I prepare to retaliate, to say how completely untrue that is, how he's cruel at best. But then our moments together—our few, fleeting moments, pathetic because they're meaningful only to me—flicker in my mind. His warning in the office the first day, when he told me to obey my Guardian. Cautioning me to get out of the village. Warning me to steer clear of Molly. Cryptically discussing the books. Leaving one on my bed. All of it.

"If Garnet knew I felt anything for you, she'd ruin you. Both my dad and I know that. Hell hath no fury like a woman scorned, right?"

"Is that why she made Harper the lead for the Art Walk? Because she saw the two of us in the library the day Molly died?"

He nods. "I've tried to stay away from you for your sake," he continues. Huge droplets of water cascade down his nose and chin as, tenderly, he strokes my wet hair from my face. "We were all warned before you got here that there'd be hell to pay if any of us let on about the truth. But it's never seemed right, keeping you in the dark. Not for a second. That day outside Valedictorian Hall, when we talked about books, I was on the brink of giving you a serious hint. But then Villicus showed up." He shakes his head, scattering raindrops. As mud pools around us, we wisely but grudgingly get to our feet again. "In his office later, Villicus told me he'd punish me severely if I revealed anything to you. *Severely*."

"Why? Why is it so important to hide the truth from *me*? Everyone else gets to know. And I've figured so much out on my own already!"

"That's one of the amazing things about you. How many people would put this together, Anne? Who'd believe they're vivified on some Maine island?" Running his hands through his wet hair, revealing his beautifully broad chest, he holds my gaze. His breathing is heavy now, as heavy as mine, his chest nearing me every time it rises. "Maybe it's because you're an artist. Or a genius. I don't know."

"I'm not a genius."

"I'm not trying to flatter you. Look, now that you know what you know, Villicus is going to cause problems for you. And he'll wonder how you figured it out. And he'll blame me. Not that it matters, but he will."

"Why you?"

"He heard our conversation that day!" he shouts, backing away from me and beginning to pace. "And Garnet saw us tonight. And so did Pilot."

"So what?"

"Pilot will tell Villicus, and he'll put two and two together."

"Why would Pilot say a *thing* to Villicus? They hate each other. Plus, it's not even true! You didn't tell me anything."

"This is Villicus we're talking about, not some district attorney who carefully weighs the facts."

Realizing he's right, I shake my head. "What will he do to you?"

"It's not about what he'll do to me. It's what he'll do to Jeannie."

"Your sister?" A new possibility occurs to me. "Is she alive on this island, Ben?"

He shakes his head, no. "But, you see, in the office after our impromptu book club, Villicus threatened to cause trouble on the *other side* for Jeannie if I told you anything." His statement leaves me flabbergasted, so he fills in the obvious blank. "In the after-life."

My teeth chatter—not just because I'm freezing. "How could he do that?"

"It's possible, Anne. After seeing the things I've seen here, I'd put my money on further examples of craziness existing."

"How could Villicus reach your sister?"

"All I know is that I have no recollection of anything that happened during the days between my death and vivification on Wormwood." He nears me again, but more cautiously this time. "It's possible the spirit world doesn't work exactly as we think it does. It's possible that Villicus could reach Jeannie. I don't know how, but I wasn't willing to take that chance with my little sister."

"But it's *impossible*."

"Look at me! Look at you! How much evidence do you need that nothing's impossible? Not when you're dealing with evil incarnate."

I turn to get my bearings, but he grabs my hands, pulling me even closer.

"The only reason I'm telling you now is because I've realized that Jeannie can take care of herself. The same way you've taken care of yourself. That courageous spirit you share. You're both fighters."

Staring through the rain into his eyes, I collect myself enough to choke out, "What did you say about evil incarnate?"

"You're freezing," Ben whispers. "Let's get you inside, and I'll explain as much as I can."

A half-minute later, we're inching Gigi's back door open, tip-toeing into the house, and creeping up the stairs. Teddy, Gigi, and Skippy still haven't returned, so the house, in all its hallowed silence, with all its empty cabinets and creaking corners, is ours.

We enter the dark attic and check to make sure the candle continues to burn in the house next door.

Sitting on a chair in the corner of my room, Ben turns away and flips through *The Prince* as I change into dry clothes. I offer him a large sweater, but he declines.

"Evil incarnate," I repeat, sitting cross-legged on my bed. "What did you mean by that?"

He holds up the book. "Did you even open this?"

"Stop deflecting."

"I'm not. I'm answering your question the best way I can, without breaking the rules."

"I thought you didn't care about the rules!"

"I swore not to tell you, Anne. But I didn't swear not to hint at it."

Groaning, not enjoying that loophole, I turn my attention to the tattered book just as he flips open the cover and removes the jacket, letting it fall to the floor. Then he holds the book up to me. It's not *The Prince* at all. It's Christopher Marlowe's *The Tragical History of Doctor Faustus.*

"I went out on a limb to give this to you," he says. "The biggest possible hint I could give you. And you didn't even read it."

"I thought it was *The Prince.* I've read that before."

"Did you think I climbed up the side of your house and through your window for fun?" he asks. "That I left this book here because I had nothing better to do?"

"Just tell me, how is *Doctor Faustus* a hint? It's about an old scholar and the devil."

"So you did read it?"

"Not exactly," I confess, fidgeting. "Before my mom got sick, she worked in a library. She read constantly. She told me the story on repeat, like it meant something to her. Anyway, it has nothing to do with bringing dead kids to life."

"Well, what is it about?"

"It's about a guy who wants a better life or more knowledge or something."

"Try again."

"I won't play your guessing game."

"And I won't just tell you."

"Fine! It's about…it's about making deals with the devil."

With that, Ben sets his eyes on mine. The pause, the sudden stillness is significant. Significant enough that I stop to think about what I've just said. And, instantly, swiftly, with the shocking abruptness of the lightning that flashes outside my window, I think about the Tuition Battle I witnessed only hours ago. The terrible exchanges parents made for their children's lives. That's what tuition is. An exchange—what Villicus wants for what a parent wants. Nothing more than a deal with the devil.

"So, we're in *Hell*, and Villicus is the *devil*?" I scoff.

"We're not in Hell."

"Then why does that book matter?"

"*You* have to answer that." Ben paces my floor now, taking care to stay away from the window. "Here's what I can tell you. Villicus has built an empire on Wormwood Island. And he's used my dad to help him, at least for the last five years. But like any dictator, he's looking for more. And now, with you, I think he's found it."

I'm reminded that Ben said his family got in a car accident five years ago. In the madness of the evening, it nearly slipped my mind. Already I've pieced together that Ben died with his sister and mother in the car that day. But the timing still doesn't make sense to me.

"Ben, answer me this. How long have you been at Cania?"

"Five years."

"But you died when you were sixteen. And you appear to be sixteen now. When we're vivified, do we not age?"

"The other students do. You will. But I don't." He leans against the wall. "I'm not a senior here, Anne. I'm just here.

That's why I don't live in the dorms. I'm not in competition for the Big V. As you may have noticed, the only classes I attend are classes I TA."

I search his face and recall something Harper said once about Ben being too old for her. "You're twenty-one."

"I am." Ben sits beside me on the bed. With a faint smile, he takes my hand in his. "Villicus trapped my dad into his service by offering him what he offers everyone."

"A second chance with their child."

"He *keeps* my dad here by promising to keep me alive, with his twist that I remain unaging. One year of my life in exchange for one year of my dad's servitude. Year after year. It keeps me out of the competition; it keeps me from graduating and permanently expiring; but it also keeps me stuck on this island, eternally sixteen." He rubs my hand between his. "I don't blame my dad. I'm sure I'd do the same thing if I were in that situation and was offered, essentially, a miracle."

"The exchange your dad made for your life was to work as Villicus's recruiter?"

"Villicus wanted access to my dad's wealthy network. At first, my dad just had to make a choice. That was the price he paid to get me in."

"What kind of choice?"

Ben lowers his head. "He had to choose which of his two children would be vivified and join him on Wormwood." His face is pale as his distressed gaze finds mine. "Jeannie died. I came back. And I don't think he's ever forgiven himself for not being able to bring Jeannie back, too."

The front door slams downstairs, startling us both.

"Anne, I have to go," Ben whispers, pulling away suddenly.

As if I could just let him leave now! He's finally answering my questions. And, with every new answer, I have a new question he needs to address.

"You can't go." I'm unable to keep my voice down as I pull at the hand I still hold, as he starts for the window. "What else aren't you telling me? You haven't even said what Garnet gave up!"

Tugging his arm free, he bolts to the window and jerks at the lock on it. "Just don't let Teddy know you know about all this, okay? Dear God, Anne, make sure he doesn't know. I'll get my dad to call your dad tonight, and we'll figure out your situation tomorrow. First thing."

Downstairs, Teddy shouts my name. The sound of footsteps bounding up the first flight of stairs follows. I scramble to join Ben at the window.

"Don't go," I plead. "I don't care if Teddy uses this as a strike against me."

"Well," Ben whispers urgently as he struggles with the window, "I do care. If you're going to stick around here, you'll need your Guardian on your side. No two ways around it."

Teddy bangs twice on my bedroom door. "You in there?"

Finally, the window gives. Ben slides it up. But he's not fast enough. Teddy is already storming up the staircase, heaving and huffing as he leaps from midway up the stairs and, arms thrown wide apart, face distorted in the ugliest grimace, explodes into my room.

"I knew it!" Teddy shouts. I've never seen his expression so twisted, his boney face so gnarly and inhuman. He turns to Ben and points an accusatory finger. "You were told to bring her directly back to your house if you found her. Were you having your way with her instead?"

"What?" I cry.

"What garbage are you filling her mind with?" Teddy demands.

Either that terrible expression or my unhinged hatred for Teddy or the events of the day have caught up with me because I fly at that skinny German beanpole before another ugly word can slither off his pointy tongue. As violently as I can, I thrust his arm down, squishing his bony finger back against his palm, using all the force my stature allows to send him staggering to the staircase.

Ben is behind me in a flash, sprinting to my side just as Teddy grabs the railing to keep from falling. "Anne, don't waste your energy."

"Don't touch me with those slut hands," Teddy growls at me.

I slap Teddy hard across the face. So hard the loose skin of his cheek flaps. So hard the smacking sound echoes through the attic. He reels back.

"I *rejected* you, you pig," I roar. "Don't you ever call me that name or any name!"

"Anne," Ben says, tugging at my arm. "He wants this from you. Villicus's demons feed on shit like this."

Still gripping the railing, Teddy pulls himself up and puffs his skinny chest out. His eyes reveal an inner madness, something more sinister than I'd given the pesky weasel credit for. He looks like he could kill Ben or kill us both.

"You told her, didn't you?" Teddy storms, his voice shrill.

"She found out on her own."

"I pieced it together."

"We'll see what Villicus has to say. You'll both be in such a hell-storm." He whirls to head down the stairs. "Expulsions! I don't care how important you think your dad is, Zin!"

"No!" I holler, tearing free of Ben and chasing Teddy down the stairs. "No, please, he didn't do anything!"

I know what getting expelled from this school means, and I can't let that happen to Ben. My heels skid over the edges of the steps until I catch Teddy. My hand braces his arm, which is fiery hot. I whip his skinny body around.

"Get your hands off me," he barks, shoving me with all his might.

With that one thrust, I lose my balance. My big toe, the only thing holding me to the stairs, succumbs under the weight of my tipping body. Without a blink, I find myself falling backward, watching Ben and Teddy disappear from my line of sight, watching as the beams of the ceiling pass by, as my hands clutch helplessly at the air while my body twists, as my heels lift up, as Ben shouts after me and even Teddy looks surprised. *I am falling*. Tumbling down. Hitting the hard edges of the wooden steps. First my back. Then my head. Then I don't know what else because all I can feel is intense, brightly colored pain shooting down my spine. I topple down the rest of the staircase—I hear myself cry out—until I land in a heaping, heaving lump at the bottom. Teddy comes up on me fast. He shoves my limp, gasping body out of his way. I reach for him. But he is just beyond my grasp. And my hand won't move. I try to scream. My voice is gone.

"Anne!" Ben calls, racing down the stairs as Teddy takes off down to the main floor.

I moan my response. The sudden pain is incredible. A white light flashes ahead. Am I dying again? I don't remember dying the first time, so it's hard to know. Is this it? Have I been in purgatory, and now I'm to be released to whichever of the two sides I've earned? Is that what those flashes of white are? Is that where the deep voice inside my ears is?

Ben stares into my eyes, whispering something I wish I could hear, but the sounds are too loud on the other side. He strokes my hair away from my face.

I hear him say only this: "Teddy's going to tell Villicus. You need to go now. And you can't ever come back. But I'll never forget you."

I shake my head, or I try to. How can I go? Where will I go? When will Ben join me there? I thought we couldn't die here, couldn't die twice.

His head lowers to mine, his parted lips closing the distance—and if I were capable of breathing, I would hyperventilate. His mouth, his perfectly formed mouth, is just an inch away. But I can't enjoy this moment, can't feel him as I want to. I try to shake my head as his unbelievable eyes come even closer, as he pauses unexpectedly.

Then, taking a deep breath, instead of kissing me, he whispers, "This is what I've wanted to tell you all along. Wake up, sweet Anne. Go home. It's not your time." His eyes search mine. "Close your eyes and wake up."

A searing pain. A flash of white. And I'm gone.

twenty-two

NIGHTTIME IN HEAVEN

BEFORE ANYTHING COMES INTO FOCUS, BEFORE THE pain in my head attacks, I notice white light. The sterile glow of fluorescent tube lighting fills the room in which I find myself. Blotches of sharper yellow pour over my body, over the white bedsheet folded neatly under my arms, over the narrow bed in which I lay, over the white walls around me, over the machines that beep and drip pale liquid into my veins. The pain follows. Behind my eyelids, I see the sharpest image of my head being split in two with an axe. I jerk my hand to clutch my head only to find my wrist restrained. I jerk my other wrist, but exhaustion owns my body, dividing my energy, dimming my movements. Straining to hold my eyelids open, I spy tethers on my wrists. My eyes discern shapes in muted colors but blur over the details as the objects in the room slowly come into focus. The pain makes me want to scream, but my throat, parched, allows little more than a moan. Inhaling deeply through my nose, I use all my strength—*so weak*—to force my eyelids wide.

Where am I?

This cannot be Hell. It cannot be Heaven. Because my dad is

asleep in the chair next to my bed. And I'm pretty sure my dad's still alive and well, living in Atherton.

"Dad?" I whisper. I can't hear myself, so I try again, try to wiggle my tongue to wet my throat enough to speak. "Dad?" I hear myself this time and smile, but it feels like I haven't moved my face in years. "Daddy?"

He shifts in his chair. Next to him are stacks of objects that don't make sense. A tower of bricks. A boom box. A tambourine and symbols. A bucket with half-melted ice floating in it. All of my favorite books, family photo albums, stacks of CDs and DVDs, school textbooks. Perhaps I'm at the gates of Heaven, and this person who looks—and snores—like my dad is an angel in disguise, and I'm about to take some sort of test using all these weird objects. The afterlife is nothing like I'd expected.

"Angel?" I try.

He snorts and crosses his arms over his chest.

The white room is quiet. With my head swooning, I drag my slow-moving eyes to a window. It's dark outside. Does it get dark in Heaven? Seems like it wouldn't. But it's always fiery in Hell, which would make it orange, not black outside. Plus, I don't think I've been very bad; I'm sure I'm not destined for Hell. So this is Heaven. It's nighttime in Heaven.

Bit by bit, I begin, in the silence, to recall everything that has just happened. Chasing Teddy to keep him from telling Villicus and getting Ben—and me—expelled. Falling down the stairs. Ben's mouth so close to mine. And the words Ben said: *Close your eyes and wake up.*

Ben told me to wake up just as Harper told me at the dance, after she'd broken my mom's barrettes. *Wake up.*

My eyes are heavy, too heavy to think any more about it. The gentle rhythm of my dad softly snoring in his chair lulls me. Sleep lures me back under.

A cell phone rings. My eyelids barely lift, my eyes resist focusing, but eventually I see my father standing in the doorway to this white room. He's talking to someone on his phone. How long has it been since I've seen a cell phone, since I've heard one ring? Feels longer than the time I've been at Cania.

And then there's the other noise in the room. The dominant noise. The *beeping*. It comes steadily from the machine that's attached by tubes to my arm.

"Am I dreaming?" I try to whisper, but my voice is so hoarse. So I stop trying to talk. Instead, I listen.

"If she wakes, I'll do whatever it takes to keep her here," my dad says to the caller. More words follow, but they fly out much too quickly for my slow-moving mind to get a hold on, to sort through, to make sense of. And then, before I can blink, my dad is snapping his phone closed and turning to me.

When did his beard get those gray patches?

His eyes are glazed over, like he's been staring at me for an eternity, even though he just looked my way.

"Dad?" I choke.

He just *stares* at me like he can't process my words. And then, after lengthy hesitation, he leaps into the air, clasps his hands in his hair, and hurls himself across the room at me, choking me in his enormous bear hug, threatening to collapse the frail bed under us both. I cough and try to breathe.

The machine next to me beeps faster, and he pulls back immediately.

"Dr. Zin just said you were on your way home," he murmurs as he kisses my forehead. He grips my cheeks in both his hands and holds my barely lucid gaze. People have always commented on how identically colored our eyes are. But his look so tired now, so puffy, as if he's been rubbing away tears for years. "I didn't believe him."

"Dr. Zin called you?" I ask.

"I just got off the phone with him." Grinning, he sits with a heaving sigh and braces his knees. "I just need a sec. This is unbelievable. It's been so long."

Like my dad, I need a moment to take everything in. So I use the next five minutes of my dad gawking, staring, gushing, running to get me water, hugging me, and gushing more to make sense of what exactly is happening here.

"My baby," Dad whispers in my ear as he crushes my head to his chest another time. I lie limp in his arms, unable to move. "Just give me more time to take in this moment, okay?"

I try to nod, but his huge hand is pressed against the back of my head, smooshing my face against his shoulder. I'm lucky I can breathe, let alone nod. He hugs me in that bear-like embrace for an eternity until, finally, his face and beard wet with tears, he draws back and collapses in the chair next to my bed. But the distance of one-and-a-half feet proves too great, and he shifts his chair so he's right next to me. Taking my hands in his. Tears still rolling down his cheeks. In my life, I've never seen him shed a single tear, not even when Mom threw a stitch-ripper at him on one of her bad days and tore the flesh near his eye. No one can prepare you for the shock of seeing your big, burly, protector dad weep at your bedside.

"Kiddo, have I missed you," he breathes, stroking my arm, evidently forgetting that I'm bound to this bed like some sort of prisoner. "Let me see those pretty eyes." As he presses his hand under my chin and searches my eyes, I can't help but drop my gaze.

"Are you dead, too, Dad?" My throat is still dry, so he lifts the glass of water from the bathroom to my lips again. I sip and pull away. "Is Mom here? Are we all here?"

"Baby, *shhh* now," he soothes. "What do you mean?"

"I'm dead. And so's Mom," I sputter. "And I guess you are, too."

Flinching, he leans back. "Dead? Oh, sweetheart, you're not dead. There was a moment, sure, when your heart stopped and you were technically dead, but you came back. That was more than two years ago, back when Mom died."

Hang on. What?

"Whatever made you think you'd died, baby?" he asks softly, stroking the hair away from my forehead like he used to do when I was little. Then he notices the tethers on my wrists and unties me, shaking his head and asking my forgiveness for taking so long.

"Because everyone else. All the others. At school." The beep-ing. The white room. "Is this a hospital? A real one? With real living people here?"

"The night nurse just stepped out on a coffee run," he says. "You're at a long-term care facility in San Mateo. You've been in a coma since the day your mom killed herself. And now, sweet-heart," he peers deep into my eyes and smiles, "now you're awake."

Lots of words fly at me in the span of the next few minutes as my dad tries to explain everything. The ones that are most frequently repeated are the only ones that stick.

Fighter is one of those words. I'm a fighter, according to my dad, because no one thought I'd make it longer than three months. It's been twenty-eight months. I'm a fighter because I've had solid brain activity the whole time I've been in a coma, when I should be brain-dead. I'm a fighter because I shouldn't even be talking yet, let alone asking my dad questions. As much as I want to care about all of that, the only reason the word *fighter* even resonates with me is because Ben once used it to describe me and his sister.

Ben knew I was in a coma this whole time, fighting to stay alive. He told me to wake up.

Another word is *sore*.

I try to squeeze my dad's hands. "I'm stiff."

My dad strokes my hair. "For now. Therapy will help with that." He kisses my cheeks, my forehead, my nose, beaming like he's won the lottery. "You wouldn't believe how much you've been jerking around in bed these last few weeks. You nearly fell out. It was mind-blowing, especially after years of just lying there. Even still, I didn't believe anything'd wake you up. Not even Cania Christy."

Those two words stick, too: "Cania Christy."

I've been mentally preparing myself for the news that Cania Christy and everyone there—everyone on Wormwood Island—was nothing more than a fantasy, an illusion dreamed up by my comatose brain. Which would mean Ben is only an illusion. I've been telling myself that my dad *didn't* say he was on the phone with Dr. Zin but with some other doctor. Could it be?

"Cania Christy?" I ask.

"You don't remember? Maybe because it happened while you were under."

"No, I remember. So you're saying he's real?" The beeping on my heart rate monitor accelerates.

"Who?"

"I mean *it*. It's real? Cania Christy?"

"Yes, sweetheart, Cania Christy is real," he breathes, smiling at the same time my monitors slow. "Best thing I ever did was sending you to that school."

I stare at him. Try to process it all. Can't.

"Water, please."

This time, I help him balance the glass near my mouth. My throat's feeling better. My voice has returned, though it's as choppy as Weinchler's. At least I know Ben is real, even if, now that I've woken, I'll never see him again; the knowledge that he was really there sustains me as my dad hems, haws, and tiptoes around the idea of telling me more about Cania Christy. Instead he talks about the state I've been in. I've been in a coma since I was fourteen. Everything I've missed! No wonder I knew nothing of Dave Stone's infamous sex scandal. No wonder I barely recognized myself in the mirror. I've missed over two years of my life lying, near death, in this very bed.

"A psychogenic coma," he clarifies. "It's the kind of coma brought on by mental trauma. It's like your brain cocooned itself to save you from the memory of something you experienced." He kisses my hands again. "I'm afraid that whatever I tell you might make you so upset, you'll fall back in."

"If you could just help me understand," I groan desperately. "How could I be there, on Wormwood Island, when I'm in a coma, and here when I'm awake?"

He shakes his head, runs his hands over his face, and glances through his fingers to make sure I'm still with him, as if he's honestly worried I'll slip away again.

"Dad, please. Don't I deserve to know what's been happening with my own life?"

At last, with a sigh so deep it could collapse his lungs, my dad launches—finally—into an explanation.

twenty-three

PORTRAIT OF
THE ARTIST'S MOTHER

"I KNEW SENATOR DAVE STONE BACK WHEN WE WERE both marines," my dad begins, "but I hadn't seen him in years. Then, a year ago this November, he came to Atherton for a funeral—his son Pilot's funeral. Do you know him, baby?"

I nod. Do I.

"Just before I was about to embalm his boy, Dave asked me to do him a favor. He paid me ten thousand dollars to keep it quiet. I'm not proud of it," he adds. "But I did what he asked, and I didn't tell a soul. We needed the money."

I gulp, though it hurts. Absently, my tongue presses against the back of my teeth, and I feel something I haven't felt in a week: my tooth is crooked again.

"Before I embalmed Pilot, I filled a test tube with his blood. I had no idea what Dave was going to do with it, but I gave a vial of his son's blood to him. And I took the cash." He rubs his hands over his puffy eyes. "When the funeral was over, Dave stuck around and we got to talking. He'd mixed a lot of Valium with a lot of Jack Daniels by then, so I asked him what the blood was for. He wouldn't tell me. Said he'd sworn an oath of secrecy and signed it with his blood. But after a few more drinks, he spilled. He had a doctor friend, a plastic surgeon who'd done Mrs. Stone's nose. This doctor was now working at a school out in Maine." He meets my eyes, and I nod. He means Dr. Zin. "What was special about this school was that its headmaster could bring kids to life again. Vivification, they call it."

"Villicus. It's really him." My voice shakes.

"Evidently, your headmaster can essentially re-create a child using their DNA." He pauses and tries to keep from smiling. "Only on Wormwood Island, which I understand Villicus has enchanted somehow. Well, months passed after that funeral. I didn't even think it could work for you. Then one night last month, after another poor examination by the doctor, I couldn't let you exist like this any longer. I called Dave. It took some gentle persuading, but I got him to admit that there's no theoretical reason Villicus's miracle couldn't work on a coma victim."

Here, I'm actually alive. There, where a vial of my blood rests, I'm only *vivified*. Reborn of dust, magic, and my blood, the core of what makes me *me*.

"So you gave Villicus my blood?"

"I gave it to Dr. Zin. He came here to see you, take your blood, and have me sign some forms. We stood over this bed, watching you sleep, talking about your future. His son is an artist, too, you know."

Oh, I know.

My dad reveals that Dr. Zin transported my vial from this hospital room across the country to Wormwood Island. Villicus met him, and I was, in a way, created then. When I think about it, I realize that I have no memories of the trip there or of anything prior to Gigi opening her front door to welcome me. My dad explains that students are normally awoken on Wormwood Island to find their parents there and are quickly told what's happened, where they are, and what their future at Cania holds for them. My case was, as everyone kept telling me, special. And, because of that, I had to figure everything out from scratch.

"Why didn't they just tell me what's going on the way they told everyone else?"

"Because," he says, "there's a code of secrecy. Villicus couldn't risk you waking up from your coma only to run around telling the world about his school, which would never survive if the world knew of it."

"It was all to keep me from talking about Cania?"

"From *painting* it, in particular. I knew I'd have to tell you eventually. What's important," he continues, "is that we *keep* the code of secrecy." Stroking my arm, he searches my face, his eyes pleading. Villicus's distrust of me is finally making sense. "No matter what, you must never speak of this to anyone for as long as you live. You mustn't create art reflecting it. Can I trust you, honey?"

I nod.

"I just wanted more time for you," he continues, his grip vice-like. "The odds of you waking here were one in a million. Cania was my only option. Please forgive me for forcing you to keep this secret, but you must. You must."

As my dad presses my palms to his face and sobs deeply, I wonder why, if there was even the chance of me waking up and revealing this secret, Villicus would let me in at all. Why? Why bend the rules for me? Why *want* me, as Gigi said?

Watching my dad shake his head, knowing he would do and give anything for me, my conversation with Ben just an hour earlier returns to me. Ben had said that Villicus used him to manipulate his dad, and that he wanted the same with me. The day I was supposed to be expelled, Teddy said the school wanted to retain me *and* my dad. What would Villicus want with my dad? It's obvious what he'd want with Dr. Zin: his influential connections.

But my dad's nothing but a tortured widower, a desperate father. A poor, lowly mortician...

...For the wealthiest zip code in the United States.

Suddenly, I get it. Villicus wants my dad to be his newest recruiter. That must have been what he exchanged to get me into the school.

My hands cling to my dad's face, and he pulls them back to look at me. At once, I have an urge to hug him, to rest in his arms where everything's always felt so safe. Throwing my arms around his neck, I pull him to me and, too quickly, run out of energy to hold him as tightly as I want to, but that's okay because he holds me close, then gently releases me, smiling ear to ear.

"Dad?" I struggle to keep my heart rate steady so the monitors don't squeal. "About my tuition."

"Mm-hmm."

"Did you agree to recruit rich dead kids for Villicus in exchange for my second chance?" I blurt.

He looks bewildered. "Of course not. Parents are *lucky* to get their kids into Cania. Villicus doesn't need anyone to recruit besides Dr. Zin, who must love his job. It's like telling people they've won the world's greatest lottery."

"You don't think it's sort of creepy and wrong, what he's doing?"

"What's *wrong*," he replies, looking hurt, "is good people losing their children. What's wrong is never getting the chance to tell someone you love how deeply you love them. What's wrong is having someone you were born to protect ripped from your life. I've seen a lot of sad people, honey. What Villicus is offering isn't wrong."

"I'm sorry. I know." Fidgeting, I finally return to my question. "If you're not going to be recruiting for him, what did you agree to give up to get me in?"

"Oh, honey, that doesn't matter," he says, smiling with his big brown eyes. "The less you know at this point, the safer you'll be."

But keeping me in the dark hasn't protected me yet.

"I'd give up anything for you," my dad continues.

"Dad, please tell me."

"If Villicus could do the same for your mother, I would have given up anything for her, too."

The mention of my mother nearly derails my brain. I can't help but think that I've never had a chance to mourn her. My monitors race. My head hurts like someone's scraping the insides of my skull.

"Baby?" my dad asks, alarmed. "What's the matter? You need to calm down."

I'm trying, but it's like the thought of my mom is tearing my mind to shreds. I shake my head weakly, trying to clear it. My dad mistakes the action as a *no* and, to my surprise, caves like he hasn't caved since I was a two-year-old holding my breath to get candy.

"Okay!" he exclaims. The beeping on my monitors returns to normal. "What I agreed to exchange for your vivification is very small. Minor. I'd do it again in a heartbeat. I'd do anything for you." He darts his gaze all over the room like he's trying to track an invisible hummingbird. And then he just says it. "I swore I'd never love again. Not another woman. Not another child. That was it." No beeping. The room goes silent. "It was so minor, I can't believe how lucky I am."

I flat-line. But only for a moment.

"Annie!" My dad throws himself on me.

I'm stunned. I knew my dad's love for me ran deep, but I had no idea. My dad loves me so much, he agreed to be alone *forever*. Just for the chance to know I was alive on some distant island for two more years, where he could visit once in a blue moon and call bi-weekly.

"Don't do that, sweetie, please," he says, watching my face. "None of that quivering lip. You know how that kills me."

I try to stop the tears, but that just makes my chin tremble.

"You're awake now, so I'll always have you to love. You just have to stay with me."

Nodding quickly, I want to agree and believe it's that easy. But I know, in spite of what my dad believes, that a man like Villicus—a man with power like this—will get what he wants. And I'm damn sure he wants my dad to help him fill his school and, in doing so, take everything he can from the wealthiest people on earth. As long as Villicus has my vial, he's got what he needs to trap my dad.

I need to get back to Wormwood Island. I need to destroy my vial.

"Our little girl," my dad whispers. "I read to you every day while you were asleep. Told you everything that was going on. Tried to wake you up by banging these bricks and cymbals. First thing every morning, I'd drive out here to rub ice on your wrists, which they say can shock your system awake." He points to the cymbals, the bricks, the bucket of ice. And suddenly my moments of dizziness and the extreme cold all make sense. Passing out and seeing him over me makes sense. "Dr. Jones said it was a long shot, but we tried. And now, here you are."

"What happens if I fall back into a coma?" I breathe, hoping he doesn't catch onto my secret agenda. I need to know if I can go back there.

"Let's not worry about that. Just stay with me until the nurse gets back, and she'll call Dr. Jones." His eyes are lost, as if he's worried I might go, as if the trauma he'd mentioned—the trauma the coma has been shielding me from—is so powerful, it could take me again.

"What's this coma called again, Dad?"

"A psychogenic coma. It's your brain shielding you from a traumatic memory."

"And that traumatic memory is … finding Mom?"

Sucking on his cheek, he shakes his head, *no*. Makes sense. How could I be shielding myself from that day, from walking in on my mom's suicide and tripping over her body, if I can think about it right now and not fall into a coma?

"So, what was it? What am I trying to hide from?"

"The police and I have our theories, baby." He glances at my monitors. "I don't think you're strong enough for this."

"I'm awake. I'm doing well."

"I'd like Dr. Jones to check you over first, just in case."

"I just want to know," I say. "If I'm going to get through this, it seems important to get over this hurdle." *Tell me the thing that will send me back into a coma, back to Wormwood.* "It won't hurt me. I'm here. Talking to you. Awake."

Reluctantly, he succumbs. But not before he's paced the room and stroked his beard a hundred times.

"You've always been so strong-willed. Just like your mother."

I smile weakly.

"Try to stay with me?"

I nod, lying to his face and hoping it doesn't show. His eyes flick between the monitors and me. And then he takes my hand and sits again.

"You found your mother on the floor, do you remember?" He waits for me to nod. "As far as we can tell, you tripped over her when you went to close the oven door."

I remember. Just like in my nightmares. Walking into the house with the earthquake siren roaring behind me. Stumbling through the darkness. I'd seen the oven wide open, releasing the gas that would kill her, but I hadn't seen her lying behind the island.

"You remember how Mom didn't seem very much like Mom in her last months?"

I nod, recalling the way she hurled unrepeatable curses at us day after day. It was like living with a mad stranger.

"She wanted to kill herself," he says. "The bills. The pain she knew she was causing. Her own pain. She turned on the gas while you were at school and waited to fall asleep."

"But I came home early because of the earthquake warning," I say, finishing his thought. Something is feeling very wrong in my head suddenly. I knew she killed herself this way, but there's something just beyond, some buried knowledge hidden in the darkness. The monitor beeps a little faster.

"Honey, calm down, please."

"Dad, I'm fine. Please tell me. *Please*."

Rubbing his beard, he nods. "When you tripped over her, Annie, you roused her. She wasn't gone yet." His jaw clenches. "And when she woke up, she was the bad version of herself. The very, very sick version."

As I begin to recognize—and resist—the story I've fought to keep out of my consciousness, I strain to keep my pulse even. But it's impossible. The machines beep in flurries.

"No more," he says matter-of-factly.

"Dad!" I cry out. The noises pile up in the room as dormant machines awaken, as my body resists what's happening and prepares for what's about to happen. "I need to get over this. You need to tell me."

"Absolutely not!" Without another word, he bounds to the door, pausing briefly to look back at me. "Calm down, baby. I'm going to find someone to help. You need to stay awake." And then, like that, he's gone.

I'm left to try to remember on my own, without him to fill in the gaps that will bring on the old memories my mind can't handle. Squeezing my eyes shut, I try with what little strength I have to remember what happened after my mom woke up. But the memories refuse to be found.

Desperately, I snap my eyes open.

To my indescribable surprise, I find my mother standing before me. Inexplicably.

But it's clear she is not her human self. Nor is she vivified. This is her ghost, her spirit. Why she's chosen to come to me now, I can't imagine—and I'm not given the time to.

In one elegant stroke, her beautiful, ghostly hand traces over my eyes, closing them again. I can feel her with me, bringing back the memories I need. They rush at me like enormous sledgehammers battering through the walls in my mind. Each blow is a memory.

Bang: My trip and slow-motion fall. Seeing my mom on the floor. Seeing her eyes pop open before she reaches for my throat, violently pulling me down.

Crash: She's grabbing a kitchen chair, lifting it high over her head.

Slam, slam, slam: the chair's coming down again and again. I'm horrified, shocked to see my own mother transform into a monster. I feel blood near my leg, feel my face swelling, lose focus. My mom screams that she'll kill me. Straddles me. Grips my hair.

"You tried to kill me that day," I whisper to the ghost I can't see.

There. The blackness opens for me, welcoming me into its embrace. But I've only just curled up in my safe cocoon when the soft noises of Wormwood Island steal in, drowning out the nurse's voice as she finds me asleep, drowning out my dad's voice as he begs me to come back to him, pushing away the quiet darkness of this in-between state where the blue glow of my mother's spirit guides me, and shoving me violently back into my attic room.

twenty-four

THE EPIPHANY

I WAKE WITH A START IN A HOUSE THAT IS MUCH TOO quiet. Only the sound of breathing and something like water dripping into a bucket. Where I'd expected to be lying in a lump at the bottom of the stairs, with Teddy and Villicus looming over me, there is instead my soft little bed under me and a glowing candle on my bedside table. For a moment, I watch it flicker and wonder if it's a remnant of some late-night vigil.

Here I am, back on Wormwood Island, back in my bed. Back in the body I left behind…how long ago? Glance at the clock. The power is still out. Glance at the window. My head pounds with the strain of peering into the darkness. Looks black out. Looks like a sheet of ice is coating the windowpane, with more icy rain thrumming against it; that was the sound I'd thought was dripping water. It's still raining, or it's raining again.

With an enormous sigh, with the task I have at hand boring a hole in my beaten, battered, bruised brain, I close my eyes. *Must not think about what Mom tried to do to me. Must destroy vial.* "Good luck with that," I tell myself.

"Shh," I hear Ben whisper before I even realize he's in the room.

The unexpected sound of a voice would normally send me leaping off my bed, but nothing can shock me now. Ben is lying right behind me; his heavy arm is draped over me. *Ben Zin is spooning me.* His warm hand holds mine, and his other arm rests under my pillow, supporting my neck. His sweet breath hangs in the air. No wonder my breath isn't like his, and no wonder he could change my teeth like he did; I'm only partway dead, but he's entirely deceased. I'm even more torn between worlds than he is.

"No one knows I'm in here. Keep quiet." Ben's arm tightens around me, and he rolls me gently onto my back. "Teddy left after you—after you left. Did you wake in California, Anne?"

I nod.

"You weren't supposed to come back," he whispers. His gaze pores over my face before darting to the stairs. "You were supposed to start again. Go to a normal school. Graduate as valedictorian with transcripts you can actually use."

I struggle to keep my focus with Ben so near. My eyes have started adjusting, but the throbbing in my head marches on. A low hum resounds somewhere behind my ears. Disorienting. I don't remember feeling like this the last time I came to Wormwood. I wouldn't forget a feeling like this.

"I came back for a reason, Ben," I say, watching him fiddle with a button on my Henley tee. "I think Villicus wants my dad to be his recruiter. To work with your dad."

"Or to replace my dad."

"Replace him?"

I adjust onto my elbow and, as I do, a paper I hadn't noticed crinkles under me. Absently, I pull it out, glance at it, and nearly toss it aside. But I stop short when I recognize the drawing on it.

Ben is watching me. My breath catches in my throat as I look at the sketch. In the bottom right corner are my initials: A.M.

"It's your best work, I think," he says, a smile in his tone. "You really are a fantastic artist, Anne."

"How did you get this?" I ask, my gaze glued to the page.

"My dad gave it to me."

"But I did this years ago. I was only eleven or twelve." I stroke the lines of the boy's face I'd drawn and recall everything. "He was lying in a casket, and there was no one else in the room yet, so I snuck toward him and found myself captivated by him. I remember," I say softly, reliving the moment, "being overcome by how young he was when he died. He was barely sixteen. And I remember imagining that he had beautiful eyes."

"There was another casket there," Ben tells me, triggering a memory.

"A closed casket. It was for his sister." My eyes are filled with tears when I look up at him. The impossible words find their way onto my tongue. "For *your* sister. You were the boy."

He nods and brushes my hair from my face.

"You sketched me, Anne. And then you kissed my cheek. And you tucked this sketch into my casket. My dad found it. He gave it to me when I woke on this island."

"It was you," I whisper as my head reels.

For the first time, I am beginning to understand why I've felt so connected to Ben. Even when he was cold and cruel. Even when I believed he was in love with Garnet. My heart has been his since that stolen kiss so many years ago.

"You left an impression on me that day," he replies, bringing his lips to my cheek and, slowly, trailing them down my jaw to my chin. "I've been looking for a charming, artistic blonde girl ever since. You can forgive me for settling for Garnet while I waited for you."

"How long have you known I drew this?" I ask, my breath coming faster.

"I've spent five years imagining what the initials on this portrait stood for."

Just when I thought I'd sorted out what I need to do—get my vial, leave—I learn that Ben Zin is the boy I first kissed, that he's been thinking of me ever since, that we've been drawn together across the planes of existence. Everything that had to happen to bring us to this moment. If it's not a coincidence, what does that mean for my plan?

"When I heard your story," he continues, "I put the pieces together. And when I saw you that first morning outside Villicus's office, while that pig Pilot was throwing himself all over you, it erased any doubt I had. I would have been overjoyed to see you at last, had I not been so tormented by the circumstances of our meeting."

I catch myself smiling and shake my head. "But you wanted me to leave. To wake up."

"I want you to live again, yes. Even if it means I won't get to be with you."

"Ben, when I was awake just now, back in California, I—I think my mom *wanted* to send me back here." Before he can say a word, I race on, trying to explain my train of thought. "Her spirit was there. She sent me back into my coma. If she wants me here, Ben, and if you're here, and if we have this history that we have, maybe—well, maybe this is all meant to be."

His face is instantly whitewashed. "No, Anne. You don't belong here."

"Maybe I do."

"You need to go back. You need to live a full, rich, happy life. Not to battle it out for the next two years under a tyrant like Villicus, especially against the likes of the students here."

"But you just said! You've been thinking of me for five years." I throw the covers off and sit just as he does, facing him directly. "Am I not what you remembered?"

"You're better than I could hope for, Anne. I connected to your spirit that day, but I fell for you as you are, here and now. And I'll think of you for the rest of my existence. But you deserve so much more than this."

My stomach knots. "Is this because you're worried about my dad replacing your dad? Because I would never let that happen!"

"Shh!" Glancing at the stairs, he sighs. "My dad will die an old man under Villicus's rule. Even if I begged and pleaded for him to let me die, my dad's too guilty about the car accident to give up on me, and Villicus needs him too badly to let that happen."

Foolishly, I'd allowed a tiny spark of hope to ignite. Hope that Ben could live. Hope that I could wake up in California, graduate, and find a way to be with him. I can almost hear that spark fizzling now, can almost see it fade out.

"You need to worry about you and your dad," he says. "Not about me."

Feeling tears rising again, I drop my eyes and swallow down everything I'm feeling.

"Villicus wants something from you, Anne. Sure, he wants your dad, but I know in my soul that he wants *you* even more. I have no idea what's motivating him, but I'm sure that he'd be happier to have you dead and trapped at Cania than any alternative. Even if it means sending one of his peons out to your hospital just to—"

"Slit my throat? Smother me with a pillow?"

"Something less direct," he says, releasing his grip on me. "I've done a lot of reading on the subject. And although I don't think Villicus or his lot are allowed to take human life, just as they can't create it from scratch, I do believe Villicus could be hatching a plan right now to end your life. That's why my dad called, to warn you guys."

"No one would kill me."

"*Any* of his employees would try to. The faculty. The secretaries. The housemoms and lunch ladies. All of them. They'd do something that would cause your death. They're all in his control. He's not just a man to them. He's their king."

"Ben, he *is* just a man. Evil, true. Insane, definitely. Paranormally gifted, yes. But only a man."

"Explain his power to vivify us," he whispers hoarsely, shifting closer to me and searching my face desperately. "He smells like fire. His glare is soulless. When he touches you, it's like being thrust into a nightmare. He makes us sign ourselves over to him in blood. *Blood*, Anne. He gets sick thrills out of forcing a man to tattoo his forehead. He builds us a beautiful cafeteria knowing the vivified don't have appetites. And Garnet offered him her soul if he would give her twenty-four years with me on this island."

That stuns me.

I shake my head, unable to believe it. "She traded her soul?"

He nods.

"Okay," I concede. "Villicus has a *fascination* with evil."

"No, he *is* evil. Can't you see? Hell is empty. All the devils are here."

"If that's true," I blast, "then if he wants me dead, if he wants my dad to work for him, nothing will stop him. I'm as good as dead. That's it."

A rustle outside startles us both. We pause, and, in the stillness, with the rain pelting the roof, I hear our hearts thumping.

"Not necessarily," Ben says quietly. "Don't think I haven't thought this through. We could force you to wake up again. Is your dad a reasonable man?"

"Aside from the fact he thinks Villicus is a godsend."

"Do you think you could convince him to sell the funeral home?"

"It was my mom's family business. I don't know. Maybe." I start working through his plan in my head. "So you think that if my dad gets disconnected from his network of rich mourners, Villicus might find us less interesting."

"It's worth a shot. Until we can figure out what Villicus wants with you. It might buy us some time."

I nod but, when it occurs to me that Ben will be trapped here forever with Villicus, I change my mind. "You would just stay here? Trapped?"

"Don't worry about me. I'll have the memory of two weeks with you to keep me company." A slow smile spreads across his perfect face, changing something inside me, driving home exactly why I can't just turn my back on him. "Let me do this for you. Let me protect you as I couldn't protect Jeannie. Anne, I've been here for five years for all the wrong reasons. Let me spend the next fifty here for the right ones."

"Fifty!" I try to keep my voice low, but it's hard. "What about this? I wake up right now, tell my dad to run away so he's protected, and kill myself. Then come back here. Where you are. We can sort things out from there."

"That's not even on the table," he stammers. "Not when you still have a chance at a real life. You're talking about killing yourself. Suicide."

"Pulling the plug," I counter. "Euthanasia. A mercy killing. I've been in a coma for years. If it weren't for the hospital, I'd be dead anyway."

"Don't talk like that."

"Just be honest, then. Just tell me it's because you don't want me to be here with you." I square my shoulders. "Not because you're trying to be noble."

With a short laugh, he leans back and watches me. "Crazy girl."

"Stop looking at me like that."

"I want you to leave *only because* I know what's here for you. I've had a long time to learn about everything on Wormwood, and none of it's good." His hand strokes my arm again. Softly. Then with pressure. "I only want what's good for you. Doesn't that tell you something?"

"*You're* good for me."

"I'm *terrible* for you. The worst," he adds forcefully.

And just as our eyes meet, before I can breathe another breath, he thrusts me against my headboard, holding my gaze as he moves my whole body with absolute ferocity. My heart pounds. The length of his body presses against mine as our tangled bodies stretch across my bed. His hands lock my arms in place. His lips are so close. The anticipation. The all-consuming, heart-stopping anticipation.

"You came back for me, risking your life," he growls. "That's my fault."

"Doesn't matter," I gasp.

"I should have left you alone the moment I realized you were *A.M.* You wouldn't be considering euthanasia if I had."

"Doesn't matter."

"I turned Garnet against you, Anne. Don't tell me that doesn't matter. If you were to stay, she would do anything to keep you from becoming valedictorian."

"Doesn't matter."

His eyes burn as he rattles off the many ways he thinks he's wronged me. But his lips are so near. And his beauty, overwhelming from a distance, is intoxicating up close, making my mind hazy and driving logic, reason, fear—everything but the desire to be as close and as connected as possible to him—into a distant realm.

Still gripping my arms, he shakes his head. "I called you dumb."

I pause. "Okay," I whisper, smiling. "*That* matters."

His soft lips finally brush mine, promising more, but he pulls away. With my pulse racing, I try to reorient myself, try to make sense of what *that* was. He looks mystified, torn even. And then I realize he's listening for something. Slowly, he brings his finger to my lips. His eyes dart back and forth as we listen. The cottage is creaky at the best of times, and the wind and hail against the side of the house aren't helping. But then I notice it. A more deliberate creaking. Unnatural creaking.

"Teddy's back," Ben whispers. "I have to go."

Pausing again, we both hear another groan. Sounds like it's coming from the landing on the second floor. Which means someone's at the bottom of these old attic stairs. Just outside my door. *Teddy.* Maybe with Villicus. And they're getting closer, approaching tentatively, as if they know I'm awake again and not alone.

"Play dead," Ben says, smirking. "When Teddy's gone, come over to my place, okay? I'm sure my dad can help us figure out a way to rouse you awake back home."

Another creak. Is that someone's hand on my doorknob? My eyes widen. I recline on the bed, pulling the covers up as Ben starts away. He watches the staircase. So do I. From where we are, we can just see the top of the door. It's still closed. He shimmies the window, which gives, and looks back at me.

"Come over the moment you can," he whispers. "I'd like to say good-bye properly."

The window slides up, and he's gone, creeping down my rooftop the same way he must have crept in when he left that book on my bed.

A squeak interrupts my thoughts. Someone is opening my bedroom door. Teddy? Villicus? Both? My heart pounds madly as I watch the shadows contract near my door, as a thin sliver of light replaces the darkness. I squeeze my eyelids shut. A faint scuffle on the stairs. And another. The soft pad of feet on my floorboards. It sounds like there's only one person. But there could be two. They cross the foot of my bed and stand at my bedside table. Look down at me. I can feel their eyes, feel my heart thumping so loudly, there can be no doubt in their minds that I'm very much alive, back from

California. I can only hope they're seeing what I want them to see. The signs of sleep. My heavy breathing. My eyelids twitching as if I'm mid-dream. Calm, sleeping girl with no concerns that she is the latest target of a madman. Of pure evil.

The person pushes my arm, shoving me awake, and I brace myself to be thrown down the stairs again as I open my eyes.

Gigi stares down at me. She is alone. Her hair is wild. Her eyes are bloodshot. She reeks of booze. I'd be relieved to see her if she didn't look so feral.

"When I die," she says, her tone flat, "throw my body off a cliff. I don't want to be cremated."

I nod, keeping my gaze fixed on her.

"Cremation is so permanent. I like to think my body might float out to sea, spend a little time there, and float back again one day. Then I'll be reborn as the perfect version of myself. The beauty I once was."

With a raspy final breath and nothing more, she recedes. A creak of the stairs. And the closing of my bedroom door.

Like a tightly wound spring released, I pop out of bed. Gigi's words, spoken quietly, scream about the power Villicus will have if he keeps my vial in his possession. Waking from my coma and getting my dad to quit the business is good, but it's not enough. Not if Villicus wants more from me and my dad than we know.

Nothing has ever been so clear to me as what I feel right now. What I *know* right now. And that is this: I need to get my vial. Gigi may be okay with the randomness of waves determining if she is or isn't vivified here, but I can't risk anyone having control of my destiny but me. Even if it separates me from Ben; I know I won't let us be forever parted.

"My vial or bust," I whisper, stuffing my hair into a quick bun, pulling on my shoes, slipping on my school cardigan. I shove my hands into my cardigan pockets. And there I feel it. Like someone put it there for me.

I pull it out. The key to the closet off Valedictorian Hall. I forgot to put it back today when I ran from Teddy. What follows can only be described as an epiphany.

Valedictorian Hall is kept locked for a reason. The plaque outside the hall—I read it once, thinking it was a word game. What did the rubbed letters spell again? It started with the word *via*, but then it got messy. Could it have been *vials*?

I'll find out soon enough. That's where I'm headed.

As I jimmy the window up again, I glimpse the book Ben left for me; it's open on my dresser. *Doctor Faustus*. I scoop it up and glance at the highlighted section on the page:

MEPHISTOPHELES
That I shall wait on Faustus whilst he lives,
So he will buy my service with his soul.

FAUSTUS
Already Faustus hath hazarded that for thee.

MEPHISTOPHELES
But, Faustus, thou must bequeath it solemnly,
And write a deed of gift with thine own blood;
For that security craves great Lucifer.
If thou deny it, I will back to hell.

As I read, I recall the words Teddy shouted that first day, when he and Villicus were pushing me to sign my forms in blood: "Thou must bequeath it solemnly!" And I recognize the final line—"If thou deny it, I will back to hell"—which I'd seen in Ben's notebook, at the bottom of one of his sketches. Both phrases spoken by Mephistopheles, prince of Darkness, the demon who took Faustus's soul…

I throw the window up. Holding onto the ledge, I teeter out onto the roof's slick surface as rain continues down and freezes instantly. How Ben navigated this, I don't know. And I don't have time to think through every step. Plus broken bones heal fast here, right?

So I let go.

Feel my body slip through a cold blast of air.

And land in a heap on the ground, something cracking.

As I stagger to my feet, I hear a gun fire inside Gigi's cottage and look up. Briefly, I think that perhaps Gigi came up to my room to shoot me. But I know that's not true. I know how unhappy she was. And I know now that her speech only moments ago was not merely the rambling of an old drunk. She needed to escape Villicus's hold on her—on her entire enslaved village—as much as I do. But rather than dragging her body to sea, as she wanted, I run.

To the school. To Valedictorian Hall. To find and destroy my vial before Villicus, evil incarnate, gets me.

twenty-five

STRANGER THAN FICTION

IT'S BLACK OUT, WET, ICY COLD. THE ROAD IS SLICK, AND rain pours.

Bounding along at midnight, I realize that once Teddy knows I'm gone, I'll have maybe half a second before Villicus tracks me down. And I'd better be damn ready to get out of here then. That means I'll need to have my vial in hand. And a solid plan to destroy it—whether burning it like Molly was burned or throwing it off the island like Villicus threw Lotus's and like Gigi, who may already be vivified in her cottage, wanted for her body.

"Say good-bye to Ben," I tell myself, choking up as my fists cut through sheets of slushy rain.

Rain cascades over my face and clothes, but even if it didn't, I'd be chilled to the bone with the thought of whom I'm abandoning Ben to. The more I think about it—and I really shouldn't think about it—Villicus can only be some otherworldly evil being. As unfathomable as that is. Which means this is no fairy tale. And I am no hero, protected by the goodness of her intentions, en route to slay a common villain. I'm just a half-dead kid trying to outsmart a man who has powers over life and death. If I'm not smart, I'll be dead before I know it.

With my pulse pounding like a villager's drum, I arrive, chest heaving, at the enormous locked doors of Valedictorian Hall. I fly toward the plaque I noticed last week, shove the vines aside, and let my eyes skip over the missing letters:

-aled-ctori-n, you shine, you exce-,
Now to each of your peer-, bid a blessed f—well
From this isle of -ope to success, do proce-d,
Eve- active, ever after, with endl-ss Godspeed.

"*Vials are here,*" I piece together.

But my stomach quickly sinks. *Why* are the letters rubbed away? Students over the years must have tried to do exactly what I'm doing now. To retrieve their vials and escape Villicus. How did those valiant attempts end?

Racing around the side of the building to the closet, I fumble with icy fingers for the key in my cardigan, which is slicked against me now. Clumsily, I shove it into the keyhole. Storm in. Leap over boxes and brooms. Pull the cord for the light.

Still high on adrenaline, I shove a heavy steel shelf directly under the opening in the shaft and scurry up it like I'm climbing a ladder.

I hop in the opening. Shimmy through the ducting.

I'm moving so quickly, I barely notice the end of the shaft: it's wide open. The cover into Valedictorian Hall has been removed. I'm a half-foot away from it when it occurs to me that this is a very, very bad thing.

At exactly that moment, a long, thin arm reaches into the duct, clutches my hair, and yanks me forward. I half-scream, half-choke on dust as I'm jerked out of the shaft and, stunningly, with incredible force, thrust fifteen feet down to the floor.

My bones crunch.

A sob pushes out of me with the last breath in my lungs. Gasping, I lift myself to my knees and turn.

Standing before me is the girl with the bobbed brown hair. She is alone in here. And she is dressed in her smartly pressed school uniform, as if it's the beginning of a school day, not the middle of the night.

"Hiltop?" I choke out.

"Hiltop P. Shemese—a pleasure," she says, making an unnecessary formal introduction.

My gaze darts back to the duct she just ripped me out of. It's high on the wall, much higher than she could possibly reach. Yet, somehow, she did. Without a ladder. A cold sweat washes over me, head to toe, although the room is sweltering, lit end to end by candles. Thousands of them. The heat they emit quickly dries the icy water that soaked my hair and clothing. "What are you doing here?" I ask.

Tilting her head sweetly, she crouches next to me and caresses my hair. Even before her soft touch changes, even before her hand clasps my curls, every cell in my body comes awake—and I realize that *Villicus* may not have been the problem.

"Please," Hiltop sings, gripping my hair at the roots, "*come in.*"

With that, she drags me, grunting and kicking, by my hair across the vast wooden floor and, with strength unfathomable, flings me smack into the center of the room. I cry out and grasp at the lacquered floor to slow myself; as my cries fade, I spin, struggling to get a grip, and eventually stop revolving. Dizzy, I notice that the rows of chairs I saw yesterday are gone. The hall is bare, save the candles, the perimeter of oversized framed portraits of valedictorians, me, and her.

At the far end of the room stands the wall of tiny drawers, nameplates on each, running the height of the arched ceiling.

That wall must be used to store our vials. Those nameplates are ours. My vial—my freedom—is in there.

I hear a waltz I recognize by Franz Liszt. Fingers on an unseen piano pound furiously, dance madly. The music sends a shiver like an electric current through me as I watch this thin, simple-looking girl pace the floor just beyond my reach. I search the empty hall. The only way out is through the front doors, which are impossibly far away and always locked.

"How can it be *you*?" I haven't yet caught my breath when I try to scream at her, "Who are you?"

"Look closer," she begins, smoothing her skirt. "That's your *prosperitas thema*, after all. It's ambitious, to say the least. Too bad for you, you're not ambitious enough to rise to it."

"I got here, didn't I? I figured this much out." I counter, my veins filling with electricity. "It barely took me two weeks to learn, on my own, the truth about this place."

"The truth? Coming from a girl who's been asleep for over two years just to *hide* from the truth." She smiles as Liszt turns gay and light. Surrounding her are more than fifty years of valedictorians, also smiling in their portraits. "Enlighten me."

"I know everyone's dead. I know they're vivified here. I know the villagers would rather be killed than sent to this hellhole."

"*And*? Do you know about this?"

Hiltop snaps her thin fingers. The doors to the hall fly open with a gust of wind that sends me careering helplessly backward. I gain my balance and peer at the doorway. Panicked whispers sneak in from the darkness, beyond where I can see. And then two people float in from beyond the doorway. Followed by another two. And another.

Except they aren't people at all. They're translucent apparitions.

Dressed in cap and gown, they march into the hall.

Then, all at once, they *stop*. In unison, the ghostly graduates turn silently my way, their shadowed, decaying faces gawking, their long teeth yellow and exposed in their mouths, dark like coal. Deep, sorrowful gashes crease their faces. And their eyes. Empty sockets flickering as they follow my every flinch.

"Fifty candidates attend the graduation ceremony," she calls over the wind. As the last apparitions enter, the doors slam shut. "Only one walks out, free to roam the world at will. Did you know *that*?"

Returning her glare, I boldly nod. "Yes, I know all about the Big V."

Her grin thins. "Someone told you."

"No one told me."

I can see that she doesn't want to believe I was capable of figuring things out on my own, as if her demonic mind can't allow me to show any signs of intelligence. So I decide not to tell her that I know our blood needs to be on this island to vivify us. Because it might wake a bigger beast than I can handle, and because I don't want to tell her that I know our vials are kept in the wall behind her—the wall I need to get into.

She saunters toward me, staring at me on my knees. With a violent shove I didn't see coming, she sends me onto my back and swiftly lowers her small foot onto my chest, pushing firmly down on me, so firmly I sputter while trying to exhale. For the most endless moment, she holds me there like a beetle whose leg she's caught under her shoe.

"Did you know about *me*, Miss Merchant? Do you know who I am?"

"You," I stammer, "are a surprise."

That pleases her, and she lets up on me, turning to walk toward the wall of drawers.

"The Zin boy didn't tell you about me?" she calls back. "I know he tried, sweet little lovesick moron. The literary game you played outside this very hall. The book he left on your bed. If it wasn't for his father's utility, your pathetic boyfriend would be dead. Again."

"Ben didn't do anything or tell me anything. I promise."

Spinning back to me, Hiltop feigns a gleeful grin and pulls her hands to her chest, mocking me, mocking Ben.

"Oh, *love!*" she cries. "How *wonderful* that you would protect him now when he has never protected you. He's more worried about his dead sister than he is about you—even though you still have the chance to live! Dear, sweet Ben had nothing but time to simply tell you the truth about me. He lived next door to you. He had limitless access to you. And yet he gave you only hints and chose to protect Jeannie. What kind of love is that?"

"Don't act like you *know* about love," I hiss. "Ben trusted that I could figure everything out in time, and I did."

"Not everything," she tsks.

Suddenly, she dashes at me and, holding my fists, straddles me. Her impossibly hot hands slide to grip my wrists as she pins me to the floor. Under her unnatural weight, I can't budge, not even to kick, a fact that infuriates me and delights her.

"You don't know *this*," she says.

And then Hiltop's transformation begins.

The plump, firm skin on her youthful face droops and runs like a mudslide. Deep wrinkles etch like streams around her eyes and mouth. Her irises turn from daylight to the inky night sky. My breath catches as I witness her grotesque transformation: she has, without a sound, morphed from a shy student to the hideous secretary I encountered on orientation day.

My lips form a curse that goes unspoken. I can't utter a word.

Her metamorphosis continues, accompanied now by her dark, pointy smile. Her face swells; her cheeks balloon. Dark, curly brown fur spreads over her aged body in patches that swiftly interlock, as the fingers that hold me become claws, and the hands paws. To my horror, her nose and mouth extend and become a snout, mouth wide open, gray tongue hanging above my wide eyes. Her dark eyes are small black beads lit by an unseen fire. She has transformed from the secretary into a dark *poodle*.

"If you'd read the book," the poodle says, "you'd know who I am. The name you know Hiltop by is merely an anagram."

My mind is unraveling now. I shake my head, shake away this unreal reality. The book this ungodly *thing* is referring to is *Doctor Faustus*. I've known it all this time. I just haven't wanted to.

Her next visage is a Nazi soldier. And then a hoofed demon with horns.

But it is not until she becomes *him*—the man I'd expected to see the moment I was yanked from the duct—that I truly know who Hiltop P. Shemese is and am ready to call this *thing* by name.

As I find myself pinned under Villicus, I whisper, "Mephistopheles."

I squirm, wheeze, and dodge his fiendish glare. Villicus seems to be deciding whether to squish me now or prolong the agony. He stands and retreats, training his eyes on my face as he backs away. A treacherous grin spreads across his dry face, cutting with the power of an earthquake through cold stone.

Villicus leers at me. "You know my name."

My body, head to toe, is shuddering—not with fear, as he would believe, but with whatever efforts my father is making back home to rouse me from my coma.

"Mephistopheles," I shout, glaring up at his grimace. "You're Mephistopheles."

"Prince of Darkness. The Great Exchanger. Problem Solver for the impatient, entitled, and bored."

"But you're fiction, a fable," I whisper, staggering to my feet again and thinking of the story *Doctor Faustus*. Of the book Ben tried to slip to me. The book he said was the biggest hint he could provide. The book about a foolish man named Johann Faust who traded his soul to a demon named Mephistopheles in exchange for twenty-four years of magical powers, infinite intelligence, the admiration of his peers, and beautiful women. When his time was up, Mephistopheles claimed Faustus's soul. "You're just a character in a *story*."

"A story?" He backs away, still watching me. Quivering even in the heat, I nod. "Is *this* a story?" he shouts. With the flick of his wrist, he throws an enormous flame my way. It tears through the ghostly graduates, eliminating them, and lands at my feet.

Shrieking, I stumble away.

The fire swells, burns, but doesn't spread. "Is that fiction?"

"Stop!" I scream.

He leaps into the air—up, up, spreading his arms wide like a bird in flight. He shoots up to the ceiling, dragging his fingertips along the enormous beams as I watch from the ground, cringing, waiting for an end I can't escape; I can only anticipate it. Death at the hands of Mephistopheles. I stare up at him, unable to tear my gaze from a floating, hovering demon.

"I am not *fiction*. Hell does not cease to be because you fictionalize it. No more than dark ceases to be because you flick on the light," he growls from above. "It's time you started believing in Hell and all of its demons, Miss Merchant. You're separated from them by the thinnest layer. You're so close to them—" he throws himself down, directly at me, halting inches over me "—they're practically touching you."

His draping cloak strokes me. I cringe, shielding my eyes. But with one swipe of his hands, he throws my arms away from my face.

"You! Wrapped in your shield. You, the worst offender, protected by your coma from the truth you don't want to face. You fictionalize what you can't handle. As though that might erase reality!" His voice rings through the room, and he bounces away from me, lurches toward the wall of drawers. "You don't know the life you've surrendered just to mourn your mother! When you could be so much more, Anne. *So much more*."

My breath is barely coming now. My eyes are strained and

sore, locked in his wicked glare. Mephistopheles is real. He's been making exchanges for decades on this very island. And for hundreds of years prior to that.

"You gluttonous fools *want* what I can give," he continues. "Since the Dark Ages, well before Marlowe, Goethe, and so many others relegated me to fiction, you've wanted me. You know you should resist me, but, oh, how I entice you! I have the power to give any person exactly what they want. The problem for this world is when I take what *I want* in exchange." He cocks his head. "The world *needs* to believe I returned to Hell with just Faust's soul and never came back for more. But ask yourself, why would I go back there when I am so good at what I do here?"

Waltzing in time back in the direction of the wall of drawers, he casually recounts a handful of the exchanges he's made over the years.

The Salem witch trials: he details how he watched them string those girls up to extract their confessions. "That exchange was my first love story. The son of a village elder named Donnan couldn't get the girl. So he called on me. Asked me to publicly torture her. In exchange, he was enslaved to me for sixty-six years, during which time I had him gather over one thousand innocents to be tried and tortured as witches."

The sinking of the *Titanic*: Villicus made an exchange with a deckhand named Tom Finnegan, who wanted to destroy a first-class passenger who'd spit on him. This exchange ended with the *Titanic* snapping in two. "Pity Tom's escape boat sank, too.

"You see, before I came to Wormwood, I had my hands full. The Great Depression. The *Hindenburg*. And my masterpiece."

I know "his masterpiece" before he says it. Gigi essentially told me. And the medals in his office spoke volumes.

"World War II," I whisper.

"*Guten*! Yes, that was my finest work. It took an impressive series of exchanges to bring that war to life, exchanges beginning as early as the eighteen hundreds. Of course, it was not until a man named Adolf Hitler approached me that I really hit my stride. Amazing what one bitter failed artist is willing to do for success. Yes, every gun, every battle, every murder, even the Weimar Republic was the result of an exchange with me. At the end of it all, I fled on a boat that arrived on this very island. And a new opportunity was born."

With his back turned, I dart my gaze to the door, to escape. The hall is so long, so vast, so impossible to cross if I risk bolting now he'd be on me in a flash. And although I could heal from the wounds he'd inflict, I'd still feel the pain—*all* the pain.

"You call manipulating people an *opportunity*?" I cry.

He whirls back to me. "If you searched your soul, Miss Merchant, you'd find that you do, too."

"You had Molly killed."

"All part of the exchange."

"She'd rather die than go to Cania."

"Alas, she'd have to die *to* go to Cania. Death is the only option for breaking my rules. She simply opted to die without the chance to attend my fine institution thereafter. You see, the rule is that anyone who crosses the red line is mine. Rules are rules. Dear Ted caught wind of Miss Watso entering the Zin premises, which, you'll note, is beyond the red line."

"So you killed her!"

"Every day, her grandfather and mother made a decision to keep her on this island. They could have sent her to Kennebunkport, where the most frightened villagers fled. But they wanted her with them. And they had to stay because they are contractually obligated to invite me to their island each morning."

My head whirls. "That's what they do for you? *That's* why you pay them?"

"We have very basic rules in the world of demons and angels," he says, sounding more like a headmaster than ever. "I must be called by name to enter the earth and walk among you. Faust, Donnan, Tom Finnegan, Hitler—they all called on me. *Mephistopheles!* And I appeared. The soldiers that brought me here called me by name each day, and I appeared. The day a renegade German boat raided this island and the daughter of the Abenaki chief was killed in the crossfire, I vivified her—and they called me back each day thereafter."

This is what Gigi was rambling about yesterday, I realize. The village girl who set off a series of miracles and horrors that now shape my world.

"We made an exchange then. I would fill Wormwood Island with the power to vivify all who die on it if the villagers would lease the land to me, calling me by name every day. They agreed to secrecy, because I operate best in the shadows. After the pact was signed, all the bodies buried here—the soldiers, old husbands and wives—were vivified, and the US Navy abandoned Wormwood, leaving me and the villagers."

"Which suited you fine!" I storm. "You could have total control of them."

"Control? Miss Merchant, I only did as they asked me to. And I asked for so little. I just wanted to stay here until I could work out my next gig."

I shake my head, amazed at what lengths people will go to and what evils they will overlook to get what they want. The shortsightedness of it!

"In time, the villagers began to question my righteousness. Such is the natural human response to indulging in what one wants—this need to withdraw, punish oneself for giving into temptation, and turn to a virtuous life." He has scaled the wall of drawers. He hovers midway up the wall, a dozen feet of air between him and the floor; a drawer is open. "They told me they wanted me to leave. They destroyed the remains of those I'd vivified. I was nearly forced from the first permanent home I'd had—so when a government official called on me for a favor, I had him abolish whaling for the Abenaki. Their means of feeding themselves disappeared." He smiles. "They came around to me then. They agreed to look the other way on the condition that I stay out of their village and compensate them handsomely for their troubles. The next time a wealthy person called on me, I asked not for his soul but for his riches. It just so happened that the first such person to call on me begged to have their dead child vivified. And thus Cania Christy was born. And soon, my empire shall expand."

"What does that mean?"

"Another school. Your father will take over as lead recruiter for Wormwood Island, and Dr. Zin will be moved to a new location." Anticipating my reaction, he sneers. "I know your thoughts, Miss Merchant, as a parent knows a child's. I know you're planning to escape me. But I have different plans. And mine, as you might imagine, trump all others."

"It won't work!" I cry halfheartedly, knowing that it will. Because, thus far, it has. "I'll kill myself before I let you use me to trap my dad."

"I'll bring you back!" he flares bitterly. "And then I'll end you when I'm damn well ready. Just like I end everyone when I'm damn well ready."

A vial glints in his hand as he closes the drawer next to him. Everything in my body shrieks for me to run. But I can't. I'm positive he's got my vial in his clutches. What he plans to do with it, I can't imagine, though I'm sure he won't be burning it—that would end his hold over my dad.

Scurrying along the wall, he swiftly pulls another vial out of a drawer.

Before he can explain his intent, the doors fly open again.

Someone storms in, racing, soaking wet. He stops just feet from the fire.

"Pilot!" I scream, *beyond* overjoyed to see him. All this time, I've been holding my breath, wondering how I'll do this alone. And now, seeing him, I exhale so hard I nearly slump to the floor. I won't have to fight Villicus alone. I almost smile.

"Am I late?" Pilot asks, huffing.

It takes me a moment to realize he's not asking *me*.

twenty-six

CIRCLING VULTURES

"I APOLOGIZE, GUARDIAN," PILOT SAYS TO VILLICUS. "I just returned to my dorm room and found your instructions."

"We will address matters of punctuality in our next one-on-one."

Then Villicus and Pilot turn their gazes on me. And just like that, I can't breathe again.

Ahead of me, Mephistopheles waits to kill. But, at this moment, I see nothing but Pilot. Pilot, my only friend. Pilot, complaining that he'll always be the disappointing son. Holding tissue flowers to his chest and grinning. Denying any interest in being valedictorian—knowing its reward is life—and telling me not to try for it either.

Pilot has a Guardian after all. *Villicus*. Which means Pilot—pious Pilot—is, in fact, in the race for the Big V. And has been all along.

"Don't give me that look, Anne. We're all competing. It's a matter of life and death."

Pilot strolls toward the fire, which burns without spreading, and stops feet from me. I can't move. This betrayal is colder than all the sheets of ice I ran through tonight. Colder than the chills that consumed my body every morning since I arrived here. The coldest.

"So you always wanted to be valedictorian?" My tone gives away my repulsion.

"Naturally," Villicus answers on Pilot's behalf. "The moment I saw the darkness surrounding this boy, I knew only I could be his Guardian. And I swiftly determined his PT."

"*To use deceit, ruthlessness, and dishonesty to get ahead,*" Pilot says, reciting his PT. "Very Machiavellian. My father is so proud. Wrap your true intents in a fluffy white cloud of nobility, and nobody, not even you, with your *I'm-looking-closer* PT, will question it. Add to that a sob story about your dad being disappointed? You've got the makings of a successful life."

"A successful life under the mentorship of Mephistopheles!" I fire.

"Mr. Stone has a bright future in politics," Villicus says. "What better mentor than I?"

Together, Pilot and Villicus snort out a few laughs. Gritting my teeth as I watch, I make a pact to myself. To beat them at their own game. Whatever it takes.

"Explain how Miss Merchant fits into your PT, boy," Villicus commands.

"Easy," I interrupt. "Our entire friendship was a lie."

"There's a little more to it than that."

Pilot explains how, since arriving here last year, he's been publicly lying about having no PT in order to give himself a competitive edge—to trick everyone into revealing their PTs so he could use those against them.

"Like a snake in the grass," I spit.

"Like a successful politician. Don't take it personally, Annie."

"Why me? Why befriend me and turn on me? You could've done that to anyone."

A blush washes his face, bringing a bashful grin with it. "Honestly? You started out as a favor to Harper."

"Harper?"

"Before you came here, Villicus told everyone about you so we'd know you to see you. You were someone we had to keep a secret from, until the day you finally croaked, which…?" He looks from me to Villicus, who shakes his head, confirming that I am still alive in California. Pilot rolls his eyes, as if my coma is *so annoying*. "So we knew your story. We knew about the art shows you had."

"Ha! There were no art shows!" I say, throwing what little I can in his face. "That was a lie my dad told to get me in here."

He and Villicus exchange another glance.

"You were in a coma for two years, Annie. A gifted art prodigy who might die any second? Art investors ate that up. Like any artist, you're worth more dead than alive. There *were* art shows. A half-dozen. Your piss-broke old man needed the cash to keep you in the hospital."

I cringe at how lightly they throw around life and death.

"Knowing that, Harper saw you as her biggest threat. The first day she saw you slutted-up in your little uniform, she thought you might join her clique, where she could destroy you slowly like Plum and the others." He smiles wistfully. "Then I told her your PT, and she realized you'd be no good in her group. So she told me if I could just keep you out of the running for the Big V—which she thought I was out of, too—she'd keep me in constant… Well, let's say I don't have to worry about dying a virgin."

"You lied to me so you could get with Harper?"

"I lied to you for my PT. Harper was just a perk."

How I've failed at my own PT. Why did I blindly accept his friendship? The only other "friends" at Cania are the members of the Model UN from Hell. Yet I believed Pilot and I were friends. Stupidly, foolishly believed it.

"So every time we skipped class together," I continue. "And every time you said you hated what the competition was doing. And every time—"

"Lies," Pilot says, cutting me off. "All lies. So many you don't even know about." Sucking his cheek, he gives it some thought. "Oh, you thought I came here after I died trying to rescue a girl from a fire, right?"

A shiver runs down my spine.

"Not so. I set her house on fire while she slept. She thought she was so hot. Never looked at me once at school. But that night, when I stood in her bedroom with the flames I'd set all around us, she saw me then." He smiles at the memory before noticing my expression. "Come on, don't act like you're new to the world of deceit."

"Me?"

"You led me on. And then I saw you with Zin on the beach tonight."

"That's hardly comparable."

"Since you bring up the topic of Mr. Zin," Villicus interjects. He tosses a vial at Pilot, who catches it and turns it over, reading the label.

Pilot groans. "I've always hated that name. *Ebenezer.*"

Ebenezer? It's Ben's vial?

Then, out of nowhere, another vial is flying—this one in my direction. Fumbling, I nearly drop it. Just before it hits the flames, I close my fist around it. Turn it over. Read it.

"Pilot Aaron Stone," I whisper.

"Now then," Villicus says, curling his lips into a snarl, "it's time the two of you sorted out an exchange."

Pilot glances up, his eyes suddenly watering. How quickly his emotions have changed.

I, on the other hand, feel like I've finally got a shot at this game. I know what cards are on the table. That puts me light-years ahead of where I've been since arriving on Wormwood. If I've survived this long in the dark, surely I can do that much better now that I know what's up.

"This is your chance to shine, Mr. Stone," Villicus says.

"Why not *her* vial?" Pilot asks, looking confused. "Why his?"

"The girl wants her vial destroyed. But she'd be heartbroken if Mr. Zin were to vanish from the earth. And you, of course, want yours."

"Let's talk this out," Pilot says, relaxing his tone as he turns to me. I see the old Pilot in his expression, as if he, like Mephistopheles, has masks he can put on and take off at will. "I know what you must be thinking, but if you throw my vial in the fire, Annie, you'll kill me. And I'll have no choice but to kill Ben, too."

"If you're fast enough." The audacity he has, trying to manipulate me again, to prey on my emotions.

"I don't think you could live with my blood on your hands."

"My mother almost killed me," I retort coldly, ignoring the flash of pain that splits my forehead at the thought of her. "I can live with a lot. And, Mephistopheles," I turn to Villicus, "I don't care about Ben's vial. I only care about mine."

That shuts Pilot up. Villicus looks impressed.

"Perhaps *selfishness* would have been a fine PT for you," Villicus says.

Pilot searches my face—a poker face that would thrill Molly—and then Villicus's, looking for a hint if not an answer to the dilemma he's been placed in. My only prayer is that I figure out what to do before they figure out I'm bluffing.

"Let's just do a pure exchange," Pilot suggests. "On the count of three, we hand each other the vials and be done with it."

"I already told you," I say, "I don't want Ben's vial."

"So I could throw it in the fire?" Pilot dangles Ben's vial over the flames.

"You could. But it would leave you empty-handed, which wouldn't give you much bargaining power. If I were you, I'd stop trying to make an exchange with me and figure out how to get Villicus to give you my vial. That's the only way you'll get me to give you yours."

Glowering, Pilot turns to Villicus, who looks as disappointed in him as he once pretended his own father was.

"Mephistopheles," Pilot begins, bowing respectfully, "I ask you for the vial of Anne Merchant in exchange for the vial of Ben Zin."

"He's never gonna go for that, Pilot," I interrupt. "You need to give him something of *greater* value."

I'm outplaying Pilot, which Villicus doesn't seem to be missing.

"If you don't pull up your socks, Mr. Stone," Villicus says, "I will insist that Miss Merchant expel you promptly."

"But this little game wasn't part of our plan, Guardian!" Pilot whines.

It strikes me then that they're distracted. Villicus is frustrated and growing angry with his supposed prize pupil, and Pilot is wracking his unimpressive mind for a worthy exchange. And here I stand, temporarily forgotten. The door is just beyond them, and it's still wide open, thanks to Pilot.

They're holding Ben's vial. I've got Pilot's. I don't have mine—but I know now that I'd rather give Ben his and let him decide his fate than escape so selfishly. And I can use Pilot's for leverage, if it comes to that. First, I need to get Ben's vial. To do so, I'll have to run through the fire to scoop it from Pilot's hand. Quickly. While they're distracted.

Without another breath, I go for it.

I dash through the flames. I throw my hand out, and instantly my side is consumed by a hellish blaze that shocks my system. With a loud *whomp*, the flames ignite my clothes and my hair. Running on adrenaline only, I grab Ben's vial out of Pilot's fist.

I leave him and Villicus dumbfounded behind me.

With both vials, I run toward the still-open door. Fast. Faster than my stunned body, now in flames, can comprehend. I am a human torch, racing to the doorway in three long strides. Bursting into the dark night, into what has become a torrential hailstorm with buckets of rain that douse my clothes and hair. I glance at the vials in my fists. They're still intact. My skin, though, is bright red.

"Help me!" I scream as smoke pours off me. The dorms are filled with parents. Surely one will hear me and help. Or the Coast Guard! They were around here hours ago. "Somebody help!"

I zoom like a bat out of Hell. I should run to Ben's, give him his vial. But Pilot is after me, racing and screaming at me. If I change direction, if I even look back, I'll be caught.

"*Help!*"

With everything in me, I claw at the air as if that might pull me forward. My feet slide over the slick grass. But miraculously, I stay upright. I bolt across the quad and behind Goethe Hall. The cliffside comes into view. My heart pounds furiously. My voice is gone. My head can't keep up with what's happened— with the cold vials in my hands and the heat on my skin—so I go on autopilot, blasting through the parking lot, blasting forward and up. Up. Through the brush that tries to hold me back. Up. To the top of the cliff.

With a quick glance over my shoulder, I see the lights in a half-dozen distant dorm rooms. Silhouettes stand at the windows. And, in the second I look, I see them, one by one, draw the shades.

No one will help me. Not against the likes of Villicus. Not when he holds such power.

Turning back to the hill, I almost lose my footing when I catch a shadow racing, slithering by at lightning speed. Pushing harder,

I grunt to force myself up the hill, knowing Mephistopheles will be waiting for me.

I burst into the rocky clearing.

Whirling, I spy Hiltop. She's replaced Villicus, who is just one of Mephistopheles's characters, the one that could reasonably pass as a headmaster. Hiltop is perched at the edge of the cliff, standing motionlessly, hands folded, watching me like a bird of prey waiting for its catch to expire. Behind her, the infinite waters are gray, vast, furious, and filling with ice.

"Nothing good will come of this," she calls to me. "I still have your vial back at Valedictorian Hall. Come with me, Anne, and we'll make a small exchange for it."

Before I can respond, someone shoves me from behind. I collapse, nearly dropping both vials. I rush away and, holding the vials to my chest, look up through the sleet at Pilot. My eyes flick between an unflinching, deceptively normal Hiltop and a scarlet-faced, infuriated Pilot.

"You *bitch*!" he bellows, his face distorting in his rage, thick rain flooding it in unholy streams until he's unrecognizable. "Give me my vial *now*!"

But before I can holler back at him, he flies at me. With a shriek, I roll away, barely escaping him. I land within feet of Hiltop. My scream fills the air at exactly the same time Ben, soaking wet, appearing from nowhere, sees Hiltop standing over me, and hurls his body at her. The two wrestle and tumble to the cliff's edge, tearing at each other as I scream Ben's name. Without a moment to spare, Ben catches a thick, exposed tree root and clings to it. Hiltop slides soundlessly by him, over the cliff's edge, and out of sight.

I scramble to my feet.

I back away from Pilot, who's lumbering toward me. His eyes bulge as he homes in on the vials I hold.

"Give me…my vial."

I stumble over a loose branch at my feet and, livid, grab it quickly, swinging it at him. "Stay back!"

"Give it to me," Pilot snarls. He doesn't care about the branch or the pain it could inflict. He's invincible. The only way to hurt him is to destroy him. "Annie, you know the last thing I ever wanted to do was hurt you."

"The *last* thing?" I repeat, rain washing my face. "It still made your list."

At once, Ben's at my side. Running entirely on willpower has left me so jerky, I nearly fly out of my skin when he wraps his arm around me. As he takes the branch and swipes it boldly, powerfully at Pilot, my exhausted body collapses against him.

"Stay back, Pilot," he bellows over a thunderclap.

"This has nothing to do with you, Zin," Pilot fires, shirking away but stealthily, on guard, continuing to close the distance. "I just want what's mine—my *life*!"

When Pilot lurches at him, Ben brings the heavy branch down on his shoulder, sending him reeling back. We watch Pilot collapse to the ground, where he writhes in pain.

"I've got his vial," I explain feebly to Ben.

"What are you planning to do with it?" he asks me.

Shaking my head, I feel my throat choke up. I clench my jaw, but there's no stopping the tears. "All this time, Pilot was lying."

Ben holds me closer. "I know. I saw his PT. Why do you think I hated him so much?"

Feeling myself growing fainter every moment—and loathing myself for it—I look into Ben's eyes and add, with a small smile, "I've got yours, too. It's your chance to escape." The shiny silver label is soaking wet on his vial as I hold it up to him. *Ebenezer Joshua Zin.* "I'm going to stay on Wormwood. My dad will work for Villicus. And, Ben, if you want to join Jeannie, this is your chance to do it. To free yourself."

"And leave you now that I've found you?" Ben smiles sadly. "I won't let you sacrifice yourself for me. You still have a real life to lead. Your dad deserves to have you with him."

Before I can argue, with a grand *whoosh*, Hiltop swoops over the mountainside, over the cliff. She comes crashing down to the earth with a tremendous rumble. Behind her, Pilot gets to his knees and slowly to his feet.

With a gasp, I stagger back; Ben keeps me stable, but barely.

In one unnaturally fast move, Hiltop plucks Ben's vial from between my fingers. I cry out, but Ben doesn't even flinch. I search his face urgently as Hiltop backs away and smiles. I know that the only leverage we have now is Pilot's vial, but that doesn't feel like enough. Just as I'm about to offer *anything* Hiltop wants in exchange for Ben's vial, Ben shakes his head softly at me. He's anticipated my next move, but he won't let me sacrifice myself for him.

"Are you ready to go, love?" he asks me.

That word, *love*. Could he mean it? If we'd had a chance, even a small chance to be together, would there have been a future for us?

"No. I'll stay."

I need to stay with Ben as long as I can. Even if it means living under the cruel tyranny of Villicus. Even if I can feel myself fading. Even if, every time I blink, I wonder if I'm not about to open my eyes in that hospital room again.

"Just give me my vial, Zin," Pilot stammers furiously. "And Hiltop will give you yours."

"That's not going to happen." Ben pulls me into the warmth of his body, shielding me, and turns to Pilot and Hiltop, who are both uncomfortably close. I can hear Pilot's heaving breaths, smell Hiltop's rancid odor even in the rain. Bit by bit, Ben inches us away, through the sleet, to the cliffside. "I'm going to stay here, and Anne's going to go back to the life she deserves."

"To free her, you'd need to destroy her vial, Zin," Hiltop reminds him. "Are you planning on running back to the hall?"

When we're just at the edge of the cliff, when my back is to the water, when I'm forced to stand on my tiptoes to keep from tumbling into the hungry, howling waters, Ben reaches into his jacket with his free hand and pulls out a single vial. I make out its label: *Anne Elizabeth Merchant.*

"When you all raced out of Valedictorian Hall," Ben says, with the smallest hint of that crinkle-nosed grin I love, "you forgot to lock up."

Ben has my vial. I have Pilot's.

Hiltop has Ben's. She locks her gaze on mine and, knowing what's about to happen, mouths to me, "*You'll be ba-ack.*"

And then it all happens in a blink. Ben wraps me in his arms, holds me against his chest, and leaps with all his might into the air. The ground disappears from under our feet. With that, Ben and I are soaring, flying, leaving Wormwood Island behind. Ben will return, but I won't. Not the way Hiltop wants me to.

We leave Pilot behind. He watches in horror, waiting for his vial to hit the water just as I'm waiting for mine to hit, for his second life to end just as mine will. I have somewhere to wake; I have no idea what will become of his spirit once his vivified body is destroyed.

We leave Hiltop behind. She'll still have Ben and Dr. Zin, but she's just lost me and my father. With a piercing cry, knowing she's been outsmarted, she raises her leg and sends it crashing into the cliff, splitting the thick rock in two. She disappears into the gash, returning to where she came from.

And Ben and I? We fall, fall, fall blissfully toward the water.

Everything slows. The spinning of the world. The rushing of the sleet and hail. The crashing of the waves. There's nothing more than Ben and me. In spite of everything, I'm smiling. So is he. But as slowly as time is moving, there's not a spare moment to talk, to say everything I need to say as I feel this temporary body of mine fade the further we drop. Soon, I'll be gone. When I wake in California, it will be for good this time. I'll have left Ben behind to continue a life he hates, and I'll have to trust that it was the right decision—at least until I can find a better way. Alive and awake in California, I'll be able to do more than I can dead and trapped at Cania.

But now.

Now, as we fall.

Now, as our eyes lock and we cling to one another. *Now* is my chance. I won't waste it this time. I press my hands to the back of his head, marvel at the endlessness of his green eyes, pull him to me, and softly—ever so softly, as our toes near the ocean—lower my mouth to his. The softness, the indescribable warmth of his lips. It's perfect torture. Perfect, as he leans into me with all his strength, with more desperation than I could have imagined, and steals my breath. Torture, as I feel my body weaken, anticipating my end. We plunge into the icy sea, squeezing our eyes shut and opening them in the unexpectedly calm water beneath the waves. The force of the water tears us apart, tears me from this world, tears me from the only boy I've ever kissed.

Waking now is nothing like when I woke in this hospital bed hours ago. I know where I am now. I know what's happened.

But it's more than that.

Waking now, I find my father's chair empty. He may have left with the doctor. He may have gone to find some new method of waking me—maybe an ice bath in which he can shock me awake. I don't know.

Waking now, I find I am not alone, however.

It takes a moment for my eyes, wet with tears, to focus on

Teddy's face hovering over me. But as soon as I register that he's here and what that must mean, I see, to my sickened surprise, that his thumb is on the plunger of a syringe. A syringe filled with a clear fluid. A syringe that juts out of a tube planted in my arm. On my bedsheet, in stark contrast to the white of it, are three vials filled with my dark red blood, which he must have taken while I slept.

"Don't speak, and don't protest," he whispers to me. His thick German accent is gone. His tongue doesn't seem to slither as it once did. "Your mother was here earlier. She had more to say to you, but there was no time."

"How can you know that?" I ask with trepidation. There's something very odd about his behavior and his countenance. His gaze connects with mine. The anger, lust, and violence once contained in that gaze have vanished. His expression is borderline kind.

"Pentobarbital," he says matter-of-factly, gesturing to the syringe he holds and ignoring my question. "It's for medically induced comas. I've arranged to have a nurse on staff keep you in constant supply."

"Stop. How did you know about my mom's spirit visiting me here?"

"It's part of the plan."

"What plan? Please, don't do something you'll regret. Let me—"

"You, too, are part of the plan. The biggest part. Which is why you must return. Your time at Cania Christy isn't over yet, Anne. Everything in your life has been building to this. We need you."

Whatever this is, it's happening too fast. "Who's *we*? You and Mephistopheles? What do you plan to do with me?"

"I am *not* aligned with that monster," he states, holding my gaze until it's clear to him that I believe him, which takes some time. His thumb begins to depress the syringe. Voices outside grow louder.

"Wait!" I plead. "You said my mom had more to say to me. What was it?"

Swiftly and with a brief apology, Teddy injects the plunger.

As I slide defenselessly back into darkness, I feel him sweep the vials of my blood from the bed and I hear him whisper, "Your mother trusts me. You should, too."

ACKNOWLEDGMENTS

I'm forever indebted to my editor, Glenn Yeffeth, and his brilliant team at BenBella. To Jason Anthony, my persevering virtuoso of a literary agent, thank you for reinventing the word *dedicated*. To Lance, you are a gift to me. To Tina, Sarah, Paul, and Jake, to Nana, and to Angela, thank you for filling my life with the most complex characters. Thank you to my teachers: Greg Hollingshead, Bert Almon, Janice Williamson, Tom Wharton, Mrs. Shukin, and Mr. Fred. To my favorite teacher, Dad, I wish you could be here for this. Above all, my love and humble gratitude to the Great Teacher. And to you, dear reader, my full and heartfelt thanks.

ABOUT THE AUTHOR

Joanna Wiebe is a graduate of the University of Alberta's Honors English program, where she received the James Patrick Folinsbee Memorial Scholarship in Creative Writing. She lives in Victoria, British Columbia, with her partner, Lance. *The Unseemly Education of Anne Merchant* is her first novel. Find her online at joannawiebefiction.com.